Praise for t
Bestsel

"Rife with poli romance never lacks for suspense. . . . This dynamic, heavily embellished history lesson manages to do what few can—illuminate and entertain."

—*Publishers Weekly*

"Few writers incorporate such rich historical detail into their romances as Henley, and Wolf and Brianna's story will appeal to fans of the sensual romances of Bertrice Small and Susan Johnson." —*Booklist*

"Henley's at the top of her form, balancing history and passion to perfection. . . . This is what historical romance is all about: getting your romance in perfect harmony with history." —*Romantic Times* (4½ stars)

Infamous

"Few authors combine historical personages and events with a passionate love story as brilliant as Henley."

—*Romantic Times* (4½ stars, top pick)

Unmasked

"Once again Henley has brought history to life—and another couple to true love." —*Booklist*

"A merry chase . . . historical romance layered with a healthy dose of intrigue makes for a book that will keep readers unable to stop turning the pages."

—The Romance Readers Connection

"U story in a way that ke e story."

oundtable Reviews

continued . . .

"Henley's gift for bringing remarkable women to life in colorful, turbulent times is what turns her romances into keepers. Henley heats up the pages with her love scenes, and her skill at portraying actual historical personages with humanity while maintaining historical accuracy wins our minds. Henley knows what historical romance is all about and always gives the readers what they want." —*Romantic Times*

Insatiable

"Dangerous games, Machiavellian manipulations, and political maneuverings. . . . Lusty and lavish."
—*Booklist*

"As twists of fate contrive to keep the two apart—intrigue, backstabbing, the bubonic plague—readers will hanker for them to live happily ever after."
—*Publishers Weekly*

"If you like history-rich characters that come to life in your own imagination . . . then Ms. Henley is one author you cannot dismiss!" —Romance Designs

Undone

"Heartstopping excitement, breathless tension, and tender romance." —*Rendezvous*

"All the sensuality and glitter of a more traditional romance, but enriched by the plot's complexity and the heroine's genuine growth." —*Publishers Weekly*

"A gently suspenseful tale . . . filled with satisfying historical detail and actual characters from this intriguing period." —*Booklist*

"Extraordinary characters, rich historical details, and a romance . . . [set] the pages on fire."
—*Romantic Times* (top pick)

Previous Books by Virginia Henley
Available from Signet

Infamous
Insatiable
Unmasked
Undone
Ravished
Notorious

THE DECADENT DUKE

Virginia Henley

A SIGNET BOOK

SIGNET
Published by New American Library, a division of
Penguin Group (USA) Inc., 375 Hudson Street,
New York, New York 10014, USA
Penguin Group (Canada), 90 Eglinton Avenue East, Suite 700, Toronto,
Ontario M4P 2Y3, Canada (a division of Pearson Penguin Canada Inc.)
Penguin Books Ltd., 80 Strand, London WC2R 0RL, England
Penguin Ireland, 25 St. Stephen's Green, Dublin 2,
Ireland (a division of Penguin Books Ltd.)
Penguin Group (Australia), 250 Camberwell Road, Camberwell, Victoria 3124,
Australia (a division of Pearson Australia Group Pty. Ltd.)
Penguin Books India Pvt. Ltd., 11 Community Centre, Panchsheel Park,
New Delhi - 110 017, India
Penguin Group (NZ), 67 Apollo Drive, Rosedale, North Shore 0632,
New Zealand (a division of Pearson New Zealand Ltd.)
Penguin Books (South Africa) (Pty.) Ltd., 24 Sturdee Avenue,
Rosebank, Johannesburg 2196, South Africa

Penguin Books Ltd., Registered Offices:
80 Strand, London WC2R 0RL, England

First published by Signet, an imprint of New American Library,
a division of Penguin Group (USA) Inc.

First Printing, November 2008
10 9 8 7 6 5 4 3 2 1

Printed in the United States of America

PUBLISHER'S NOTE

This is a work of fiction. Names, characters, places, and incidents either are the product of the author's imagination or are used fictitiously, and any resemblance to actual persons, living or dead, business establishments, events, or locales is entirely coincidental.

The publisher does not have any control over and does not assume any responsibility for author or third-party Web sites or their content.

Chapter 1

Buckingham House
Pall Mall, London

"I *hate* that you are being married today!" Lady Georgina Gordon blinked back tears and threw her arms around her sister.

Lady Louisa looked stricken. "Don't be sad, Georgy. I know you'll miss me, but we shall visit each other often." The bride's other three sisters quickly pulled Georgina away and readjusted Louisa's bridal veil.

Georgina could have bitten off her tongue. The last thing she wanted was for her closest sister to feel guilty about getting married. "Don't be daft! Of course I won't miss you."

Lady Louisa exchanged a glance with her other sisters, Charlotte, Madelina, and Susan. "Then why are you sad?"

"I'm not sad." She dashed away her tears with determined fingers. "I'm blazing mad that your wedding day has arrived!"

The lovely, Titian-haired bride looked uncertain. "Georgina, this is supposed to be the happiest day of my life."

"Pay her no mind, Louisa. You know she's as contrary as a cockroach." Charlotte rolled her eyes. "It's bad form to shed tears of jealousy on your sister's wedding day."

Georgina's jaw dropped. "Jealousy? Allow me to inform you that these are tears of pure self-pity. Now that the rabid Duchess of Gordon has bludgeoned poor Charles Cornwallis into making Louisa Lady Brome, I will become the solitary focus of her motherly attention. She will relentlessly pursue every marquis and duke between the ages of nine and ninety until she bags me a bloody husband."

"Charles is marrying me because he loves me," Louisa declared.

Georgina's tears turned to whoops of laughter. "Love has absolutely nothing to do with it. You are a Gordon and rank is the only thing that counts. You cannot deny that Mother set her sights on the Duke of Manchester for Susan and the heir to the Duke of Richmond for Charlotte, and hunted them until she ran them to ground."

"Georgina is queer in the head," Charlotte said dismissively. "It comes from being the runt of the litter."

"If I'm the runt, you are the oldest bitch," Georgina teased.

"*Countess* bitch, if you don't mind."

"Yes, countess; it all started with you. When you bagged Colonel Charles Lennox, Earl of March and heir to the Dukedom of Richmond, Mother's ambition for the rest of us suddenly knew no bounds. Her thirst for titles became insatiable."

"We cannot deny it," Charlotte finally admitted. "Mother's instincts are more mercenary than maternal. We were all brought up with one aim in life, to marry with the maximum status. And I freely admit that if I were not the daughter of the Duke and Duchess of Gordon, the Earl of March would never have proposed."

"Not marriage, at any rate," Georgina said lightly.

The sisters all laughed at her witticism. She was the adored baby of the family, and the precocious little beauty had been much indulged and pampered by her siblings. The entire brood had had a most unconventional upbringing. Their time was divided between fairy-tale Castle Gordon in the Scottish Highlands, an elegant townhome in Edinburgh, a large unpretentious farmhouse at Kinrara beside the wild River Spey, and the spacious mansion in Pall Mall, where they were all presently gathered for the summer wedding.

Jane Gordon swept into the bedchamber and let out a deep sigh of relief. "Prime Minister Pitt and dearest Henry Dundas have just arrived. I also spied the Prince of Wales and the Duke of York making their way through the gardens from Carlton House."

Their arrival wasn't the cause of her overwhelming relief. It was the young groom and his father that she hadn't been completely sure of. The Marquis Cornwallis, a top general in the king's army and member of the Privy Council, had objected to the engagement, fearing the infamous taint of Gordon madness, until the duchess had privately assured him, in the strictest of confidence, that there was not a drop of Gordon blood in Louisa's veins.

"Is Charles here?" Louisa asked.

"What a silly question, my wee lass. Of course yer eager bridegroom is here, as well as yer future father-in-law, the marquis. What great good fortune that the Bishop of Lichfield and Coventry is the Marquis Cornwallis's brother and has agreed to officiate today."

"It will be the wedding of the Season." Georgina winked at her eldest sister.

"The Season? It will be the wedding of the *decade*! An even more impressive affair than they gave the Princess Royal," their mother declared.

Charlotte said dryly, "I believe that is the whole intent."

Louisa reached for her bridal bouquet. "We'd better hurry."

"Nay, that's the last thing we must do. We shall be fashionably late, and make them all wait for a glimpse of the blushing bride."

"I warned my husband to keep his distance from

Frederick. The last thing we want is pistols at dawn." Lennox had fought a duel with the Duke of York only months before he had wed Charlotte.

"A wedding duel would guarantee that we go down in the history books," Georgina jested.

Jane Gordon threw back her head and laughed with gusto. "I warrant that graze with the bullet improved Frederick's looks."

"That wasn't the only benefit," Georgina pointed out. "If Lennox hadn't been posted to Edinburgh for his audacity in shooting the king's son, he never would have married Charlotte."

The duchess raised her eyes heavenward and murmured with mock piety, "Amen to that."

"Did your archrival, the Duchess of Devonshire, show up?"

"Not yet, Susan, though I doubt she'll be able to resist."

"A wager!" Georgina announced gleefully. "A guinea says she'll be in the ballroom by the time we make our entrance, and that she'll be sporting the Prince of Wales's feathers atop her wig."

"I'll take that wager," Charlotte declared. "I warrant the Gordon clan en masse is far too formidable and intimidating."

Georgina's wry glance swept the chamber. "You lot certainly intimidate me."

"Little liar," her mother refuted. "Yer afeared of neither man nor beast, Georgy!"

"Enough folderol," Charlotte said firmly. "Let us proceed with the nuptials before the groom has a chance to escape. I shall lead the way."

"Remember to smile sweetly," Duchess Gordon directed, "and though capturing young Cornwallis has earned us the well-deserved envy of the *haut ton*, I order you to banish all traces of smugness from yer lovely faces."

"Dearly beloved, we are gathered together here in the sight of God and in the face of this congregation," intoned the exalted Bishop of Lichfield.

And in the face of the formidable Duchess of Gordon, Georgina added silently. She glanced at her brother, Lord George Huntly, who had escorted their mother to the place of honor. *He looks so handsome in his kilt.* She returned the devilish wink he gave her.

"Charles Cornwallis, wilt thou have this woman to thy wedded wife?" the Bishop of Lichfield charged.

Charlie looks so young and vulnerable. Georgina felt a rush of pity rise up in her. *We Gordons are a rum bunch—poor bugger doesn't know what he's letting himself in for.* She glanced at the florid face of Marquis Cornwallis. *The groom, already dominated by his father, will now add his wife's mother to the list . . . From the frying pan into the bloody fire!*

The bishop adjusted his purple miter and cleared his throat. "Louisa Gordon, wilt thou have this man to thy wedded husband?"

My sister will make Charlie happy, and coax him from being so timid. Louisa and I had such rowdy fun together—I shall miss her sorely. Georgina's thoughts flew back to the time their mother had taken her two youngest daughters on her now famous Gordon Highlanders recruiting mission. The daring duchess had wagered with King George that she would enlist more soldiers than any of his royal recruiting officers. Dressed in Highland bonnets and the new Black Watch tartan, the beautiful Gordon ladies, accompanied by six pipers, had visited every market and fair held on the vast Gordon lands. They offered a kiss and a guinea to each and every male who would join the regiment.

At some of those fairs the atmosphere was so racy and flirtatious, Louisa and I behaved like teasing coquettes. The braw Highlanders were so eager to taste our mouths, we recruited a thousand men in less than three months.

"Who giveth this woman to be married to this man?"

Proudly attired in his dress kilt, Alexander, fourth Duke of Gordon, stepped forward. "I do."

Georgina watched her father join her mother. *They*

make a handsome couple. This is the longest they've been together without coming to blows since the last wedding. I wish they could stomach each other. I have my father's black hair and my mother's vivacious personality, and God help me, I love them both dearly.

"Forasmuch as Charles and Louisa have consented together in holy wedlock, I pronounce that they be man and wife together. In the name of the Father, and of the Son, and of the Holy Ghost. Amen." Bishop Cornwallis closed his prayer book and bestowed a sanctified smile upon the newlyweds.

Across the ballroom, George, Prince of Wales, murmured to his close friend the Duke of Bedford, " 'Tis a *fait accompli*, Francis, so you may breathe easy. Congratulations on escaping the clutches of Duchess Gordon and skillfully evading the dreaded institution of marriage yet one more time."

"Jane certainly had me in her sights for Louisa, but red hair never did attract me for long. After an initial skirmish, my interest waned. As for being leg-shackled, my brother John's marriage has given me such a horror of wedded bliss that I have vowed to avoid it at all costs."

Prinny shuddered as he thought of his own disastrous nuptials to his cousin Caroline of Brunswick. *I needed so much brandy to face the ceremony that the only thing I recall is my dear friend Francis Russell propping me up.* " 'Tis the world's greatest pity that *amore* and marriage do not go hand in hand."

"*Au contraire!* Making love to a wife is one of life's sweetest pleasures, so long as I'm not her husband," Russell quipped.

"Lady Melbourne looks particularly ravishing today." Both the prince and Bedford had enjoyed her sexual favors, and each had fathered at least one of her children. Prinny's glance moved to the lady who had accompanied Elizabeth Melbourne, and a heartfelt sigh escaped him. Though for years he had professed his deepest love to Georgianna, Duchess of Devonshire, and had given her a lock of his hair, she always refused to become his mistress. He had been forced to settle for her devoted friendship, which they openly displayed before their aristocratic friends. Prinny raised his eyes from Georgianna's opulent breasts, and they flooded with sentimental tears when he saw that she was sporting the Prince of Wales's feathers. Like iron to a lodestone, Prinny gravitated toward Georgianna, and Bedford followed.

She wafted her ostrich feather fan and sketched a graceful curtsy. "Your Highness . . . Francis . . . I am delighted you both condescended to attend. 'Twill banish our boredom."

The Prince of Wales took her outstretched hand to his lips in a theatrical show of affection. "My dearest Georgianna, I am ever at your command." He bestowed an elegant bow upon Lady Melbourne. "Lizzie, you look charming, as always."

"Ravishing," Bedford said with a leer. "I know a surefire cure for banishing boredom."

"Devil roast you, Francis. Your cure takes nine months," Lady Melbourne drawled. "Do try not to gloat over your bachelorhood. You will be ensnared in the tender trap sooner or later."

The Duchess of Gordon, well versed in protocol, came to greet His Royal Highness, the Prince of Wales, before she acknowledged her other guests. "Such an honor, Yer Highness." Her words were calculated to stress that the honor was his, not hers. Then to prove her point, she dipped her knee and afforded the gentlemen an eye-popping view of her lush breasts.

"Jane, darling," the Duchess of Devonshire gushed, "you've outdone yourself. Young Cornwallis is quite a catch."

Jane glanced at Francis Russell. "You should have seen the one that got away." She slapped her thigh and laughed at her own wit.

The men and Lizzie, thoroughly amused, joined in her laughter.

"Georgianna, dearest, it won't be long before you

are husband hunting for yer own daughters. Shall I lend you my rope and teach you how to tie a Gordon knot?"

"My dear Jane, the Devonshire girls won't need a noose," the duchess said sweetly.

Jane Gordon was too good-natured not to laugh at the riposte. "Yer wit is exceeded only by yer beauty," she said generously.

"Dare I hope that you will be serving your magnificent Highland salmon, my dear duchess?" Prinny was almost salivating.

" 'Tis the thing that makes a Gordon invitation the most sought after in London—that and our famous whiskey punch." The duke owned a salmon fishery on the River Spey, and the wagons that arrived from Scotland always carried barrels of Scotch whiskey.

The Gordon sisters gathered around the bride. Georgina kissed Louisa's cheek. "You are now Lady Brome, freed from Mother's control. I urge you to spread your wings like a butterfly."

Charlotte scoffed. "You two young hellcats were never under her control. Whenever the two of you conspired, mayhem and madness were sure to follow."

Louisa protested, "Georgy was the instigator. I but followed her brilliant suggestions for diversion."

"I have no trouble believing you. She is a triple threat. The little baggage has Mother's beauty, breasts, and boldness."

"You forgot my bawdy sense of humor," Georgina protested.

"You got that from Mother too." Charlotte nodded her head in their mother's direction. "Look at her, she's got a royal audience at the moment." She spied the Duchess of Devonshire. "Ah, I believe I owe you a guinea, Georgy."

"I don't want your guinea . . . what I *do* want is an invitation to Marylebone Manor, where you're staying for the summer. I don't fancy being the lone chick in the nest with Mother for a while. You don't think Lennox will object to my visiting, do you?"

"Lud, no. He's engrossed in the infernal Marylebone Cricket Club that he founded in Dorset Fields. The children will be avid to have you, so I suppose I can force myself to endure you for a fortnight."

"Georgina, you're always welcome at Kimbolton Castle," her sister Susan reminded her.

"Oh, never fear, you and the handsome Duke of Manchester will be next on my list."

"Hmm, handsome is as handsome does," Susan declared with a toss of her head to show that married life was not all blissful.

"Oh, please, no complaints in front of the bride. You will give her a disgust of marriage," Charlotte declared.

Georgina hooted. "If she doesn't have a disgust of marriage from observing our parents, the Duke and Duchess of Manchester's trivial tribulations won't make much of an impact."

"You speak the gospel truth." Charlotte looked at their sister Madelina, who had been widowed and remarried within the past year. "You're on your second husband. Surely you can conjure some words of encouragement and wisdom for the bride."

"Live in the country and keep your husband away from London politics, prostitutes, and private gaming houses."

"Lud, Madelina, your life must be dull as ditch water. Still, I suppose one of us had to take after Father." The Duke of Gordon preferred the country life on his Highland estates and came to London only when it was absolutely necessary. Alexander and Jane had been living separate lives for the past decade.

Georgina glanced across the room at her mother. *I find politics as fascinating as she does, thank heaven.* Jane was holding court with the prince and the Duchess of Devonshire. *The two rivals have far more in common than they would ever admit. Both are leading political hostesses who love being the center of attention. Each is a beauteous, sensual woman, who sets the fashion in clothes, decor, food, and entertainment. Both are married to powerful dukes of the realm who have shamed them by being blatantly unfaithful with more than one mistress.*

Georgina closed her eyes until the tightness left her chest. In spite of her gregarious personality, her parents' estrangement since she was a child had left her vulnerable and often insecure. *I shall never get trapped in a loveless marriage,* she vowed. *I'll never allow myself to become a victim!*

Georgina moved among the throng of invited and uninvited wedding guests with ease, despite the grandeur of their titles. She saw the Marquis of Lansdowne with two of his sons, and knew they would both be eager to partner her when the dancing began.

Georgina paused to speak with Lord and Lady Holland and make them feel welcome. "Beth, it is lovely to see you again. Henry, I insist that you partner me in a Scottish reel when the dancing commences." Henry and Beth had met and fallen in love on the Continent, despite the fact that the lady was already wed. Because of the romantic liaison, her husband was granted a divorce and Henry Fox did the honorable thing and married her immediately.

Georgina spotted Lord and Lady Jersey too late to avoid exchanging pleasantries. She strived valiantly to keep a straight face. It vastly amused her that George, Earl of Jersey, was the Prince of Wales's lord of the bedchamber, while at the moment Frances, Countess of Jersey, was *mistress* of Prinny's bedchamber.

The countess lifted her lorgnette. "You're the young one, if I'm not mistaken. Such a pretty little thing."

"Why, thank you, Lady Jersey." *You're the current one, if I'm not mistaken.*

Frances Jersey's eyes narrowed as she watched Georgina greet the prime minister and Henry Dundas, the home secretary, with casual familiarity. The young one stood on tiptoe to bestow a kiss on each gentleman. "I still haven't fathomed whether Jane Gordon is sleeping with William Pitt or Henry Dundas. What do you think, George?"

"I think people who live in glass houses shouldn't speculate."

"Rubbish! Risqué speculation is the spice of a woman's life."

Georgina spied her brother speaking with a fashionably dressed male who affected an air of haughty superiority. "Hello, George. Promise you'll partner me in the first strathspey?"

"My pleasure, sweetheart," Lord Huntly assured her.

Francis Russell glanced down at the exquisite female whose shiny black curls were piled atop her head and adorned with rosebuds. She wore an elegant white empire gown that displayed her lush upthrust breasts to perfection. His arrogant indifference rapidly dissolved as his cock began to harden, and he experienced a throbbing erection.

"Huntly, I demand an introduction to this lovely young goddess you have been keeping to yourself."

"She is my sister and strictly off-limits to you, Bedford. She hasn't even come out yet."

Georgina gave the Duke of Bedford a saucy smile. "When I do come out, I shall be delighted to make your acquaintance, m'lord."

The buffet tables in the two supper rooms were laden with every delicacy known to fashionable society, as well as a goodly supply of more hearty fare that would appeal to males with healthy appetites and the royal princes who overindulged in the deadly sin of gluttony every day of their lives.

The Duchess of Gordon's liveried servants plied the guests with champagne and her famous whiskey punch, inducing them to lose their inhibitions for when the musicians began to play.

After a couple of hours, the elegant contradances and cotillions gave way to more lively country dances, and the crowded ballroom rang with the joyous laughter of people who were truly beginning to enjoy themselves.

At midnight, the bride and groom cut the wedding cake and were feted with toasts wishing them happiness and fruitfulness. All the guests trooped outside to wave the newlyweds off on their honeymoon. Then, en masse, they hurried back to the ballroom to indulge in the raucous and decidedly scandalous Scottish reels and strathspeys, where arms and legs became entangled, breasts bounced indecently and threatened to escape their confines, while skirts and kilts swung high to display frilly undergarments and the occasional bare buttock.

The festivities did not end until six o'clock in the morning. The Gordon sisters linked arms with their mother as they bade their exhausted guests good-bye.

Georgina watched the Prince of Wales sway precariously as he made his way down the front steps and murmured to her mother, "I warrant he's had one sip too many of that which is fermented!"

Chapter 2

Georgina's lashes fluttered and her eyes flew open. *What the devil was that?* She heard a crash, followed by raised voices. *Damn and blast—they're at it again!* Her heart sank at the realization that her parents were having one of their vicious rows. Their tempers were so volatile that neither Jane nor Alexander Gordon spared a thought for either family members or servants who might overhear them.

"Not one penny more!" The duke's deep voice rumbled like thunder. "Nay, not a brass farthing more!"

"You unreasonable swine! I cannot manage on the annual pittance you allow me." The duchess was primed and ready to do battle.

"Pittance?" Alex bellowed. "Only an avaricious vulture like ye would call four thousand pounds sterling a pittance!"

"Scot skinflint! Penny-pinching miser! You are one of the wealthiest dukes in the realm, yet you expect yer duchess to live like a bloody pauper. I cannot hold my head up in society."

"This *miser* has just laid out two thousand to pay fer yer fancy firkin society weddin'. Yer head is so high, 'tis in the clouds. If yer no' careful, ye *will* be a bloody pauper."

"Don't threaten me, you uncouth Highland bully," Jane screeched.

Georgina, whose bedchamber was directly over the

library, drew up her knees and laid her forehead against them. *Please stop!*

"I'm generous to a fault, woman. I provided Louisa with a dowry of three thousand pounds and she isna even ma' daughter!"

"How you have the bare-faced gall to cavil over Louisa's legitimacy when you have at least half a dozen of yer bastards living at Gordon Castle is beyond belief!"

"Ye refuse to share ma bed," he accused. "I'm a mon, not a bloody monk!"

Georgina pulled the covers over her head with trembling hands.

"Alexander Gordon—Cock o' the North! I wouldn't touch you with a ten-foot pole!" Jane vowed.

The library door crashed and Georgina sprang from her bed, threw open her wardrobe, and began to pack her clothes into a large traveling trunk. When it was full, she threw a bed robe over her nightgown and made her way into the east wing, where most of the guest bedchambers were located.

She paused at her sister Charlotte's door and tapped lightly.

"Come."

Georgina turned the knob and the door swung open to reveal her eldest sister struggling to sit up against her pillows. "Oh, you're still abed."

"Of course I'm still abed. What the devil time is it?"

"It's after nine. I've been packing." Georgina hesitated. "Didn't you hear the row?"

"I heard something, but Lennox's snoring blotted it out." She glanced at her sleeping husband. "What were they rowing about?"

"Money. As usual."

"I should have known." Charlotte saw her sister's pallor. "Don't be upset, Georgy. You'll feel better once you've eaten. I'll come along to your room, and we'll order some breakfast. That'll give Champagne Charlie here some time to sleep it off."

The sisters made their way back to Georgina's spacious bedchamber and Charlotte pulled the bell rope. She inspected her sister's packing. "You'll need sturdy walking shoes. The whole area surrounding Marylebone Manor is quite countrified."

A maidservant answered the summons. She bobbed a curtsy. "The duchess asks ye to join her downstairs fer breakfast."

"How did she know Charlotte and I were up?"

"She didn't. The duchess said any of her daughters would do."

"Lumped together like a gaggle of bloody geese," Charlotte snorted.

"Speak for yourself," Georgina protested. "I'm a swan."

Charlotte sighed with resignation. "She most likely feels in need of reinforcements. You may tell Mother we'll be down."

The sisters didn't bother to dress; they went down in their bed robes and slippers. Unconventionality reigned supreme in the Gordon household, and each member felt free to dress and speak exactly as she pleased.

"Good morning, my wee lassies. I think you will agree the wedding was a triumph! I can't wait to read what the *Times* will have to say." Jane showed no visible signs that the row had ruffled her feathers or cast the slightest shadow over her spectacular social achievement.

"You have the true stamina of a Highlander. You amaze me. I don't know how you do it," Charlotte declared.

"You forget . . . I was a Maxwell long before I was a Gordon. Resilience was bred into my bones."

As Georgina watched her mother lift the silver covers on the sideboard and fill her plate with gammon ham, lamb kidneys, and eggs, she suppressed a shudder. She served herself with a bowl of oatmeal and poured on a liberal amount of cream and honey. "Charlotte has invited me for a visit, and I have accepted," Georgina said in an attempt to forestall any plans her mother might conceive. *I invited myself, but Mother isn't to know that.*

"I thought we might go to the play tonight, or perhaps Ranelagh, but apparently the pair of you are abandoning me to my own devices."

"It'll give you a chance to spend some time with Father," Charlotte said with a straight face.

"You know he can't abide London for more than five minutes. He's returning to Fochabers."

"When?" Georgina dropped her spoon.

"Already left for all I know . . . or care," Jane said lightly.

Her youngest daughter jumped up, almost oversetting her chair. *I can't let him go without saying good-bye.* Georgina rushed upstairs to the bedchamber her father always occupied when he stayed at the Pall Mall house. She saw to her dismay that it was empty and that the sheets had already been stripped from the bed. She ran to the window and saw that the black traveling coach was standing outside the stables and the team of Cleveland bays had already been harnessed for the long journey.

Georgina flew down the stairs, hurried through the kitchen, and ran as fast as she could toward the berlin coach. "Father, surely you weren't leaving without saying good-bye?"

Alexander took his breathless young daughter into his arms. "Ma wee lass, I thought ye'd still be sound asleep. Will ye miss yer old dad?"

She pressed her face against his caped greatcoat. "You know I will. I was hoping to sketch you in your kilt. You looked so grand in your wedding finery yesterday."

"All my lasses have had drawing lessons, but ye are the only true artist, Georgy. I treasure that sketch ye did of me fishin' in the Spey. Next time ye come to Fochabers, we'll go fishin' again—just the two of us."

"I'll come before autumn is over, I promise."

"Good lass. Well, I'm away—can't wait to get the

stink o' London outa ma nostrils and fill ma lungs wi' the invigoratin' air o' Scotland."

Georgina stood waving until the black coach went through the gates and turned toward Piccadilly, unmindful of the stable hands gaping at her *dishabille.*

Three hours later, Georgina stepped up into her sister Charlotte's carriage, which bore the ducal arms of Richmond on its door. Charles Lennox, mounted on a Thoroughbred, saluted his wife and took off at a gallop.

The carriage lurched forward. "Wretched driver," Charlotte complained. "My stomach is queasy before we even start."

Georgina gave her a speculative look.

"Yes, I'm breeding again." She sighed heavily. "I've produced six children in the past eight years, and now I'm caught again. All Lennox has to do is throw his trousers on the bloody bed."

"Well, at least they are all fathered by your husband." Georgina smiled at her fondly. "That must be some sort of a record in London society."

Charlotte laughed wryly. "I have neither time nor inclination to take a lover."

"No doubt a diabolical plan by Lennox to keep you for himself," Georgina teased. She tentatively ran her tongue around her lips, and then blurted out, "Who is Louisa's father?"

Charlotte stared at her youngest sister for a full minute, then recounted what she knew. "When Mother was your age, she fell madly in love with an Edinburgh lad from the Fraser clan. He was sent to fight the war in America with the Fraser Highlanders and it broke her heart when she got word that he had been killed.

"Her Mother insisted she accept a proposal of marriage from the wealthy, powerful Duke of Gordon, since such a miraculous offer from one of Scotland's highest nobles would never come her way again. After a year of mourning her first love, Mother gave in to the relentless pressure and did her mother's bidding.

"When she was about six months pregnant with me, she received a letter from Fraser in America. When she realized he was very much alive, she collapsed from shock and suffered some sort of a breakdown. I don't think Father ever forgave her for preferring another man over him."

"It would be a devastating blow to his pride to be thought second best," Georgina said with heartfelt compassion. "So you believe that her childhood sweetheart returned to Scotland and he and Mother became lovers?"

"Putting two and two together, that's the explanation I came up with. Louisa has the distinctive Fraser auburn hair and, approximately nine months before she was born, the seventy-first Fraser Highlanders regiment returned from America."

Georgina jumped in. "The Fraser ancestral home is in Struy, not too far from her beloved farm in Kinrara, where Mother has always spent her summer months."

"Exactly. Though Fraser returned to America years ago."

"We are lucky she didn't run off with him," Georgina said.

"And give up her exalted position as Duchess of Gordon? I think not. When she married Father, she decided that her head would rule her heart, and she's brought us up to do the same. It's the wisest choice, Georgy, when all's said and done."

But they are not happy together! Georgina kept a wise silence. *Perhaps Charlotte's head ruled her heart when she wed the future Duke of Richmond.* She closed her eyes. *I will never do that. I will never marry a man unless I love him with all my heart!*

A chorus of "Mama! Mama! Georgy! Georgy!" greeted the two sisters when they entered Marylebone Manor. Charlotte's young children outran their two nursemaids. Lord John and Lord James, four-year-old twins, and three-year-old Lady Sarah wrapped their arms about their mother's skirt and jumped for joy. Lady Mary, who was five, almost six, threw herself at her favorite aunt and said with a beatific smile, "I didn't know you were coming!"

Georgina picked her up and twirled about. "Surprise! Surprise!" She absolutely adored children and couldn't wait until she had her own. She suspected that being a mother was the only part of marriage that she would truly enjoy. A nursemaid came forward carrying a baby girl who was not quite two. Georgina asked Mary, "What's the baby's name . . . I have forgotten."

Mary giggled helplessly. "Her name is *Georgina*!"

"Such a strange name . . . I can never remember it." Georgina counted the children aloud, "One, two, three, four, five . . . someone is missing."

"It's Charles. Papa came home, and they went to the stables."

"He likely prefers male company now that he's almost nine."

"This year I'll be six, and next year I'm going to be *seven*," Mary said importantly. "Can I try on your hat, Aunt Georgy?"

"*May* I try on your hat?" Georgina corrected.

"I'm not wearing a hat, silly," Mary said, giggling.

"So you're not. In that case, have mine." She set Mary's feet to the carpet, removed her large-brimmed straw with its pretty ruched satin ribbons, and placed it on her niece's head. "You look absolutely divine, Lady Mary."

"Why, thank you, Lady Georgy."

"I hate to break up your mutual-admiration society, but I need you to come upstairs and decide which bedchamber you prefer."

"We prefer the pink room," Mary said without hesitation.

"Thank you, Mistress Know-all," Charlotte declared.

"Come on." Georgina took hold of Mary's hand,

and they followed Charlotte. The three younger children trailed after them, navigating the stairs on hands and knees. "Be careful you don't fall," she cautioned over her shoulder.

"If they fall, they'll pick themselves up. How else are they to learn?" Mary said wisely.

"Nobody picked up you and me," Charlotte reminded her sister, "and look how self-sufficient we turned out to be."

"We were undisciplined hellions." Georgina chose the pink bedchamber.

Mary gazed up at Georgina with a rapt look of adulation. "Will you teach me to be an undisciplined hellion?"

"I shall," she solemnly promised. "Your lessons start tomorrow."

An hour later, Georgina had finished unpacking, and she joined the children in the nursery for their tea. By this time young Charles had returned from the stables.

"Hallo, Aunt Georgy. Will you play a game with us tonight?"

"Of course. What shall we play? Hide-and-seek?"

"No, the babies always hide in plain sight. We'll play tag."

"Ha! You think you can catch me?" Georgina challenged.

"I'll give it a good shot," Charles declared, cramming half a scone into his mouth.

"Oh, well, if you're going to use a gun, that's taking unfair advantage."

He choked with laughter, and Georgina thumped him on the back.

"I don't like raspberry jam. It has too many seeds," Mary complained, determined to regain her aunt's attention.

"Raspberry seeds give you magical power," Georgina said as she spooned jam onto Mary's scone.

Her eyes went round as saucers. "I need some of

that." Mary changed her mind about the jam and proceeded to eat the scone.

Charles wrinkled his nose. "Warm milk is for babies."

"I'll ask your father to send some ale immediately."

The young heir laughed so hard, he fell off his chair.

The moment the nursery maid cleared the table, Charles said, "I'll count to ten to give you a head start."

Georgina jumped up, and ran like the wind. The nursery was located on the ground floor, where the late-afternoon sunshine flooded in through the west windows. She raced down the hallway, through the formal dining room, rushed past the library, and on into a large sitting room.

George Finch, Earl of Winchilsea, a great friend of Lennox who was also a cricket enthusiast, stepped from the library to view the runners. He was amazed to see a beautiful young hoyden climb up and over the backs of two sitting room chairs in a mad dash to escape from two squealing children in wild pursuit.

"Don't mind the racket, George. It's always bedlam when my young sister-in-law visits."

"A tempting sylph I wouldn't mind pursuing."

"A sticky wicket, George. She's not out yet."

The earl cocked a rueful eyebrow. "Forbidden fruit."

"She's not ripe for plucking—as you can see, Lady Georgina still prefers children's games."

"Just my luck." Winchilsea held out his glass for a refill.

That night at dinner the elegant young woman in the tasteful gown presented a very different picture from the madcap creature that had been vaulting over the sitting room furniture.

When she was introduced to the Earl of Winchilsea, her expressive dark green eyes lit up her face. "I am delighted to meet you, George. I shall look forward to a lesson in how to whack a cricket ball tomorrow." Her mother had taught her to pander unscrupulously to the male ago and to treat gentlemen informally, no matter their noble rank. Therein lay the secret to charming the male of the species.

"Lady Georgina, would you really deign to play cricket?"

"Why not? I play tennis, and when I'm in Scotland I often play golf."

The earl was completely captivated by the vivacious beauty and hung on her every word. At the end of the meal, when they had finished eating and Georgina dipped her fingers into her crystal finger bowl, he murmured, "Your sweet touch could turn water to wine. I'm almost tempted to drink it."

Georgina murmured back outrageously, "When I wash my feet tonight shall I have the maid save the water for you?"

Next morning, Georgina awoke to find Mary curled up in bed with her. "How did you get here?"

"Magic power," Mary said solemnly.

"Ah, from eating raspberry jam, I warrant. What would you like to do on this warm, sunny day?"

"Can we go for a ramble through the woods? Just us two?"

"*May* we go for a ramble?"

"Yes, we *may*!" Mary's face lit with rapture.

Georgina took one of Mary's chubby feet in her hand and inspected it. "Are you a good rambler?"

"I can walk miles and miles," she declared.

Georgina took hold of the child's big toe. "This little piggy went to market." She moved on to the next one. "This little piggy stayed home. This little piggy had roast beef. But this little piggy had none," she said sadly.

"Aw, poor piggy, eh?" Mary said with heartfelt compassion.

Georgina transformed her face from sad to happy. "This little piggy cried wee, wee, wee, all the way home." She dropped the foot and tickled Mary's tummy.

The child giggled and wriggled, the pillows went flying, and the pair rolled off the bed with laughter.

A maid arrived with a breakfast tray. "There you are, little Miss Mischief. Nanny's been looking for you."

"I'm a *big* girl," Mary protested.

"Tell Nanny that she's safe and sound with me. The big girls are spending the morning together."

"Very good, my lady." The maid bobbed a curtsy and left.

"I'll soon be as big as you, Georgy." Mary stood on tiptoe beside her aunt. Since Georgina was on the small side and still had some growing of her own to do, Mary's head came just below her breasts. "I'll soon be as tall as your titties."

Georgina hid her amusement. "You have a way with words."

The big girls soon devoured everything on the breakfast tray.

"Go and get dressed. Choose an old smock that won't get ruined on our ramble, and don't forget to put on some shoes."

Georgina donned her plainest gown. It was an oyster-colored batiste cotton that looked rather drab. *It won't matter if it gets soiled. I warrant the dirt won't even show.* She drew on her stockings and slipped into her sturdy walking shoes. She brushed her dark curls and left them loose about her shoulders.

The pair of nature lovers set off on their ramble and soon left the gardens of Marylebone Manor behind. They began to climb the wooded slope known as Primrose Hill, and clouds of tiny midges gathered above their heads. Georgina broke off a couple of leafy branches and handed the smaller one to Mary. "Swish it about like a magic wand and the midges will disappear . . . poof!"

In imitation, Mary wafted her wand. "Poof! Poof!" The child laughed with delight. "It really is magic!"

They crested Primrose Hill and gazed downward. "The lower woods are perfect for deer. We must proceed quietly."

A field mouse scurried under some large burdock leaves, and Mary squealed with laughter. The noise alerted a pair of squirrels, and a brown rabbit that had been nibbling a fern bolted away in fright. Mary put her finger to her lips. "Sshh!"

They stopped and listened. Georgina could hear running water and the voices of shouting boys. They descended the hill and emerged from the woods into a meadow through which ran a wide stream that was a tributary of the Thames. Two boys were standing on the bank holding fishing rods.

"Noisy buggers!" Mary muttered.

Georgina knew it was a word her little niece shouldn't use, but she also knew from personal experience that in a household with a large number of children, swear words were relished.

As they drew closer to the stream, Georgina saw that the boys were almost as tall as she, though she guessed their ages to be only eleven and twelve. Then she saw a much younger boy sitting on the bank, and guessed all three were brothers.

"Any luck?"

"No. They're not biting," the eldest told her.

"That's because it's too shallow. If you want to catch fish, you should wade out to the middle, where the water runs deeper."

"Are you sure?" the dark-haired boy with the serious face said.

"Of course I'm sure. When I fish in the River Spey in Scotland, I always wade out. Let me show you."

"William, give her your rod," the eldest brother directed.

"Mary, sit down on the bank and watch." Georgina kicked off her shoes, kilted up her skirts, took the rod William handed her, and waded out to where the water came up past her knees.

After only two or three minutes she got a bite, and the fish on the hook began to splash about.

"You got one! You got one!" The two boys, filled with excitement, waded out to get a closer look.

Georgina handed the rod back to William so he could have the joy of the catch. The two children who had been sitting on the bank joined them in the water. "My name is Johnny," the little one said shyly.

"Hello, Johnny. You should have taken off your shoes."

"I took mine off," Mary said importantly.

Suddenly, a man's harsh voice rent the air. "Francis! William! What the devil are you about?"

Georgina whirled, slipped on a stone, and lost her footing, thoroughly wetting herself. Striding toward them was an extremely tall man with a powerful build and jet-black hair, and she could see that he was angry. She had often seen her father lose his temper, but the dark look of fury on this man's face made him seem far more dangerously threatening than the Duke of Gordon.

The two older boys quickly scrambled from the water, but the young one froze.

"You two devils are supposed to protect John from danger!" he thundered. "It's a damn good thing I came to see what you were up to." His dark, accusing eyes swept over the bedraggled Georgina. "Little girl, have you no more sense than to lure my sons into the middle of the river?" he demanded.

"It's just a stream," she protested.

He removed his shoes, rolled up his trouser legs, then waded out into the water and picked up his son. "John, you'll be ill again." He towered above Georgina, and his wrath turned his face dark and ominous.

Georgina found the man extremely intimidating. It wasn't just the fury he displayed that was frightening; it was the deep-suppressed anger in his black eyes that he kept reined in that daunted her. *If he ever unleashes his rage, it will be like opening the gates of hell.*

"Little girl, go home! And take your sister with you. It's a wonder you didn't drown!"

Georgina was highly offended. *Little girl, indeed!* He spoke to her as if she were a ragamuffin instead of a duke's daughter.

"Did you hear me, little girl? Go home!"

She had to summon all her courage to answer him back. Georgina flung her hair back over her shoulder, raised her chin, and shouted insolently, "Go to the devil . . . *old man!*"

He looked as if he wanted to strike her, but she glared back at him defiantly. He carried his son from the water, but Georgina noted the two older ones had fled. She took Mary's hand, and they waded from the stream. They put their shoes on over their wet stockings and Mary, mimicking Georgina, shouted, "Old Man!"

Chapter 3

John Russell carried his soaking wet son across Dorset Fields toward the house he had leased for the summer in Dorset Square.

"I'm sorry, Papa," Johnny said contritely.

"It's all right. It's your mother who will have a fit. You know she's not well." He remembered the harsh words he'd said to his wife when she had objected to the boys going out into the fields: *Elizabeth, for God's sake, let the boys be boys. They're cooped up all year in school. This is their summer holiday. You are being overly fearful to believe they'll come to any harm.*

John entered the house and hoped to get his youngest upstairs before Elizabeth saw him.

"Is Johnny wet?" Her voice rose hysterically. "He'll come down with pneumonia! I told you he shouldn't go outside."

"He will be fine," John reassured her. "Please don't upset yourself."

"You never listen to me. I have these dark premonitions come over me, and I know something dreadful will happen to Johnny."

"Yes, I know all about your dark thoughts, Elizabeth. I'll take him upstairs and get him into some dry clothes."

John Russell's wife suffered from acute melancholia, which had become more pronounced with the birth of her third child. For almost nine years she'd been deeply depressed and low in spirits. Her husband had tried everything to dispel her gloom and her fearful anxiety, yet nothing rid her mind of its dark shadows.

John took his son into his bedchamber, and a maidservant came forward to help. He waved her away, closed the door, and removed the boy's wet clothes. He took dry garments from the bureau and handed them to his son so that he could dress himself. "You won't get pneumonia, John. Your mother can't help her fears."

"I wish she could be happy," he said wistfully.

"Yes, but you mustn't let her fears stop *you* from being happy."

Johnny looked up from buttoning his shirt. "Wading in the river made me happy," he murmured.

A bark of laughter escaped from John. "I'm glad—but don't go in the water again unless I'm with you."

His two older sons pushed open the door and came into the room. They had already changed into dry clothes. Francis said, "We came in the back way and crept upstairs so she wouldn't see us and become upset."

Anger rose up in John that his sons had to creep about quietly, and it took him a minute to control it. *I should have left her at home in Devon.*

Their sons attended prestigious Westminster School and when they finished for the summer, John brought Elizabeth to London to be with the boys and to also see a physician. They had gone to his family's ancestral town house in Russell Square, but Elizabeth had become agitated with the London noise and fearful of the traffic. On the doctor's advice, John had leased a house in the more rural outskirts of the city, in the hope that the bucolic setting would calm her nerves.

The doctor had told him privately that his wife looked consumptive and would benefit from fresh air and country walks. Though John was highly skeptical about consumption, he knew that languishing on a couch in a darkened chamber would only foster his wife's ill health. Elizabeth had given up riding years ago, and now she even refused to walk outdoors. *She enjoys being an invalid, sunk in sepulchral gloom. I should have left her in Devonshire.*

"There's a cricket match on Saturday. Would you like to go?"

"Yes, please!" William was on the junior team at Westminster.

"Just the four of us?" Francis asked, eagerly.

"Yes, just us men. Your mother doesn't care for sports."

Charlotte welcomed the drooping buttercup and daisy bouquet Mary had picked for her. "Thank you for the flowers, darling. They're lovely. I can see the pair of you had a fabulous time."

"How did you know?" Mary asked, wide-eyed.

"Children are happiest when they are dirty or wet." She eyed Georgina. "Even grown children. Since the pair of you are dirty *and* wet, a fabulous time was had by both!"

"We saw a bad man," Mary declared. "A bad *old man* who told us to go home. Georgy told him to go to the devil."

"Really?" Charlotte's lips twitched with amusement. "What happened to Lady Georgina's fatal charm that renders men weak?"

Georgina declared, "He was totally impervious to it. The surly sod addressed me as *little girl*! I wanted to kick his shins."

Charlotte laughed. "What stopped you?"

"The thought of breaking my toe," Georgina replied ruefully. *The man was definitely dangerous! The dark, dominant brute looked quite capable of giving me a thrashing.*

In the early afternoon, Georgina strolled out behind the stables to where her brother-in-law had set up permanent wickets so that he could practice.

She was wearing a crisp blue linen dress and had brushed her dark curls back and tied them with a ribbon. With a warm smile, she greeted her brother-in-law, who was pitching the ball to his friend George Finch. "Charles, cricket isn't your hobby. It is your obsession," she teased.

"Mea culpa," he said with a grin. "Winchilsea and I have a match on Saturday." Since Lennox was the member of parliament for Sussex, he played for the Sussex team.

The earl completely missed the ball because his attention was focused on the vision in blue. Young Charlie Lennox ran to retrieve the ball and return it to his father.

Winchilsea asked, "Would you like to come and watch the match?"

"George, I would enjoy it above all things."

"Jolly good! How about that lesson I promised you? Come over here, and I'll show you how to hold the bat."

Georgina knew exactly how to hold a cricket bat, but she wasn't about to spoil the earl's pleasure. She winked at Lennox standing on the mound and joined Winchilsea.

He handed her the bat and placed his arms around her. "There's a special knack to it, you know. Above all else, you must keep your eye on the ball."

"I feel most honored that you are willing to share your secrets with me, George." She held him in thrall with flattery.

Lennox watched the interaction between his friend and his young sister-in-law and thought perhaps he had been wrong yesterday. Georgina just might be ripe for plucking.

Elizabeth Russell, as always, withdrew early to her own bedchamber, and John dined with his sons. After dinner, the two older boys played a quiet game of chess. At bedtime, John read to his youngest son, and then in his own chamber, he did paperwork that dealt with the needs of his constituents.

His grandfather had instilled in him that wealth and

privilege brought great responsibility to those less fortunate. John thoroughly enjoyed representing the people of Tavistock, and worked tirelessly in the House of Commons to better the lives of his working-class constituents. If the government turned down his proposals, he paid for improvements out of his own money.

That had always been a bone of contention with Elizabeth. She was adamantly against any of their wealth being *squandered*, as she called it, on the *lower* classes. As a result, John had learned to keep his own counsel and to never discuss politics with her.

John finished his paperwork and went to bed. About an hour after he fell asleep, his recurring dream began. *He was astride his hunter, riding through a sun-drenched meadow filled with wildflowers. Their heady scent, combined with the exhilarating feeling of freedom he experienced, was intoxicating.*

The female companion riding beside him was a joyous creature who loved and lived life to the fullest. She had a passion for nature, and children, and animals, and he never tired of hearing her laugh. They were racing their horses toward a hill, and John knew he would let her win for the sheer pleasure of watching her exult in her victory.

Suddenly, they were drenched by a summer shower, but the lady did not even slow down. She galloped up the hill, slid from her saddle, and climbed up on a high boulder. She raised her arms and exultantly lifted her face to the rain, as if it were the elixir of life.

John dismounted at the base of the boulder and he held up his arms. "Jump! I'll catch you."

Her silvery laughter was the loveliest thing he'd ever heard. Without hesitation she flung herself with total abandon into his waiting arms. He caught her and then rolled with her until he had her pinned beneath him in the wet grass.

When he captured her soft, warm mouth it tasted of delicious laughter and sensual anticipation. It was heady intoxication to know that she wanted him as much as he desired making love to her. The reaction her eagerness stirred in him was a potent spur to possess her body and soul and lure her to surrender her essence to him.

She was that rare female who could blot out his pain and anger and the dark thoughts that tortured his mind. He could lose himself in the tempting, honeyed depths of her body, where she allowed him to indulge any wicked fantasy for which he thirsted and craved.

He enjoyed the seduction because it heightened their desire and brought the blissful, almost unendurable pleasure that allowed him to escape as nothing else could.

The intense delirium his lovemaking aroused in her took him to a place where only rich, dark sensation existed. He indulged a passion so powerful, it brought exquisite pleasure, followed by peace and deep contentment.

John awoke with the usual sense of acute loss. He knew he had had the recurring dream again because the details were so vivid. The only thing he could never recall was the face of his joyful companion. And though he did not often allow himself the indulgence of introspection, he realized he could never remember what she looked like, because she was a mythical creature—there was no face, no woman. His dream was a manifestation of a suppressed longing for more laughter, joy, and freedom in his life.

On Friday evening at Marylebone Manor, Thomas Lord was a guest at dinner. The match on Saturday was being played at nearby Lord's Cricket Ground, which Lennox and Winchilsea had backed financially when it opened. Once again the subject of cricket monopolized the men's conversation.

By the time dessert was served, Charlotte had had enough. "Lady Georgina and I will take our dessert in the sitting room," she told the footman. "Really, gentlemen, I believe the conversation in the nursery would be more stimulating."

The gentlemen stood and offered their sincere apologies as the sisters left the dining room. Georgina tucked her legs underneath her on a sofa and picked up a scrapbook of newspaper clippings. She briefly scanned the articles about Charles Lennox, Earl of March. They hailed him as a renowned cricket player, both as a wicket keeper and a right-hand bat. She flipped over the pages and found something much more to her liking.

"Oh, here is an article from the *Times* about the grand ball at the Pantheon given to celebrate the king's recovery from his devastating malady. You and Mother were patrons of the event. I was pea green with envy because I was too young to attend. It sounds like it was a most opulent affair: *More than two thousand guests danced the night away, drank champagne, and sang 'God Save the King.' The Duchess of Gordon and her daughter, the Countess of Lennox, decreed that all the guests should wear white and gold. The ball was opened by Jane, Duchess of Gordon, on the arm of Prime Minister Pitt to the sound of loud applause.*"

"It was a mad crush, and unbelievably expensive. Ostensibly, the ball was to celebrate King George's return to sanity, but in reality it was to mark the political victory of William Pitt."

"Yes, the Prince of Wales and his friend Charles James Fox thought they could secure control of the administration when the king became incapacitated. But the brilliant Mr. Pitt introduced the Regency Bill in parliament to limit the prince's power. The arguments in the House, both pro and con, delayed any action being taken, and before it was passed to the House of Lords for a decision, King George suddenly regained his sanity."

"You have quite a grasp of politics for a young lady of fashion," Charlotte said with admiration.

"How could I not? Mother's liaison with Henry

Dundas, the prime minister's home secretary, gives me a front-row seat about what's going on in the government. I have to admit that I am fascinated by politics."

" 'Tis said that power is an aphrodisiac . . . Mother's long-standing intimate friendship with the Scot statesman proves it."

"Louisa and I regularly went up in the House of Commons gallery to listen to the speeches. Disguised as males, of course, to add to our enjoyment. I shall have to find another partner in crime to aid and abet me."

"Surely Huntly will accommodate you, and with our brother as escort, you needn't disguise yourself."

"I suppose that will be the great advantage to my coming out. I will no longer be excluded from moving about in fashionable circles. I shall also be able to attend balls and entertainments thrown by the *haut ton*'s leading hostesses." Georgina wrinkled her nose. "Unfortunately, being thrust onto the marriage market will be the great *disadvantage.*"

"When I came out, Mother set her sights on her dear friend and ally, William Pitt, believe it or not. She was so determined to make a match between us that she began to take me with her to visit him at his house in Wimbledon. Though William paid respectful attention to me, it never progressed to the amorous stage, and I believe it finally dawned on Mother that the prime minister was a confirmed bachelor."

"Oh, that's priceless. I'm so glad you didn't allow her to choose your husband for you, Charlotte. I too intend to decide whom I shall marry."

"Don't delude yourself, Georgina," her sister said dryly.

"I wish . . ." Georgina's voice trailed away.

"What do you wish, my dear?"

"I wish Mother and Father weren't estranged. Do you suppose they were ever in love?"

"I don't know. They had a strong physical attraction at one time. They were certainly in lust—I don't know about love."

"She was unquestionably a good wife and mother. Though the Maxwells were far lower than the Gordons in noble rank, she made him a magnificent duchess. She certainly devoted herself to helping the Gordon tenants, and by doing so made Father's fortunes grow. She started the local industry of weaving, and introduced the wearing of tartan into fashionable society, which in turn boosted Highland manufacturing. She taught the cottagers how to grow and dress flax. She urged Father to build mills, then convinced other nobles to start mills in their own Highland towns."

"The spinning, dying, and weaving of wool have certainly helped to alleviate the scourge of poverty that is so prevalent in Scotland," Charlotte agreed. "She even became an advocate for children to be educated in how to grow crops, so they can take over their fathers' farms."

"She became political only when she realized that more long-term solutions were needed to cure poverty. She was also a tireless patron of the arts in Scotland and then in England. Mother is an unparalleled hostess. No man could ask for a more accomplished partner."

"True! Yet Father has rewarded her with a passel of bastards—there's thanks for you."

"I know I complain about her, because of her shameless pursuit of titled husbands for her daughters, but I am extremely proud of her accomplishments. She is a force to be reckoned with."

"You are very like her, Georgina."

"Well, she has brought us all up in her own image to be unabashed sensualists and enjoy life to the fullest."

"As well as her vivacity, you have her great beauty. Of course, you are more delicate and refined, and thankfully far more cultured. Mother has a coarseness about her that you didn't inherit, praise heaven! I assure you that the runt of the litter turned out to be quite a dazzling jewel."

"Your praise is far too generous, Charlotte. I have

myriad flaws that I don't always manage to keep hidden."

On Saturday they arrived early at Lord's Cricket Grounds, and much to Georgina's amusement, she watched as a herd of sheep were rounded up and driven from the field. They were allowed to graze at Lord's to keep the grass short. "You gentlemen had better acquit yourselves well in the match today, or it will be said that the sheep have a better right to the grass than you do."

"Cricket fanatics are impervious to insult," Charlotte assured her. "Let's stroll about before the match starts. It will give us a chance to show off our elegant hats and make disparaging remarks about the other ladies' dresses."

Georgina was adorned from head to foot in pristine white. As well as a fashionable large-brimmed hat, she had brought a frilly parasol to shade her from the sun.

The two sisters made their way through the crowd, exchanging greetings with friends and acquaintances gathered to watch the sporting event that was gaining popularity with the upper classes.

"Lady Stafford believes she looks quite fetching in that bilious shade of green, when in actual fact it is simply retching!" Charlotte looked over her shoulder. "Now, where did that boy get to?" She had brought her eldest son to watch the cricket match.

"Charlie is with his father," Georgina assured her. "He's at an age where being thought a mother's boy is anathema."

The ladies circled back to where they had left Lennox and Winchilsea, and found them conversing with a group of men who were obviously cricket enthusiasts.

Suddenly, Georgina stopped in her tracks. *Hell and damnation!* The dark, dominant, and dangerous devil she had encountered yesterday was deep in conversation with her brother-in-law. The two spoke as if they were friends. *They obviously know each other. The last thing I want is another encounter with the uncouth brute.* She turned her head and adjusted her parasol so that the tall, dark male would not recognize her.

"Is something wrong?" Charlotte asked.

"I think I must have dropped my gloves back there somewhere. I'll go and have a quick look, and catch up with you."

Georgina walked back the way she had come, determined to put distance between herself and the authoritative male who had accosted her. The thudding of her heart in her eardrums was so loud that it blocked out the noise of the people in the crowd. *Why are you running away? Only a coward would retreat,* her inner voice accused. *I'm not running away,* she assured herself, *I'm simply avoiding an unpleasant encounter. I cannot abide imperious, domineering males who think they have God-given dominion over females.*

Georgina did not return to her sister until Charlotte was sitting in the stands and the match was about to begin.

"Did you find your gloves?"

"No. Perhaps I forgot to wear gloves today." Her glance roamed the stands, surreptitiously searching for the dark man with the stern features. She finally spotted him standing close to the action. He had found an advantageous spot for his three sons to observe the game close-up. She deliberately moved her parasol to block him from her vision.

During the match, Georgina found she could not concentrate on the game. Her mind kept wandering to the dark stranger, and she grew most annoyed that he drew her thoughts like a magnet. Though she felt intense dislike for him, she could not deny that her curiosity was piqued. She lost track of the runs, and at the end of the game she had no notion which team had won.

"Charlotte, your husband played a first-class game."

"Thank heaven the Sussex team won or there would be no living with him tonight. Let's find the carriage. Lennox and Winchilsea will be hobnobbing and celebrating for hours."

* * *

Later that night, at dinner, Georgina tried to satisfy her curiosity. "Before the match today, I saw you talking with a big fellow with black hair," she said casually.

"I spoke with a lot of chaps," Lennox acknowledged. "Can you be more specific?"

"He had rather dark, arrogant features. He appeared to have his young sons with him."

"Ah, that was John Russell, Lord Tavistock. He's the member of parliament for his district in Devonshire. He's quite a forceful speaker—has a commanding presence on the floor of the House. He's a sincere chap, with strong views. Seems to thoroughly enjoy representing the people."

Forceful and commanding describe him to a T.

"John Russell? He's the Duke of Bedford's younger brother," Charlotte said. "The Russell brothers were orphaned at an early age, and brought up by their grandparents, the Marquis and Marchioness of Tavistock. Strange how dissimilar brothers can turn out to be. Marriage is anathema to Bedford, yet John couldn't wait. Against his grandmother's express wishes, he wed Elizabeth Byng in Brussels when he was only nineteen. He was a young ensign in the Footguards, and fought in Belgium."

"Speaking of grandmothers, Elizabeth Byng's *grandmere* was a Lennox," Charles remarked. "So John's wife is a distant relative of mine."

"Lud, I wouldn't be surprised if the entire British aristocracy was related through intermarriage," Charlotte said dryly.

"Charlie is about the same age as John's youngest. They got along so well today that I invited him to visit us. He's taken a house for the summer close by on the other side of Dorset Fields."

Hell and damnation! I must avoid the surly devil at all costs. With any luck he won't come.

"I think we should extend an invitation for the Russells to come to the August races at Goodwood."

Goodwood House was the seat of the Duke of Richmond, near Chichester in Sussex. The opulent mansion was filled with priceless treasures and had its own racecourse.

Georgina's spirits sank. She was sorry she had ever asked Charles who the man was. She assured herself she didn't have the least interest in the churlish lout. *I shall make a point of missing the Goodwood races this year.* "Speaking of the Duke of Bedford, he flirted outrageously with me at Louisa's wedding. Our brother gave him a set down. It was most amusing."

Georgina had managed to change the subject, and she made a determined effort to dismiss Bedford's brother from her thoughts. That night, however, John Russell haunted her dreams.

Georgina was fishing in the River Spey with her father. She waded out to the deeper water where the salmon were fighting their way upstream. The spring thaw had made the rushing river far more dangerous than usual, and Georgina slipped on a stone and lost her footing. Her head went beneath the swirling torrent, and she found herself out of her depth and in serious trouble.

Suddenly, a powerfully built man with black hair appeared from nowhere. Without hesitation he forged his way into the raging water, and swam to her side. His arms closed around her, and he lifted her high against his powerful chest.

Georgina clung to him, weak with relief, as he carried her from the river. His arms were so strong that she had never felt this safe in her entire life.

"Little girl, it's a wonder you didn't drown!"

She smiled up into his dark eyes. He was angry, but he knew she was a woman grown. Calling her "little girl" was a term of endearment. She loved the idea that he had rescued her, and wanted to protect her from danger. She had never experienced such tender concern from a man before, and it was intoxicating.

"Thank you, 'old man,' " she whispered provocatively.

Chapter 4

"How are you feeling, Elizabeth?" John Russell crossed to the sitting room window to let some fresh air into the stuffy chamber.

"Please don't open the window. Drafts are very bad for me. I actually felt tranquil while you were all away this afternoon. I believe the boys are too much for me."

John heard the plaintive note in her voice and strived for patience. *What sort of a mother cannot bear the presence of her own children?* "I hope you'll be joining us for dinner."

"No, I'm not hungry. All I want is peace and quiet. I think I shall go up to bed and have Gertrude bring me a tray."

"If you wish." John removed her lap robe and helped her to rise. He felt her stiffen at his touch, and quickly withdrew his hands. She had permitted no intimacy in almost nine years.

John accompanied his wife as she slowly climbed the stairs. Young Johnny, who was standing at the top of the staircase, smiled sweetly at his mother. "It was a great cricket match!"

"Your mother's not feeling well."

"I'm so sorry, Mama. Would you like me to read to you?"

"No! I have a vile headache. Leave me be, Johnny."

John saw the happy smile leave his young son's face, and he bit back a cruel retort. "I'll send Gertrude to you," he said curtly. *I should have left her in Devon. Sooner or later I'll lose control of my temper. If I hold it in much longer, it will erupt like bloody Vesuvius.*

The next morning, John suggested that William get out his bat, and the four of them would enjoy a game of cricket. He cut some wood, made makeshift wickets, and then spent the next three hours pitching the ball to them. Not only did it give the boys much-needed exercise and fun in the fresh summer air, it kept them out of the house and away from their mother's continual disapproval.

When they returned, he sent them upstairs to clean up before lunch. He found Elizabeth on her usual chaise huddled beneath a lap robe. The sitting room shades were drawn to keep out any vestiges of sunshine, and John forced his hands behind his back to stop himself from lifting the blinds and flinging open the windows. "I hope you are feeling better today."

"My chest feels tight. I have this constant fear that I won't be able to breathe. I'm terrified of suffocating."

I'd suffocate too if I spent hours in this overheated room. "I'm sorry, my dear. Perhaps if you stepped outside for a few minutes and strolled in the garden it would help you to breathe."

"The scent of the flowers always brings on my headache, and what if I was stung by a bee? It happened once when I was a child. They seek me out for some reason I cannot fathom."

There's no point in my asking her to join the boys and me for lunch—she would conjure an excuse to reject my request. "I ran into Charles Lennox and his wife at the cricket match yesterday. He and his family are close by at Marylebone Manor for the summer. He invited us to drop in for a visit. John is around his oldest son's age."

"Charles is married to one of those dreadful Gordon women. Married him for his money, no doubt, and his prospects of becoming the next Duke of Richmond."

"But she is a duke's daughter. Alexander Gordon has vast wealth and lands in Scotland."

"And by-blows aplenty." Her mouth tightened with disapproval. "His faithlessness reminds me of your brother, Francis."

John clenched his fists. He had a very close bond with his brother because their parents had died when he and Francis were so young. "Francis is unwed, not unfaithful. Shall I accept the invitation?"

"They have a whole brood of children, probably all unruly. I couldn't stand it. You know my poor health won't allow me to socialize. It's out of the question, John; don't ask it of me."

"Of course not. I understand. I think I'll take them up on the invitation. The boys would enjoy it. I'll give Lady Lennox your regrets."

"Yes, that would be best." She pressed a languid hand to her head. "You'll be glad when I'm gone."

How often have I heard that plaintive refrain? "We'll go tomorrow. It will give you some peace and quiet."

Georgina was on her way to the stables for a morning ride. Charlotte had offered her favorite filly, Barleybree, since the dread of morning sickness prevented her from joining her sister.

At the familiar *clip-clop* of hooves, Georgina glanced toward the gates of Marylebone Manor and saw four riders approaching. The sight of an adult male accompanied by three boys mounted on ponies threw her into a panic. "Good God, it's *him*!"

Georgina looked down in dismay at her old divided riding skirt and ran her hand across the sleeve of her shabby tweed jacket. She turned on her heel and fled back to the house.

She ran up the stairs to the pink bedchamber and threw open the mirrored doors of the wardrobe. "I need something that will make me look like an elegant lady of fashion." Her hand hesitated over her dresses. "I need to look older . . . I need to look taller. Oh damnation, nothing is suitable!"

Georgina finally chose a morning gown in a lovely shade of apricot. The sleeves and hemline were embroidered with a Greek key design in a deep shade of amber. Its slim empire line was elegant and sophisticated, rather than frilly and girlish.

She took the hairbrush, swept up her curls to give her height, and anchored them with a pair of tortoiseshell combs. Then she put on a pair of dangling amber earrings. She powdered her nose, darkened her eyelashes with kohl, and added a touch of lip rouge. Makeup was deemed scandalous for a young lady who had not yet made her debut, but Georgina did not even pay lip service to convention. She picked up her small ivory fan and examined her reflection in the mirror.

She nodded to her image. "Lady Georgina, you look at least two years older and two inches taller." Before her confidence deserted her, she left the bedchamber and descended to the main floor.

Children and dogs dashed across her path in a mad rush for the great outdoors. Charles and Charlotte were engaged in conversation with their guest, and Georgina heard him say, "My wife sends her regrets. Elizabeth is feeling a bit under the weather these days."

"The last time I saw her was at court at one of the queen's receptions. It seems years ago. Do give her my fondest regards." Charlotte caught sight of Georgina, and her eyes widened. "That was a short ride."

Georgina opened her fan. "I changed my mind."

"John, let me introduce you to my sister."

He turned toward her and his dark, compelling glance swept over her from head to toe. His brows drew together as if he were puzzled. "Have we met before, my lady?"

Georgina wafted her fan. "Not formally, my lord."

Charlotte made the introduction. "May I present

my sister, Lady Georgina? As you must have guessed, this is John Russell, Lord Tavistock."

"Please forgive me for staring. You look familiar— I'm sure I've seen you before," he said.

"You have a very short memory, Lord Tavistock. It was only a few days ago that you gave me a brow-beating."

"Forgive me, my lady, I am at a loss—"

"I shall neither forgive nor forget . . . *old man.*"

Georgina had the satisfaction of watching his face as incredibly he made the connection between her and the girl he had berated at the stream.

"I humbly apologize," he said smoothly.

"Liar! *Humble* isn't in your repertoire."

Charlotte felt the hairs rise on the nape of her neck. The undercurrent between Russell and Georgina was palpable.

Charles ended the awkward moment of silence that descended. "My duties as a host are remiss. Come into the sitting room, John. I have some freshly brewed ale I'd like you to try."

"If you will excuse me," Georgina said coolly, "I prefer to join the children and reacquaint myself with your sons."

John Russell's jaw clenched, and he gave her a curt nod.

With satisfaction, she noticed the glint of anger in his eyes. With a shiver, Georgina wondered what it would take to provoke him enough to unleash that controlled fury that lurked beneath his polished surface.

After Georgina left, Charlotte led the way into the sun-drenched sitting room, and as her husband poured ale, she gave John Russell a quizzical glance.

He smiled ruefully. "I met your sister the other day. She and my sons were in the middle of the Tybourne stream, fishing."

"Ah, that explains everything! You are the *surly sod* who called her *little girl* and told her to go home."

John joined in her laughter. "And she told me, in no uncertain terms, to go to the devil!"

"She took high offense at your words. She has been teased all her life for being the runt of the litter, and is rather sensitive about her lack of height. You must forgive her, John. She is very young."

"I'm afraid your sister won't soon forgive *me*."

"It's really not like Georgy to get up on her high horse. She's ready for mischievous fun and games at the drop of a hat."

When the men had finished their ale, Charles got to his feet. "I'll show you that horse we spoke of. The young mare would make an excellent mount for Francis if, as you say, he considers himself too old for a pony."

"He'll be thirteen by the time school term starts again. He is convinced ponies are for children."

"And rightly so," Charles agreed. "At thirteen you likely thought yourself a man. I know I did."

"True. At that age I was convinced I was ready for the army."

Georgina had set up a croquet game on the lawn and had divided the players into three teams. Francis and William Russell were pitted against Johnny Russell and Charlie Lennox, while she partnered young Mary.

Though Johnny confessed he had never played before, he was delighted that he and Charlie were winning.

"I think I prefer cricket," William declared.

"That's because you're losing," Georgina teased.

"Boys are sore losers." Mary rubbed salt into their wounds.

"So are girls. Everyone likes to win," Georgina said. "Just as in cricket, the secret is to keep your eye on the ball. You and Francis are swinging your mallets too hard."

"Don't give them tips, Georgy, or John and I might lose," Charlie protested.

It was too late for the older boys to catch up, and John and Charlie claimed victory. Francis spotted his father heading to the stables with Lord Lennox, and asked Georgina to excuse him from the game.

She agreed, and watched Francis and William take off in the direction of the stables. "I think we have lots of time for another game before lunch," she told the younger boys. She had so enjoyed watching Johnny's delight in winning that she decided she wanted him to win again. "I have an idea. Why don't I ask the cook to prepare you a picnic lunch that you can eat out here on the lawn?"

"Hooray!" Charlie cheered. He swung his mallet and hit his own foot. "Damnation!"

John looked stricken, but when he saw that Georgina laughed at the curse word, the corners of his mouth turned up.

When the game was over, Georgina retrieved her fan from the garden seat. "Don't pout, Mary. The young gentlemen beat us fair and square." She headed toward the kitchen entrance and Mary followed. Georgina found Charlotte speaking with the cook. "I thought it might be a good idea if the young people could have a picnic on the lawn. The Russell boys might be equally uncomfortable eating in the nursery or joining the adults in the dining room."

"That's an excellent idea, Georgina." She instructed the kitchen maids to prepare the children an alfresco lunch, and then she gave her sister a speculative look. "Do you intend to be civil in the dining room?"

"I hadn't planned on it," Georgina said lightly.

"How about a wager?" Charlotte challenged. She was well aware that Georgina could never resist a bet. "A guinea says you cannot charm John Russell the way you mesmerize other men."

"I don't want to charm him! Perhaps I'll remain outside and eat with the children."

"Don't you dare, Georgy. That would be like a slap in the face to our guest."

"He looks brutish enough to slap me back. I warrant he wouldn't cavil at striking a woman."

"Ah, you are afraid of him."

"Afraid? You must be jesting! Lead on, Macduff. I'll take that wager." Georgina felt a tug on her skirt.

"I want to eat with you," Mary said.

Georgina bent down, and lowered her voice. "I have to eat with the *old man.* Wouldn't you be happier having a picnic with the boys? If there's something you don't like to eat, you can slip it to the dogs."

Mary didn't have to think twice about it. "Will you come out and play with us again after lunch?"

"Wild horses couldn't keep me away."

When John Russell entered the dining room with his host, he found that the ladies were there before them. Good manners prompted him to hold Georgina Gordon's chair, but he braced himself for a rebuff. To his surprise, the young lady thanked him with a gracious smile.

He took his own seat and turned to his hostess. "Lady Lennox, the lawn picnic was an ingenious idea. My sons will truly enjoy the novelty of having lunch outdoors."

"It was my sister's idea. At our mother's farmhouse in Kinrara we used to picnic outdoors every day that the weather permitted."

"Children love to be carefree, and nature provides the perfect setting for all sorts of exciting fun and games," Georgina added.

I wish my sons had more opportunities to be carefree.

"We ran wild, like mad demons, I'm afraid," Charlotte said.

"Some of us still do." Georgina's green eyes sparkled. She turned her full attention upon John Russell.

Why is she staring at me with such rapt attention?

"Forgive me for staring, my lord. My curiosity outweighs my good manners. Will you enlighten me about something?"

"I will do my best, Lady Georgina."

" 'Tis the fashion for gentlemen to wear wigs, yet you wear your own hair. Do you look hideous in a wig?"

He ignored the barb. "It is a political statement to show my opposition to Pitt's decision to tax powder," he said bluntly.

Georgina's eyes widened. "It is a mark of sympathy for the poor who need flour for bread. How courageous of you, my lord."

"Oh, Lud, don't get her started on politics, John. She eats and sleeps the stuff," Charlotte declared.

John's eyes met Georgina's. *You're a Pitt Tory and I'm a Whig. We'll be at daggers drawn any minute.*

"Are you a parliamentary reformer?" she asked avidly.

"I am." He could not keep the challenge from his voice.

"How splendid! And what about Ireland? Are you for her independence?"

"I am." His deep voice conveyed his strong conviction. "My political philosophy is based on the principle that all governments should be made for the happiness of the many and not for the benefit of the few."

Charlotte and Charles exchanged a glance. It was as if they were suddenly invisible and their guests were alone together.

"You fight an uphill battle," Georgina warned.

"I have the temperament for it," John declared.

Georgina smiled into his eyes. "I have no doubt of it."

You are intentionally flattering me and hanging on my every word. Lady Georgina Gordon, you may be very young, but you are a practiced coquette. His deliberate glance roamed over her curvaceous figure and came to rest on her full, sensual lower lip. *You are actually wearing makeup.* The thought shocked him that one so young would employ artifice. *I warrant you are shrewd and manipulating. At the moment you are as sweet as honey, but I know from experience, Lady Georgina, that you possess a hot temper.*

Suddenly, she seemed to become aware of the others at the table. "I am monopolizing your guest. Do forgive me."

John heard her compliment her sister on the food—something about the curried prawns—and for the first time he became aware of what he was eating.

When she withdrew her attention from him, he felt the loss acutely. Then he cursed himself for a gullible fool. He had been captivated by her feminine wiles. She had deliberately lured him to talk about himself, playing him on the end of her line like a trout. John was amazed that he had ever taken her for a little girl. She was as age-old as the temptress Eve.

The ladies began to talk about their sister Louisa's wedding and some of the guests who had attended. "I'm so glad that Lord and Lady Holland accepted the invitation. I admire Beth so much. She showed great courage ignoring the gossips, and she wasn't the least jealous when Henry partnered me in the Scottish reels."

"Lord Holland is a good friend of mine," John declared.

Georgina once more gave him her attention. "Henry is a great sport and he has such charming manners."

You are hinting that I have neither charm nor manners.

"I met another charming gentleman at the wedding. The Duke of Bedford begged my brother, Huntly, for an introduction."

"My brother, Francis, is a great favorite with the ladies."

"Ah, if his reputation is racy, that explains why my brother refused the introduction."

Francis's taste in the opposite sex runs to older, vastly experienced married women. It is unthinkable that he would compromise an innocent young lady, no matter how flirtatious she acted . . . at least, I hope it is unthinkable.

"I am to make my debut into society soon. I promised His Grace of Bedford that when I came out, I would be delighted to make his acquaintance." Her eyes glittered with mischief.

"You are incorrigible," he murmured.

"Flattery, begod! Charlotte, you owe me a guinea."

John's eyes narrowed dangerously. He wanted to put the little hellcat over his knee and tan her arse.

To fill the ominous silence, Charles jumped in and changed the subject to horses. "Why don't we let your son Francis try out the horse we looked at, to see if it's a good match?"

"An excellent suggestion," John agreed, turning away from the spoiled young beauty who had amused herself throughout lunch by deliberately baiting him.

The moment dessert was finished, Georgina stood up. "As always, you set a delightful table, Charlotte. The food was delicious and the conversation stimulating. I'm off to help the children play havoc."

"A pastime that suits you to perfection," Charlotte said dryly.

Georgina ran upstairs to change her clothes before she went back outside. She glanced in the mirror at the elegant apricot morning gown. "You served your purpose in showing the *old man* that I'm a grown woman, but it's back in the wardrobe for you. I refuse to spend the afternoon in a corset."

When she emerged onto the lawn, wearing her old riding skirt, the servants were removing the remnants of the picnic. "Where is everyone?" she asked Mary.

"The nursemaids have taken the babies for their nap."

Johnny looked up from the pug dog he was feeding. "My brothers have gone with Father and Lord Lennox to try out a horse, my lady."

"Call me Georgy. All those in favor of a boat race on the carp pond, say aye, aye, Captain."

"I want to be captain," Charlie asserted. "Let's be pirates."

"I want to be captain," Mary argued.

"You can all be captains. Charlie can be Captain

Cutlass, Mary can be Captain Contrary, and Johnny can be Captain Cutthroat."

Johnny smiled shyly, clearly pleased with his name.

"What about you, Georgy? Who will you be?" Charlie asked.

"I'll be Captain Cuspidor." She spat on the grass, and the boys roared with laughter.

"I'll go and get my boats," Charlie offered.

"Why don't we make our boats? There's lots of stuff that floats." She produced a knife from her pocket, and the three children were off and running to the trees. They found a half-rotted log and Charlie broke off a piece of wood for his boat.

"I'd like a piece of bark for mine. It might be lighter and faster," Johnny said.

When Georgina handed him her knife so he could cut it, he looked thrilled to bits.

Mary found an abandoned bird's nest and insisted on using it for her boat even when Georgina warned it might not float. "I'm Captain Contrary . . . don't argue with me!"

They used twigs for masts and leaves for sails, and Mary filled her nest with hawthorn berries.

"I need a cutlass," Charlie informed Georgy.

"As does Captain Cutthroat." She cut some branches and stripped off their leaves.

"You have to spit every time you speak, Captain Cuspidor," Mary reminded her.

They carried their pirate ships out to the carp pond for the contest. The boys made waves to carry their crafts on the current. In less than half an hour, Mary's vessel sank, but when the little red berries bravely floated on, she took it well.

The two boys doubled their efforts to win, banging their cutlasses on the water to create giant waves. When it turned out to be a draw, the race became a sea battle that thoroughly drenched the two male captains. Mary joined Georgy in urging them on to victory, alternately cheering and spitting.

When their games were done and the children had

wrung every last ounce of fun out of the afternoon, Georgina led the way back to the house. Charlotte rolled her eyes when she saw their bedraggled state.

"We need a fire. How about the library?" Georgina asked.

"By all means—once you have removed your soggy shoes. I'll get some dry clothes."

All four removed their shoes and carried them to the library.

"John, how would you like the honor of kindling the fire?"

John's eyes lit up at the mere thought of such an adult responsibility. Charlotte arrived with dry clothes, deposited them inside the door, and quickly departed.

Georgina removed her stockings, and the children followed suit. She promised to hide her eyes and vowed not to peek while the boys changed into dry shirts and pants. When they were all sprawled comfortably around the fire, Georgina said, "How about a story? These library shelves are filled with great adventures."

The afternoon light was leaving the sky by the time the men and older boys returned from their ride. Francis was overjoyed that his father had purchased the horse for him, and William had high hopes that his father would soon consider a new mount for him.

John Russell thanked Charlotte for a lovely day. "It was most generous of you to entertain Johnny. Where might I find him?"

"It was our pleasure. Come again, anytime." She pointed down the hallway. "You'll find him in the library."

John heard his son's voice before he got to the library door. Johnny was reading aloud from Daniel Defoe's *Robinson Crusoe* while his audience sat before the fire, mesmerized by his words.

John's glance was drawn to Georgina. The rapt look on her face as she listened to his young son showed that she was enraptured by the way he read the fascinating tale.

Georgina was the first to notice John Russell standing quietly in the doorway. "John, your father is here. Thank you so much for entertaining us. You read better than many adults I know."

Reluctantly, Johnny closed the book and handed it to Georgina.

She gathered up his dry clothes and handed them to his father.

"I'm sorry, my lord. We were playing in water again, in spite of the fact that I know you thoroughly disapprove of such wicked, wanton pleasures."

He knew her words were chosen to provoke him, so rather than react to the provocation, he merely took the clothes and nodded politely. He hid his amusement when he saw a fleeting glimpse of disappointment cross her face because she had not been able to goad him into an angry retort.

On the ride home, John hung on to his youngest son's reins.

"I had a wonderful time, Father. Georgy is such fun."

"You mustn't call her that. Her name is Lady Georgina."

"Yes, I know. But she doesn't seem like a lady."

"Indeed, she does not." *She is an outrageous minx.*

Chapter 5

John Russell fought to keep his fury under control. "As soon as I opened the bedchamber door, the smell of laudanum hit me in the face. Gertrude, did I not expressly forbid you to feed my wife any more of the filthy stuff?" he demanded.

"My lord, I *swear* I did not give it to her."

"Yes, it's enough to make anyone swear," he said curtly. His wife's maid looked terrified of being dismissed on the spot. "Very well, I'll take care of it."

He went back upstairs to his wife's chamber and began to search. He opened every bureau drawer and every cabinet. He looked in the cupboard of the night table and the washstand. He opened her wardrobe and searched every pocket of every garment. When he found the brown bottle in one of her hatboxes, he uttered a foul oath.

He crossed to the bed and stared down at the sleeping figure of his wife. She looked pale and ethereal, like a saint with her eyelids closed in gentle repose. *The doctor suspects she is consumptive. He would never dream that such a respectable lady is an addict.* John paced the room, debating what he should do.

He considered asking his wife's sisters for advice. Lucy, Baroness Bradford, might be persuaded to come for a short visit. He could send a note to Park Lane, but Lucy was most likely at Bradford-on-Avon this summer, rather than her London town house.

Isabelle, her other sister, was the Marchioness of Bath. She was likely at Longleat for the summer. *How could I confide my wife's secret to her straitlaced sister Isabelle? She considers any hint of scandal worse than being buried alive.*

The only one I can confide in is my brother, Francis. There's little that shocks him. I'll take the boys to Woburn—it will get them away from here for a few days. I'll get a nurse to watch over Elizabeth. It's obvious Gertrude cannot stand up to her.

"Good God, that carriage looks like it's in a chariot race. Who the devil could be arriving at this hour of the morning?" Charlotte and Georgina were in the stillroom adjacent to the conservatory, making perfume from summer roses and jasmine.

Georgina went to the door for a better look. "I'm afraid it's Mother. Gird your loins, she looks as if she's on the warpath." The sisters hurried through the conservatory and made their way to the reception hall.

Jane Gordon strode through the front door and brushed aside the footman. She needed no fool servant to announce her. She threw off her cloak, but kept on her beribboned bonnet, which now sat at a cockeyed angle due to her haste.

"I'm ruined! I shall be a laughingstock! As the leading Tory hostess, I am being held up to ridicule by this jackanapes!"

"What? How? Who?" Charlotte followed her mother into the sitting room, and Georgina tried not to laugh at the comic scene.

"This!" With a melodramatic flourish, she thrust a book at them. She was panting with outrage, and her face had turned a florid red that clashed alarmingly with the purple of her bonnet.

Georgina took the book. "*A Winter in London* by T. S. Surr."

"I willna' stand fer it!" Jane screeched, lapsing into Scottish brogue.

"Then sit, Mama," Charlotte urged dryly.

Jane paced across the room, turned and paced back. "I'll ne'er sit again until the swine is brought to justice. Devil take the wretch. If I were a mon, I'd challenge him to a duel!"

Georgina opened the book and began to read aloud. *"When the Duchess of Drinkwater appeared on the London scene, the Duchess of Belgrave was not amused."* She grasped immediately that it was a satirical novel. *Mother recognizes herself as the Duchess of Drinkwater.*

"Go on . . . read it!" Jane's hat tilted over one eye.

"The Duchess of Drinkwater appeared upon the field of fashion and threw down the gauntlet of defiance to Belgrave: an event which produced upon the fashionable world an effect precisely similar to that which the natural world sustains from the convulsion of an earthquake; or which the moral world experienced from the French revolution.

"Before this challenge was given, to have doubted that the will of Belgrave was the law of fashion would have been deemed an abrogation of loyalty itself. What, then, must have been the surprise, the horror of a people cherishing such sentiments when they beheld the Duchess of Drinkwater erecting her standard of revolt against the object of their allegiance and their worship, and promulgating with undaunted zeal a code and creed diametrically opposite to the principles of their former obedience and faith."

Jane snatched the book from her daughter and pushed her hat back from her eye. "Listen to this: *The duchesses never met without betraying some signs of approaching hostilities. The patroness of reels cracked the shoulder straps of sixteen dresses by exercising herself in shrugs at the Duchess of Belgrave. At length the war was openly declared by both parties, and the first blow was struck by the Duchess of Drinkwater, who gave a grand gala the same night on which her rival had previously announced one.*" She slammed the book closed. "There is no rivalry between the Duchess of Devonshire and myself. We are the dearest of friends! How dare the miscreant write such slanderous codswallop?"

"I don't think anyone will recognize you," Georgina said in her most reassuring tone.

"He called me the *patroness of reels* fer Christ's sake!"

"There is that," Georgina acknowledged.

"He casts you in a better light than the Duchess of Devonshire. She clearly comes off the loser," Charlotte assured her.

"Do you think so?" Jane asked, trying to see it through the critical eyes of society.

"Put it on the back of the fire, and dismiss it as scurrilous tripe. Then go to the theater, and hold your head up high. Better yet, attend one of the Duchess of Devonshire's entertainments," Charlotte advised.

Georgina gasped as her mother threw the novel into the fire.

"Georgy, pack yer things. We shall do both."

"But Susan invited me to Kimbolton," Georgina protested.

"The entertainments the Duke and Duchess of Manchester give at Kimbolton are far too sophisticated fer you. Their guests are allowed uninhibited freedom of speech and action, and illicit liaisons are encouraged. You may visit them once you have been introduced at court, but until then a sojourn at Kimbolton Castle could very easily sully yer reputation."

With a sigh of exasperation, Georgina gave in to her mother's demand. "I'll go upstairs and pack."

Charlotte followed her sister from the sitting room.

"Why the devil did you tell her to throw it on the fire?" Georgina asked. "I was dying to read it!"

"I have a copy in my bedchamber. I'll lend it to you, but you must promise to give it back once you've read it."

"You devious witch! Why didn't you tell me?"

"It could very easily sully yer reputation," Charlotte teased.

Mary arrived in the pink bedchamber, breathless

from her hurried climb upstairs. "I don't want you to leave, Georgy!"

"If you were listening behind the sitting room door, as I suspect, you must know that Grandmama gave me no choice."

"Who is the Duchess of Drinkwater?" Mary whispered.

Georgina removed her garments from the wardrobe and began to fold them. "She is a Titan who must be obeyed."

"It's Grandmama, isn't it?"

Georgina nodded. "But you must promise not to tell anyone."

Mary crossed her heart. "It will be our deep, dark secret."

The Duchess of Gordon, decked out in a fashionable gown of striped *crêpe de chine*, her hair decorated with bejeweled feathers, stepped from her carriage in the Haymarket. Georgina followed, wearing a simple empire gown of white gauze over green with a matching wrap. Her dark curls were piled high and held in place by green ribbon and a jeweled dragonfly.

They entered the King's Theatre. With her head held high, the Duchess of Gordon led the way to her private ground-floor box, where mother and daughter took their seats.

"I don't think you'll enjoy this Mozart opera, Mother. *La Clemenza de Tito* is a dark tale about a woman who plots the assassination of the Roman emperor Titus."

"I am here to be *seen*, not to *enjoy* the opera. It's all in Italian anyway—I shan't understand a word, nor will many of the *haut ton*, believe me."

"I don't think you'll find many ladies of the *ton* here tonight. Only true aficionados of opera will be stoic enough for this one."

"Why, there's Prime Minister Pitt. There is such a refined elegance in his taste." Jane raised her chin, smiled archly, and was most gratified when William

Pitt graciously stood and bowed his head in acknowledgment.

Just as the overture began, the Prince of Wales and his good friend Charles James Fox entered the royal box, which was directly opposite the Gordons' box.

"Oh, how very fortunate I chose to wear the Prince of Wales's feathers tonight. You are quite wrong, Georgina. I am enjoying the opera immensely."

Georgina amused herself by watching the audience and counting the number of patrons who dozed off. She had almost given herself up to the arms of Morpheus when the burning of the Roman capital revived her.

When her mother saw Prinny's fervent applause, she began to clap with great enthusiasm. "The Prince of Wales is often censured for his profligate habits, but there is no denying that his taste in the arts is perfection itself."

Georgina gathered her fan and her wrap and stood to leave.

"There's no hurry, dear. We must time things so we will meet the prince in the foyer."

"In that case I have time for another snooze. It will take both Prinny and Fox an aeon to navigate their bulk from the royal box to the theater lobby."

"Georgina, that was unkind . . . vastly amusing, but unkind."

Jane's timing was perfect. She'd had considerable experience in maneuvering as she climbed the social ladder. Since Fox was with the prince, she surmised their next stop would be a place where they could gamble. "Your Royal Highness, the opera tonight was a triumph. Not in the common taste, of course. Only a devout opera aficionado could fully appreciate it."

"Your Grace, what a delightful encounter." He drew her proffered hand to his lips with a gallant flourish. Prinny never forgot that when his debts had become astronomical, and King George disowned him, Jane Gordon had arranged a truce between himself and his royal father. She had persuaded the king to give his son the revenues of the Duchy of Cornwall, which George had usurped for his own use. King George settled his son's debts on condition that parliament grant the prince an allowance of one hundred thousand pounds a year. Without the Duchess of Gordon's influence, he would not have been able to indulge his passion for building, and Carlton House would not be the most magnificent residence in London.

Jane confided, "I have an open invitation from our dearest mutual friend, the Duchess of Devonshire. Since the night is young, I thought I might pop in for a friendly game of faro."

"By an amazing coincidence, Charles and I also are on our way to Devonshire House."

"Then we shall take the liberty of joining you, Your Highness. It would be unthinkable to pass up the honor of a royal escort. I shall instruct my driver to follow your carriage." She turned to Fox. "You are looking well, Charles. This is my youngest daughter, Georgina. She's not out yet, but I'm sure you both remember how unnecessarily restrictive the mores of society are at her age."

Both gentlemen kissed Georgina's hand with marked gallantry.

Mother is a master of manipulation. The prince is putty in her hands. When we make our grand entrance at Devonshire House, I wager that Duchess Drinkwater will tell Duchess Belgrave that His Royal Highness insisted that we join him.

Francis Russell, Duke of Bedford, had spent the entire evening in one of the sumptuous reception rooms at Devonshire House that was used exclusively for gaming. He and his hostess, along with Sir Robert Adair and the Earl of Lauderdale, were playing his favorite game of lanterloo. As usual, Francis was winning and the duchess was losing.

The pot had grown to five hundred guineas. Francis took another trick with his last trump. Georgianna

Devonshire discarded in desperation, and replenished her hand with a new card from the deck. She was still unable to take another trick, and as a result lost the whole amount of the pot to the winner, Francis.

"Oh, Loo, you have the devil's own luck." Loo was her pet name for Bedford, since he loved the game and usually won. She stood up. "The game of loo is a jinx to me; I don't know why I play!"

Francis got to his feet and came around the table. "The pleasure of your company is reward enough." He lowered his voice. "You owe me nothing, my dearest lady."

"Loo, you forget that discreet loan of six thousand a year ago. I'm distraught that I've not been able to pay you back one penny."

I don't forget, Georgianna. I know Devonshire has refused to pay any more of your gambling debts, and I am realist enough to know you will never be able to pay back the money I lend you.

Their attention was diverted by some new arrivals. "Ah, it is darling Prinny and—" The Duchess of Devonshire's jaw literally dropped when she saw that the Prince of Wales had the Duchess of Gordon on his arm. She floated across the room, her flowing gown billowing like a sail, her immense coiffure threatening to topple.

"Your Highness . . . Your Grace . . . I am honored."

While Prinny kissed Georgianna's hand with reverence, Jane spoke up. "The honor is mine, I assure you. It's been far too long since I visited Devonshire House. If I stayed away longer, the gossips would begin to insinuate that we are rivals."

"Ah, you have read that dreadful piece of trash by Surr. The man should be pilloried! There is not the least rivalry between us, as anyone with a soupçon of intelligence would know."

"That is why I accepted His Royal Highness's offer to escort me to Devonshire House. It will display our friendship to the world at large and give the lie to that scurrilous novel."

The Duchess of Devonshire gave her hand to Charles Fox, a man of enormous charm and warmth. "I welcome you with open arms, my lord, since you are the only man of my acquaintance who gambles more recklessly than I."

"And with the same devastating results." Fox kissed her hand. "I stand a greater chance of breaking another leg than breaking the bank, Your Grace." Two years ago he had broken his leg in the Devonshire House gardens, competing in a silly race.

Francis Russell crossed the room and greeted his friends.

"Loo, here are some worthy partners for you. I shall change games and try my luck at faro with my friend Jane."

Francis had been lured, not by his friends, but by the young beauty who stood quietly behind her mother. "We meet again," he murmured as his eyes undressed her.

"You look nothing like your brother," Georgina blurted.

"You know John?"

"Not intimately. Why are you called Loo?" she asked innocently.

"Because I always win at lanterloo." *Damn, one whiff of this female and I'm aroused.* He was amazed that he felt lust for one so young.

"Then gardez-loo!" Georgina murmured, and her eyes brimmed with wicked amusement.

The Duchess of Devonshire suddenly noticed Jane Gordon's daughter. "Georgina dear, you'll find my daughters and Caroline in the music room." She summoned a footman wearing scarlet and sepia livery, gave him instructions, and Georgina followed him up the marble staircase.

On a devilish impulse she turned around and looked back. Just as she suspected, Bedford was gazing after her with a hungry look of lust on his face. "I'll be damned. I think I've made a conquest," she murmured. "One Russell detests me . . . the other fancies me!"

"Dorothy, it's Lady Georgy!" Harriet Cavendish cried happily.

"What a lovely surprise." Georgianna Dorothy Cavendish went by her middle name to distinguish her from her mother.

"A surprise, at any rate," Caro Ponsonby said acidly.

The girls all took dancing lessons together in preparation for the balls they would attend after their debuts. The Duchess of Devonshire's eldest daughter was no beauty, but she made up for it with a sweet, gentle personality.

Their cousin Caro, who had lived at Devonshire House since she was a child, was the antithesis of sweet. She was thin as a rail, with a jealous nature and a waspish tongue.

"Mother says I may make my debut a year early, so we will be coming out together! Isn't it exciting, Georgy?"

"Well, it's exciting that we'll be invited everywhere, but I don't look forward to being put on the marriage market."

"I don't think you have much to fear," Caro sneered. She was only fifteen and pea green with jealousy that she would have to wait another year or two before she was presented to the queen.

"Pay no attention to Caro. I think you are absolutely bewitching, Georgy. Are there any interesting gentlemen visiting downstairs tonight?" Dorothy asked avidly.

"Mother and I came with the Prince of Wales and Charles Fox."

Caro wrinkled her nose. "They are both so fat and florid, I'm amazed you can tell them apart."

"Charles is older than Prinny," Georgina said dryly.

"I find His Royal Highness to be both handsome and warmhearted, and he absolutely adores Mother,"

Dorothy declared. "Who else did you see downstairs?"

"I was quickly whisked upstairs by a footman, so the only one I had a chance to see was Francis Russell."

"The Duke of Bedford?" Dorothy asked breathlessly. "I've only seen him from afar, but he's reputedly the most eligible bachelor in England."

"I think you secretly worship him from afar," Harriet teased.

Her sister blushed pink. "No I don't, silly. But I do look forward to being introduced to him . . . as well as all the other eligible bachelors, of course."

"I've met his brother," Georgina confided. "There's something about the Russells that set my teeth on edge. They act like gods gazing down from Olympus at us inferior mortals."

"Some of us *are* inferior," Caro said pointedly.

"In your case, I promise to overlook it, Caroline."

"Touché, Georgy!" Harriet giggled.

"Why don't we go to the top of the stairs? Perhaps we'll catch a glimpse of some of Mother's guests," Dorothy suggested.

You are simply dying for a glimpse of Bedford, Georgina realized with surprise. *I suppose he is the premier duke of the realm, but his attraction eludes me completely.* A vision of his brother, John, sprang into her mind. His black hair, dark eyes, and dominant personality seemed in complete contrast to his brother, Francis. She wondered why the surly devil kept popping into her head and made a firm decision that from now on she would banish the old man from her thoughts.

Chapter 6

Two days later, John Russell and his three sons were ready to depart for Woburn Abbey in Bedfordshire. Before he left, young Johnny went to bid good-bye to his mother.

The moment she laid eyes on him, she rose up on her hands and knees in the wide bed and snarled at him like a wild animal. "I have been ill for nine long years because of you. I wish to God that I had never had a third son!"

Johnny stared, aghast, at her words. "I'm so sorry I caused you to be ill, Mother. With all my heart I wish you were well."

"You are a hateful little liar. I gave birth to a *demon* when I had you! Like your father, you can't get away fast enough. You'll both be happy when I'm dead and gone."

Johnny's face drained of all color, leaving him pale and shaken. "Please don't die, Mother."

John Russell entered his wife's bedchamber with the new nurse he had employed. He watched Elizabeth compose her features from anger to sorrow. She slipped back beneath the covers and lay like a wounded martyr, ready to accept her suffering without complaint. "Good-bye, my dear. The house will be nice and quiet when we leave. It will give you a chance to rest and recuperate."

"Be assured you leave your lady in good hands,

Lord Tavistock," the nurse declared in a calm, capable voice.

"Are you ready, Johnny?" His son looked small and pale, and he knew a few days at Woburn would do him good.

John had decided to drive the carriage, not because of his wife's morbid objection to the boys going on horseback, but because his brother had a well-stocked stable of Thoroughbreds.

He heard his two older sons fighting over who would sit next to their father, but when Johnny slipped his hand into his and gave him a pleading look, John appointed his youngest son to the seat of honor.

The traffic along Marylebone Road was heavy and took all his attention. As they left London behind, however, John was free to let his mind wander.

Elizabeth's fears are irrational. He relived the angry words they'd exchanged when she found out he'd bought a horse for young Francis. "You are tempting fate! Surely you've not forgotten your own father was killed by being thrown from his horse? I have these dark premonitions that bedevil me. They tell me that one of my sons is sure to die the same way, John. Why do you purposely do things that fill me with dread?"

"Your dark premonitions come from a bottle," he accused.

"You are so pitiless! Why do you deny me the only medicine that calms me and allows me to sleep in blissful peace?"

John bit his tongue and strived for patience. "Francis will be thirteen when school term starts again. If he is the only youth in his class with a pony, the other boys will poke unmerciful fun at him."

"There is no need to remind me that the male of the species is cruel, my lord. I am a faithful wife who has given you three sons, and what is my reward? You deliberately choose to live apart from me in London for most of the year."

"Elizabeth, we have been through this before, ad nauseam. I am the member of parliament for Tavistock. If you would act as my political hostess in London, I would like nothing better. It would be most beneficial to me and the people we represent. The family house in Russell Square is a mansion most women would envy, but you have made it plain you cannot abide living in London. *You* are the one who chooses to live apart in Devonshire."

"Perhaps I won't live much longer. Then you'll be happy! I have a distressing feeling that I am not long for this world."

It took a deal of control not to roll my eyes at that one; I've heard it so often.

"Father . . . am I . . . am I a demon?"

His son's small, earnest voice startled him. He smiled down at him. "I'm afraid not, Johnny. You are a mere mortal like your father, with the added advantage of a vivid imagination. Were you reading about demons?"

He shook his head. "No, sir."

Johnny sounded extremely troubled. "Then what brought demons to mind?"

He shook his head again and tightened his lips.

"Johnny, I hope you know you can tell me anything."

He hesitated for a long time, then finally blurted, "Mother . . . Mother said she gave birth to a demon . . . She said that I'm the one who has made her ill for nine years."

Christ Almighty! How dare the madwoman poison his mind! "Johnny, your mother doesn't mean the things she says. It is the medicine that makes her say such terrible things. Her illness has absolutely nothing to do with you. You must believe what I say. Promise me you won't brood about the things she has said to you."

"I promise," he whispered solemnly.

John let the horses have their head, and they bowled along at a great pace. *Why don't I simply let the bitch have all the opium she craves? Sooner or later she would overdose, and I would be free of her.* John shook his head to rid himself of the dark thoughts that would shame the devil himself. *I must not allow myself to indulge evil thoughts, no matter the provocation. I must learn to keep my fury under control.*

The speed of the galloping horses helped to diffuse his anger. He glanced down at his son, and saw that Johnny still looked pinched about the mouth. He gradually pulled back on the reins until the horses slowed their pace. "Would you like a go?"

Johnny's features turned eager. "You mean, drive the team?"

His father nodded and lifted his son into his lap. Then he handed him the reins and encouraged him with a confident smile. After a mile, John began to sing, and when his sons joined in it lightened his heart. He reflected on the relief he felt at being away from his wife for a week. When he felt a nagging twinge of guilt, he forcefully banished it.

When they arrived at Woburn, John turned the carriage over to a groom at the stables, and his two older sons helped him unload their traveling bags.

"May we look at the horses, Father?" Johnny asked eagerly.

"I think it would be better if Uncle Francis were with you when you make your mad dash through his stables." He handed him a small valise. "Do you think you can carry this piece of luggage?"

Johnny's smile conveyed that he was happy to be useful.

They hadn't walked more than a dozen yards from the stables when a pair of horses came thundering into the courtyard. Francis Russell and the woman who accompanied him reined in their blooded mounts. "John, this is a surprise! I only returned from London today." He dismounted and threw his reins to his female companion.

John nodded curtly to the woman. "Mrs. Hill."

She was one of his brother's many mistresses, reputed to be an old madame. Francis did not take her into society, but had installed her in a cottage on the grounds of Woburn. She was a bruising horsewoman with whom he enjoyed not only bed sport, but also hunting and riding about his wooded acres.

Francis welcomed his nephews and clapped his namesake on the back. "You've grown apace since I last saw you. I hope you are making the most of your summer. It won't be long before you're off to Cambridge, in the Russell tradition, right?"

"Right, sir. I'm in my senior year at Westminster."

"William, you too are growing like a weed." He glanced at Johnny, and his eyebrows drew together in a frown. "How old are you . . . seven?"

"I'm eight, almost nine sir."

"The runt of the litter. Let's hope you start to grow soon."

Johnny stepped closer to his father in a defensive move.

"He has an oversize intelligence," John told his brother, "and a keen thirst for knowledge. Johnny is a voracious reader."

"I don't believe I opened a book until I was twenty-four," Francis declared facetiously.

"You say that as if you are proud of it," John said bluntly.

"Pride is a Russell strength, not a failing," Francis drawled.

When they entered Woburn, they were met by Mr. Burke, the majordomo, who directed members of his staff to take the visitors' luggage, plenish bedchambers, and prepare for four more at the evening meal. The Duke of Bedford was served so well by Mr. Burke that he seldom had to issue orders to Woburn's plethora of servants.

A footman appeared with refreshments for the newcomers. Mutton pasties and fruit tarts were accompanied by ale for the men and glasses of dandelion and burdock for the boys.

"Father bought me a horse," young Francis said proudly.

"About time you retired that pony. How about you, Will?"

"I live in hope," Will replied.

"Leave it to me. We'll mount you on something worthy of a Russell. What do you say, John?"

"We'll see," his father said, refusing to make a commitment.

"Why don't you fellows go and inspect the horses? At least pick out mounts you can ride while you're here."

The three brothers needed no urging, but did look at their father, hoping for his permission.

"Go on, then. We'll be along shortly. Keep your eye on John."

"I thought I'd find you at Russell Square. What happened?"

"Elizabeth grew agitated in London, so on the recommendation of the doctor I leased a house in Dorset Fields."

"Did it help the situation?"

"No, not really. The physician confirmed her melancholia and said she looked consumptive."

"Well, there you are. Perhaps that is the root of what ails her."

"Looks can be deceiving. She *looks* like a bloody angel, but I assure you she is anything but."

"Then you don't think it's consumption?" Francis asked.

"It's laudanum. She's addicted to the filthy stuff!"

"So she suffers from the blue devils? I'm so sorry, John. Opium eats the brain, you know."

"What can I do? If I asked her sisters to come and spend time with her, they would learn her secret. They are so straitlaced, it would shock them out of their minds. You're the only one I can be frank with. I've had to employ a nurse for Elizabeth's own well-being while I'm away."

Francis poured two brandies and handed one to his brother. "If she's not too far gone, abstinence is the only answer. You'll be able to keep a vigilant watch while you're home for the summer, but what about when parliament opens?"

"Exactly," John said, gazing over the rim of his glass.

"Keep her off the stuff for a month, and when you have to go back to work, send her to Bath to take the medicinal waters. Many ladies go to Bath for one cure or another. Both her sisters have beautiful homes near there. Elizabeth should stay at Longleat; it might bring her out of her melancholia. Let the Marchioness of Bath take some of the responsibility off your shoulders. What if she *is* shocked? Do you really give a goddamn?"

"Not really. It will be a miracle if Isabelle can put up with her deep depression and dark portents. I've had it up to my bloody epiglottis, and my gorge is rising." John finished his brandy.

"Grandmama was deadset against your marrying her."

"Yes, I know, but in my youthful ignorance I thought I was madly in love. Marriage certainly cured me of believing in anything so ridiculous as love. If it exists at all, which I gravely doubt, it is deceptively fleeting."

"If only you'd listened to the domineering old girl and not gotten Elizabeth with child," Francis reminded him.

"Well, I can never regret my sons, Francis. Becoming a father was the best thing that ever happened to me. Unfortunately, after Johnny was born, Elizabeth became mentally afflicted with melancholia. Sometimes I fear she is going mad."

"Though I don't covet your wife, I do envy you your sons."

"You mean you covet *legitimate* sons."

"Exactly. I have bastards aplenty. But the beauty of by-blows is that you are not married to their mothers."

"How can I argue with such faultless logic?"

"Have another brandy."

"I think we'd better go to the stables and check on your nephews' antics. Brothers can get up to all sorts of trouble, if you remember."

By the time they got to the stables, both Francis and William had chosen mounts for themselves and were eager to try them out in Woburn's park. Their uncle directed the grooms to bring the horses from their stalls, but the brothers saddled up themselves.

Johnny was stroking a stable cat. "Don't you have any ponies, Uncle Francis?"

"I'm afraid not. Let's find you a suitable colt."

Johnny glanced at his father uncertainly.

John experienced a moment of doubt. *What of Elizabeth's dark premonition? My father did lose his life when he was thrown from a horse.* John ruthlessly thrust aside his fear for his son. Life involved risks every day. "I'm sure Francis has a palfrey you can handle. How about Grey Lady over there?"

"A most mannerly creature. Let's get her saddled up, and you can give her a trot round the park. If you can handle her, we'll all go for a hunt tomorrow. Woburn has three thousand acres."

"No promises," John said firmly. "First things first."

As it turned out, Johnny was able to handle the docile Grey Lady with confidence, and his father was proud of him. After some persistent persuasion from his sons, John finally agreed to a hunt the following afternoon.

The three brothers spent the rest of the day happily mucking about with the farm animals. Woburn had cattle, oxen, sheep, pigs, goats, geese, game birds, and a herd of domesticated deer. Its large kennels had foxhounds for hunting and some greyhounds.

That night, after his sons went to bed, John and Francis sat sipping brandy before the fire in the large, comfortable Woburn library. "I want to thank you for giving the lads such a happy day. Because of their mother's melancholy condition, their holidays haven't been much fun so far."

"Boys their age need freedom to laugh, and shout,

and fight, and generally horse about, like you and I did."

"We went to a cricket match at Lord's last week. Charles Lennox was playing, and he invited us to spend a day at Marylebone Manor with his family. Their eldest son is close to Johnny's age. In fact, that's where I bought the horse for young Francis."

"Lennox married Lady Charlotte Gordon. By God, there's a family for you! The Duchess of Gordon is nicknamed 'the whipper in.' She's absolutely shameless in the pursuit of ducal husbands for her daughters. She was after me for Louisa, but caught Charlie Cornwallis instead. I recently attended their wedding."

"You managed to escape the Gordon knot."

"Mind you, the youngest daughter, Lady Georgina, is a vivacious beauty. I've got my eye on that one . . . tempting as bloody sin!"

A picture of Georgina appeared full blown in John's mind. He was shocked at his brother's words. Francis had always been attracted to older, experienced women, like Lizzie Melbourne. John had often thought it was because he sought out mother figures. "I have met the lady. She is extremely *young*." His tone was forbidding.

"She's a little saucebox. At the wedding I asked Huntly for an introduction to the lovely goddess he was keeping to himself. He told me she was his sister and strictly off-limits to me, and wasn't even out yet. Georgina gave me a teasing smile and promised: *When I do come out, I shall be delighted to make your acquaintance.* She was obviously attracted to me."

John's imagination allowed him to hear her saucy words clearly. "She's extremely young," he repeated.

"Young or not, she won't be off-limits once she comes out. A hundred guineas says I'll bed the little hellcat."

"Damn you, Francis, I won't wager with you about bedding a virgin. Whatever gives you the remotest idea that you can accomplish such a shameful thing?"

"I managed to bed Louisa Gordon," he said with a

leer. "Next on the agenda is Lady Georgina. She's got a delicious pair of dolly-knockers, old man."

Old man! That's what Georgina called me. John got to his feet abruptly. "I think I'll call it a day. Good night, Francis."

As John Russell disrobed, he was gripped by a cold anger. Because they had lost both their parents by the time John was three, the brothers had formed a special bond of unusual strength.

Francis led the promiscuous life of a bachelor, and John had never condemned him for the numerous mistresses he kept. Each one seemed to fulfill a different need in his brother, and John had always excused him for his sexual excesses.

When Francis returned from his grand tour, he'd traveled from Paris with Lord and Lady Maynard and lived in a ménage a trois with the couple for many years. The older woman had a notorious past, although she was well educated.

Nancy Maynard's appeal was more than physical. She taught him to appreciate literature and poetry, and as a result Francis can recite Ovid by heart. The thought of his brother reciting Ovid to Georgina Gordon only fueled John's anger.

Naked, he paced across to the window and gazed with unseeing eyes into the dark night. *Why the devil does Francis's prurient interest in Georgina Gordon infuriate me? The young woman means absolutely nothing to me.* In spite of what he told himself, the fact remained that he was incensed over his brother's attempted wager to bed the lady. *I would be offended no matter who the female was, if she were young and innocent.* An inner voice nagged: *Are you sure, old man?*

Francis acknowledges his bastards without qualm. As well as one with Lizzie Melbourne, he has two with Mrs. Marianna Palmer, his current mistress, who entertains him when he is in London.

Illegitimate children are commonplace with the beau

monde, *from the Prince of Wales down to those of the lowest noble rank. It's almost considered fashionable, for Christ's sake. I have always turned a blind eye to my brother's peccadilloes. Why do I suddenly find it bloody reprehensible?*

John knew the answer. Lady Georgina Gordon. The little beauty might be high-spirited and saucy in the extreme, but she was a young innocent girl who deserved to be protected from the debauchery of an older man who was a premier duke of the realm. There was nothing noble about his brother's intentions, and tomorrow he would tell him so.

A movement outside caught John's attention. A nerve ticked in his jaw as he watched Francis leave the house and follow a path that would take him to the cottage of Molly Hill. His vivid imagination pictured Francis, complete with riding crop, enjoying a lusty sexual gallop with his horse-faced harridan. *Tallyho!*

That night, John's sleep was fitful to say the least, but finally after tossing and turning for hours, he drifted into a dream. *He was alone, riding through the forest on a warm summer day. He felt free and alive and amazingly tranquil. Then, suddenly, he heard a cry of distress and, thinking it was an animal caught in a trap, he began a search to track it down. The hunt took him deeper into the forest, where the trees grew closer together, making it difficult for his horse. He was relieved when a clearing opened up before him, but his relief was short-lived.*

The cries of distress were not from an animal; they were from a young girl who was being ravished by a man. She was fighting him wildly, but was no match for the powerful male. In a flash, John dismounted, grabbed the man, and smashed him in the jaw. To his horror he saw that the raptor was his brother, Francis, and in cold anger, he gave him a brutal thrashing.

When his brother fled, he turned to the young girl, and his heart constricted as he recognized Lady Geor-

gina Gordon. He quickly stripped off his shirt and covered the naked beauty.

Georgina flung the shirt away. "Go to the devil, old man!"

John stared, mesmerized by her slim legs, tiny waist, and lush breasts. Hot desire rose up in him, and he had no inclination to control his hungry craving to possess the tempting beauty. His dark eyes licked over her creamy flesh like a candle flame.

"Your sister informed me that you were ready for mischievous fun and games at the drop of a hat. I intend to put it to the test, little girl."

The tip of her tantalizing tongue touched her lips in a provocative gesture. "Nature provides the perfect setting for all sorts of exciting fun and games."

"I hereby warn you that I intend to make love to you."

She tossed her saucy curls and challenged, "You will be fighting an uphill battle."

"I have the temperament for it."

Georgina smiled into his eyes. "I have no doubt of it."

John closed the distance between them and took the exquisite beauty into his arms. Just as he took possession of her sinfully tempting lips, he felt a hand on his shoulder. He turned to stare into the face of his brother, Francis.

My God, our roles are suddenly reversed. John stiffened, bracing himself for his brother's fist to smash him in the jaw.

To his amazement, Francis did not hit him. Instead he handed him a hundred guineas. "I lose. You win the wager, old man!"

John woke up in a sweat. It was a few minutes before he realized he was not in the woods, but in bed at Woburn. He was relieved that the episode was not real. It was only a dream. And yet he pondered why on earth he had dreamed such a thing. The part where he had smashed Francis in the jaw for his attempted ravishment of Georgina Gordon was explained easily enough. He had gone to bed angry with his brother for his prurient interest in the girl. What baffled him was his own seduction of Georgina.

He put it down to the sexual drought he had endured for the past nine years. Perhaps unconsciously his physical needs had been transferred to his dream. *That still doesn't explain why Lady Georgina Gordon was the object of my desire. She is more child than woman. I'm fifteen years older than the girl.* John grimaced. *That's why she calls me old man.*

Until nine years ago, John Russell had been a faithful husband. Since then, though he'd had an occasional slip, he had never taken a mistress. His friendship with Lady Sandwich had resulted in an intimate interlude upon rare occasions, but what he felt for widowed Lady Anne was affection and respect, rather than any deep-rooted passion.

Because of his own lapse of infidelity, he had never condemned his brother's multiple liaisons. Francis belonged to the inner circle of the Prince of Wales, and loose morals ran rampant in that crowd. Now, however, John felt disgust at his brother's lecherous interest in young unwed girls. When Francis revealed that he had bedded Lady Louisa Gordon, John had been thoroughly shocked. A picture of Louisa and Georgina Gordon flashed into his mind. *The Gordon daughters have been brought up in a most unconventional manner. Perhaps Jane Gordon has urged them to go to any lengths to trap wealthy, noble husbands. Perhaps the little honeypots have been taught that beauty and promiscuity are an irresistible combination.* The thought angered him further.

The following morning, after breakfast, John made a suggestion. "Why don't we have a game of tennis on that grand indoor court of yours, Francis? A game of doubles will be good practice for the boys."

"I'm glad you suggested it, John. My namesake and I will take on you and William. What do you say, Francis?"

"That sounds jolly good, sir, if you have the patience to play with a rank amateur."

"Your youthful vigor will make up for your lack of expertise."

They all went along to the indoor tennis court, and Johnny offered to retrieve the balls. They tossed a coin for first serve, which Francis lost.

John smiled with anticipation and allowed his fierce anger full rein. With little help from his partner, he had Francis gasping for breath as he desperately tried to return the ball, and John trounced his brother badly. The battle was fought and won quickly; he beat Francis by sheer dint of will and fury.

"When the devil did you become so good at the game?" Francis demanded. "I'm glad we didn't have a wager on the outcome."

"Since you like fun and games and enjoy wagers so much, let's have a hundred guineas on another match. It'll give you a sporting chance to redeem yourself."

"Well, if I can take William for my partner this time."

"Done!" John was chafing at the bit. Ordinarily, he was no match for Francis, but today he felt an insatiable need to beat the devil out of him. Even if it was only symbolic.

By the time the match was over, Francis had had the wind knocked out of him and was pressing his hand to a tender spot in his belly that had plagued him on and off since boyhood.

"Are you all right?" John asked with concern.

"Bloody hernia popped out. I'd have trounced you soundly otherwise."

It took the pleasure from John's victory. His brother could not bear to lose and always had a ready excuse. He felt most of his anger against Francis melt away. Most, but not all, he realized, and decided to tell him bluntly that his dishonorable intensions toward Lady Georgina were not only shameless, they were unacceptable.

Chapter 7

Georgina stood patiently while the fashionable modiste fitted her for the court gown she would wear when she was presented to Queen Charlotte.

"It must be kept simple," the Duchess of Gordon stressed.

"White is most flattering for Lady Georgina because of her lovely coloring," Madame Chloe said truthfully.

"Yes, I quite agree. Some of the other debutantes, one in particular who shall remain nameless, will look gauche and washed out in a plain white gown."

Before her mother divulged she was speaking about the Duchess of Devonshire's daughter, Georgina said, "I would prefer a little decoration . . . perhaps a lace edging around the sleeves and a white rose at the high waistline, beneath my breasts."

"Ah yes," her mother agreed, "a flower just coming into bloom."

Georgina's eyes sparkled with mirth, but she managed to keep from laughing out loud.

"How soon can the gown be ready, Madame Chloe?"

"I have orders for so many court gowns," the modiste said vaguely.

"But surely you will put the Gordons at the head of your list?"

"Mother, there is lots of time."

"Indeed there is not. You are to have your portrait

painted in the gown before you are presented to Queen Charlotte. This is one of the most important occasions of your entire life, Georgina. I have only one daughter left to launch into society. We have saved the best for last. We must plan down to the finest detail. You must start working on your guest list immediately."

"Guest list?"

"For your coming-out ball, Georgina. Since it will be one of the most eagerly awaited debutante events of the winter season, we must make it a very grand affair."

Lud, I shall be paraded before an endless line of prospective husbands so that Mother can maintain her reputation as the most accomplished matchmaker in London.

Georgina felt as if a trap were closing in on her and the need for escape rose up and made her short of breath. A plan ran through her head like quicksilver. "Perhaps you could have the gown ready by Friday, since Mother has already arranged for me to sit for my portrait next week."

Jane gave her daughter an approving glance.

As soon as the portrait is done, I'll go to Scotland and visit Father. I'll beg him to return with me for my presentation at court. He likely won't bother to come if I don't cajole him. The thought that her father had little interest in her drained away her confidence and was replaced by an overwhelming vulnerability. She closed her eyes and made a wish. *Now all I have to do is talk Mother into letting me go.*

"The bracken has already started to turn color." Georgina gazed from the coach window, drinking in the unparalleled beauty of the Scottish countryside.

Helen Taylor, the Scotswoman who had been her wet nurse when she was a baby, was her traveling companion. "Aye, the last half of August is still summer in London, but up here autumn is already painting the landscape and, come September, the nights will be verra chilly, ma lamb."

"We won't be able to stay long. I gave Mother my word of honor that I would be back in London by the middle of September. That's the only reason she allowed me to come." *That, and the fact that I promised to ask Father to pay for my coming-out ball.*

The coach driver maneuvered through the narrow streets of Edinburgh, where they planned an overnight stay before continuing to the Highlands. When he pulled up before the fashionable town house in George Square, a familiar manservant hurried down the steps and opened the coach door.

"Welcome tae Edinburgh, Lady Georgina. His Grace didna' tell me he was expecting ye."

Her eyes lit up. "Father is here?"

"His Grace has business up on the rock, but he'll be back afore long. Let's get yer baggage inside and get ye settled."

Inside, Georgina greeted the housekeeper. "Would you order a bath for Helen, please? After that unforgiving coach ride, she needs a long soak in some hot water."

"Both me and ma old bones bless ye, ma lamb."

"A tot of whiskey wouldn't be amiss, either," Georgina directed. "I shall unpack for us."

When the Duke of Gordon returned, Georgina ran into her father's arms. "I'm so happy to find you here in Edinburgh. It will save me that arduous journey to Castle Gordon. I . . ." Her words trailed off as she saw the woman who accompanied her father.

Jean Christie, Alexander's longtime mistress, bobbed a curtsy. "Lady Georgina."

The plain female was meekness itself, exactly opposite to the flamboyant Duchess of Gordon. Her father had never hidden the woman, and Georgina had met her on many occasions, but today she was taken aback by the fact that she was ripe with child. *Dear God, how many is this, the fourth or the fifth?*

"Please excuse me, my lady. I know ye'll both wish to be private," Jean said before she quietly withdrew.

Georgina quickly tried to mask the dismay she felt. The Duke of Gordon was Keeper of the Great Seal of Scotland and often had official business at Edinburgh Castle, but surely he hadn't taken his mistress with him. "You were up at the castle?" she asked.

"Aye, while Jean was visiting the doctor. I brought her to the city while the weather is still good. Will ye no' travel back to Castle Gordon with us? Ye can join me for the annual autumn woodcock shoot." He noticed her suppress a shudder. "We'll talk about it at dinner, my wee lass. Then ye can tell yer old dad what's troubling ye."

As Georgina bathed her hands and face and changed her clothes, she realized that the joy she had felt at coming to Scotland to see her father had begun to ebb away. But she went down to dinner determined to keep disappointment from taking over.

She was relieved that there was only the two of them in the dining room for the evening meal.

"Ye look very grown up tonight, lass."

"I had my eighteenth birthday last month."

"Really? I canna keep track of birthdays."

Too many children by too many mothers, Georgina thought. "I just sat for my portrait wearing my court gown."

"Since I didn't get ye a gift, I'll pay fer the portrait. Who painted it?"

"John Hoppner."

"Just like yer mother to pick someone expensive. Did he do a good job?"

"Yes, I like it very much. It makes me look alluring."

"Isn't the object of a debutante's first portrait to make her look young and innocent?" he asked with a twinkle.

"Convention would have it so, but then I come from a most unconventional family," she said pointedly.

"At least on yer mother's side," he agreed.

"Don't expect me to be disloyal to Mother. I love you both."

"And that's how it should be, my sweet lass. Now, what's upset ye enough to send ye running off to Scotland?"

How the devil do I answer that? I can't say that Mother will ruthlessly shove me on the marriage market and sell me to the highest title without sounding disloyal to her. "I realized this would be my last chance for a holiday before the winter season starts with a vengeance. And I also came to make sure you come to London for my court presentation to Queen Charlotte."

Alexander frowned. "Aye, well, that might prove a bit tricky. Jean's bairn is due to be born in early October."

The disappointment Georgina had been holding at bay now flooded over her. Her mouth went dry, and she swallowed with difficulty. "I understand," she said quietly.

"Good lass. Now, why don't we go trout fishin' tomorrow in the River Esk? It's not the Spey, but it's the best around Edinburgh."

"I'd enjoy that, Father. I'll bring my sketchbook."

"And I'll wear ma kilt. We'll have an early start, say five o'clock?"

Georgina smiled. "I'll be ready. I'll ask the cook to pack us a picnic lunch."

Upstairs, she told Helen that she was going to bed early so she could be up at five. "I hope it won't be difficult for you to be here without me. Jean Christie is here."

"Och, the woman is so self-effacing, she'll present no problem to me, ma lamb. Does she make ye feel uncomfortable?"

"No, no, not really. I was just taken aback when I saw she was having another baby."

Helen nodded with understanding. "What canna be cured must be endured."

"You are a wise woman." Georgina sighed. "Good night, Helen."

* * *

During the course of the next fortnight, the Duke of Gordon and his daughter enjoyed countless hours together. They fished in the River Esk, went sailing in the Firth of Forth, and played golf. Her father had a kilt made for her in black-and-white Gordon plaid, along with a bonnet and a black velvet doublet. He bought her a sterling silver brooch fashioned like a thistle with a huge purple amethyst at its center.

When her father went to Holyrood Palace on official business, Georgina accompanied him. It was a place that fascinated her because of its compelling atmosphere. As always, she went to the chambers that had been occupied by Mary, Queen of Scots, and stared at the bloodstain on the wooden floor where Mary's husband, Darnley, had reputedly been murdered.

So much misery has been caused by the adultery of husbands and wives. I don't want a marriage like you had, Mary. Nor do I want a marriage like my own parents have. Georgina closed her eyes and made a fervent wish for a husband who would love her so deeply he would never look at another.

Alexander took his daughter to a popular oyster cellar in the Cannongate, where the famous fiddler Neil Gow played, and the Scottish dancing began at ten o'clock sharp. To honor the Gordons, who had long been his patrons, Gow played a strathspey that the duke himself had written.

"Oh, I wish Neil Gow could come to London to play at my coming-out ball," Georgina said wistfully.

"So yer mother is throwing one of her fancy balls, is she? Ye'd better warn her not to stick me wi' the bill."

Georgina tried not to feel hurt at his blunt words, but she didn't quite succeed. He was one of Scotland's wealthiest nobles, and could well afford a party to celebrate the debut of his youngest daughter. *But I'm not his youngest daughter—he has others who are not legitimate. Is it possible he loves Jean Christie's children more than he loves us?* She quickly pushed the thought away. *Stop feeling sorry for yourself, Georgina Gordon!*

After two weeks she could tell her father was itching to get back to his Highland castle and his autumn woodcock shoot. Georgina bade him a fond good-bye as she and Helen Taylor boarded their coach to go back to London. It had been a bittersweet visit, though she had thoroughly enjoyed the activities she and her father had shared.

She had made numerous sketches of him, and she was gratified that he wanted to keep them all. She did keep one she made while he was fishing in the River Esk. As the carriage bowled along at a brisk pace, she took out the drawing and examined it.

"This sketch of Father reminds me of someone," she told Helen. "Who the devil can it be?"

"The duke is an authoritative figure, yet extremely handsome with his black hair blowing in the wind."

Georgina suddenly knew whom her father brought to mind. *John Russell, Marquis of Tavistock! Though younger, the surly sod is an authoritative father figure with jet-black hair. Damnation, I wanted to frame this sketch and hang it in my bedchamber, but every time I look at it, I shall be reminded of the old man.* She quickly thrust the offensive likeness back into her drawing case.

"I'm happy to see you are a young lady of principle. You said you would be back by mid-September, and here you are!" Jane said. "I shouldn't be surprised . . . You take after me in every way."

"Father was in Edinburgh, so I was saved a long journey."

"Really? What was he doing in Edinburgh, pray tell?"

Georgina had more good sense than to mention Jean Christie. "I believe he was visiting Edinburgh Castle and Holyrood Palace in connection with his duties as Keeper of Scotland's Great Seal."

"I see. And did the great man agree to pay for your coming-out ball, by any remote chance?" her mother asked dryly.

"Father offered to pay for my portrait."

"As he should. I already informed Hoppner that the Duke of Gordon would foot the bill. What about the expense of the ball?"

Georgina did not repeat his warning about sticking him with the bill. "I'm not even sure he will be able to come to London for my presentation at Court." *In fact, I know he won't!*

"Hmph! Other fish to fry, I warrant."

"He no doubt has pressing business matters."

"Funny bloody business, if I know the Cock o' the North!"

Georgina laughed. *Funny bloody business indeed. If I didn't laugh, I'd cry.*

"Well, now that you are back we must not waste a moment. I'll send a note around to Madame Chloe and ask her to come tomorrow. You must be furnished with an entire new wardrobe, Georgina. I shall do all in my power to make your Season a spectacular one. I warrant it will be the best investment I will ever make."

Georgina's emotions hovered between resentment and resignation. *Successful Seasons are measured by marriages, not fancy gowns and balls.* She sighed. *Ah, well, as Helen wisely said, what cannot be cured must be endured.* "I shall put myself entirely in your hands, Mama."

After she unpacked and hung her things in the wardrobe, Georgina took the sketch she had made of her father from her drawing case. She stared at it long and hard. "I was just being fanciful. It looks nothing like John Bloody Russell!"

She had made a sketch of her brother, George, in his colonel's uniform. She removed it from its frame and replaced it with the one of her father. She hung it up on the wall, and stood back. Alexander, Duke of Gordon, Cock o' the North, his hair blowing in the wind, stared back at her. Georgina fingered the silver and amethyst thistle pinned at her throat. *You do love me! I know you do!*

Next morning, Georgina sought her brother in the breakfast room. "Hello, George. I need a special favor from you."

"Anything for you, Georgy. What is your pleasure?"

"This morning I have to consult with Madame Chloe about my new wardrobe, but this afternoon I would like to go up in the visitors' gallery at the House, and I need an escort."

"Ah, got your eye on someone, have you?" he teased.

"Of course not! Louisa and I visited regularly to listen to the speakers. I take a keen interest in politics, George."

He ignored her denial. "Better not set your cap for someone in the House of Commons—only the members of the House of Lords will measure up to Mother's standards."

"Since both Houses are now back in session, I shall visit the Lords next week, if you will be good enough to escort me."

Jane came into the breakfast room. "There you are, Georgina. Madame Chloe has just arrived."

George winked at his sister before their mother dragged her away to be measured, fitted, and pushed, pulled, and pinned.

Though it was traditional for young debutantes to be gowned exclusively in white, Georgina insisted her new wardrobe must contain some color.

She knew exactly what shades complemented her dark hair and creamy complexion. Pale hues of peach, primrose, lavender, and green were most flattering. When her mother objected to the vivid peacock Georgina lusted for, she compromised and agreed to a sheer white overskirt that would mute its brilliance.

She needed fans and slippers to match every outfit, as well as cloaks and capes, some of which were edged with swansdown or white fox fur.

"I have a coiffeuse coming this afternoon. You definitely need a couple of new wigs and some jeweled ornaments. I shall be fitted for a new one myself, while she is here," Jane declared.

"Sorry, I'm going out with George this afternoon."

Jane did not argue with her daughter. If George were with his sister, he would be safe from the man-eating females who ran shamelessly after him. "I'll have the coiffeuse come tomorrow."

Georgina, garbed in her best walking dress of cream linen with a summery hat adorned with flowers, matched her steps to her brother's as they made their way to the House of Commons. "It has occurred to me that Mother's obsessive determination to give away her daughters in marriage does not extend to her only son."

"Her possessiveness is fanatical. She has interfered in my life every bit as much as she has in yours and your sisters'. Of necessity, I have learned to be secretive about my interest in the opposite sex. Mother put an end to every relationship I sought if the young lady were suitable, and shoved me into the arms of females who were highly unsuitable, if you get my meaning."

"Yes, I do. She encourages your rackety life, hoping to keep you sated with pleasure so that you will never marry. She believes that no lady breathing is good enough for you."

"Well, of course she's right," he teased.

Georgina grinned. "I've heard you referred to as the Prince of Wales of the North."

"A most unflattering comparison. Prinny must weigh at least ten stone more than I do."

Georgina's eyes sparkled with curiosity. "Is there a special young lady you are secretly interested in?"

He winked. "If I told you, it wouldn't be a secret."

They climbed the stairs and entered the gallery, which wasn't too crowded today. There were one or two wives present to listen to their husbands, and a few male heirs viewing their fathers below on the floor of the Commons.

Georgina did not take a seat, but stood at the rail and looked down. She saw him immediately. He was the only member of parliament not wearing a wig, and his black hair stood out in stark contrast to the white powdered heads.

Her glance moved to Mr. Pitt, who stood on the floor with a sheaf of papers in his hand. "Though we successfully put down the attempted Irish rebellion, we must not be complacent. If solutions to the religious and political problems in Ireland are not found, malcontents will try again and again to overthrow the monarchy. I firmly believe the only answer is a union of Great Britain and Ireland."

Loud shouts, both agreeing and disagreeing with the prime minister, broke out. And it took a few minutes for order to be restored.

Georgina watched John Russell get to his feet. He did not need to climb on the bench to be noticed. He was a head taller than most members.

"The house recognizes the honorable member from Tavistock."

John Russell spoke without notes, and his deep, somber voice carried easily to the gallery. "Mr. Prime Minister, honorable members. You are well aware that my vote is for full Irish independence."

Cheers and jeers met his words.

Unperturbed, Russell continued. "Since most of you are still living in the Dark Ages and will not even consider this, I would throw my weight behind Prime Minister Pitt's suggestion of an Act of Union, providing . . . *providing* we allow Catholic emancipation."

Once again there were cheers and jeers.

Pitt held up his hand. "Irish Catholics have been permitted to vote since 1790, but any bill allowing

Roman Catholics to become members of parliament will be blocked by His Royal Highness, King George III. I remind you we serve at the pleasure of the king."

"The king is mad!"

Georgina couldn't tell who made the shocking declaration, but pandemonium reigned as members banged their shoes on the benches.

Charles James Fox got to his feet and held up both arms. The members quieted so that he could be heard. "Once again, I humbly propose a Bill of Regency."

His words were met with laughter and cheers from his fellow members of the Whig opposition.

Mr. Pitt responded. "We are aware of the honorable Member's ambition to become prime minister of this House. Sadly, I cannot accommodate you at this time."

John Russell's deep voice rose above the mirth. "It is no laughing matter that ninety percent of Irishmen are excluded from sitting in the Irish parliament because they are Catholic. And you are right, Mr. Pitt—we do serve at the pleasure of the king. But I respectfully remind you that the *king* serves at the pleasure of the *people*." The entire House broke into applause.

Georgina hung on to his every word. *I find the man himself detestable, yet I totally agree with his sentiments.*

"Are you watching Charles Lennox?" her brother asked.

Georgina blinked. *I didn't even see Charlotte's husband.* Her glance roamed across the benches. *Why, there's Lord Holland. How on earth did I miss seeing Henry?* She knew the answer all too well. She had eyes only for John Russell. She grudgingly admitted the surly sod was the sole purpose of her visit today.

Georgina was disappointed when the parliamentary session ended abruptly and it was ruled that the members would address the subject tomorrow and thereafter until they reached a resolution.

George was in no hurry to leave the gallery, and by the time they descended the stairs, the members of parliament were also leaving. "Don't rush out, Georgina. Let's wait for Lennox. I'd like a word with him."

She acquiesced against her better judgment. She didn't want John Russell to know she had been in the gallery today.

"Charles. Over here!" George raised his voice and waved.

Lennox spoke over his shoulder to a couple of men behind him, and they cut through the crowd toward George.

"How about attending the Newmarket races this weekend?"

"I'd love to, George." Charles turned to Lord Holland. "How about you, Henry? Newmarket this weekend?"

"Why not? I haven't been to the races in an age." He turned to his friend John Russell. "How about you, John?"

"Sorry. My sons are back at school, and I promised to visit with them at Westminster this weekend."

Georgina's eyes met Russell's. She looked away quickly, and smiled at Lord Holland, who never missed a chance to lightly flirt with her. "How are you, Henry? I took great delight in watching you from the gallery this afternoon."

"You know exactly how to flatter a man, Lady Georgina. But John here was the one to watch today." He addressed Russell. "Your brother, Francis, invited Beth and myself to the Woburn races the following weekend. I hope you can attend Bedford's annual affair. Beth and I haven't seen your wife in ages."

"My wife is visiting her sister, Lady Bath, but I hope to be at Woburn for the annual races." John's dark glance swept over Georgina and came to rest on the brilliant poppies decorating her hat. A muscle ticked in his jaw. *The bold young hussy is deliberately flamboyant so she can catch every male eye and be the center of attention.*

"Then the plans are set," George declared. "Newmarket this weekend and Woburn next."

"Will you be joining your brother, Lady Georgina?" Lord Holland asked. "Beth would enjoy your company."

Georgina saw the dark frown of disapproval on the old man's face.

"No," George said firmly. "My sister doesn't make her debut until the first week of October."

Georgina's glance swept over Russell's face, and she smiled sweetly. "All plans should be made for the happiness of the many and not for the benefit of the few."

John Russell knew she was deliberately mocking him. He had said those words in connection with the government when they had dined together at Marylebone Manor. *The girl needs her arse tanned.*

Chapter 8

It seemed like every hour of every day was taken up with plans concerning Georgina's coming debut. There were fittings for her new wardrobe as well as shopping excursions to Bond Street. She spent an entire day on the guest list for her coming-out ball, but the following day her mother pointed out just how many important people she had overlooked, and together they amended it.

"The list totals three hundred!" Georgina protested.

"There is no point in having a coming-out ball unless it is on a grand scale. And you can be sure the Duchess of Devonshire will invite everyone in fashionable society, including his brother, to the ball she throws for her daughter Dorothy."

Under no circumstances must the Duchess of Belgrave be allowed to outdo the Duchess of Drinkwater! "That reminds me, I have a dancing class at Devonshire House this afternoon."

"No, I have arranged for the dancing master to come here for the next two weeks. The Cavendish girls will have to have their lessons here for a change."

"Oh dear, this is shaping up to be a battle of the maternal rivals," Georgina said with amusement.

"Rubbish! We have collaborated so that our daughters' coming-out balls fall on different nights of the week. I'll have the invitations printed immediately so that our footmen can deliver them personally."

The following day, Georgina enjoyed a respite from discussions of gowns, guests, food, and flower arrangements for her ball, when her brother escorted her to visit the House of Lords, as promised.

As she looked down from the gallery, she recognized some of the faces. "There is the Duke of Devonshire."

"Good God, there's an aberration for you. The man leads a nocturnal life and spends every night at Brooks's Club swilling booze until his back teeth float. This will likely be his sole appearance in the Lords all year."

"He never smiles." Georgina felt pity for his family.

"He can't smile. The muscles of his face have been paralyzed by sugar of lead that he applies to conceal the redness."

"I am getting an education today." Her avid glance moved about the benches. "There's Susan's husband. I must say, the Duke of Manchester looks bored to death. I don't think he's listening."

"Of course not. William is far too athletic to sit still and listen to a debate on the Irish problem."

"He is an extremely handsome man." *Susan did well for herself.*

"Yes, women go mad over him."

Then perhaps she didn't do well for herself!

"Francis Russell is about to enter the debate."

Since this was the man whom Georgina had come to observe, she focused her attention on him and listened. *Though his argument is solid enough, the Duke of Bedford is addressing his opponent with utter indifference.* She watched as he gave sneering replies to his adversaries. "Bedford treats everyone with contempt."

"Oh, Francis has atrocious manners."

It must run in the family!

"Fortunately, he is wealthy enough to get away with it."

She changed the subject. "The House of Lords is supposed to keep a check on government by scrutinizing its activities. And it also has the power of veto over the House of Commons, I believe."

"I'm amazed you have an interest in this political rambling."

Georgina gazed down at Francis Russell. *He is better looking than his stern-faced brother, John, and he is certainly a fashion plate, but there is a debauched look about him somehow. He gives off the scent of lechery. I warrant he's a self-indulgent devil, but as the richest duke in England, how could he be otherwise?*

At four sharp, the debate ended. The noblemen had far more important interests to pursue than government matters. Their clubs beckoned, where they were free to indulge their twin vices of drink and gaming.

George tried to catch up with his brother-in-law as he left parliament, but the Duke of Manchester's carriage was at the door waiting for him.

Georgina stared after William Montagu. "Who the devil was that woman in William's carriage? It certainly wasn't Susan."

George shrugged. "One of his *petites amies*, I expect."

Georgina was shocked, and felt outrage for her sister.

"Huntly, what are you doing here?" Francis Russell asked as his glance licked over Georgina.

"Oh, hello, Bedford. I just missed Manchester. I was going to ask him if he was going to your races at Woburn this weekend."

"Yes, Manchester accepted my invitation. Dare I hope that Lady Georgina will be joining us?"

"You may always hope, Your Grace," Georgina said coolly.

"She will *not* be joining us. My sister is teasing you."

"She certainly is," Bedford drawled.

"We visited the Commons last week, where I observed your brother addressing the Irish problem."

"How do we compare?" Francis asked smugly.

"Your brother is far more passionate."

"Not in all things." His words were deliberately *risqué.*

"That remains to be seen, Your Grace. Good day."

George hurried to catch up with his sister, who had walked away. "You shouldn't banter with Bedford like that. He is a known womanizer."

"From what I've observed lately, what nobleman isn't?"

"He's more profligate than others. His mistresses are legion. I'd just like you to be careful, Georgy. After your debut, the men will be swarming about you like bees round a honeypot."

"I am in no hurry to be leg-shackled, George, especially to a man with a string of mistresses."

"Leg-shackled is a term used by the male of the species."

"Until now. Perhaps I'll set a new fashion."

"You underestimate Mother's husband-hunting abilities. They don't call her the 'Whipper-in' for nothing."

Mother caught a powerful noble for herself, and great titles for my sisters, but I wonder if any of them are truly happy? Georgina shivered and sent up a silent prayer.

"Are you cold?" George asked with concern.

"No, no. Just a goose walking over my grave."

Francis Russell returned to the Bedford London mansion in Russell Square. Not only did the Russells own the mansion and the entire square, they owned all of Bloomsbury. The brothers used different wings of the mansion whenever they were in London, but they often supped together in the evenings after their parliamentary sessions.

Francis drove through the wrought-iron gates and turned his phaeton over to a stableman. As he was walking through the gardens toward the house, he ran into his brother. "Hello, John. Why the frown?"

"Francis, these gardens are in a hell of a state. The

place is like an overgrown jungle. I thought you were going to get someone in here to redesign them and make the place look civilized."

"Never seem to find the time. You worry about things too much. You always put duty before pleasure and expect me to do the same."

"If you can't find the time, Francis, I'll do it. Humphrey Repton is a great landscape gardener—just the man we need."

"If Repton suits you, he suits me. Let's go and eat. Would you like to join me at Brooks's tonight?"

"No, thanks. I'm working on a speech I intend to deliver in the House tomorrow. This Irish matter must be resolved."

"There you go again—duty before pleasure. With your wife off visiting her sister, you should take time for something pleasurable."

"I am—I'm coming to Woburn this weekend for the annual races."

In the dining room, over dinner, Francis eyed his brother with speculative eyes. "Do you know, wearing your own dark hair is rather striking. I've been considering leaving off my wig. It could set a new fashion."

"I wear my own hair to protest the tax on flour. It has nothing to do with fashion."

"But if I did it, John, it would have everything to do with fashion. You know I'm all for pleasure before duty."

"I am well aware, Francis."

"You say that as if I am derelict in my duty."

"In one thing you are absolutely derelict. As the Duke of Bedford you need an heir. You have vast wealth, enormous property holdings in London, as well as estates in the shires of Bedford, Buckingham, Cambridge, Devon, and Northampton. You need a son and heir to pass all this on to, and to carry on your name."

"I would need to *marry* to beget an heir," Francis said dryly.

"You would indeed. At thirty-six, soon to be thirty-seven years old, surely it is time to start looking about you for a suitable wife?"

"You never seem to tire of nagging me on this subject, but as usual, John, though I hate to admit it, you are right. I just cannot contemplate limiting myself to one woman."

"I doubt you could, or that you would even try. Nevertheless, your need for an heir grows with every passing year. You also need an official mistress for Woburn, and only a legitimate wife can fulfill that role."

Francis sighed and drained his glass of claret. "A political alliance between the leading Whig duke and the daughter of the leading Whig hostess would no doubt fulfill society's expectations."

"Good God, the Devonshires' daughter is little more than a child. Francis, what can you be thinking?"

"The young lady is making her debut soon. I'm invited to her coming-out ball at Devonshire House."

"That makes her eighteen at most," John protested.

"Wasn't Elizabeth eighteen when you married her?"

"Yes, but I was nineteen, not a middle-aged man of thirty-seven."

"For Christ's sake, John! First you urge me to marry; then, when I agree to consider the matter, you throw obstacles in my path and do all you can to deter me."

John put up his hand. "I'm sorry, Francis. I have no right to interfere in your life. I just wanted to prod you into at least thinking about marriage. I will refrain from advising you on your choice of wife. God knows, my own marriage gives me no authority to set myself up as an example."

"No need to apologize to me, John. You have always been a steadying force in my life. Your resolve is like a rock." He changed the subject. "Prinny is coming to Woburn for the races, as well as Prince Edward. I have a huge wager with Edward on each and every race. The foolish fellow is addicted to gambling."

John's dark brows drew together, puzzled that Francis did not recognize his own obsession with gaming. *Bite your tongue, John.*

"I fancy a long drive in the country this weekend. The autumn leaves will be spectacular." Jane Gordon took it for granted that Georgina would fall in with her plans.

"Where did you have in mind?" Georgina knew her mother seldom did anything without an ulterior motive.

"Kimbolton, as a matter of fact. Your sister, the Duchess of Manchester, has a magnificent collection of Georgian silver that I wouldn't mind borrowing for your coming-out ball."

"Surely all you need do is drop Susan a note, and she will bring whatever you fancy when she and William come for my presentation to Queen Charlotte."

"True enough, my dear. But Kimbolton has such treasures; I warrant I may see other things I could use to impress the *haut ton* who will be coming to our ball."

Georgina smiled her secret smile. *There's her ulterior motive.*

When the carriage stopped in the courtyard of the ancient Abbey of Saint Albans to water the horses, Georgina and her mother took the opportunity to stretch their legs.

The Duchess of Gordon made a small, charitable donation to the Benedictine monks prior to climbing the famous tower. It gave them a spectacular view of the majestic Chiltern Hills that were garbed in their scarlet, orange, and yellow autumn finery.

Georgina saw her mother's eyes glisten with tears. "It reminds you of Scotland . . . Try not to let it make you feel sad."

"I didn't get to visit my beloved Kinrara this summer," Jane said wistfully. "I missed seeing the woods filled with fawns."

"Your precious memories are etched forever in your heart and soul. You will enjoy it twice as much next summer."

"Yes, I shall be free as a bird by then . . . if we get you happily married, of course."

I have no doubt you will do your damnedest to get me wed, Mother. How happy I will be, however, will depend upon my own determination and resolve.

Before they departed, the ladies refreshed themselves with the famous ale brewed by the Benedictine monks. Jane allowed their coachman a large mug to quench his thirst before he climbed back up to his seat.

Georgina removed her cloak because the late morning had warmed considerably since they'd left London, and sat back against the velvet squabs to admire the view. After a minute or two, she glanced at her mother. "He's taken the wrong road, I think. The town of Baldock is north; then we go through Tempsford before we reach Kimbolton Castle."

"It's all right, Georgy. I told the driver my change of plans."

"What change of plans?"

"It suddenly occurred to me that this weekend is the Woburn races. Susan will most likely be accompanying Manchester to the great sporting event. It could be a complete waste of time to go to Kimbolton."

Suddenly occurred to you, my arse! I knew you had an ulterior motive, but didn't guess how devious you could be. I'm not nearly as shrewd as I imagined.

"How fortunate that the Woburn races will be chockablock with eligible bachelors, Georgina."

Not the least of which will be the lecherous Duke of Bedford. She opened her mouth to protest, then bethought that the dangerous devil, John Russell, would be there. Georgina suddenly decided to keep a wise silence.

* * *

"Well, I'll be damned," George Gordon declared when he fell in beside his young sister as she trailed behind her mother, making a direct path to the Woburn racecourse. "The Whipper-in has already laid her plans for the fox hunt of the Season. How the devil did she get you to agree to come?"

"She outfoxed me! Allegedly, Kimbolton was our destination. Her maneuvers are so bloody transparent, I am humiliated," Georgina said with a blush.

"Well, you and I know what she's up to, but perhaps no one else will guess."

"They're not idiots, George." Georgina saw Prinny laughing with his brother Edward at the antics of a pet monkey dressed up as a jockey. "I am mistaken—they *are* idiots."

"She's dangling the bait in front of Bedford, but I don't think you'll come to any harm with your mother, brother, and a pair of your brothers-in-law present. The bait looks delicious, by the way."

"I wore this outfit thinking I was going to Kimbolton Castle. It's rather dramatic for a race meet."

"It's decidedly racy," he punned with a wink.

"Father had this Black Watch kilt made for me in Edinburgh. It reveals my legs. I didn't know I'd have an audience."

George laughed. "All the gentlemen will be praying for the wind to pick up."

"If it does, I shall simply put my cloak back on." She returned his wink. "Or perhaps, on a whim, I won't."

"Scotland forever!" they said in unison.

Georgina saw that her mother had joined Susan near the grandstand and decided it was her chance to slip away from parental control. Her brother told her that they had arrived too late for the first minor race, but that the second would be run shortly. "Lend me a guinea, George, and point out a bookmaker; then I shall happily allow you to escape."

"Done!" he said, fishing in his pocket for the coin.

The fellow taking the bets was in conversation with

the Earl of Lauderdale and seemed to be having difficulty understanding the Scot's thick brogue.

"I'll act as your interpreter, James, if you'll tell me who's running in this race."

"Lady Georgina, ye've saved ma bacon. Tell this laddie I want tae place a bet on ma own horse, Strathspey."

"How much?"

"A hundred guineas."

"Is that all? You are ever the frugal Scot. Surely you have more confidence in your own animal than that, James?"

"Go on, make it two hundred. Strathspey canna lose."

Georgina arranged the bet for Lauderdale and gave him a saucy smile. "Thanks for the tip." She listened carefully as he named the other horses in the race and turned back to the bookmaker. She proffered her own guinea and placed her bet. Then she headed toward the grandstand so she could watch the race.

As she walked along, she was aware that every head turned to stare at the young lady sporting the kilt and doublet. She fingered the large amethyst in her thistle broach. *Father, you have made me the talk of the Woburn races. I can run and hide, or I can thumb my nose at drab respectability and act with bravado.*

Georgina caught up with Lord Lauderdale. Since he was a Scot, and a widower to boot, she felt safe with him. She bit her lip with vexation as he hailed his great friend Francis Russell. As she had anticipated, the Duke of Bedford's lustful eyes lingered on her legs with appreciation before he raised them to her face.

"What a delightful surprise. Your brother told me in no uncertain terms that you would not be accepting my invitation for the weekend."

"Ah, I'm afraid I'm not here for the weekend, Your Grace. It was imperative that Mother contact my sister, the Duchess of Manchester, on a family matter. We shall be leaving shortly."

"Surely not before you watch the main event for

the Woburn Gold Cup? I insist you stay and partake of my hospitality. It will be an honor to serve as your escort, Lady Georgina."

She relented a little. "Well, I shall certainly watch the upcoming race, since I have placed a wager on it."

Lauderdale clapped Bedford on the back. "Strathspey's the horse tae beat. I hope ye have money on him, Francis."

"I do, James, since I don't have one of my own horses in this race. The odds are only two to one, but there is a thrill to backing a winner that has little to do with money."

Only a man with more riches than Croesus would think that. Georgina stepped closer to the rail. "It's about to start!" She watched avidly as the horses swept past them, raising a cloud of dust beneath their thundering hooves. At the same time, she was acutely aware that Bedford's eyes were focused on her. *Mother too will be watching me with bated breath. Please don't get your hopes up, Duchess Drinkwater.*

The ending of the race was exciting, and a great babble of voices rose up as Strathspey and another racehorse galloped neck and neck down the stretch. A collective sigh could be heard when Strathspey lost by only a head.

"Hellfire and damnation!" Lauderdale shouted, visibly crestfallen. "I'm sorry, lassie, ye've lost yer bet."

"James, please don't be sorry. I didn't lose. I won!"

"How did ye win?" he puzzled as Bedford listened intently.

"I didn't bet on Strathspey. I placed my wager on Silky Sullivan. An Irish horse will beat a Scottish horse every time. I thought that was common knowledge, but perhaps not, since the odds were twenty to one."

Francis Russell threw back his head and roared with laughter. He laughed even harder when he saw his friend's face turn purple with ire. "The joke's on you, James, to let a slip of a girl beat you at your own game!"

"And how much did you lose, Your Grace?" Georgina asked pointedly. "Oh, I forgot. It isn't about the money . . . it's about the thrill of victory or the agony of defeat."

Francis placed his fingers beneath her chin and looked at her. He made no effort to conceal the hot desire in his eyes. "You enjoy being cruel to me. The shoe might be on the other foot someday, mistress, and you will beg for mercy."

"Do you often delude yourself, Your Grace?" she asked sweetly. "I know you gentlemen will excuse me while I go and collect my winnings."

Georgina walked away from them so rapidly, she was panting by the time she found the bookmaker and presented her ticket. When he put the twenty guineas in her hand, she felt rich beyond her dreams. She'd never had more than a sovereign in pocket money.

She turned away quickly and almost collided with John Russell, who had also come to collect his winnings.

His dark, disapproving glance swept over her in the short kilt, and she felt her cheeks burn. She wanted to sink through the turf. Her pleasure at winning was wiped away. *Why the devil does he make me feel like an audacious baggage?* She raised her chin and said defensively, "I bet on the winner."

"Congratulations. Making wagers is obviously a game you enjoy. I too bet on the Irish horse."

"Twenty-five quid pays five hundred, m'lord." The bookmaker inquired if he'd placed his bet on the Woburn cup race.

"Not yet. You can put my winnings on Gimcrack."

"How about you, m'lady?"

"I don't know who's running."

The bookmaker handed her a list.

She felt Russell's disapproving eyes on her. *The dark devil has a dangerous look, as if he'd like to shake me until my teeth rattle.* The thought prompted her bravado to assert itself. "I'll have fifteen guineas on Thunderpot!" she said defiantly. "I believe the name is a euphemism for Pisspot."

John Russell did not laugh. "You have a penchant for vulgarity. It is decidedly inappropriate in a maiden."

"Are you totally devoid of a sense of humor, Lord Tavistock?"

"Not entirely." His glance deliberately wandered over her kilt and doublet. "I find an endless number of things that amuse me." He bowed politely. "Good day, Lady Georgina."

He bested me again—I wish I'd kicked him in the shins. Picturing the act brought a smile to her lips. *My kilt would have flipped up to expose more than my legs!*

She joined her mother and her sister in the grandstand. "If Susan has agreed to bring her impressive silver service for my coming-out party, I see no reason to remain much longer."

"We are not leaving before the main event," Jane declared. "I have a wager on the Prince of Wales's horse, Royal Charger. I got the tip from Charles James Fox."

"That's taking quite a risk. If it wasn't for bad luck, Fox would have no luck at all."

Susan laughed at her sister's apt remark. "I asked William to place my bet on Godolphin. He's a magnificent stallion."

"William or Godolphin?" Georgina asked innocently.

Susan's smile disappeared. "Both, I'm afraid. Sometimes I wish it wasn't so."

"How about a private wager? I'll bet five pounds on Gimcrack."

Susan agreed. "That's the favorite. It belongs to Bedford."

"I didn't know that." *John Russell has bet five hundred pounds on his brother's horse.*

"I'll put my money on Messenger," Susan declared, assessing the racehorses as they made their way to the starting post.

"I saw you bantering with Francis Russell, Georgy. I hope he indicated that he will be attending our grand ball," Jane said.

Georgina smiled sweetly. *Since I tore up his invitation, it will be a miracle if we will have the pleasure of the Duke of Bedford's company.* "He gave me no indication, Mother."

"They're off!" Susan grasped Georgina's arm in her excitement.

"Come on, Messenger!" she cried with great enthusiasm.

"Royal Charger is in the lead," Jane cried, surging to her feet. "I shall be able to join Prinny in the winner's circle while he receives the gold cup!"

Georgina saw that Gimcrack and Thunderpot were running neck and neck. *If Thunderpot wins the race, I'll collect an amazing sum!* Gimcrack pulled ahead of her horse and, suddenly, perversely, she wanted Gimcrack to win. Her excitement increased apace as Gimcrack moved to the rail and inexorably moved past each horse that was ahead of him. By the time he took the lead, she was jumping up and down and screaming his name. "Gimcrack! Gimcrack!"

"He won! He won!"

"Georgy, the odds were two to one. I only owe you ten pounds. Hardly an amount to get so excited about."

John Russell won a thousand pounds! I am delighted for him. I don't give a fig that I lost fifteen guineas on Thunderpot.

"How fortuitous that Bedford's horse won. It is only fitting that we go down to the winner's circle and congratulate him."

Georgina cursed silently and rolled her eyes at Susan. She pictured Francis Russell presenting the Woburn gold cup and quipped, "Bedford will be beside himself."

Chapter 9

The first week of October sped past so quickly, it all seemed like a blur to Georgina. The day before she was to be presented to the queen, her sisters and their spouses arrived en mass at the Pall Mall mansion. The ladies spent a delightful afternoon showing one another the gowns they would be wearing to court. The men withdrew to the card room and discussed the merits of various racehorses and the amounts they had lost at Newmarket and Woburn.

That night, Georgina lay abed, too unsettled to fall asleep. She got up, walked to the window, and gazed at the stars in the midnight sky. "I wish Father had come," she whispered wistfully. She knew the apprehension she felt about being presented at court was magnified because her father would not be there to give her moral support. Her confidence was at low ebb. *People will think his absence shows a lack of love or caring for me. But that's not true!* She saw a shooting star and made a wish.

The following morning Georgina slept late, and when she went down for breakfast found the room filled with her siblings, all talking at once. For the most part they ignored her as she pushed her food around her plate listlessly.

Finally, Louisa took her hand and squeezed it. "What's the matter, cockroach?"

"No appetite," she murmured.

"Nerves!" Charlotte declared with her usual wisdom.

Georgina managed a wan smile for Louisa. "Are you happy?"

"I'm Lady Brome, and someday I'll be a marchioness. Of course I'm happy."

Georgina stared at her pretty, Titian-haired sister. *Are titles truly what make a woman happy? Without a grand title, am I doomed to unhappiness?*

Louisa squeezed her sister's hand again to reassure her. "Not to worry, Georgy. I have every confidence you will outdo us all!"

"You are the beauty of the family," Charlotte said briskly. "We expect great things from you."

Georgina's heart sank. She desperately wished she could vanish into thin air.

One by one they all left, completely occupied with preparations for this evening's royal ceremony at Saint James's Palace. Georgina sat alone, overwhelmed by inertia. Gradually, because the servants began to rush about, she became aware that someone of importance must have arrived. She shook off her lassitude and left the breakfast room. As she passed a window, she saw a huge black traveling coach standing on the driveway.

Georgina rushed through the entrance hall, flung open the front door, and ran down the steps, her lethargy forgotten. "Father! Father! You came! Oh, I am so happy and so excited. Isn't it an absolutely glorious day?" She flung herself into his outstretched arms, laughing and crying at the same time.

"Do ye see who I brought wi' me, lass?"

Georgina looked at the man climbing from the coach. "Mr. Gow! Mr. Gow! You've come to play the fiddle for my coming-out ball tomorrow night. Welcome to London, Mr. Gow. Father couldn't have brought me a better present."

Alexander, his arm around his daughter, headed for the house. "How many are invited to this grand ball?"

"Three hundred," she admitted reluctantly.

"I hate these damned affairs, so dinna expect me

to be host to these English society snobs. But I will escort ye to court tonight. It will give me pleasure to present ye to the queen."

She smiled into his eyes. "Thank you, Father."

The Duke and Duchess of Gordon, in a show of solidarity, rode the short distance from Pall Mall to Saint James's Palace in their carriage. With them were Huntly, their son and heir, and their youngest daughter, Lady Georgina. Behind them were the carriages of the Duke and Duchess of Manchester, Lord and Lady Lennox, Lord and Lady Brome, and lastly Madelina and her husband, Sir Charles Palmer.

When they arrived at the palace, there were so many carriages clogging the entrance that the Gordon entourage was forced to wait over thirty minutes before they could alight. The Duke and Duchess flanked Georgina, and the rest of the family followed.

In the large crowd slowly making its way to the presence chamber where the debutantes were to be presented to Queen Charlotte, Georgina caught sight of the Duchess of Devonshire's towering wig, decorated with ostrich feathers. Her glance slid over the Duke of Devonshire's stiff, pale face, and finally she saw their daughter, Lady Dorothy. Her friend was wearing an exquisite white muslin gown and wig, similar to her own, but her appearance was marred by the gawkiness of her tall, ungainly figure and her mouth that had a tendency to gape open.

Georgina sent her friend a fleeting smile of encouragement. *I'm glad my father is here. His presence gives me so much more confidence.* She looked around and caught glimpses of the dozen or so other young ladies who were being presented tonight. She knew their names because she had seen the list, but she was far more familiar with their parents, who often attended entertainments given by her mother at their Pall Mall mansion.

She saw the Duchess of Devonshire's sister, Lady Bessborough, who had brought her daughter, Caro

Ponsonby, and Harriet Cavendish to watch Lady Dorothy be presented to the queen. Georgina smiled at the girls, but Caro stuck out her tongue. Unfortunately, Jane Gordon saw her and, in retaliation, she gave Lady Bessborough a haughty snub.

When the doors of the presence chamber were finally opened, the throng filed into the long room hung with royal portraits and rich tapestries and stood against the walls. The royal chamberlain would announce the nobles and the name of each debutante being presented in alphabetical order. Then, in turn, each girl was to leave her parents and walk the length of the chamber to where Queen Charlotte sat enthroned.

Behind her fan, Jane murmured, "I'm gratified to see that dear Prime Minister Pitt has come to pay his respects." Then she bristled slightly. "It's too bad that our daughter will be presented *after* the Devonshires' daughter."

The chamberlain waited until Queen Charlotte, seated at the far end of the presence chamber, finished speaking with Lady Henrietta Coyningham; then he read from a card: "Lady Dorothy Cavendish, daughter of the Duke and Duchess of Devonshire."

The duchess gave her daughter a push, and Lady Dorothy moved forward with an ungainly, hesitant gait. Her head stuck out before her, like a tortoise from its shell.

When Georgina heard her mother murmur, "Here's my head—my arse is coming," her heart ached for her friend. Then she saw her mother hand the chamberlain the invitation card printed with her name, and knew she was next. She closed her fan, adjusted her gloves, and proudly raised her chin.

"Lady Georgina Gordon, daughter of the Duke and Duchess of Gordon of Banffshire, Scotland."

Georgina felt as if she were surrounded by an aura of light. Her lips parted in a half smile, and she had the sensation that she was floating down the long presence chamber. When she arrived before Queen Charlotte, she swept down into a graceful curtsy and waited until the queen raised her.

"It is a special pleasure to meet the youngest daughter of our dear friends the Duke and Duchess of Gordon," the queen said.

With a sweet smile, Georgina replied, "It is a great honor to be presented to you, Your Highness."

The captive audience gave a collective sigh at the young debutante's radiant beauty and grace.

Once all the young ladies had been presented, Queen Charlotte arose and led the royal guests to a reception room where buffet tables lining the walls were laden with hors d'oeuvres, rich desserts, and German wines.

Jane Gordon, a great favorite of the queen's, brought her a glass of golden Rhenish wine. She noticed a look of panic cross Queen Charlotte's face when the king entered the room to join the guests. "What is amiss?" she murmured.

Queen Charlotte whispered, "The king isn't feeling quite himself tonight. Could you help me, Lady Gordon?"

Jane looked over at King George, who was wearing what looked like a purple dressing gown. He had recognized Alexander and was deep in animated conversation with him. "Leave it to me, Your Highness. The Duchess of Devonshire desires your attention."

Jane signaled William Pitt, and together they approached the king and the Duke of Gordon. "If you don't want a Regency on your hands, you'd better get His Highness out of the room."

The pair saw that Alexander had an alarmed look on his face as he listened to King George's rapid staccato speech, punctuated with "What? What?" every few seconds.

Prime Minister Pitt made an elegant bow to the king and suggested smoothly, "Why don't we go somewhere private so we can discuss the matter further, Your Highness?"

George's bulbous blue eyes stared at Pitt until he recognized him, then his head nodded rapidly. "Just so! Just so! Just so!"

Flanked by the prime minister and the Duke of Gordon, King George withdrew from the reception room.

Jane returned to Queen Charlotte's side and lavishly complimented the Duchess of Devonshire on the presentation of her daughter. "At Georgina's coming-out ball tomorrow evening, Lady Dorothy could very easily steal my daughter's thunder."

Susan overheard her mother and murmured to her sister, "How can she utter such blatant claptrap to the Duchess of Devonshire and expect her to believe it?"

"All mothers are convinced that their geese are swans," Charlotte said dryly, "even ours."

By eleven o'clock the reception was over and the Gordons were in their carriage returning home.

Jane asked the duke, "What happened when you left with the king?"

Georgina saw her father place his hand over her mother's. "I'll tell you about it when we are alone," he said.

They are on friendly terms tonight. Life is much more pleasant when they are being civil to each other. If only they can remain like this until Father leaves. That would make my coming-out ball truly a success. Georgina crossed her fingers and made a wish.

When all the family arrived back at number 91 Pall Mall, Jane Gordon instructed a footman to bring champagne. When the glasses were filled, she proposed a toast. "Here's to Georgina! Her presentation was a raging success. She was by far the most beautiful debutante at Saint James's Palace tonight."

"Hear! Hear!" Alexander raised his glass. He was the only one who had been served whiskey. "I would like to propose a toast to my wife, Jane, who has done a magnificent job bringing up daughters and a son worthy of a duke."

"To Mother!" her offspring chorused.

Georgina saw her mother blush at the rare compliment her husband paid her. *She is vividly attractive tonight.*

More toasts to the debutante followed, each more outrageous than the last. Finally her brother raised his glass. "Here's to a successful Season. I wager Georgina will win the gold cup in the race to the altar."

"Devil take you, George! You make me sound like a filly that's ready to be harnessed and ridden." Georgina added wickedly, "I shall at least wait until after my coming-out ball."

Everyone cheered at her saucy wit; then one by one, the couples went upstairs to their bedchambers. Georgina watched as her father whispered something to her mother. Jane picked up the decanter of whiskey, and then they too began to ascend the staircase. Georgina set her empty glass down and followed.

When she saw her parents enter her mother's bedchamber, she told herself fiercely, *They only want to be private to discuss the odd behavior of the king.* Georgina left her door ajar so that she would know when her father sought his own bedchamber in the east wing. After half an hour had passed, she distinctly heard her mother's throaty laugh.

Dear God, Mother would never let him share her bed if she knew that he'd gotten Jean Christie with child again. I should have told her—I shouldn't have kept my mouth shut! Guilt washed over her. She stopped brushing her hair and gazed into the mirror. Suddenly she realized that Jean Christie must have safely delivered the baby, or her father would not have come to London. *I should have known.*

She went to her bedchamber door and listened, trying to reassure herself. *They are only talking about the king.* Georgina's conscience was pricking her unmercifully, and she felt the need for advice from her sisters

Susan and Charlotte. They would know whether she had done the right thing in keeping the upsetting news from their mother.

She slipped along the corridor to Susan's room, tapped softly, opened the door, and stepped inside. Georgina gasped at the sight that met her eyes. Clothes were strewn all over the bedchamber, and Susan and William were coupling stark naked in the middle of the floor. "Christus! You're riding him!"

Montagu, lying supine on his back, grinned at her. "You're the one who put the idea into her head, Georgy. Care to join us?"

Georgina backed from the room and closed the door. It was the first time she had been exposed to a sexual encounter, and she was shocked. She realized she had made a terrible mistake in seeking out Susan. The one to advise her was Charlotte, with her practical common sense. She hurried to the east wing, past her father's empty chamber, and stopped at her eldest sister's door. "May I come in?" She turned the knob and the door swung open.

Charlotte, wearing a modest nightgown over her distended belly, sat on the side of the bed. A naked Charles was standing before her with his cock in her mouth.

"I . . . I . . . I'm sorry," Georgina stammered.

Charlotte made a choking sound, Charles flushed red to the roots of his hair, and Georgina fled.

Five minutes after she reached her room, Charlotte knocked and entered. "You're pale as a ghost. Come and sit down."

Georgina allowed her sister to lead her to a chair.

"You're upset about what you saw." Charlotte sat on the edge of the bed and rested her hands on the mound of her belly.

"I shouldn't have come bursting in on you."

"And I should have locked the door. There, now that's out of the way, let's talk about what you saw."

"I didn't know . . . I never imagined—"

"Truly? I had no idea you were such an innocent. You *do* know what happens between a male and a female . . . how babies are made?"

"Of course I know about coupling—at least in theory. And at the farm I've seen many a ram mount a ewe."

"Between men and women there are many forms of intimacy. When intercourse becomes difficult during pregnancy, men seek sexual relief in other ways. Males get very randy if they don't have a physical outlet. If you don't keep your husband satisfied, he'll soon find a woman who will. It's as simple as that."

"So you're telling me that a wife has to submit to her husband's demands, no matter how disgusting?"

"Georgy, sex isn't disgusting, not with the right partner. At times it can be glorious, at other times deeply satisfying. We are all sexual beings with varying degrees of lust. The trick is to find a good match, and that's what courtship is for."

Georgina tried to digest what Charlotte was telling her.

"What about love? Is there such a thing?"

"If you're lucky. But in any relationship between two people, one always loves more than the other."

"Or *lusts* more than the other."

"Exactly."

"I came to your room to ask your advice about Mother."

"Mother?" Charlotte laughed. "She should be the one advising you. What has she done now?"

"She's allowed Father into her chamber, and likely into her bed. If I'd told her what I know, she never would have done that. And now my conscience is playing merry hell with me."

"What do you know?"

"When I went to Scotland, I learned that he'd fathered yet another bastard on Jean Christie. When I asked him to come for my presentation, he said he couldn't because the baby was due in October. He likely came because she's been safely delivered. I never breathed a word to Mother. I didn't want to hurt her."

"For what it's worth, I wouldn't have told her either. I think you did the right thing, Georgy."

"But he's using her. He's seduced her because he's 'randy,' as you call it."

"Perhaps she's randy too, tonight."

"Do you think there's a chance that they will forget their differences and get back together?"

"I'm sorry to dash your hopes, Georgy, but there isn't a chance in hell of that happening. Mother would never give up her life in London as the leading Tory hostess, and Father would never give up his life in the Highlands of Scotland. His great passions are hunting and fishing."

"And *fucking*," Georgina spat.

Charlotte didn't even raise an eyebrow at her language. "When two people have been trapped for years in an unsuitable union and divorce is impossible, it is only natural for them to seek partners outside the marriage. That's why affairs are so commonplace in our society."

Georgina gave her sister a tremulous smile. "It was naive of me to expect a lasting reconciliation."

"Naïveté is a charming quality in a young debutante." Charlotte kissed her sister's brow. "Good night, darling."

Georgina undressed, got into bed, and lay quietly contemplating the things she had learned tonight. *Well, at least I am considerably less naive than I was this morning!*

Jane Gordon rolled onto her back and opened her legs in invitation. When Alexander moved between them, she groaned with anticipation. She reached down between their bodies and cupped his heavy sac. Then her fingers firmly gripped his hard cock, and she slid them up to its swollen head and squeezed.

It was Alexander's turn to moan. "I always could make ye hot fer me, lass." He buried his face between her opulent breasts and relished the scent of her aroused body. Then he thrust up inside her with one forceful push.

"Yer randy as a bull tonight. 'Tis plain ye've been starving fer the body of a real woman." She wrapped her thighs about his buttocks and moved with him as he plunged in and out with a driving force that was far more satisfying than the fingers he'd used to arouse her and bring her to orgasm earlier, before she'd even undressed.

Jane and Alexander's goal was the same. Each wanted the other to be moaning and frenzied, reeling with the hot carnal need for each other. Both were determined to prove that they alone could satisfy the other's raging sexual needs.

With grim determination, Alex hung on, clenching his fists and his teeth, in an effort to delay his climax until he felt his wife's sheath begin to tighten with strong pulsations. Only then did he allow himself to spend. With a groan of satisfaction he collapsed on top of her, and lay still, enjoying the feeling of satiety this voluptuous woman brought him.

When he finally summoned the strength to roll off her, he watched Jane arise from the bed and walk across the room to pour him a dram of whiskey. The gesture made him decide it was a good time to confess. "Jane, I have to tell ye something."

Georgina had just fallen asleep when a screech rent the air, followed by angry voices. Then she heard the sound of glass shattering. Georgina jumped out of bed. *Mother threw the decanter at him!*

She opened her door and came face-to-face with her father wearing a dressing gown and clutching the formal clothes he had worn to the palace. Georgina nervously licked her lips. "I swear I didn't tell her."

"I told her myself."

"*After* you seduced her!" his daughter accused.

"She seduced me in a shameless attempt to get me to foot the bill fer this bloody ball she's throwin'."

For once Georgina was on her mother's side. "And pay you bloody well should, Alexander Gordon. Think of it as conscience money." She shut the door and went back to bed.

Chapter 10

"Lord have mercy, Susan, just looking at those corset strings you are pulling gives me a bellyache," Charlotte said.

"I don't feel the least bit pinched," Georgina said, laughing, and held up her arms so they could slip her gown over her head.

"Perhaps you are numb. If you start to feel dizzy it's because the blood has rushed to your head," Charlotte warned.

"Giddy, yes . . . dizzy, no," Georgina assured them.

All three of them gazed into the mirror at her reflection, as the gown slid over Georgina's hips and fell to her ankles. It was a delicious confection of gauzy white silk trimmed with silver.

"Your titties are well exposed tonight. Could this be the chaste debutante who was presented to Her Royal Highness not twenty-four hours ago?" Charlotte teased.

"I'm less innocent than I was, after being *exposed* to some shocking sights last night," she said with a straight face. Then added, "At the palace, I mean. I thought the Duchess of Belgrave's breasts were in competition with each other to see which would pop out of her gown first, the left or the right."

"Then the Duchess of Drinkwater removed her cloak and took first prize," Susan declared.

The sisters sobered when Georgina refused to put on a wig.

"I shall wear my own hair and set a new fashion. I have a pair of silver sequined butterflies for decoration."

"Well, you have such pretty black curls, it's a shame to cover them," Susan conceded.

"It's your bloody ball—do as you please!" Charlotte declared.

The invitations said that the ball would begin at the fashionably late hour of ten, but many of the guests began to arrive early. The Gordon family formed a receiving line in the spacious foyer to welcome their guests. The noble hostess Jane had taken the precaution of asking George Grenville, the Marquis of Buckingham, from whom the Gordons leased the Pall Mall mansion, to act as official host.

"You do us great honor, George. The duke finally arrived from Scotland, but I doubt Alex will make more than a token appearance."

"The honor is mine, Your Grace. To host a ball with the leading social hostess is a great feather in my cap. Ah, here comes the Prince of Wales and his brother Prince Edward."

"Good evening, Your Royal Highness. It gives me the greatest pleasure to welcome you to Lady Georgina's special ball."

Prinny kissed her fingers. "Wouldn't miss it for the world. Hello, Buckingham. Whenever you officiate, fun is guaranteed."

"Prince Edward, welcome." Jane dipped her knee in a second curtsy. "Now you have arrived, I believe the ball can begin."

The royal brothers moved down the receiving line and when they reached Georgina, each took one of her hands and led her to the ballroom, where over two hundred guests were already gathered.

The throng broke into applause when the guest of honor arrived, and with a radiant smile, Lady Georgina slowly circled the room to thank everyone for coming.

More guests were arriving by the minute and Georgina stopped to speak to Lord and Lady Holland. "Beth, Henry, I'm so glad you could come. I declare you are the handsomest couple in the room."

"Don't flatter him; he's conceited enough," Beth teased.

"Conceited enough to beg to partner you in the first strathspey, my dearest Georgina."

"Done! I won't need to write your name on my dance card. I won't forget you, Henry." Georgina saw that the gentleman standing next to Lord Holland was Francis Russell.

"Your Grace." *You came without an invitation!* She offered him her hand and he raised it to his lips and kissed her fingers.

His glance lingered on her breasts as he drawled, "It would be a distinct honor to partner you in the opening dance, Lady Georgina."

"Indeed." She smiled sweetly. "And the distinct honor has been granted to Lord Henry Petty."

The Duke of Bedford's eyes narrowed as the youngest son of the Marquis of Lansdowne came to claim the beautiful debutante and lead her out in the first dance, which was a lively tune played by the renowned violinist Neil Gow.

"Conceited young puppy," Francis remarked.

"Petty is the same age as Lady Georgina. No doubt the duchess orchestrated the opening dance with the young nobleman."

"Doubtless you are right, Henry. I shall partner your lovely wife and allow you to cool your heels."

The demand to partner Georgina increased with every dance, until there was a waiting line of eager gentlemen. Before midnight, she danced with the prime minister and every Tory member of parliament. After midnight she started on the Whigs.

The Earl of Winchilsea, whom she'd met at Charlotte's, finally claimed her. She smiled up at him. "George, I swear more than half the gentlemen here are named for the king."

"I'm sorry it is such a common name, my lady."

"Pray, don't be sorry. I'm named for the king myself!"

Prince Edward partnered her in the mazey dance, where the couples lined up and the top couple raised their arms to form an arch. Then all the couples tripped beneath the arch, reversing the order of the line. The mazey dance always caused confusion and a great deal of laughter ensued.

The laughter encouraged the Marquis of Buckingham to announce a game of ballroom blindman's buff, and Lord Huntly volunteered to be blindfolded first. Dorothy Cavendish, who was enamored of Georgina's brother, made sure she was the one he captured. Because of her squeals, it didn't take him long to guess her identity. When it was Dorothy's turn, she caught Lord Holland, who in turn caught and identified Georgina.

"I think you were cheating, Henry. I warrant you could see that it was me all the time."

"What man wouldn't cheat for a chance to get his hands on you, my dearest Georgina?" Lord Holland put the blindfold on her and secured it so that she couldn't see, then turned her three times.

With the crush of gentlemen crowded round her on the dance floor, it didn't take her long to catch someone. Georgina realized immediately that it was Francis Russell, and she knew that he had planned it. "Is it His Royal Highness, the Prince of Wales?" she asked innocently. She knew the guess would offend Bedford, since Prinny was exceedingly stout.

"No, no, no!" everyone shouted. "Guess again!"

"Is it Lord Lauderdale?" She named another portly friend of Bedford's. "No? Then I give up." She removed the blindfold and pretended great surprise.

"You little witch . . . you knew my identity," Francis accused.

"Surely you don't want me to tell the truth and shame the devil, since I suspect *you* are the devil?" she teased.

When Buckingham saw that Bedford was disinclined to don the blindfold, he signaled the orchestra to play a Scottish reel.

Georgina relented and smiled at Bedford. "I promised when I came out I would be delighted to make your acquaintance."

"And do you always keep your promises, m'lady?"

"I do, m'lord."

"In that case I will partner you in this dance, if you promise you will allow me to escort you to supper later."

"I'm sorry, but I already promised Prince Edward."

Francis Russell took her hand to lead her onto the floor. "I shall simply tell the prince to bugger off."

"I was warned your manners were shocking."

He gave her a look that was close to a leer. "Do I shock you, Georgina?"

"Not at all. I know someone with far more atrocious manners than you."

The duke looked offended. "Name him."

"John Russell."

She looked up and saw her father. "Here's the Cock o' the North come to partner his daughter in the first reel." She took back her hand. "I'm sure you'll excuse me, Your Grace."

Supper was not served until three in the morning. A knot of young gentlemen surrounded Georgina and escorted her into the supper room. Both Prince Edward and the Duke of Bedford were annoyed at the competition.

The more Georgina Gordon teased Francis Russell and rebuffed his overtures, the more determined he became to ensnare her. Her fresh beauty was a stark contrast to his aging mistresses. To the duke, her challenge was irresistible.

"You're a betting man, Edward. A thousand guineas says I can tempt the little vixen into a liaison before you."

"You're on, Bedford. A prince trumps a duke any night of the week. It'll give me a chance to win back some of the money I lost to you at the races."

* * *

In Russell Square, the Duke of Bedford used his key to open the front door. His brother, John, who had just come downstairs, eyed his evening clothes. "Good morning. You're just in time for breakfast."

"Couldn't eat a thing. I'm stuffed to the gills." Nevertheless he followed John into the breakfast room. "I'll tell you one thing, the Duchess of Gordon put on a sumptuous spread. It's no wonder the royals never miss one of her entertainments. You should have come with me. Everyone we know was there."

"Why would I wish to attend a coming-out ball?"

"For the food . . . for the music . . . for the delightful company. John, you are in danger of becoming a dry old stick. These affairs are not simply to dance with the debutantes."

"But surely that is expected. It would be bad form to *not* dance with the debutante."

"Bad form, yes. That's exactly why I didn't dance with Lady Georgina. I seldom do what is expected. The saucy baggage told me I had shocking manners."

"The young lady could use some lessons in manners herself."

"I wouldn't mind giving her a few lessons, but manners wouldn't be on the agenda," Francis drawled.

"I didn't think your taste ran to virginal debutantes."

"Oh come on, I warrant you wouldn't mind having a go at her. The two of you have crossed verbal swords. You must find her attractive, and by what she said about you, you certainly piqued her interest."

"What did Georgina Gordon say about me?"

"She said that she knew someone with far more atrocious manners than me. When I asked her to name him, she said, *John Russell.*"

John chuckled as he recalled their first encounter, and their last.

"There, you *are* capable of laughter after all. Come

to the Devonshire House ball with me tomorrow night. I guarantee you'll find plenty of things to amuse you."

It was two o'clock in the afternoon before all the Gordon ladies arose and gathered in the breakfast room to read the society pages of the various newspapers.

"Listen to what the *Times* has to say." Georgina licked her lips and read: "*Fair and lovely as the rest of the duchess's female offspring are undoubtedly, Lady Georgina seems to outrival them all. Her eyes with magic power endued, fired many a youthful heart and produced many a wistful glance.*"

Charlotte read from her paper: "*Georgina's fascinating form, grace of gesture, and pleasing manner quickly inspired the whole company and made them totally forgetful of the severity of the season or the cares of the world.*"

Jane interrupted. "Never mind the weather report. What does it say about me?"

"Here it is," Susan said: "*Mirth and plenty reigned around. The noble hostess herself, who was all attention, pleasantry, and conviviality, looked not for these ten years past more engaging or more youthful.*"

Pleased as Punch, Jane remarked, "The *Times* can always be counted upon to print the gospel truth."

"There's more about me. They describe how I opened the ball with Lord Henry Petty and mention the lively tunes played by Neil Gow, who was brought especially from Scotland. "*The Marquis of Buckingham officiated, and where he presides hilarity and good humor are diffused on every countenance.*"

Charlotte added: "*The ladies eager to resume the mazey dance soon summoned the gentlemen from the supper room. After two or three country dances, Scotch reels commenced, which did not finish till six in the morning, when each with seeming regret separated from a society in which all were delighted.*"

"Such a triumph!" Jane declared. Her ecstasy lasted

only a moment. "Was there no mention of the Prince of Wales and Prince Edward attending?"

Susan picked up another society page and scanned it quickly.

"Yes, it's all here. They go on to remark that it was a stylish occasion and mention all the ladies' dresses and hair ornaments."

"Read the last bit," Georgy insisted.

Susan continued: *"The incomparable Lady Georgina outshone all the other debutantes."*

"Lud, there'll be no living with the little cockroach," Charlotte declared.

"*Incomparable* little cockroach, if you please!"

Jane's brows drew together in a frown. "Georgina, I did not see the Duke of Bedford partner you. I am sure you could have enticed His Grace to dance, if you'd encouraged him with your irresistible charm."

"I did my utmost to *discourage* him."

"I beg your pardon, Georgina? I sincerely hope that was a facetious remark. Surely I do not need to remind you that the Duke of Bedford is the most eligible bachelor in the realm?"

"Francis Russell is not interested in marriage," Louisa said with a toss of her auburn curls.

"Not many dukes are," their mother pointed out. "Because you failed to snare the prize is no reason to discourage your sister. Georgina, it is up to you to ply your feminine wiles and engage his attention. That is the first step. Once you pique his interest, I will do my utmost to encourage and promote a relationship."

Georgina shot a look of alarm at Charlotte.

"She was in great demand by all the gentlemen last night. Surely it is far too early to set her sights on just one."

"Dukes are few and far between, Charlotte, especially unwed dukes with vast wealth and property. We cannot allow this one to slip through our fingers. We must all make a concerted effort on Georgina's behalf. Each of you must plan an entertainment in the coming weeks and make sure Francis Russell receives an invitation. We will coordinate our strategy."

"Mother, you make it sound like a military campaign," Georgina protested.

"And so it is," Jane assured her. "You must engage the enemy; then, en masse, we will overcome his defenses, and when he is most vulnerable, you deliver the coup de grace."

Georgina licked lips gone suddenly dry. "And what is the finishing blow?"

"You seduce him, of course." The duchess gathered up the newspapers so she could read them again. "Georgina, what are you planning to wear tomorrow night to the Devonshires' ball?"

"I haven't had a chance to catch my breath from my own ball."

Charlotte commiserated. "Poor Georgy. From now on you'll be plunged into a continual and frenzied social swirl of entertainments. Thank God I'm only expected to put in a token appearance at Devonshire House. Then we are off to Goodwood so the children can spend time with their other grandparents."

"Goodwood House will make a spectacular setting for your ball, Charlotte. The Duke and Duchess of Richmond's opulent mansion filled with priceless treasures is just the sort of place to impress the Duke of Bedford. I'm sure Her Grace of Richmond will do her part to launch our incomparable Georgina."

"Well, enjoy yourself at Devonshire House, Georgy. We are off home to Kimbolton as soon as I'm packed. I miss the children," Susan admitted.

"Kimbolton Castle is the perfect setting for entertaining. With all those bedchambers, it is a simple matter to accommodate weekend guests. I am counting on you, Susan," Jane admonished.

"Get lots of rest, Georgy," Susan advised. "Whenever you accept an invitation, you won't see your bed before six in the morning."

Chapter 11

John Russell opened the note that a parliamentary page handed him and read: *I would greatly appreciate a word in private.* It was signed with the initial P, and John knew it was from William Pitt. At the afternoon recess, he made his way to the prime minister's private chamber.

William Pitt shook his hand. "Thank you for coming, Russell. Please have a seat. Though we are on opposite sides of the floor, at the moment we have common interests."

John nodded. "The union of Great Britain and Ireland."

"I want to propose an Act of Union. If you can work behind the scenes and guarantee me a dozen Whig votes, I believe we can get it passed in the House of Commons. Once we have a union, Catholic emancipation will quickly follow."

"What about the king's objection?"

Pitt steepled his fingers. "That is a delicate matter, and one I would not discuss with any other Whig. Can I trust your integrity? Will you work for the common good, rather than cry for a regency that would bring down the House?"

"I pledge you my word."

"I have been in King George's company on several occasions recently and have come to realize he is no longer capable of a detailed interference in politics."

"Simply put, you will not mention emancipation to him."

"Exactly."

"The Act of Union will have to be passed by the parliaments of both countries," John cautioned.

"Chief Irish secretary, Lord Castlereagh, assures me their parliament will agree to the union if, once it is passed, we promise to allow Catholics to become members of parliament, and if we remove the duties on Irish goods sold in England."

You will achieve it through the age-old Tory method of patronage and bribery, which are against my principles. Still, I am quite willing to hold my nose to achieve Catholic emancipation. "I will get you your Whig votes, Mr. Prime Minister."

Pitt rubbed his nose. "Your brother Bedford is an intimate friend of the Prince of Wales and Charles James Fox, is he not?"

"Point taken, sir. I will keep to myself what you have told me in strictest confidence about the king."

Pitt rose and shook John Russell's hand. "My deepest thanks, Lord Tavistock."

On his way home to Russell Square, John decided his good friend Holland would be the first Whig member he would approach. *For some reason Henry hasn't been in the House for the past two days. I'll visit him at home tonight.*

Francis greeted him when he arrived. "Hello, John. I hope the rain holds off. Are you sure I cannot persuade you to come to the Devonshires' ball tonight?"

"No, I'm off to Kensington to see Henry tonight."

"The Hollands won't be home, John. They'll be at Devonshire House, along with everyone else we know."

"Do you think so?" John asked skeptically.

"I *know* so. They were at the Gordons' ball until six in the morning. Lady Holland certainly won't pass up an invitation to Devonshire House."

"That explains why Henry wasn't in the House for

the past two days. Francis, I've changed my mind. I will attend the ball."

It was after ten o'clock when the Russells' carriage arrived at the gates of Devonshire House. Empty conveyances filled the courtyard and were lined up on the long driveway, so John suggested that their driver take the carriage home.

A battery of footmen stood in the entrance hall, waiting to take the guests' cloaks. John tried not to stare at their scarlet and sepia livery. *Francis wasn't exaggerating when he said I'd find plenty of things to amuse me.*

"Loo!" The Duchess of Devonshire swept forward to embrace Francis. "Your presence guarantees that my daughter's coming-out ball will be a triumph."

"Your Grace, I took the liberty of bringing my brother, John."

"Lord Tavistock, you do us great honor."

John kissed her outstretched hand, and with iron determination kept his glance from straying to her towering wig, adorned with pink ostrich feathers. "The honor is mine, Your Grace."

She turned her attention back to Francis, tucked her arm beneath his, escorted him to the ballroom, and led him straight to her daughter.

John followed them to the ballroom entrance, spied his friend Lord Holland, and made good his escape.

"Henry, you're just the man I want to see."

"John, I'm glad to see you here. Beth will be delighted. She's off dancing with Richard Sheridan. Let's go and have a drink. There are three rooms set up with refreshments."

Over a glass of burgundy, John turned the conversation to politics. "Pitt is going to propose an Act of Union, and put it on the floor of the House for a vote. If you and I and a few more Whigs vote in favor, it will pass."

"You can count on my vote, John. What about Lennox? He's here tonight. Well, speak of the devil, here comes Charles now."

"Join us in a glass of wine," John invited, "while I shamelessly solicit your vote."

"You caught me just in time. Charlotte longs for her bed. We put in a token appearance only to repay a social obligation."

John explained to Charles that his vote was needed to pass the Act of Union.

Lennox was more than happy to oblige. "We are on our way to Goodwood tomorrow, so let me know when the vote is to take place, and I'll be there."

Georgina bade her sister good night.

Charlotte whispered in her ear, "Your beauty is so vivid tonight, you put the other debutantes in the shade."

As Charlotte and Lennox departed, the Duchess of Gordon turned her attention to her youngest daughter. "The Duke of Bedford is here, though our hostess has shamelessly monopolized him since the moment he arrived."

"I didn't notice. I was dancing the cotillion with Prince Edward." *And had a devil of a time with his wandering hands.*

"Royal princes cannot offer marriage—dukes can," her mother pointed out. "You are naturally flirtatious, Georgina. When Bedford addresses you, I'm sure you can entice him to dance."

"I will do my best." *Mother will never stop nagging me until I dance with the arrogant duke, so I'd best get it over with.*

Georgina saw her friend Dorothy and joined her. "You are in great demand tonight. You haven't missed a dance."

"Your brother partnered me. He's so handsome!"

Georgina spied Francis Russell heading straight for her. She took a deep breath and smiled.

The Duke of Bedford ignored her completely.

"Lady Dorothy." He gave an elegant bow. "Would you do me the honor of allowing me to partner you in this dance?"

Lady Dorothy giggled and allowed him to take her hand.

Georgina was amused. *He is paying me back for the deliberate snubs I have given him.* She saw her friends Beth and Henry Holland and walked toward them. Before she reached them, a gentleman garbed in elegant black joined them. She blinked in disbelief as she recognized John Russell.

Lady Holland suddenly became all aflutter. "John, my dear, how delightful to see you here."

Russell raised her fingers to his lips. "Beth, you look lovely tonight, as you always do."

She slapped his sleeve with her fan. "Flatterer."

Good God, Beth is acting kittenish. She actually finds the dark devil attractive.

Russell's glance moved politely to Georgina, and to her utter dismay, she felt herself blushing as usual. *Damn you to hellfire; you always have this disquieting effect on me.*

Beth said prettily, "Allow me to introduce my friend Lady Georgina. She has just made her debut."

John's eyes met Georgina's. "The lady and I are acquainted."

"Oh, how silly of me," Beth said, laughing.

Without taking his eyes from Georgina's, he said, "May I partner you in the next dance, my lady?"

"Thank you, John," Beth replied. "I would love it!"

Georgina knew he had meant her. He gave her a rueful smile of apology. *We just communicated without words. We read each other's minds.* His smile left her feeling strangely breathless.

Lord Holland said happily, "That leaves me to partner the most beautiful debutante of the Season. I've been waiting all night."

When the floor cleared and a contradance was announced, Henry said regretfully, "Just my luck."

"Sorry, Henry. It's too bad there won't be any reels tonight."

The gentlemen led the ladies out and the couples formed two lines facing each other. In a contradance, everyone changed partners. Before it was over, each man would partner every lady.

When Georgina realized that her next partner would be John Russell, she experienced a small ripple of panic. As they stepped toward each other and he took her hands, she blurted, "Is your wife here tonight?" Then she blushed again. *Damnation! The arrogant devil will think I have a* tendre *for him.*

"Why do you ask?"

"Because once again my curiosity outweighs my good manners. I'd like to know what she looks like."

"My wife looks like an angel."

His tone had finality about it, warning her that he did not wish to discuss his wife with her. He placed his hand on her waist to swing her around, and she imagined she felt the heat of it seep through the delicate material of her gown. She flushed again, and shivered. His dark eyes saw and her blush deepened.

Georgina felt weak with relief when he moved down the line to the next lady. She saw that her new partner was the Earl of Lauderdale, and it gave her a chance to recover her composure.

He winked. "Scottish lassies make the best partners."

"Do you mean in the dance, Lord Lauderdale, or in marriage?"

"Call me James. In both, come to think of it. I wish these musicians would play us a rousing reel."

After the partners changed half a dozen more times, Georgina saw that the next man in line was Francis Russell. She masked her amusement that he would no longer be able to ignore her.

He nodded politely, but did not smile.

"Your Grace, it is such an honor."

"The honor is mine." His tone was cool and detached.

"Yes, indeed it is."

A fierce light kindled in his eyes, proving he was neither cool nor detached. "You are playing a teasing game of cat and mouse." He placed his hand on her waist and squeezed. "I would enjoy playing other games with you, Georgina."

He's flirting outrageously with me, yet I feel absolutely nothing, apart from distaste. "Lanterloo, perhaps?" She tried to keep the sarcasm from her voice, knowing she would be rid of him in a moment or two.

"We could play for forfeits," he said with a leer.

Georgina heard the echo of her brother's words: *You shouldn't banter with Bedford like that. He is a known womanizer.*

When the contradance ended, Georgina's mother cornered her.

"When Bedford partnered you, I hope you encouraged him."

"He needed no encouragement. His manner was most familiar."

"Splendid! I knew if you plied him with charm, he wouldn't be able to resist you."

"Lady Gordon," a Scots voice boomed. Lord Lauderdale bent his head confidentially toward Jane. "This ball canna compare to yours. These musicians dinna know how to play reels."

"James, you are too kind."

Georgina saw John Russell walking a straight path toward her and went suddenly weak in the knees.

He nodded politely to her mother. "Lady Gordon." Then he spoke to Lauderdale. "James, if I can steal you from the ladies, I'd like you to join me in a drink."

"There's an offer I never refuse. Holland told me ye were looking for me." He bowed gallantly to Jane and Georgina. "Please excuse us, ladies?"

The uncouth brute totally ignored me. She was highly offended and stared after him, feeling strangely abandoned. *If the surly sod does ask me to dance, I shall refuse him outright!*

Georgina was rescued by the Earl of Spencer's son, Lord Althorp. Jack, Lady Dorothy's cousin, was a red-haired scamp of eighteen and a fun-loving friend of Georgina's.

"Jack, I'm so glad you are here. I looked for you earlier, but couldn't find you."

"I've only just arrived. There was a hell of a row at Spencer House tonight. Since the Duchess of Devonshire is Father's sister, he insisted that we must attend. Mother adamantly refused because she detests her sister-in-law."

Georgina laughed. "Poor Lavinia lost the argument."

"Absolutely not," Jack said with a grin. "She went off to the theater instead with an old admirer."

After she danced with Jack, she felt thirsty and headed toward a refreshment room. She encountered John Russell at the doorway.

A look of amusement crossed his face. "Are you by any chance looking for me, Lady Georgina?"

Conceited swine! "Sorry to disappoint you, Russell. The only thing I'm looking for is a glass of champagne."

The amusement left his face. "Aren't you a little young for champagne, mistress?"

"God in his goodness sent the grapes to cheer both great and small; little fools will drink too much, and great fools none at all," she quoted.

John felt the urge to protect her. "Wine can steal the senses and lead a young lady into trouble."

"I certainly hope so. Trouble is my middle name."

"Must you always be so *extreme*?"

"Indeed I must. Extremes are sharp black and white . . . that's why I love them."

Georgina returned to the ballroom, where Prince Edward partnered her again. He tried to lure her into a rendezvous, and she gave him a set down. Nevertheless, the prince's advances made her feel vulnerable and she sought the safe company of Lord Holland. After Henry partnered her, Georgina's confidence was restored, and she went on to dance with Lord Petty and the Earl of Winchilsea. After that, Lord Granville Leveson Gower asked her to dance.

After so many dances, Georgina found the ballroom extremely warm and stuffy, and she fanned herself to catch her breath. She saw her mother, who'd been in deep conversation with their hostess, raise her head and search the ballroom with her eyes. *Lord, she's looking for me.* Georgina slipped out onto a balcony and drew in a deep breath of fresh air.

She lifted her face to the dark sky and gazed at the glittering stars. After a few moments of blissful solitude, she noticed the aroma of tobacco and sensed that she was not alone. She glanced across the stone balcony and saw the glow of a lit cheroot.

"I'm sorry, I didn't mean to disturb you."

"You don't disturb me, *little girl.*"

She drew in a swift breath as she recognized the deep voice.

"You!" she accused.

"Obviously you were expecting someone else."

She was outraged at his accusation. "Surely you don't suspect me of arranging a tryst out here on the balcony?"

"I suspect you are capable of arranging anything you damn well please, Georgina Gordon."

Her anger flared. *Why are we like flint and tinder whenever we meet?* The answer was obvious. The shrewd devil knew her too well. She had no defenses against him.

"Go to the devil, *old man*!"

Chapter 12

"Georgina! Don't you dare fall asleep. I am most disappointed in you." Jane Gordon shook her daughter's arm.

Georgina had dropped off to sleep the moment she sat down in the carriage on the way home from the all-night ball.

"Lady Dorothy somehow persuaded Francis Russell to partner her in four dances, while all you managed was two minutes in the contradance."

"It's not a competition, Mother."

"That is *exactly* what it is—the Gordons against the Devonshires—and we are losing. Badly!"

"What makes you think that?"

"The Duchess of Devonshire smugly informed me that they have invited the Duke of Bedford for a visit to Chatsworth next week, and that Francis Russell has *accepted*!"

A wave of relief washed over Georgina. If the duke was courting Lady Dorothy, she could cross him off her list of prospective suitors.

"Well, two can play at that game. I shall write to Susan and have her issue Bedford an invitation from the Duke and Duchess of Manchester to visit Kimbolton Castle the moment he returns. Cambridgeshire is far more convenient than a trek up to Derbyshire at this time of year. Why, his Woburn estate is just a stone's throw from Kimbolton."

Georgina climbed from the carriage, eager to reach the sanctity of her own bedchamber. Her mother followed on her heels as she ascended the stairs, rattling off plans to snatch the marriage prize of the decade from the clutches of the Duchess of Devonshire. *Hell and furies, all I want is my bed.*

"I'm glad you talked me into going to the Devonshires' ball last night, Francis. There were more Whigs there than in the House of Commons."

"It's always like that. Devonshire House is like our own private club, complete with gaming. I'm invited to visit Chatsworth next week."

"Will you go?" John asked his brother.

"Well, they're obviously offering their daughter. I need to assess Chatsworth and its treasures to see if it compensates for the sacrifice that marriage would demand."

John did not utter the biting remark that sprang to his lips. Instead he sorted through the post that had just been delivered and opened a letter from his wife.

> *Since you cannot bring yourself to write more than one letter per week, you make it abundantly clear that you no longer love me. The absence of your letters demonstrates your complete rejection.*
>
> *Your sentiments of tenderness have been entirely wanting for some time. It is obvious that you no longer value my friendship and have come to despise me because of my lowness of spirits.*
>
> *I have been quite happy here with my dearest sister, Isabelle. I believe it would be better for both of us to live apart.*

John stifled a curse. He knew Elizabeth meant exactly the opposite of what she had said about living apart.

Each week he had visited his sons at Westminster School and had written her in detail about their progress. *She never asks about their welfare, or even men-*

tions their names in her letters. The sole purpose of her correspondence is to condemn me for the treatment of my poor, neglected wife.

"From Elizabeth?" Francis asked.

John looked up. "Yes. I must make time to drive to Longleat and visit her."

"Duty calls to both of us, I'm afraid. You're for Longleat and I'm for Chatsworth. First, however, I intend to pay a visit to my darling Marianna. Her ministrations will fortify me against the night starvation I'll suffer when I trek north."

After Francis left, John put his wife's letter in the fire and watched the flames devour it.

I'll be able to tell Pitt I can deliver the votes he needs. Once the Act of Union passes, I'll drive down to see Elizabeth.

"There, I've written to Susan, and for good measure I've penned a note to Charlotte asking her to coordinate her Goodwood ball with the grand entertainment at Kimbolton," Jane Gordon declared. "We will show the Duke of Bedford what hospitality is all about."

Georgina chose her words carefully. "I'm not sure we should pursue the Duke of Bedford, Mother. George told me that Francis Russell is a known womanizer. His mistress is Marianna Palmer."

"Mrs. Palmer is just a commoner. You cannot expect a duke who has reached his midthirties to be celibate. That would be most peculiar. A man of the world is exactly what an inexperienced young noblewoman needs in a husband."

"But I don't have my heart set on a duke. Charlotte married an earl and she's extremely happy. I always have great fun with Jack Spencer and he's heir to his father's earldom."

"Lord Althorp is just a boy. It would be years before you became a countess."

"I met a lot of other gentlemen at Devonshire House. Charles, Earl Grey, is quite attractive."

"You couldn't have chosen someone more unsuitable if you'd tried. Grey happens to be the Duchess of Devonshire's lover."

Georgina's eyes widened. "I had no idea."

"You are innocent in the ways of the world, and that is as it should be."

"I may be inexperienced, but I am not completely innocent, Mother. My own father has had more than one mistress, and I have reason to suspect that the Duke of Manchester is not entirely faithful to Susan."

Jane did an about-face. "I warrant it's beneficial for a young lady to know these things. A noblewoman must learn to accept and overlook the frailties of her husband."

"Frailties? I think you mean excesses!" Georgina recalled another young man who had made a favorable impression on her. "I danced with another earl who had delightful manners . . . Granville Leveson Gower."

"I said you couldn't have chosen anyone more unsuitable than Lord Grey, but I was wrong. Lord Granville is rumored to have fathered two of Lady Bessborough's children."

Georgina gasped. "Not Caro?"

"No, not Caro . . . Two of the younger Ponsonby offspring."

"If I'd known, I would not have allowed him to partner me in the dance."

"If you eliminate every noble who has by-blows, you will sit like a wallflower all night. Polite society turns a blind eye to these things, and you must do the same, Georgina."

I wish Louisa were still at home so we could share the gossip. Such sexual misconduct would shock her beyond belief.

The next morning, Georgina received flowers from Lord Henry Petty along with an invitation to attend Drury Lane Theater with his family that evening. Since the play was Richard Sheridan's *The Rivals*, she immediately sent a note of acceptance.

Lord Petty arrived and helped her into his carriage.

"Did your parents change their minds, Henry?"

"No, they went on ahead. I wanted a chance to be alone with you, Georgina." He took her hand and sat gazing at her.

She was both bemused and flattered, and since it was only a short ride to the theater, she let him hold her hand.

Lord and Lady Lansdowne awaited them in the lobby, and when they took their seats she found herself between Henry and his father. Once the play began, however, she forgot them as she was transported to Bath and the world of Lydia Languish and Jack Absolute. The heroine was obsessed with the romantic ideals of love, so the wealthy hero pretended to be a poor soldier.

Georgina laughed with uninhibited enjoyment. Sheridan used his characters to satirize society, and in Mrs. Malaprop, who wanted Lydia to marry for financial reasons, she saw the resemblance to her own mother.

On the ride home, Lord Petty again took her hand. "Henry, I had a marvelous time. Sheridan's characters are vastly amusing."

Henry pulled her into his arms and kissed her.

Georgina did not struggle. It was a nice kiss, and she thought him sweet. But when the carriage stopped in front of her Pall Mall residence, she gently pulled away from him.

"Lady Georgina . . . Georgy, I'm in love with you. I want to marry you," he blurted. "I'm sorry, that's not the way to propose." He began again. "My lady, will you do me the honor of—"

Georgina was stunned. She quickly placed her fingers against his lips. "Oh, please, no, you mustn't propose to me, Henry." *Dear Lord, I mustn't hurt him. He's so young and so earnest.*

"I'm sorry," he said miserably. "It's too soon. I should have asked permission to court you first. Please forgive me. It's just that I will have so many rivals for your hand—"

"Henry, my Season has only just begun. There are no rivals. It is too soon for me to consider marriage to anyone." He looked so dejected that her heart ached for him. "I would like us to be friends."

He helped her from the carriage and escorted her to the door. "Good night, Georgina. Thank you for a wonderful evening."

"Thank you, Henry." She kissed his cheek and went inside.

"Did you enjoy the play, my dear?" her mother inquired.

"Yes, I did, but I feel just awful. On the way home, Henry told me that he loved me, and I had to stop him when he started to propose to me."

"Lud, it's most fortunate that you stopped him. Such audacity is beyond belief. Petty is a younger son, with not a hope in Hades of coming into his father's title of Marquis of Lansdowne."

It's not his lack of title that stops me from considering him. It's his age. "Henry is little more than a boy."

"Exactly. A mature nobleman like the Duke of Bedford would be a far more suitable husband."

It was not a picture of Francis that came full-blown into Georgina's mind. It was an image of John Russell.

The following week, William Pitt put the proposal for an Act of Union on the floor of the House of Commons for a vote, and it passed by a sizable majority.

"Congratulations, Mr. Prime Minister." John Russell shook Pitt's hand. "This is a huge step forward for Ireland."

"I owe you a debt of gratitude for your support and the Whig votes you rounded up."

John Russell felt good about the outcome and the small part he'd played in it, knowing Catholic emancipation would follow. He spotted Charles Lennox. "Thanks for coming back to London for the vote today. I appreciate it."

"You can return the favor by attending the ball Charlotte is planning for her sister. Lady Georgina's

Season must be a roaring success or the Duchess of Gordon will hold the entire family responsible and make our lives pure hell."

John was saved from making a commitment when Lord Holland joined them. "What say we celebrate at Brooks's tonight?"

"Sorry, Henry," John said with a laugh, "I'm barred from the club because I refuse to wear a wig. Now that the vote has been taken, I shall drive to Longleat tomorrow to visit Elizabeth."

John returned to Russell Square, where he ate alone and then caught up on all his paperwork pertaining to Tavistock and his constituents. He considered it a privilege, rather than a burden. Representing the people of Tavistock, Devonshire, gave him a great deal of personal satisfaction.

He retired late, and as he lay abed he gave a fleeting thought to Francis, who had left yesterday for his visit to Chatsworth. Try as he might, John could not picture Lady Dorothy Cavendish as his brother's bride. *I feel sorry for the naive young woman if he does wed her. Francis would install her at Woburn and neglect her shamelessly for the rest of her life.*

His thoughts progressed to the other young debutante, Georgina Gordon, and he could not help comparing the two. There was certainly nothing naive about the vivid beauty, and he could not picture her as a complacent wife, no matter whom she wed. *The audacious hellcat will lead all her suitors on a merry chase. Whoever catches her will have to tame her.*

Thoughts of Elizabeth intruded. He recalled her letters complaining of neglect, and knew there was some truth in them. *I hope the visit with her sister has been an antidote to her melancholia.* He knew her dark thoughts were a mania that sometimes bordered on madness, and he wished she could be cured for their sons' sakes, as well as her own.

I kept her off laudanum for a month before I took her to Longleat, and she's now been there for five weeks. I should have warned Isabelle about her craving for the soporific, and the terrible effect it has on her condition, but I'm certain her sister won't have provided her with the filthy stuff.

John wondered if he was deluding himself that his wife could be permanently weaned off laudanum. He was convinced it would improve her melancholia if her addiction could be cured. He put her from his mind, turned over and finally fell asleep.

He was awakened by a knock on his bedchamber door. He sat up and lit the lamp. "What is it?" He knew it was not yet morning.

"I'm sorry to disturb you, sir, but a courier has just arrived with a message. He says it is urgent."

"Is it for me or Francis?"

"He says it's for you, sir . . . from Longleat."

John's brows drew together. *Trouble with Elizabeth, as usual.* "I'll be right down. Make sure there's a fire in the drawing room. The fellow has had a long, cold ride."

John, who slept naked, grabbed a dressing gown and followed the servant downstairs.

The courier stood in the entrance hall, stamping his feet. "My lord, I bring an urgent message from the Marchioness of Bath."

"Come in here man, and get warm." John took the letter and led the way into the drawing room, where the footman had replenished the fire and lit the lamps. John poured the messenger a whiskey.

He broke the wax seal, took the note from the envelope, and held it beneath the lamp.

Lord Tavistock:
Come immediately with all possible speed.
Elizabeth has suffered a terrible setback.
The situation is dire.
Isabelle, Marchioness of Bath

"My wife suffers from ill health. I will go immediately. The note is brief. Can you tell me anything more?"

"The doctor's been twice. That's all I know, my lord."

"I'll take my carriage. You can leave your horse in the stables." He spoke to the footman. "While I pack a bag, will you kindly see that this good fellow gets something to eat?"

John decided he would make better time if he drove his phaeton, and before he reached Richmond, the messenger was sound asleep. Though he stopped only to water and rest his horses and grab a bite to eat at an inn in Basingstoke, it took all day to get to Longleat House in Warminster.

On the long drive, he'd had lots of time to ponder what Isabelle meant when she had said the situation was dire. He knew from experience his wife often warned of impending danger, and the dark portents of doom and imminent catastrophe might well seem dire to someone who'd not been exposed to Elizabeth's ravings.

John hoped that her illness was nothing serious. He felt confident that if it were just a manifestation of his wife's melancholia, he would be able to soothe her and calm her fears. Most likely her sister Isabelle wanted to be rid of her and had summoned him for that purpose.

Longleat was a magnificent Tudor house, far more impressive than many castles. John turned over his team of grays to a stableman and asked him to give them a good rubdown.

The majordomo took his caped greatcoat and led him down a long hall to the Marchioness of Bath's private sitting room.

"Thank the Lord you came." Isabelle clutched her hands together tightly. Her face was a mask that told him nothing.

"Tell me what has happened."

He heard a cry, and for the first time became aware that his wife's other sister, Lucy, was in the room. When Lady Bradford covered her face with her hands and began to sob, John became anxious. "Take me to Elizabeth."

"I cannot go and see her again," Lucy moaned.

John's anxiety turned to alarm.

Isabelle did not look him in the eye. "Come with me, John." She led him to the main staircase and they ascended to the second floor. She opened the door to a guest bedchamber and allowed him to enter before her.

John strode across to the bed, where his wife lay still with closed eyes. "Elizabeth." He knelt down and reached out to touch her. For a moment, he thought his wife was dead. Though lifeless, however, her flesh was still warm. He stared up at Isabelle, trying to control his anger. "She's unconscious. How long has she been like this?"

"Yes, I know. When I could not awaken her, I sent for you immediately."

"When did this happen?" he demanded. "*How* did this happen?" He got to his feet and stared down at Elizabeth, imagining he was seeing her corpse.

"We had been in Bath for a week, taking the waters. Sadly, the cure did not help her condition. She fainted early yesterday, and I summoned my doctor. We put her to bed, and he gave her some medicine. At dinnertime she could not be roused, so I sent again for the doctor. When he arrived, he said there was nothing he could do—that she would regain consciousness on her own, or not," she finished ominously. "Dr. Neville ordered me to send for you immediately."

John's eyes fell on the brown bottle on the bedside table. "What medicine did he give her?" he demanded.

"Elizabeth asked him for laudanum. She said it was the only medicine that eased the painful symptoms of her consumption and allowed her to sleep."

"My wife does not have consumption! She has an addiction to laudanum. It is an opiate. That is what has almost killed her!"

"How *dare* you accuse my sister of such a wicked

thing? I am outraged that you would even *insinuate* that she has an addiction." Isabelle's face registered horror, and she moved toward the door. "I shall leave you with your wife, so you may beg her forgiveness."

John stepped back to the bed and stared down at Elizabeth. "I do need to ask your forgiveness—for not being more vigilant. I should have weaned you from your addiction." He felt anger at himself, his wife, her sister Isabelle, and the doctor. All were to blame that his sons had almost lost their mother.

Angrily, he tore back the bedclothes and hauled his wife's torso up over his shoulder. He secured her body with a powerful arm across the back of her thighs. Her head and arms hung limply down his back. John strode to the door, flung it open, and marched down the hallway until he came to a bathing chamber. He went inside and slammed the door closed with his foot.

He lowered his wife to the floor and bent down to turn the tap and fill the bathing tub with water. He paid little heed to regulating the temperature of the water, reasoning that if it were cold enough, it might shock her back to consciousness.

When he gauged that the water was deep enough, he picked up Elizabeth with ungentle hands and submerged her. When there was no response, he pulled her head above water quickly. He cursed vilely and plunged her under once again. Still nothing. Her head flopped to one side, resting on her shoulder.

The third time he pushed her beneath the surface, she began to cough. He raised her head from the water and slapped her face. When she coughed again, he bent her forward and, with the flat of his hand, hit her sharply on the back three or four times.

She moaned, her eyes fluttered open, and then closed again.

"You pathetic bitch—wake up!" he shouted. John cupped his palm about her cheek, then gave it half a dozen sharp slaps. He moved his hand to the opposite cheek and repeated the action.

Elizabeth gasped and moaned again.

"Can you hear me?" he thundered. "Can you hear me, Elizabeth?"

Her eyes opened to half slits, and she slowly nodded her head.

John took hold of her shoulders and he shook her. "Don't you dare go back to sleep. Speak to me!" he ordered.

"Don't . . . hurt . . . me," she begged weakly.

"You are hurting yourself, you stupid creature!" *Easy, John. If you don't control your anger, all hell will break loose.*

"Don't . . . drown . . . me." She clutched at his hands.

"I ought to drown you," he muttered. He lifted her from the water and tried to stand her on her feet. Her knees buckled and her body sagged against him. He tore off her soaking-wet nightgown and lifted her naked in his arms.

John carried her back to her bedchamber and again slammed the door shut with his foot. He sat her in a satin-upholstered bedroom chair and ordered, "Sit up, damn you—don't slump over." He went to the wash-stand and found a jug of water. It was for washing, but at the moment he didn't give a damn for niceties.

He poured a glass and held it to her lips. "Drink!"

He saw her eyelids close and she nodded off.

He dashed the water in her face and she spluttered awake.

He poured another glass, put it to her lips, and this time forced her to drink. "We have to wash it from your system."

John was so adamant, she had no choice but to obey him. He looked down at her straggling, wet hair and rail-thin body with distaste. *I don't want her. Why in Christ's name am I trying to save her?*

It took him the better part of four hours to get four glasses of water into her. Now, long after midnight, she was hissing and spitting, and wide-awake. She was also ready for a fight. And John was willing to oblige.

"You are a brutal swine!"

"I kept you clean of your filthy poison for a month. I hoped a sojourn in Bath with your sister would help you to overcome your addiction. But, as always where you are concerned, my hopes were in vain."

"You won't be happy until you have killed me!" she screeched.

"In your soporific state, it wouldn't take much."

"I hate you! I hate you!" Elizabeth cried.

"Hate is often a two-way street, madam."

"You are so dominant and controlling, you wield a heavy hand, overruling all my wishes." She flung the accusation dramatically.

"Truth be told, Elizabeth, you are the one who manipulates and controls with your addiction to opium."

"You make my life unbearable!" she screamed.

"You make my life hell on earth." Suddenly John realized what he must sound like. Not only would his wife's sisters be able to hear him, but also Longleat's large staff of servants would be privy to this vicious quarrel.

John went to the bureau, took out a clean nightdress, and went to put it on his wife.

"Don't touch me!" she cried in a screeching voice.

"Believe me, to touch you is almost more than I can stomach." He pushed her arms through the sleeves and pulled it down over her naked body. Then he turned on his heel and left the chamber. Because of his anger, he crashed the door closed.

John sought a bedchamber a few rooms away down the hall. He flung himself into a chair, far too overwrought to lie down on the bed. He leaned his head back in an effort to calm himself. In a couple of hours it would be dawn, and he would have to start his vigilance all over again.

In her own bedchamber, the horrified Marchioness of Bath lay rigid in her bed. She had heard Elizabeth accuse her husband of trying to drown her. Heard her cries and moans. Heard angry voices quarrelling. Heard crashes and bangs. It sounded as if John and

Elizabeth were killing each other. Isabelle kept her distance from the combatants for fear of becoming embroiled in the horrendous situation.

I'm thankful Elizabeth has regained consciousness. In the morning I shall demand that they leave. I will not have my household thrown into turmoil in this sordid manner.

Chapter 13

John roused from a dreamless sleep when a maid knocked on his door. He brushed the hair back from his forehead. "Yes?"

"I'm sorry to disturb you, my lord, but I have knocked on your wife's door several times, and there is no answer."

He rose from the chair and opened the door. "Thank you. I will look after her," he said quietly.

The housemaid followed his footsteps down the hall. John strode across to the bed, where his wife lay still with closed eyes. "Elizabeth." He knelt down and reached out to touch her. She was cold and stiff and lifeless. "Good God, my wife is dead!" he said with stunned disbelief.

The maid gasped and threw her apron over her face. "I'll tell her ladyship we'll need the doctor!"

John stared down at Elizabeth's corpse, trying to comprehend. He instinctively glanced at the bedside table, where another brown bottle sat. He picked it up and found it empty. "Christ!"

Isabelle came hurrying to the door, but stopped on the threshold. "Can it be true? Is she . . . ?" She looked at John with accusing eyes. "May God forgive you!"

He stared down at Elizabeth, his brain trying to grasp the fact that she was really dead. He tried to gauge how much time had elapsed since he left her spitting and screaming. He knew it could be only two hours, no more than three. *She killed herself!* Whether it was deliberate or accidental, he could only guess.

"I've sent for the doctor!" Isabelle informed him sharply.

John looked up in time to see her disappear. Again he stared down at his wife. Her fair hair had dried in delicate wisps about her face. *She looks like an angel.*

He paced the room as it sank in that his wife and the mother of his children was dead. He put a clamp on his emotions and began to make a mental list of the necessary arrangements he would need to plan. The Russell family church and burial place were at Chenies, a few miles from Woburn. It would be a private funeral for family members only. He paced to the window and gazed out at the gardens with unseeing eyes.

After some time had elapsed, a knock brought him back to the present. Dr. Neville entered and approached the bed. John saw him feel for a pulse, but knew he would find none.

"I offer my condolences, Lord Tavistock." He reached into his bag. "I will make out the death certificate. If it is any consolation, your wife passed away most peacefully."

Apparently you haven't been told of our vicious quarrel. Dr. Neville handed John the death certificate.

"You have the cause of death as consumption. My wife did not have consumption, Dr. Neville. She had acute melancholia and an addiction to the laudanum that you supplied," he said bluntly.

"Since this tragedy has happened at Longleat, it will be far more circumspect for the Marchioness of Bath if the official cause of her sister's death is consumption."

"I don't give a damn about the Marchioness of Bath. I'm not the sort of man who covers the truth with lies because the facts are inconvenient. You cannot invent an illness to save face."

"The situation is delicate, my lord. An overdose

could be construed as suicide by those prone to gossip, or even something far more sinister."

Dear God, is it possible her sisters think I killed her?

"Apart from the Marchioness of Bath, think of your brother, the Duke of Bedford. You would not wish any scandal to touch him."

"My brother was aware of Elizabeth's addiction."

"Then I beg you to think of your sons, my lord. For their sake, surely you would not wish any stigma attached to their dear mother? It will be extremely difficult for them, and I am sure you will want to do all in your power to save them pain."

John's eyes were bleak. He was awash with guilt. *For the boys' sake, I will do what I have to do.* He folded the death certificate and put it in his pocket. "If you will excuse me, doctor, I have arrangements to make."

"The news was such a shock. I came as soon as I could." Francis Russell embraced his brother. He had not arrived back at Woburn until after the funeral.

"I didn't see the necessity of holding back the burial, Francis. Her sisters wanted her interred as soon as possible and were anxious to return home. My relations with them are strained to the breaking point. If it were not for abhorrence at the taint of scandal, I believe they would have accused me of having a hand in my wife's death. I owe a debt of gratitude to Mr. Burke. He helped me make the arrangements at the church, and accommodated Elizabeth's family with superb efficiency."

"He's always like that. Woburn is run like a well-oiled machine. Was Elizabeth's death a suicide, John?" he asked bluntly.

"She died from an overdose. I have no proof that it was deliberate, though sadly, I suspect that it was."

"For God's sake, John, don't flagellate yourself over this." Francis changed the subject. "Are the boys here?"

"Yes, I decided they must attend their mother's funeral to say good-bye. I determined a few days out of school wouldn't hurt, and I wanted to spend some time with them. I'll take them back to Westminster soon. I want their lives to be as normal as possible, under the circumstances."

"And you too should resume your normal routine as soon as possible. It's the best way to cope with bereavement."

John nodded. "It's the only way." *My sons are bereft, but what do I feel?* He examined his emotions. *If I am brutally honest, anger and guilt far outweigh my sorrow.*

"I should like to propose a toast." The Duchess of Gordon lifted her champagne glass and the dinner guests followed suit. "Congratulations to our worthy Prime Minister Pitt on getting the Act of Union passed into law last week."

"Hear! Hear!" chorused the Tory members of parliament Jane had invited to a celebratory dinner party.

Georgina, seated between Pitt and Lord Apsley, turned to the prime minister. "How many seats will the Irish members have?"

"One hundred seats in the House of Commons and thirty-two seats in the Lords. And, as I promised if the act passed, I have now proposed that we allow Catholics."

"That will be an admiral achievement." Georgina had a strong sense of justice and always supported the underdog. *Mr. Pitt is as proud as a dog with two tails tonight. And John Russell will be a happy man. Though it's not Irish independence, I wager he is adamant about Catholic emancipation.* She smiled, remembering their conversation. *When I warned him independence would be an uphill battle, he declared he had the temperament for it. He has a strong will. I admire that about him.*

Lord Apsley cleared his throat to gain her attention, and Georgina suddenly remembered that her mother had seated him beside her because he was heir to the

Earldom of Bathurst and a fifteen-thousand-acre estate in Cirencester. She favored him with a smile. *He's rather pleasant looking, if you like fair skin, pale brows, and blue eyes. Personally, I prefer dark, dangerous-looking men.*

George Canning turned to William Wilberforce. "I'm surprised that Henry Addington isn't here tonight."

Jane Gordon overheard. "Henry sent me a note that he would be late. He was called to the palace to tend the king tonight." Henry Addington, as well as being speaker of the House, was one of King George's physicians. "His Royal Highness has not been himself of late. I'm sure we are all anxious to hear how the king is faring. I pray for a swift recovery."

Henry Dundas patted her hand. "Amen to that, my dear."

When the dessert was served, Georgina had to mask her amusement. Lord Apsley's adoring gaze watched every mouthful she took so, wickedly, she kept licking her lips to taunt the poor devil. When she was finished, she murmured, "Dare I have another?" She saw an eager look kindle in his eye. "No, I mustn't be greedy." When she saw his disappointment, she felt contrite and vowed to stop teasing him.

The company was about to take their drinks into the drawing room when Addington arrived.

"Henry, you've missed dinner. Do sit down and I shall order you a plate," Jane invited, "and you can tell us about the king."

Henry Addington looked agitated. "My dear duchess, I couldn't eat a thing. Actually, I would like a word in private with the prime minister, if I may?"

"We are all friends here, Henry, and loyal Tories. There is no need for secrecy. We all understand that the king suffers bouts of distress where he is not quite lucid," Pitt declared.

"Actually, tonight His Royal Highness was most lucid and suffering from a bout of anger." Addington hesitated; he should not discuss his patient's condition, but the king was not ill. He was furious. Henry felt he had no choice but to inform William Pitt what the king had ordered.

"What has angered him?" Pitt prompted.

"The Act of Union. Well, not the act per se, but your promise to emancipate the Catholics. The king insists you should not have proceeded without consulting him, and he intends to block it." Henry took a deep breath and blurted, "His Royal Highness has ordered *me* to become his prime minister."

Everyone in the room sat stunned.

Georgina glanced at her mother, thinking that they should excuse themselves so the Tories could discuss the matter privately, but the duchess shook her head and put her finger to her lips. The ladies sat quietly and listened.

The members all spoke at once, voicing their outrage and disapproval. Then George Canning made a suggestion to William Pitt. "For the time being you must drop the proposal for Catholic emancipation."

"I made a solemn promise, in good faith, that if I got enough votes to pass the Act of Union, I would guarantee that Catholics could become members of parliament. My word is my bond; my political reputation would be in ruins."

"All will know it is the king who blocks it and not you."

Pitt got to his feet and proudly raised his head. "The mistake was mine, gentlemen. I was so confident of my influence, I failed to consult with the king. Since I cannot fulfill my promise, I have no choice but to resign my office."

Georgina suspected that it was William Pitt's overabundance of pride that prompted him to make such a dramatic decision. The king's insult, asking Addington to become his prime minister, could not be borne.

The members argued against such a drastic step, while Addington stood wringing his hands.

Pitt cut through the arguments to the heart of the matter. "I will resign, and the speaker of the House will become prime minister, as His Royal Highness wishes. To do otherwise would bring down the Tory party and put the Whigs in power. If we do not want Prince George and Charles Fox as our masters, we must do the king's bidding."

The Duchess of Gordon left the room and came back with a cask of Scotch whiskey. She poured a dram for every member, knowing they were in need of fortification. After they drained their glasses, the party broke up and everyone departed.

"Such dreadful news is beyond bearing. The Gordons have always been staunch supporters of King George. We have given him our love and our devotion, but I fear our monarch is mentally deranged. Your father told me as much on the night you were presented to Queen Charlotte."

"The situation is so sad. I feel sorry for the queen."

"The situation is appalling. William Pitt is the finest prime minister this country ever had. His skills surpass those of his father by a mile. Addington will never fill his shoes."

Georgina's brother came into the drawing room. "It has only just struck midnight. Did your dinner party break up?"

"I have dreadful news that is beyond bearing."

"Hello, George. You're home early," his sister declared.

"I have news, too. I ran into Lord Holland at Brooks's. Henry told me that John Russell buried his wife a few days ago."

"Oh no." Georgina's face went pale.

"Great heavens! It never rains but what it pours!" Jane refilled her glass with whiskey as her mind grappled with the inconvenient news. "Elizabeth isn't a blood relative of the Duke of Bedford, so he likely won't go into official mourning. There is no reason why he should curtail his social calendar. I shall write to Charlotte and Susan immediately and have them postpone their balls until next month."

Georgina was deep in her own thoughts and did not

hear one word her mother said. *John Russell will be devastated. It must be a terrible shock to lose a wife at such an early age.* She immediately thought of his three sons. *How on earth will the man cope?* A picture of young Johnny came into her mind. *He's so sweet and so shy.* Her heart went out to him, and a lump came into her throat that made it difficult to swallow.

"I wonder if the duke's visit to Derbyshire was curtailed? The moment he got the news, I'm sure he would return to Woburn."

"Holland said he got the news directly from Francis Russell, so he must be back in London," George said.

"I wonder if anything developed between the duke and the Devonshires' daughter during his visit? I'm sure the duchess would press him to make a commitment. That was the whole idea of the invitation to Chatsworth. I shall be on tenterhooks waiting for an announcement. With a death in the family, a declaration might be postponed. Oh dear, was anything ever so vexing?"

"I'm sure you'll find a way to ferret it out, Mother," George said. "What is the other news that has upset you?"

"Oh, yes, upsetting news indeed. Mr. Pitt has been forced to resign as prime minister."

Georgina withdrew quietly as her mother went into detail about the political upheaval.

After she undressed, she went and stood before the sketch she had made of her father. "There really is a resemblance to John Russell. I wonder if I was thinking about him when I drew the picture." *The man does jump into my thoughts at odd moments.*

Now that tragedy had touched Russell and his sons, she felt wretched about the rude things she'd said to him. It had been an amusing game really, to utter cutting, cruel remarks. One he had seemed to relish. Now she regretted being deliberately unkind. She had the impulse to write him a letter of condolence and glanced at her writing desk. *No, it would be better if it came from the family, not just from me.*

* * *

"It's been a long day." In Russell Street, John joined his brother in the library and set a bundle of letters of condolence on the desk unopened. He poured himself a drink. "I took the boys back to school. I had a word with each of their teachers, who assured me they would report anything amiss. I had a meeting with the headmaster, then stayed at Westminster to have dinner with Johnny. It was a wrench leaving him—I hope he'll be all right."

"Of course he will—boys are resilient," Francis assured him. "Did you hear the news?"

"About what?" John drained his glass.

"William Pitt resigned today!"

The weary look on John's face was replaced by one of surprise.

"The king is blocking Irish Catholics from becoming members of parliament, so Pitt stepped aside in favor of Speaker Addington."

"Damnation! I should have known Catholic emancipation was too much to hope for."

"Why on earth would he resign his prime ministership?"

"On principle, of course. It was also a very shrewd move. If he opposed the king, it could bring down the government and put us Whigs in power. Pitt made the sacrifice for the Tory party."

"Sacrifice is a concept that is beyond me," Francis said dryly. "I am on my way to Carlton House. Prinny will be prostrate that the government didn't fall. He will need me to bolster him against the cruel winds of fortune."

After Francis left, John contemplated what the House would be like under Henry Addington. He surmised that things wouldn't go smoothly. Though he was deeply regretful that the Irish problems were no closer to being resolved, he clearly saw that the political mess would divert him from dwelling on his own turmoil. John poured himself another drink, hoping it would induce sleep, and went upstairs to bed.

Just before dawn, his recurring dream began.

He was astride his hunter, riding through a sun-drenched meadow filled with wildflowers. Their heady scent, combined with the exhilarating feeling of freedom he experienced, was intoxicating.

The female companion riding beside him was a joyous creature who loved and lived life to the fullest. She had a passion for nature, and children, and animals, and he never tired of hearing her laugh. They were racing their horses toward a hill, and John knew he would let her win for the sheer pleasure of watching her exult in her victory.

Suddenly, they were drenched by a summer shower, but the lady did not even slow down. She galloped up the hill, slid from her saddle, and climbed up on a high boulder. She raised her arms and exultantly lifted her face to the rain, as if it were the elixir of life.

John dismounted at the base of the boulder and held up his arms. "Jump, Georgy! I'll catch you."

Her silvery laughter was the loveliest thing he'd ever heard. Without hesitation she flung herself with total abandon into his waiting arms. He caught her and then rolled with her until he had her pinned beneath him in the wet grass.

When he captured her soft, warm mouth it tasted of delicious laughter and sensual anticipation. It was heady intoxication to know she wanted him as much as he desired making love to her. The reaction her eagerness stirred in him was a potent spur to possess her body and soul and lure her to surrender her essence to him.

She was that rare female who could blot out his pain and anger and the dark thoughts that tortured him. He could lose himself in the tempting, honeyed depths of her body, where she allowed him to indulge any wicked fantasy for which he thirsted and craved.

He enjoyed the seduction because it heightened their desire and brought the blissful, almost unendurable pleasure that allowed him to escape as nothing else could.

The intense delirium his lovemaking aroused in her took him to a place where only rich, dark sensation existed. He indulged a passion so powerful, it brought exquisite pleasure, followed by peace and deep contentment.

John knew he had never felt this happy in his entire life. The laughter and the newfound freedom made his heart overflow with joy. "Georgina, you must know I want to marry you."

She laughed up at him, her green eyes sparkling with amusement. "What took you so long?"

"I wasn't free until now!"

John awoke with a start. He knew he'd had the recurring dream, but this time his female companion had a face, and a name. *Georgina Gordon.* He pushed the dream away, not wishing to analyze it. Not daring to. The joy and happiness he had felt quickly evaporated and left behind a dreadful, guilt-ridden remorse.

Chapter 14

"Charlotte and Charles are back in London." Jane Gordon handed the note from her eldest daughter to Georgina so she could sort through the rest of the morning post that had just been delivered.

"Charlotte says she couldn't put up with the cold fog that constantly shrouded Goodwood House. Chichester is too close to the coast for the weather to be anything but gloomy in November."

"Fife House in Whitehall will be far more convenient for the guests she invites to the ball that she is planning for you. We must go over there and settle on a date."

Mother will make the plans for her. Poor Charlotte will have to bow to her wishes.

"We have a number of calls to make today. I need to visit Henry Addington's wife. He will have told Mary Anne far more about the king's condition than he divulged to us at dinner last night, and since I am a dear friend of the royal family, I warrant she will tell me everything. In strictest confidence, of course."

"Of course." *Then you will tell Henry Dundas, who will waste no time passing it along to William Pitt.*

"Next, we must pay a call on George Canning's new wife. He will have confided in her how all the Tory members feel about the shocking state of affairs that has come to pass."

"Are you sure he will have discussed politics with his bride?"

"I am certain. Joan is an heiress, and therefore she controls the purse strings. Canning would not dare make a move without confiding all and asking her advice."

"Your shrewdness amazes me, Mother."

"A woman needs to be shrewd to get anywhere in this man's world, Georgina. You will do well to learn from me." Jane summoned a footman and ordered that their carriage be made ready directly after lunch.

"Last, but by no means least, I intend to pay a visit to Lady Spencer. The Duchess of Devonshire's sister-in-law will tell me if anything noteworthy transpired between the Duke of Bedford and the Devonshire girl while he was at Chatsworth."

"But Lavinia Spencer doesn't speak to her sister-in-law. She won't know anything."

"Au contraire, my dear. Lavinia will have made it her business to know *everything.* Ah, here is lunch."

Her mother's keen interest in the Duke of Bedford made Georgina think of John Russell's bereavement. She hadn't been able to get him or his sons out of her mind since she had heard the tragic news. *I cannot imagine how alone he must feel at such a sad time.*

Georgina pushed her food around her plate. Her mood had affected her appetite, and nothing appealed at the moment. She smiled apologetically as the maid came in to take her dish. When she declined dessert, her mother frowned.

"It is this dull, overcast weather that is affecting you. Before we pay our calls, I want you to go upstairs and put on one of your new hats to brighten up the day."

By four o'clock in the afternoon, Georgina was ready to scream. During the visit with Mary Anne Addington, they had discussed the king's health ad nauseam. It was plain from the doctor's report that poor old George was again tottering on the brink of madness.

The visit with Joan Canning had seemed endless. She discussed every single Tory member and revealed all sorts of personal details about their wives and children. Jane avidly took it all in, but Georgina found it offensive. When they rose to leave, she decided she had had enough. *Mother can visit Lavinia Spencer without me. One more serving of tea and gossip will make me spew.*

She waited until her mother climbed into their carriage. "We are close to Whitehall. I think I will drop in on Charlotte and make plans for the ball. If I am with you when you quiz Lavinia Spencer about the Duke of Bedford, it will make me look desperate, as if I am hunting him down."

"Very well. Tell Charlotte to prepare for at least two hundred. And be sure to have Charles drive you home."

Georgina took off her gloves and stuffed them into her reticule. Then she walked down Tothill Street toward Parliament Square. Fife House, Charlotte's imposing town residence on Whitehall Place, was only about half a mile away. *The walk will clear my head.*

John Russell spent most of the day in parliament and left just after four. *What a bloody waste of time! Absolutely nothing got done in the House today, and by all the futile discussions and hand wringing, it will be a miracle if things get sorted out before the start of the new year. Both Whig and Tory members huddled in groups, whispering like a bunch of old women!*

John shrugged off politics and thought of his sons. Westminster School was close by, and as he walked toward Parliament Square, he debated whether to drop in and check on their well-being, or whether his visit would cause an emotional upheaval. *I should at least make sure Johnny is all right.*

John turned to go back toward the school and came face-to-face with Georgina Gordon. He stopped abruptly, and the shocking details of his sensual dream flooded his senses.

Her surprise at seeing him was palpable. "Lord Tavistock . . . John . . . please accept my heartfelt condolences for your sad loss. Your concern for your children must be devastating." She put her hand on his sleeve. "You and your sons shouldn't be alone at such a harrowing time. The Christmas season will be particularly difficult. Please know that you would be warmly welcomed if you visited Charlotte and your friend Charles at their house here in Whitehall, and I offer you an open invitation to drop in at Pall Mall anytime you feel in need of company."

John pulled his arm away as if her touch scalded him. He stared with disapproval at the profusion of bright pink lilies adorning her hat. Guilt over making love to her and asking her to be his wife goaded his conscience as if the dream had been real. "My lady, I am newly widowed and not in the market for another wife." His voice was quelling, his expression rigid as stone. "Your shameless husband hunting is abhorrent to me."

Georgina gasped at the brutal insult. She wanted to slap his dark face, but decided to wound him with words instead. Her chin lifted and her glittering eyes narrowed. "It is not hard to like you, Russell—it is *impossible.* I offered you my genuine compassion, and you flung it back at me as if it were dung." She smiled sweetly. "Whatever makes you think I would be interested in a mere lord when I can attract a duke to offer me marriage?" She tossed her head, and her pink lilies danced enticingly. "And not just *any* duke, I might add. We *both* know the duke I have in mind. He has quite taken my fancy. Good day to you, Lord Tavistock."

"Georgy, Georgy!" Mary danced around her favorite aunt. "You have another new hat."

"One I'm rather partial to, so try not to muck it up." Georgina looked at her sister Charlotte. "I've had a trying afternoon. I'm so glad you're back in London . . . I am sorely in need of civilized company."

"A trying afternoon, indeed, if you think the inhabitants of Fife House are civilized."

"There, you've brought a smile to my face already."

"You've managed to escape from your keeper, I see."

"Mother's gone to pay a call on Lavinia Spencer to see if aught transpired with the Duke of Bedford at Chatsworth."

"Mary, it's time for your tea. Run along to the nursery while Aunt Georgina and I have a chat."

"You're trying to get rid of me!" Mary accused.

"And I intend to succeed. Off you go."

"I'll come and visit with you later," Georgina promised as she followed Charlotte into her sitting room.

"So if the Duchess of Devonshire hasn't snared Francis Russell, Mother intends to do her utmost to bag him for you."

"I'm afraid she's quite made up her mind."

"You don't much fancy Bedford, do you, Georgy?"

"Not in the least. But I do intend to engage his interest."

"Now you're talking in riddles. Is this solely to amuse yourself? I thought you would have preferred to spar with his brother."

"What makes you say that?" Georgina demanded sharply.

"Don't bite my head off."

"I'm sorry, Charlotte. I don't suppose you've heard the dreadful news that John Russell's wife died a week ago."

"Elizabeth? No, I had no idea. We didn't arrive from Sussex until late last night. Oh, I must write him a letter of condolence immediately. Those poor children!"

"I bumped into him just now in Parliament Square. I felt such remorse over the dreadful things I'd said to him that I gushed something about my heartfelt condolences and concern for his children. Then I babbled on about them not being alone in the Christmas season. I assured him that you and Charles would welcome them here at Fife House, and I invited him to Pall Mall if he felt lonely." Georgina's hand went to her throat in a defensive gesture. "I said it in such a clumsy way that he took immediate offense. He coldly informed me that he was not in the market for another wife."

"Whatever did you say to such a pointed insult?"

"I wanted to fly at him and scratch his insolent eyes out. Instead, I asked him sweetly whatever made him think I'd be interested in marrying a mere lord when I could have a duke."

"Good God, he might have surmised you were hinting at his brother!"

"In case he was uncertain, I removed all doubt by adding that we both knew which duke I had in mind." She bit her lip. "Charlotte, what on earth am I going to do?"

"You'll simply have to marry the Duke of Bedford."

"Ask a silly question and get a bloody silly answer. However, a thought did just occur to me . . . I don't need to actually marry the Duke of Bedford. I merely need to become engaged to him."

"Is that all?" Charlotte asked dryly. "Didn't Louisa try that route and find it a dead end?"

"I am not Louisa," Georgina asserted.

"I hear the front door. It's probably Charles. He'll have heard the sad news about his relative Elizabeth Russell and will be amazed that I already know."

"Here's something else he'll be bursting to tell you. William Pitt has resigned as head of the Tory government because the king asked Henry Addington to become prime minister."

"You are a veritable font of information."

When the Duchess of Gordon swept into the sitting room, Charlotte realized it wasn't her husband who had arrived but her mother. "I have a soupçon of good news amidst the avalanche of bad. Apparently, the Duke of Bedford made no commitment whatsoever in connection with Devonshire's daughter on his visit to Chatsworth. And moreover, he is not observing mourning for his lately deceased sister-in-law."

"View halloo!" Charlotte exclaimed. "From a view to a death in the morning." The words to Woodcock Graves's hunting ballad were not lost on either Jane or Georgina.

"Have you decided on a date for your ball yet, Charlotte? I warrant November twentieth would be ideal."

"That is only a week away . . . hardly time to get out the invitations."

"We shall write them tonight. I'll stay and help."

"That's what I was afraid of," Charlotte murmured irreverently.

"Did Georgy tell you to plan for two hundred?"

"She hadn't gotten around to that detail. We were discussing William Pitt's resignation. Why on earth did the king ask Addington to be prime minister?"

"Because he's run mad again," Jane said matter-of-factly. "We had the whole story from Mary Anne Addington when we visited her this afternoon. Didn't your sister tell you? Queen Charlotte is the one I feel sorry for. The poor lady doesn't know if she's coming or going. No wonder she looks so dowdy as she sits wilting on her throne."

"You would have made a good queen, Mother."

"No, I wouldn't, Charlotte. A queen must play second fiddle to her king, no matter how deranged he is, while a duchess is free to tell her duke to kiss her arse!"

Georgina laughed. "You make the life of a duchess sound irresistible. I believe I'm ready to chase a certain ducal fox from his lair after all."

"You are a Gordon, darling. You can do anything you put your mind to," Jane declared, "with a little help from your mother, of course. What time do we eat around here? Then we can get on with those invitations."

"This would be a good time for me to have that visit with Mary," Georgy declared. "I hope I have a daughter just like her."

"First things first. The wedding must be planned before children can be considered."

"I'm already contemplating an engagement." Georgina winked at Charlotte.

"John, the vultures have already moved in and are circling." Francis poured two brandies and handed one to his brother.

He cocked a black eyebrow. "You think I'll need this?"

"Brace yourself. Adair told me today there is speculation that you helped Elizabeth shuffle off her mortal caul."

"I'm cynic enough to have expected it. My only fear is that the boys might hear the filthy rumors. Gossip can be a feral beast, tearing people and reputations to shreds."

"I nipped it in the bud instantly. I informed Adair that your marriage was a love match, and that your heart and soul belonged to the lady you wed at nineteen. I told him you were heartbroken. I warrant word will soon circulate throughout the clubs."

"You needn't lie for me, Francis," John said wearily.

"It wasn't an outright lie. You imagined yourself in love when you first wed Elizabeth." Francis contemplated the amber liquor in his glass. "Tell you what, though. It has quite put me off marriage again. *Till death do us part* and all that."

A picture of Georgina flashed into John's mind and, perversely, he was happy that Francis had lost interest in marriage.

"Perhaps it's just as well. If you did wed a young debutante, she'd most probably outlive you."

"Bite your bloody tongue!"

John changed the subject. "How did Prinny bear up to the news that the government didn't fall?"

"Carlton House was drenched in bathos. The prince cried like a babe whose mother's teat had dried up. I poured him a very large brandy to suck on."

John looked at his own glass with distaste and set it aside.

The Earl and Countess of Lennox, along with the Duchess of Gordon, her son and heir, Lord Huntly, and Lady Georgina, stood in the reception hall of Fife House to greet their noble guests. Charlotte's children had been banished to their own wing, one story up from the elegant ballroom.

Among the first to arrive were the Hollands. "Beth, how lovely to see you." Georgina bestowed a radiant smile upon Henry.

"May I offer to partner you in the first reel, unless another has already claimed the honor?"

"Henry, it will be my pleasure," Georgina replied.

Jane Gordon greeted Lord and Lady Spencer and their son, Jack, effusively. "Lavinia, I am so happy you decided to come." The countess had only agreed to attend on condition that her sister-in-law, the Duchess of Devonshire, had not been invited.

Charlotte was secretly amazed when the Princess Royal arrived with her brother, Prince Edward. The Gordon ladies all curtsied to Augusta Matilda. "Such an honor, Your Highness."

When the princess was out of earshot, Jane admonished Charlotte, "I hope you set a lavish buffet. Tapeworm Tilly always devours enough food for ten."

Georgina tried to cover her laughter with her fan. "Gluttony runs rampant in the royal family."

Lady Melbourne was the next to arrive, escorted by her son, William Lamb. They were Whitehall neighbors of Charlotte, and she felt obligated to invite her.

Jane greeted her with enthusiasm. Lizzie would be able to tell her best friend, the Duchess of Devonshire, that Francis Russell had danced attendance on Lady Georgina. Provided, of course, that the Duke of Bedford showed up. Jane spoke to her daughters behind her fan. "Lizzie is a devoted mother, but not chaste."

Georgina almost choked on that one.

When Charles Lennox's friend the Earl of Winchilsea arrived, Georgina tucked her arm beneath his. "George, I've been waiting for you. Lead the way to the ballroom."

It was another two hours before Francis Russell arrived with his great friends the Prince of Wales and the Earl of Lauderdale. The trio had been gambling at Devonshire House, and to get away, made the ambivalent excuse that they had business at Whitehall.

Georgina and Prince Edward had just finished a rousing strathspey when Russell and Lauderdale approached. Francis raised a bold eyebrow. "No kilt tonight, Georgy?"

"Only my dearest friends call me Georgy, Loo." She taunted him with his own nickname. "Why the sudden interest in kilts?"

With a knowing leer, Lauderdale quoted Robert Burns.

"She kiltit up her kirtle weel
Tae show her bonie cutes sae sma'
And walloped about the reel
The lightest louper o' them a'!"

Georgina laughed wholeheartedly. "The words are most apt, though I doubt His Grace understands your brogue, James."

"I could hazard a guess at what your *bonie cutes* are," Bedford drawled. He elbowed his rival, Prince Edward, aside.

"I have been warned that you are a womanizer."

"Is that why you are attracted to me?"

"Actually, it's the *manse* more than the man that attracts."

"Woburn and Bedford are inseparable—you cannot have one without the other."

"Pity." Georgina found that she was enjoying the banter.

"Och, Francis, mayhap ye've met yer match in the wee Scots lassie." Lauderdale gave her a broad wink.

"And making matches is the primary purpose of these debutante balls. Run while you have the chance, Bedford," she urged.

"I never run from a challenge," he drawled.

"Ah, I hear the overture to another reel. Which one of you gentlemen shall I choose as partner?" She looked the three men over. "Just as I picked an Irish racehorse over a Scottish one, it only stands to reason that a Scot can dance a reel better than an Englishman. Shall we, James?"

Though Francis appeared to take the teasing in good nature, Georgina guessed that the arrogant duke wasn't amused.

When the reel ended, Lauderdale escorted her back to Bedford. Georgina did not demur, but gave Francis a sweet smile. He did not offer to partner her in another dance, however.

"Shall we take a stroll and see what refreshments our lovely hostess has provided?"

"An excellent suggestion." She placed her hand on his arm and allowed him to lead her to the supper room. "I believe we could both use a drink."

"Champagne?" Francis suggested.

"Perfect." Georgina raised her glass in a salute to him. She took a few sips and set it down. "I know you will excuse me. I promised to take a petit four to my favorite niece up in the nursery. I warrant Lady Mary will refuse to go to bed until I arrive with her treat."

"A stubborn little wench like her aunt, no doubt."

"*Exactly* like her aunt, I am pleased to say."

"Enticing a noble lady to bed requires certain skills only a few of us possess."

"Lady Melbourne and I were discussing that very subject earlier," Georgina said with an innocence that belied the pointed dig and the wicked sparkle in her eyes.

"Georgy! Georgy! I knew you would come!"

"And I knew you would be standing at the door in your bare feet." She handed Mary the treat, picked her up, and carried her to her bed.

"You look as pretty as this cake," Mary declared, picking off a sugared violet and licking the icing.

"And you look as pretty as a princess . . . actually far prettier than the royal princess in the ballroom."

"Is she wearing a crown?"

"A tiara, I believe."

"I wish I had one," Mary said wistfully.

Georgina removed the crown of rosebuds from her hair and placed it on Mary's head. "Your wish is my command, Your Highness."

"Can I keep it, Georgy?"

"*May* I keep it," she corrected. "Oh, what the devil . . . yes, you can."

"Did you dance with a prince tonight?"

"Yes, and he's been paying me outrageous compliments."

"I'm glad you're enjoying yourself. Thank you for coming."

"When I have a little girl and you're all grown up, you can return the favor. Good night, sweetheart."

Georgina returned to the ballroom and encountered her mother.

"I thought you went to the supper room with Francis Russell."

"I did, but then I excused myself to go upstairs and see Mary for a moment."

"You actually walked out on the Duke of Bedford?" Jane asked with disbelief.

"He is a man who enjoys the chase, I warrant."

"Return to him immediately and apologize."

Georgina shrugged a shoulder. "If you insist."

She found Bedford in the company of Prinny, who

was making inroads into the smoked salmon. "There, that didn't take long, and I made a little girl very happy." She looked for an iced cake and found they were all gone.

Francis was holding a linen napkin, which he folded back to reveal the treasure it held. "I saved you one."

Georgina took it and licked off the icing. "You *do* know how to tempt a noble lady," she acknowledged with a secret smile. When she finished, she said, "I'm ready to dance, if you are."

"I am unable to resist further temptation," he said gallantly. On the way back to the ballroom, Francis pulled her into an anteroom used for the guests' coats. He took her into his arms and captured her lips in a lingering kiss.

"Your kiss tasted of sugared violets," he murmured.

"I wager that's a first for you."

"Not a first for you . . . you've been kissed before, haven't you, Lady Georgy?"

"I have indeed, Lord Loo," she murmured, then added wickedly, "Fortunately, I *am* able to resist further temptation."

Chapter 15

"I am very encouraged with the way you conducted yourself at the ball, Georgina." Duchess Gordon, her son, and her youngest daughter were in their carriage leaving Charlotte's in the wee small hours of early morning. "The duke paid you quite a bit of attention. I know I advised you not to waste your time with Prince Edward, but perhaps Bedford noticed the young royal's interest in you, and it stirred his own."

"Bedford's a womanizer," George cautioned, as usual.

"All men are womanizers, if they are normal. It simply takes the right woman to tame them," the duchess declared.

As you did with your duke, Mother? Georgina did not voice her cynical question aloud.

Jane ignored her son and turned back to her daughter. "Yes, I am quite pleased. Capturing and holding the interest of a man like the Duke of Bedford will not be easy. As a matter of fact, you are setting yourself a gargantuan task. But if you succeed, the rewards will be beyond your wildest dreams."

Georgina weighed the pros and cons of raising her mother's hopes. Pure deviltry put her thoughts into words. "Francis Russell kissed me tonight."

"Oh, my dear girl! See what you can achieve when you apply yourself?" Jane looked as if she could hear wedding bells.

When Francis kissed me, for one moment I pretended it was John. Georgina had felt decidedly wicked when she did that. Now she shivered at the memory and went off into a reverie. *Mother thinks bagging Bedford would be a gargantuan task, but luring and capturing John would be a thousandfold more challenging. He totally disapproves of me and, I warrant, detests the sight of me. The mere thought of such a provocative and stimulating achievement fires my imagination and takes my breath away.*

"It's snowing! Look how thick the flakes are," Huntly said.

Georgina suddenly became aware of her surroundings. "Oh, how lovely! George, have the driver stop the carriage. I want to get out and walk in it."

"Are you mad, Georgy?" Jane pulled her cloak close about her.

"Indulging an impulse is good for you." Huntly banged the silver head of his cane on the carriage roof. "Georgy and I can walk home from here. The morning traffic has already begun, and it will soon turn the pristine snow to sludge."

"Thank God I'm no longer young and foolish," Jane declared.

Georgina climbed from the carriage and raised her face so that the snowflakes could fall on her lips and eyelashes.

Her brother warned her again of Bedford's loose morals.

"George, it's only a game! It serves two purposes—it pleases Mother and it amuses me vastly."

"What if Russell's affections become serious?" He heard her laugh. "You don't give a feather or a fig about him, do you?"

"Close. The word I was thinking of begins with the letter F."

George shook his head and began to walk on. When she saw him a short distance away, she decided he would make a perfect target. She scooped up a handful of snow, packed it, and pitched it at him. "Bulls'-eye!"

George turned and, laughing, made a snowball and began his own playful assault.

Georgina's joyous laughter rippled along the street. She bent and made another snowball, then flung it with all her strength at her brother.

George ducked, and the cold missile hit a young boy walking farther along the street. The lad shouted with sudden glee. Then he made his own snowball and threw it at the young lady who was having such great fun. Suddenly, he recognized her and ran toward her. "Georgy! I'm so glad to see you!"

"Johnny, is that you? What are doing at this time of morning?"

"I spent the night with Father. He's taking me back to school."

"Ah, I see." Georgina saw that indeed Johnny's father had been walking with his son. Her heart suddenly went out to the boy. "Do you like school, Johnny?"

"I like the classes and lessons, and love the books, but . . . " He hesitated, "I don't like the nights."

"That is perfectly understandable."

"I love the snow—I hope it stays around for Christmas." His eager face suddenly changed, as if he remembered Christmas would be a sad time.

A lump came into her throat. "I'm glad I ran into you."

"It was lovely to see you, Geor . . . I mean, Lady Georgina."

She approached her brother, who'd stopped to speak with Russell. She heard George say, "Please accept my sympathy for your loss."

"Thank you, Huntly," Russell said briefly.

His dark eyes swept over Georgina for only a moment, but she knew he saw the evening gown beneath the velvet cloak—knew she had been up all night enjoying herself. Then Russell and Johnny walked on.

She was annoyed that his slightest glance could quicken her heartbeat and make her pulses race when it was obvious that he thoroughly disapproved of her.

"Poor devil," George said.

"Don't pity him, for God's sake. That's the last thing he'd want anyone to do."

"He never seems to smile."

"He is the sort of man who masks his amusement," she assured her brother.

Georgina was beginning to feel the cold, so she decided to walk faster. When the pair arrived at their house in Pall Mall, George watched her climb the front steps.

"Aren't you ready for bed?" she asked, surprised.

He gave her an enigmatic smile. "I am—just not the bed at 91 Pall Mall."

You do have a special female tucked away somewhere. If my toes weren't freezing, I'd follow you.

When John Russell and his son reached the gates of Westminster School, Johnny said in a slightly defiant tone, "I like Lady Georgina. She is always so . . . " He couldn't find the right word to describe her.

"Alive?" his father suggested.

"I . . . I didn't mean any disrespect to Mother," he murmured.

"I know you didn't, Johnny. This snow reminds me that Christmas looms on the horizon. Your uncle Francis always celebrates the Yule at Woburn. Your brothers have told me that is where they would like to spend their school holiday. Does Woburn sound good to you?"

"Will you be there?"

"I'll be there until just before Christmas, but then I plan to go home to Tavistock. Over the years it has become a tradition for me to spend the Yule with my constituents. They are hard-working people who look forward to celebrating Christmas."

"Could I . . . that is, would you consider . . . " His voice trailed off, as if his hopes would be dashed.

"Would I consider taking you with me?" John finished his son's sentence. "If you think you would be happier in Tavistock than with your brothers at Woburn, of course I will take you."

"I'm happiest wherever you are, Father."

John, deeply touched, put his arm about his son and hugged him.

The social scene in the month of November had been extremely active, but once December arrived it turned into a veritable whirlwind of invitations to parties and balls.

Georgina did her best to be on hand when the post arrived so she could sort through the invitations before her mother got to see them. That way she could discard the ones she suspected would be dead boring.

Today, however, she opened one that intrigued her. It was addressed solely to Lady Georgina Gordon, and was an invitation to attend an Evening of Fashion. At the bottom in small print it said: *Masks Optional.* She did not know who had invited her, but strangely the address was fairly close by on Pall Mall.

She tucked the pink card into her reticule, and later that morning took a stroll past the tall stone house. She had no idea who resided there, but her curiosity was piqued. On the spot, she decided that she would attend.

The Duchess of Gordon received an invitation to a musical evening being given by Lady Lavinia Spencer for the same evening, which she accepted on behalf of herself and her youngest daughter.

At the last minute, Georgina complained of a headache and begged off.

"Since Lavinia and her sister-in-law, the Duchess of Devonshire, are not on speaking terms, the Duke of Bedford isn't likely to attend. I don't suppose it will hurt if you miss the party. Perhaps you should have an early night and get some beauty sleep."

After her mother left, Georgina went up to her bedchamber, opened her wardrobe, and with a critical eye, tried to decide what to wear to an Evening of Fashion.

"I wish Louisa were still at home. She'd join me in a heartbeat. We had such jolly times together." Georgina hadn't seen her sister often since her wedding, as she and her young husband lived at Brome Hall in Suffolk. Louisa had attended Charlotte's ball, but she had focused her attention on Charles the entire evening, much to Georgina's disgust.

"I suppose I ought to take Helen with me, but she would blab to Mother that I'd accepted an invitation and gone out after complaining of a headache."

Georgina smiled her secret smile. *Masks Optional.*

She donned her most sophisticated evening gown, which was the one in the vivid shade of peacock. Then, to hide her identity, she put on a wig as well as the black sequined mask that belonged to a cat costume she'd worn to a children's party years ago.

Wearing her velvet cloak, Georgina waited at the top of the stairs until the foyer was empty of servants; then she quickly descended and hurried through the front door. Feeling free as a bird, she felt like singing as she made her way along Pall Mall.

She crushed her apprehension about the unknown by dashing up the steps, and making liberal use of the door knocker. The majordomo who appeared was wearing gold and purple livery, as if he presided over a royal residence. Georgina presented her pink invitation, and in return she received a formal bow.

"This way, my lady."

She followed the footman up a spiral gilt staircase to a ballroom that was lit with crystal chandeliers. The walls were mirrored from floor to ceiling, giving it an aura of palatial opulence. The room was half full of people, with more men than women, and she noted that most of the ladies wore masks. She was surprised to see that the servants, who were carrying glasses of champagne on silver trays, were not footmen, but what could more aptly be described as *footwomen.*

The orchestra was playing a baroque piece by Handel, and Georgina saw that no one was dancing. She recognized three of the gentlemen immediately. Francis Russell was laughing with Prince Frederick and Prince Edward. She remembered that she was wearing a mask and would be incognito until she spoke with them and they recognized her voice. *What fun!*

The hostess came forward to greet her. Georgina knew she had never seen the woman before in her life. "My dear, welcome to an Evening of Fashion. The show will get underway shortly. There is something to tempt and titillate every taste. I urge you to be bold and bid on whatever strikes your fancy."

She's urging me to bid . . . That must mean the fashions will be for sale. How delightful. Georgina watched the hostess engage an older woman in conversation, and she recognized the female immediately. The gestures of Lizzie Melbourne were unmistakable. Georgina did not know the man with her, though she knew it was not Lord Melbourne.

Rather than stand alone, she decided to join a trio of masked ladies who were whispering and laughing behind their fans. They fell quiet as their hostess went to the center of the ballroom and held up her hands. "I thank you all for coming tonight. Don't forget that Christmas is coming and presents will be expected. I urge the gentlemen to be generous and loosen their purse strings. The fashions you will see tonight are unique. They have been imported from Paris at great expense to the establishment."

Everyone laughed.

"Ladies and gentlemen, I proudly present the *Demoiselles de Maison Rouge*!"

The applause was deafening, but as the first female high-stepped across the floor, the clapping turned to whistles of appreciation.

Georgina stared in disbelief. The girl was clad in a flowing red gown that was completely transparent. As she walked, the creamy flesh of her breasts and thighs was clearly visible. The tendrils on her mons showed dark red through the sheer silk.

Before Georgina could regain her composure, another girl undulated across the ballroom floor. This one was wearing a frilly white corset, a pair of lace stockings, and sequined garters. The space between her hips and thighs was completely nude. As she crossed the room, her bare buttocks bounced. She carried a red rose and tossed it toward the whistling men.

When Francis Russell caught it and immediately bid, "Twenty guineas," Georgina was shocked. The bidding was fast and furious, and it began to dawn on her that the men were buying more than the fashions.

A girl garbed in a black busk decorated with pink bows touched her breasts with the tiny fan she carried. When she drew it suggestively across her mons, two of the women present began to bid, and the laughter turned raucous.

Georgina's shock turned to anger. *Who the devil sent me the invitation?* She gazed across at Prince Frederick, who was bidding an obscene amount of money for a statuesque blonde wearing silver tassels. *Charlotte's husband, Charles, once dueled with Frederick. Could this be his way of getting even with our family?* She soon dismissed the suspicion. It had happened years ago, and the prince didn't seem the type to carry a grudge.

She wondered if the hostess was amusing herself by inviting a debutante who lived on the same street as her establishment. *What would she gain by offering such an insult to a Gordon daughter?*

Georgina's glance traveled slowly around the ballroom, and when it came to rest on the Duke of Bedford, she knew exactly who had sent her the outrageous invitation. She was not amused.

The more she thought about it, the more furious she became. She was angry with herself as well as Francis Russell. *I should not have come. I must get out of here.*

She glanced toward the door and was stunned to see her sister Susan's husband walk in. The Duke of Manchester was not alone. The woman on his arm was the one she had seen in his carriage that day outside the House of Lords.

Outraged, she hurried across the room until she reached her brother-in-law. She removed the woman's hand from his arm. "William, you must escort me home immediately."

"Christ Almighty, Georgina! What the hell are you doing in a brothel?" he demanded.

"I am here by accident. Obviously, you are here by intent. Nevertheless, I need your protection."

"Of course, my dear." He offered her his arm.

She glanced back across the room, her wicked juices bubbling. "Just one moment. I will be back directly."

With head high she marched across the ballroom until she stood before the Duke of Bedford and Prince Edward. She raised her hand and slapped Francis Russell's face. "Pig!"

She knew he recognized her green eyes glittering through her mask. The prince, who did not recognize her, took immediate offense for the assault on his friend and grabbed her arm. She shook him off and slapped his face also. "Pig's friend!"

The crowd about them parted like the Red Sea as Georgina swept across the floor, took the Duke of Manchester's arm, and departed.

As they walked up Pall Mall, Georgina said, "I warrant discretion is the better part of valor. If you won't divulge where I was tonight, I won't reveal where you were, William."

The Duke of Manchester saw her to her door and kissed her hand.

The Duke of Bedford felt both elation and desolation. *The little vixen came!* The moment Georgina slapped his face, it ignited a raging lust that ran through his veins like wildfire and spread to his loins with the inevitable result. But something else had happened when he looked into her glittering green eyes. His heart had skipped a beat as he realized the lady was utterly desirable. He experienced a twinge of despair that she might refuse to speak to him again.

"Who the devil was that bold bitch?" Prince Edward demanded, rubbing his cheek.

"Don't you know?" Francis asked, surprised.

"She just left with Manchester. Is she one of his whores?"

"I haven't the faintest idea who she was," Francis lied as an urge to protect Lady Georgina suddenly came over him. "She obviously has a grudge against you, though," he added with glee.

"She slapped you first."

"That's because I'm your friend. What female have you offended recently?"

"More than I can count on one hand," the prince admitted with braggadocio.

Francis Russell perused the females parading in dishabille and suddenly lost his appetite for the strumpet in the frilly white corset. *Now, if Georgina were wearing those white lace stockings and sequined garters, it would be another matter entirely.*

"I fancy the one you bid on, Francis," Edward remarked glumly.

"Then be my guest. I'm off to Brooks's."

It was four in the morning when Bedford returned home to Russell Square. At the club he'd lost money because his mind was not on the game but elsewhere. Thoughts of Georgina Gordon persistently intruded, playing merry hell with his concentration. Finally, he gave up, tipped the porter who summoned his carriage, and allowed his mind to fully focus on the object of his desire.

As he disrobed for bed, he played a game of "what if." John had been nagging him to consider taking a wife, and for the first time in his life, he thought about it seriously.

Georgina would be an exciting woman to bed. She is a combination of innocence and recklessness. It would be fun to teach her to be wild and wanton. His hand went to his groin. *Christ, my cock is so hard, I could crack walnuts with it!*

The only drawback is the thought of the Duchess of Gordon. Then he mused that Jane Gordon was a voluptuary, and without doubt would be rewarding in bed. The thought that the daughter would take after the mother suddenly added to her allure.

The duke realized he would never be able to sleep with an erection. He rang the bell to summon a housemaid.

Chapter 16

"Since the Duke and Duchess of Manchester are hosting the Christmas festivities for the Gordon clan at Kimbolton this year, I advised Susan to hold your debutante ball on December twentieth, so that we need not return to London after the party."

"That's a fabulous idea, Mother. Kimbolton Castle is a fascinating place. It will be fun to spend some time there. Poor Queen Katherine of Aragon was imprisoned there in her final days, over two centuries ago, and I hope to catch a glimpse of her ghost that is reputed to float through the galleries."

"Katherine's specter is no doubt restless due to the uninhibited parties that Susan and William throw at the castle," Huntly teased.

"I've no notion why you call them *uninhibited*, George. The Manchesters' entertainments are filled with innocent fun and frolic aimed at making their guests laugh and be merry."

George repeated the witty words his sister had used. "Close. The word I was thinking of begins with the letter F."

"Mother, you banned me from Kimbolton until after I came out," Georgina reminded her. "I shall be desolate if there isn't at least one illicit liaison being carried on among the guests!"

George winked. "You won't be disappointed. I'll go

and clean my guns. There's bound to be at least one shooting party."

"I dropped a hint to Susan that she invite the Duke of Bedford to stay for a couple of days," Jane confided.

"In that case, George, can you lend me one of your guns?"

"Is that supposed to be amusing, Georgina?" Jane asked archly.

"Well, you cannot deny we are on a hunt, Mother. Ah, here is the post." She tore open an envelope embossed with the ducal crest of Manchester. "Susan's invitations are exceedingly fancy; they must have cost the earth."

"That is why I aspire to a match with a duke for you, Georgy. You will be able to lavishly indulge all your fancies."

"Here's a note from Susan. She's invited the Duke of Bedford for three days, from the nineteenth to the twenty-first, so we will have to be there the day before the ball." Georgina scanned the invitation. "Oh, how exciting! Susan's ball is to be a masquerade."

"We must get to work on our costumes immediately. We have no time to lose."

Georgina winked at George. "The *sewing women* will have no time to lose. Mother speaks as if she intends to make her own."

"I heard that! Don't think I couldn't make my own. I'm very handy with a needle, and I passed my sewing and knitting skills on to my daughters, as a devoted mother should."

"I apologize profusely. You are a paragon among mothers," Georgina teased. "Why don't you go as the Goddess Diana?"

"I do get the allusion, Georgy. Goddess of the hunt would be far too obvious, even for me." Jane joined in the laughter. "You could go as Queen Katherine, since she fascinates you, my dear."

"Never! She was far too good and pious."

"Georgy would prefer to be someone wicked like Anne Boleyn," her brother jested.

"I would never portray any of King Henry VIII's wives. I'd have more good sense than to wed a womanizing swine!"

"Then why don't *you* be Diana of the hunt?"

Georgina's eyes glittered with mischief. "By God, I'll do it! I'll need a bow and some arrows. I already have the gold paint."

"Here's an envelope from the Manchesters. An invitation, no doubt." John handed Francis the post that had arrived at Woburn.

"I've been expecting this. It's been delayed because it was first delivered to Russell Square before it was forwarded on." Bedford opened the invitation. "Damnation, it's to be held on the twentieth, but I'm invited to stay from the day before until the day after the masquerade ball. What's today's date?"

John looked at the newspaper. "It's the eighteenth."

"Christ, they are expecting me tomorrow."

The thought of Francis spending three days in the company of the alluring Lady Georgina filled John with dismay.

"Send your regrets. Mr. Burke will have a servant deliver it tonight. Kimbolton is only a dozen miles from Woburn."

"Regrets? Are you mad? I wouldn't miss this for the world. Their weekend entertainments are legend. After visiting the Devonshires' mausoleum of Chatsworth, Kimbolton Castle will feel like I've been resurrected. Oh, sorry, John, ignore my allusions to death." Francis apologized with the sincerity of a hedonist. "I'll be back late on the twenty-first. You won't mind putting off your trip to Tavistock until I return, will you, old man?"

"Of course not." John amended his itinerary. "My plans aren't set in stone. It will give me a chance to spend more of the Yule holidays with young Francis and William."

"I'll need a costume for the masquerade. What do you suggest?"

"Casanova, perhaps?"

"You have a dry wit, John. Often, I don't know if you're serious or jesting. But your suggestion has merit. As a connoisseur of fine fashion, food, wine, and women, I have much in common with Giacomo."

You are absolutely right, Francis. You don't know when I'm serious or when I'm jesting.

"I have that fabulous gold brocade coat I had made in Venice. Casanova wore his own long black hair powdered and scented, as I shall do. All I need is that golden Venetian mask I brought back and a dueling pistol, and my disguise is complete."

"None will recognize you," John said without a hint of sarcasm.

"Casanova was a womanizer who used charm, guile, intimidation, and aggression to conquer women." Francis winked. "As I said, we've much in common."

"He often left behind children and debt."

Francis laughed. "Well, mea culpa on the bastards, but I have never left a debt unpaid." He glanced at the clock. "Christ, I'll never be ready to leave in the morning."

"Mr. Burke will organize everything and pack whatever you need. I hope you realize how fortunate you are to have him as steward."

"Au contraire. He's fortunate to have me as master."

You could be jesting, but I'd bet a pound to a pinch of shit you are serious, Francis.

"I've just had a brilliant idea. Why don't you come to Kimbolton and attend the Manchesters' masquerade on the night of the twentieth? I know you are technically in mourning, but if you are masked and costumed, none will recognize you."

"Brilliant indeed," John said dryly. "Don't waste your evening trying to find me."

"Not bloody likely! The irresistible Lady Georgina will occupy my evening. When I compare her to the

Devonshires' daughter, I cannot believe I entertained the idea of a match with the gauche little mouse."

John stiffened. "I'll let you get on with your packing. The boys were having a game of chess before bed. I'll go and check on them. If I don't see you in the morning, enjoy rubbing elbows with the Gordons. Don't do anything I wouldn't do."

"I intend to rub more than elbows," Francis said with a leer. "Masquerades are blatant excuses for dalliance. I warrant I'll be able to collect on my wager with Prince Edward."

With difficulty, John held on to his temper. He suspected the wager was about Georgina, and it was all he could do to control his vicious desire to smash his brother in the face. As he climbed the stairs he thought, *Francis has me pegged right—privately, I'm only technically mourning Elizabeth. My secret thoughts about Georgina Gordon would shame the devil himself.*

John found William and Francis playing cards and tried not to censure them. "What happened to the chess?"

"Johnny beats us every time," Francis declared. "The little pissant is too clever by half."

"What card game are you playing?"

"Lanterloo—Uncle Francis taught us how to play. The game isn't much fun with only two. Would you join us, Father?"

"I don't really like you to game. Do you do it at school?"

His sons looked at each other guiltily.

"Go on, deal the cards. I'll play one game with you." John picked up his cards and put a guinea in the pot. He knew each son had only a couple of guineas' pocket money. When they bet all they had, John took the final two tricks and pocketed their money.

"It's not really the gaming I disapprove of. It's the betting. Good night, boys."

He went into Johnny's room and found him in bed reading. "I hear you soundly trounced your brothers at chess."

"I couldn't believe it—both of them made terrible blunders with their rooks."

John smiled knowingly. "While they are thinking of attacks, you are thinking of *planning* attacks. By the way, our plans have changed. We won't be going to Tavistock until December twenty-second."

"I'm looking forward to our journey to Devon."

"So am I. Good night, Johnny. Don't burn the midnight oil too much longer."

"You're a wretched tease, Georgy. We invite Bedford so you can get to know each other better, and you deliberately make yourself scarce when you were supposed to be in the great hall to receive him," Susan complained.

"He arrived early—obviously panting to get a glimpse of me."

"You're a shameless hussy. Since Kimbolton stands at the head of the fen country, William has arranged a hunt."

"I shall decline. The fens are open to the winter winds."

"The winds are in March. This is only December. Get into your riding habit or I shall set the bloody dogs on you, Georgy. Three days of entertainment have been planned solely for your benefit, so you had better cooperate, Mistress Contrary."

"Since you ask so sweetly, how can I possibly resist?" *It will give me the chance to show off my new apricot velvet habit.*

Georgina took her time dressing for the hunt. After she pulled on her long black riding boots, she donned a saucy hat, which sported a black ostrich feather that curled under her chin. She picked up her sketch pad and some charcoal, then slowly descended the magnificent staircase that led down to the great hall.

"We almost left without you," her brother, Huntly, declared.

She glanced over at Francis Russell, who was finishing off a stirrup cup. "I would have been devastated."

Bedford set down his empty drinking vessel. "You make a most arresting entrance, descending the stairs." He noticed the pad of paper she carried. "Do you sketch, Lady Georgina?"

"Among other things," she replied in a suggestive voice. "I'm particularly good at capturing wildlife."

"Man or beast?" he drawled.

"I intend to sketch a fen waterfowl. A far more civilized endeavor than hunting and killing them, don't you think, sir?"

"I never professed to be civilized," Francis taunted.

"At least you are honest."

"Brutally."

The swine likes to have the last word. I've noticed it runs in the family. Georgina chided herself for thinking about John. She gave Francis a radiant smile. "Shall we go, Your Grace, before Susan and William start frothing at the mouth?"

Together they walked toward the stables, where the hunting party and their attendants were gathered in the courtyard. Bedford helped her to mount, and they walked their horses through the rustling carpet of leaves that lay beneath the great bare elms. They followed the other riders through the gateway in the wall and across the castle's double ditch. The duke glanced back at Kimbolton. "It has a grand feudal air about it."

"It was built as a stronghold, guarding the road from Bedford to Huntingdon. Bedford inhabitants must have posed a threat."

"We still do," he promised.

"Forewarned is forearmed," she replied, refusing to let him have the last word. She urged her horse into a gallop, passing Susan and her groom, and caught up to William and George.

The fen reeds were dry and the dogs raced ahead, flushing a covey of marsh ducks. They quacked their protest at being rudely disturbed, and a couple fell to the hunters' guns.

Georgina drew rein and held her mount in check until everyone in the party rode past her, including

Francis Russell. Then she doubled back and led her horse in a different direction, where she anticipated being alone to observe nature.

In a quiet spot, she dismounted and slowly made her way toward the edge of a saltwater pool. She pulled up her velvet skirts and knelt down so that she could sketch a green heron as it fished.

She caught her breath as it elongated its neck to catch a frog, then sighed with relief when it missed. In a heartbeat the heron caught a small fish instead, and tossed it so that it could swallow it lengthwise. She knew the bird had to hunt for food from dawn to dusk to sustain itself.

She sketched the heron quickly, catching the determined look in its beady yellow eye. She drew the fish in its beak and the tiny drops of saltwater that dripped from its tail. She even put in the frog as it frantically swam away.

Georgina was so engrossed in her drawing that she was startled when the heron took wing with a plaintive cry. She looked up, found Francis Russell at her side, and smiled her secret smile. Deep down inside she had expected him to seek her out.

He looked at her sketch. "You are an accomplished artist."

"Why does that astonish you? Because I'm a debutante, fit for only flirting and fu . . . fumbling?"

Christ, she was about to say fucking! "Mea culpa. You have hidden depths, Georgina."

"You may address me as Lady Georgina."

"A misnomer if I ever heard one," he drawled.

She held out her hand, and when he helped her to rise, she managed to display the entire length of her leather riding boots. "Oh, sorry, Francis, my hands are covered with charcoal. I've blackened you. Your hands now match your reputation," she teased.

He bent and washed them off in the water, then took his handkerchief, wet it, and cleansed her hands. He took a step closer and traced a finger down the black feather that curled beneath her chin.

"If you don't think *lady* is suitable, what do you suggest?"

"Cocktease."

Georgina gasped and raised her arm to slap his insolent face.

The duke caught her hand, forced it behind her back, and pulled her against him for a kiss.

She laughed in his face. "I've never heard that word before, though I know it is lewd in the extreme. But you are right. I was teasing you. Unmercifully."

He released her immediately, knowing that she was laughing at him. *You flirted, and like a besotted fool, I fumbled. Just as you expected me to do. Just as you lured me to do. But in truth, I couldn't help myself. You are a bloody irresistible piece of female flesh.*

At dinner, Susan seated the Duke of Bedford next to Georgina. Through the first three courses, Francis found it difficult to keep his hands from straying. Used to giving in to his impulses, especially where women were concerned, and knowing full well that the lady was not likely to cause a scene involving the guest of honor, he finally succumbed to temptation and surreptitiously stroked his fingers along the thigh that was so close to his own.

Georgina smiled sweetly at her dinner partner and, under cover of her linen napkin, jabbed her dessert fork into his hand.

Francis turned his cry of pain into a bark of laughter, ostensibly at some amusing remark Huntly made.

"Stab me! That was witty, George." Georgina laughed merrily. "I think a sense of humor is a very seductive quality in a man."

The Duchess of Gordon bestowed a fatuous look of approval upon her youngest daughter. "My husband, Alexander, has rather a dour, Scottish sense of humor. He thoroughly disapproves of fun and frolic. Fortunately, my daughters take after their mother."

Georgina rolled her eyes at Francis, and this time

his laugh was genuine. She joined in. "I shall be generous and forgive you your trespasses." *In a pig's eye!*

After dinner, the company moved to the gaming room, where everyone except Georgina chose Scotch whiskey to drink. "I much prefer champagne," she informed Francis.

"I shall remember when you come to Woburn."

"Shall I be coming to Woburn?"

"Indeed you shall."

"I advised William to set up a table for lanterloo," Jane Gordon informed their guest. "I know you are expert at it."

"I much prefer faro," Georgina interjected. "Surely you will indulge me, Francis?" She pretended not to see the glare of disapproval her mother directed her way. "Since you are the player most likely to put up the largest stake, you can be the permanent banker, Your Grace."

Francis bowed to the company. "If all are in agreement?"

"Oh, we always indulge Georgy's whims," Susan informed him.

"I adore being a pampered pet," Georgina murmured wickedly.

They all sat around one large gaming table, and when William laid out the complete spade suit, Georgina decided to be contrary once more. "I don't like spades. Let's use hearts"—she glanced at Francis—"or perhaps diamonds? I can never decide which I like better. I'll let the banker decide."

"I think diamonds would suit you best."

Though it sounded like a compliment, she knew it was a sly jab because she'd told him it was the *manse* rather than the *man* that attracted her. *If he's hinting that I can have the house if I'll take him as spouse, I'm not even tempted.*

They played for two hours, and when she ran out of chips, she played for favors. "I know a gentleman would never collect gambling debts from a lady," she said without conviction.

She ran the tip of her tongue around the rim of her champagne glass. "I've had enough wine, and more than enough cards. Now that Kimbolton's galleries are shrouded in shadow, I shall go and seek the shade of Queen Katherine."

"Oh, darling, it's frightening up there," her mother warned. "You need an escort with a strong sword arm to protect you."

"Would you do the honors, Your Grace?" Georgina asked with a straight face.

Up in the darkened, eerie galleries, she made a game out of being elusive. Bedford was persistent in his pursuit. "You always manage to track me down like a hound with the scent of his prey."

His arms went around her, and he pulled her against his body so she could feel his hard erection. "See what you do to me?"

"Is that the result of *any* female scent, or one in particular?"

"It's not just your fragrance that entrances me, vixen, it's your essence. You are an exciting female, and you are well aware of it." He captured her lips, and halfway through the kiss he intruded his tongue into her mouth.

"I thought a gentleman never collected gambling debts from a lady," she teased.

"I'm not a gentleman."

She pulled away, laughing. "So your brother informed me."

"That isn't the first time you've mentioned my brother."

"We are like flint and tinder. He rubs me the wrong way."

Francis promptly rubbed his erection against her mons. She pulled away. "There's no need to cock your weapon—the ghost isn't here tonight. Shall we return to the party?" She adroitly escaped his advances, knowing he would follow wherever she led.

Sometime later the ladies went upstairs and left the men to their whiskey and cigars.

Jane kissed her daughters' cheeks. "Susan, you have done an outstanding job of providing this golden opportunity for Georgy." She squeezed her youngest daughter's hand. "And I am over the moon that you are making the most of it. Good night, girls."

Ten minutes later, Georgina entered her sister Susan's chamber. She sat down on the bed, opened the book she was carrying, and began to read a speech by the Duchess of Belgrave.

"The town must be carried by storm. While such cold calculators as the Duchess of Drinkwater, with all the frigid economy of her native north, are collecting a little money and a few forces to meet us, reckoning upon our weakness, we must by a display of unbounded magnificence, taste, and expense, at once overwhelm their puny preparations and strike a blow that shall palsy every effort of our rivals for the remainder of the Season . . . I am decidedly for a grand masked gala."

The two sisters were helpless with laughter, with tears of mirth streaming down their cheeks, when William opened the bedchamber door.

"What's so funny, m'dear?"

"Men!" they replied in unison, and went off into another peel of uncontrollable laughter.

Chapter 17

"Mr. Burke, I had the idea to take my sons into the woods and select a Christmas tree for Woburn's great hall. But if Francis enjoys doing this himself, we will wait until he returns."

"His Grace never takes part in choosing a tree or putting up the Yule decorations. He leaves it to his staff and me. Since I decided we'd do that today, our plans mesh perfectly, my lord."

"Do call me John, Mr. Burke. I'll tell the boys. I suppose you take a wagon and a couple of strong footmen to carry the tree back to the hall?"

"We take two wagons, one for the tree, and one for the holly, ivy, and mistletoe that the housemaids gather. The woods at the northern edge of Woburn land have the best selection."

When John and his sons were saddled up, they led the way north, ahead of the wagons. "I'm glad it snowed last night. The drifts make the landscape beautiful."

"Can we help chop the tree down?" William asked.

"Yes, we'll all have a go. Mr. Burke put more than one ax in the wagons."

They'd been riding almost an hour when they came on a stand of tall firs. John turned to look at Mr. Burke for his nod of approval. But Burke shook his head and motioned for them to ride farther north. "I hope you're not feeling the cold, Johnny?"

"No, Father. I'm enjoying the ride. I've seen lots of hares, and Will and I spotted a pair of deer."

They rode on for a couple of miles and finally came to a wooded area that boasted some magnificent, tall conifer pine trees among the larches. The riders dismounted, and the wagons drew rein and stopped. "You fellows choose the Yule tree," John directed.

"I think Francis and William should choose. I won't be here for Christmas," Johnny pointed out.

The maids jumped from their wagon and went deeper into the woods, where the ivy and mistletoe climbed up the tree trunks.

"I won't be much good with an ax, so I think I'll help cut the ivy and gather some pinecones," Johnny decided.

First Francis then William took their turns with the axes, once their father had cut a notch in the trunk of the conifer. They gave it all they had, but managed to cut only about halfway through the sturdy trunk before they gave up and handed an ax to their father.

John took off his coat and got down to business. "You did the hard part. This shouldn't take long." There was a crack like a gunshot in the frosty air, and the boys shouted, "Timber!"

As the tree started to fall, John saw a team of horses pulling a sleigh. The tree crashed down within feet of the vehicle, and the horses screamed and reared in fright. It took a deal of skill by the sleigh driver to bring the animals under control.

John recognized his brother holding the reins of the shuddering horses, while a white-faced Lady Georgina Gordon sat beside him clutching the side of the sleigh. John was furious that Francis had put Georgina in danger. "That was a damn fool thing to do. You could have been killed!" He embedded the ax into the tree stump, strode to the horses, and gentled them.

Francis pretended nonchalance in front of his lady fair. "That would make you the new Duke of Bedford. The *ton* would never believe it was an accident, old man."

John was not amused. "Are you all right, Lady Georgina?"

"Yes, thank you. So few noblemen cut down their own Christmas trees, I could have sworn we had stumbled across my father."

Francis laughed at his brother. "What a pity, old man, that you come across as a father figure."

Georgina arched her brow at her companion. "Could *you* fell a twenty-foot tree with an ax, Your Grace?"

"I have servants to do that for me, my dearest lady."

"That's a pity, Francis." She made a moue with her lips.

"When you do that, I don't know if you are going to kiss me or spit on me," he drawled.

"I guarantee it won't be the former," she replied saucily.

It was John's turn to laugh at his brother. Yet his laughter masked his real feelings. He saw the way they looked at each other, heard their teasing banter, and felt his gut knot.

Johnny emerged from the trees. "I heard the horses scream—what happened? Oh, it's Georgy and Uncle Francis. You are having a sleigh ride . . . what jolly good fun!"

"Hello, Johnny. Would you like to have a ride?" She pretended not to see her companion's frown.

Johnny glanced at his father. "I . . . I wouldn't dream of intruding on your privacy, Lady Georgina."

"Nonsense!" She flicked a glance at his father's disapproving face. "I insist. You can come for a ride while they haul the Christmas tree into the wagon. Come and sit here between us."

"If you sit closer to me," Francis suggested, "Johnny can sit on the outside, where his view won't be impeded."

Georgina thwarted his suggestion. "I want him to sit next to you, Francis, so you can turn the reins over to him for part of the ride." She raised her hand in expectation of John Russell helping her from the sleigh so Johnny could get in the middle.

John took hold of her proffered hand and squeezed hard. Not so hard that it was painful, but hard enough to let her know that he was on to her tricks.

Georgina smiled her secret smile and knew that John saw her wicked self-satisfaction at being able to entice his brother to do her bidding. It amused her that they could silently communicate. After Johnny climbed aboard, she jumped in and the horses plunged forward.

Francis slowed them and, to please Georgina, put his arm about his nephew and handed him the reins. "Hold them in check—don't let them have their heads. They are mares, and filled with nervous energy at the moment."

"You don't approve of letting females have their heads?"

"For a special female, I might be persuaded."

"A special female might not give a fig for your approval. She might take the bit between her teeth and run rampant."

"Rampant?" he asked with a leer. "Is that a promise?"

After a ten-minute run, Francis took back the reins, turned the sleigh, and headed back. When they arrived at the wagons, Georgina jumped out and lifted Johnny from the sleigh. "You did well."

"Thank you, my lady. Thank you, Uncle Francis."

Georgina did not even glance in John Russell's direction, but she knew he was watching her.

When she climbed back in, Francis tempted, "Would you like to move closer so you can drive, Georgina?"

She smiled radiantly. "I would like it above all things."

Francis tucked the fur rug about her hips, waved to his brother, and gave him a broad wink.

John felt despair. He had seen the intimate smile she had given Francis, seen his brother's possessive hands touch her, and believed they were on the brink of falling in love.

Back at Woburn, John and his sons spent the entire afternoon helping Mr. Burke and his staff put up the Christmas tree in the great hall and decorate it. They helped the maids carry in armloads of pine branches, holy, ivy, and mistletoe. Mr. Burke went up to the attics and brought down Yule ornaments, garlands, Christmas bells, and reams of red ribbon.

After dinner that evening, John's sons wrapped presents and put them under the tree. That night they went to bed tired, but happy and excited about the upcoming festivities. John was extremely relieved that his boys were no longer overcome by grief and seemed to be settling down.

Tonight, however, John felt exceedingly unsettled. He went to Woburn's library for a book, but nothing sparked his interest. He wandered down to the ancient weapons room and marveled at the lances, maces, pikes, and shields that had been utilized in wars through the centuries. He looked at his brother's sword and gun collections and admired a few of the pieces. Against one wall a narrow table displayed antique knives and daggers on a plush blue velvet cloth with an embroidered silver border.

Normally, he could spend hours in this chamber, examining the artifacts, but tonight his mind was on Francis and the masquerade ball at Kimbolton Castle. *You cannot stand not knowing, can you?* he mocked himself. He knew the answer. Knew he could not rest until he had seen for himself. *Go! What the hell's stopping you?*

John removed the daggers from the table and shook out the cloth. He lifted down a sword and buckler and took them up to his bedroom, where he donned black knee breeches and tall black riding boots. He cut a hole in the blue velvet cloth large enough to fit over his head. *It will make a passable tabard. Let's hope I make a passable French Musketeer.* He searched through a large wardrobe that stored Russell garments from bygone years until he found a black cavalier's hat with an ostrich feather.

John bathed and shaved, but did not use the razor on his top lip. He rubbed his finger inside the lamp chimney and darkened the shadow of his mustache with soot. When he put on the tabard, hat, and black eye mask, he knew no one would recognize him.

Georgina was bubbling with excitement over attending her first grown-up masquerade ball. Since the *haut ton* was curious about Kimbolton Castle, and avid to know every last detail of a possible Bedford-Gordon alliance, all invitations had been accepted. "There are at least two hundred guests tonight . . . half of them men!"

Susan, wearing the Queen Katherine of Aragon costume she'd had made when the Duke of Manchester first brought her to Kimbolton, lent Georgina a long, golden-haired wig. "Let me tuck in all your dark tendrils. There, you make a perfect Diana. If you reveal your identity, your reputation will be in shreds with that bared shoulder and scandalous short skirt."

"What are reputations for?" Georgy asked blithely, as she donned her golden-winged eye mask. She admired her reflection in the mirror. "Actually, it isn't as short as the kilt Father had made for me."

She adjusted her quiver of arrows to rest between her shoulder blades and picked up her golden bow. "You go first, Susan. I suspect the Duke of Bedford will be lurking about outside so he will know what costume I'm wearing."

"What fun! I shall pretend to be you and lead him astray . . . well, at least as far as the ballroom."

Susan left, and before she got halfway down the hallway, she felt a man's arm around her waist and a whisper in her ear.

"It's Francis. Why don't we arrange a rendezvous, my sweet?"

"You have mistaken me for someone else, Your

Grace. I am not in the market to bag a duke, since I am already a duchess."

He caught himself quickly. "Casanova prefers a duchess to any other noble lady."

"Really? I know a debutante who will be devastated," she teased. "Would you care to partner your hostess in a dance?"

Georgina waited ten minutes, then cautiously opened her chamber door and looked out. The castle hall was empty, so, unobserved, she managed to gain the ballroom and mingle with the crowd.

The lighting was subdued, the music seductive, and a bacchanalian atmosphere prevailed. A liberal supply of drinks induced the guests to freely imbibe; laughter, whispers, risqué banter, and intimate touches were the order of the night. An aura of anticipation and indiscretion permeated the very air.

Georgina received advances from a dashing highwayman, a sultan, two kings, and a friar intent on unfrocking her. She soon singled out the most ostentatiously dressed gentleman at the ball, and surmised he was the Duke of Bedford. *Tonight, Francis is affecting even more haughty pride than usual. In the Venetian attire, I warrant he truly thinks himself Casanova!*

She watched as he sniffed around several females. All of them practically threw themselves at him, which didn't engage his interest. *He knows damn well Georgina Gordon wouldn't act that way. So here is where I have some fun!*

As she approached Casanova she swept up two glasses of Madeira wine and handed him one. In a husky voice, she declared, "I have viewed my prey and have stalked you long enough. I am about to pierce you with my arrow."

"Since I'm the greatest lover who ever lived, I warrant you have designs on being pierced with *my* arrow," he drawled. "The line forms to the left, my dearest lady."

Georgina pretended to take offense and stalked off. Because of her provocative costume, she was soon surrounded by males, and she had fun guessing who was behind the various disguises. Most were easy. Jack Spencer was Puck, complete with goat horns and tail. She finally revealed who she was, but swore him to secrecy.

Georgina had no trouble identifying Prince Edward, who was wearing an authentic uniform of a Royal Dragoon, complete with saber. He felt her bottom, made a lewd suggestion, and she knew he had already had far too much to drink. She beat him to a glass of champagne he was reaching for and cautiously moved away.

She spotted Lord Holland, complete with Roman helmet and leather tunic, and decided that if her costume could deceive Henry, she could dupe everyone else. She took an arrow from her quiver and poked him in the breastplate. "Here's *my* lethal weapon . . . Would you care to show me *yours*, dahling?"

Henry laughed heartily. "I suspect my wife has put one of her friends up to tempting me, to see if I take the bait."

"You are far too perceptive, my lord. I told Beth I couldn't lure you to do anything lewd—lascivious perhaps, but never lewd."

Because of their banter, she feared he would guess her identity, so she took the glass from his hand and began to sip his Scotch. *This will put him off the scent, since he knows Lady Georgina prefers champagne.*

She searched for Casanova and saw him in conversation with flame-haired Mary, Queen of Scots. *Damn you, Mother, you will tell Bedford I am Diana, Goddess of the Hunt.* Georgina watched him scan the room, and when his eyes came to rest on her, she felt like a butterfly pinned to the wall.

As Francis walked a direct path to her, she gulped the Scotch and got rid of the glass. She suddenly felt light-headed.

Francis took possession of her hand. "You are a wicked tease, Georgina. You deliberately amuse yourself at my expense."

"I'm so glad you have tempered your language, Your Grace. Last time you called me a cocktease." The moment it slipped out, she knew she should not have uttered the word. *Damnation, that's tantamount to flinging fuel on a fire!*

He slipped his arm about her waist and drew her close.

She tried to fend him off with the arrow. "Step back, or I shall pierce your heart."

"You've already done that, as well you know. I believe you enjoy conquest as much as I. It's high time we got to know each other better. Why don't we go up to my chamber?"

"Would Casanova be an appropriate teacher for a debutante?"

"Absolutely. I would give you riding lessons."

"Dancing induces romance, don't you think? If you partner me, perhaps later I will look kindly upon your suggestion." *Thank heaven it is a contradance, where everyone changes partners.*

Georgina misstepped and knew she'd had too much to drink. She regained her balance and warned herself to be careful. The trouble was, she felt decidedly reckless.

The Musketeer surveyed the ballroom and saw Casanova with his arm around a goddess, whispering in her ear as they danced. He suspected immediately that only Georgina would be daring enough to wear such a provocative costume. *Francis is making an assignation. Will she succumb?*

John bowed to a lady in an old-fashioned pannier gown and asked her to dance. *It won't be long before I partner the divine huntress.* He went through the motions of the contradance until Diana stood before him. He bowed formally and noticed that her curtsy was slightly unsteady. *The little minx is flown with wine. Her inhibitions will be at low ebb.*

John watched Georgina's glance roam over him with frank appreciation. She ran the tip of her tongue around her mouth, as if she were licking her lips over him. *Is she promiscuous? How far will she go?* Something compelled him to find out.

The moment the dance was finished, he walked a direct path to her. "Mademoiselle," he murmured in a seductive French accent, "would you . . . *promenade avec moi*?"

She gazed up at him and sighed. "Ah . . . walk with you . . . *oui*."

John, who knew exactly where his brother was, took Georgina's hand and led her in the opposite direction. "The castle galleries call out to the soul, *n'est-ce pas aussi*?"

Her mind was fuzzy when she tried to translate. *Is that not so? "Oui, oui, monsieur."* Mesmerized, she allowed him to lead her from the crowded ballroom and up a flight of stairs to the dimly lit galleries. The shadow of another couple moved quickly, then disappeared into the darkness.

They stopped walking. He towered above her, and the seclusion cloaked them in privacy. "You make a ravishing Diana."

He's going to kiss me. Dear God, I pray he's going to kiss me.

His fingertips caressed her naked shoulder and a frisson of desire made her shudder.

"I have seen Batoni's magnificent painting of Diana. Your costume is not quite accurate . . . one beautiful breast should be bared." His mouth descended and captured her lips.

He was so overtly masculine, Georgina was lost in a blissful fantasy where her dream lover took control of her senses. The French swordsman was all power and command, and she was weak with trembling desire.

As his kiss deepened, his fingers stole beneath the

shoulder of her tunic and slid it down her arm until it fell to her waist, baring both breasts. He cupped one with his palm and rubbed his thumb across her nipple until it ruched prettily. He had an overpowering need to take the tidbit into his mouth and taste her.

As his lips took possession, Georgina pulled away. "I . . . I'm sorry, my lord. I should not be here with you. Too much wine has stolen my senses." She pulled up her bodice and fled the gallery.

John remained where he was for a long time. *You tried to seduce her.* He wondered if Francis would succeed where he had failed. *Why in hellfire did you come to Kimbolton tonight?* He avoided answering by leaving the gallery. He decided to return to Woburn immediately.

As he traversed the ballroom, a loud voice ordered, "Halt!" A Royal Dragoon who took exception to the presence of a Musketeer suddenly confronted him.

"You filthy French coward! How dare you show your face in an English Cashle?"

John did not need the slurred speech to tell him that Prince Edward was drunk. To his dismay, everyone stopped talking and dancing and began to gape.

Prince Edward fumbled with his saber and managed to draw it from its scabbard. *"En garde!"*

"A good swordsman is not given to quarrel," John declared.

The prince raised his saber and knocked off John's plumed hat.

News of a duel spread like wildfire, and the guests clustered about the declared enemies. The Duke of Manchester, in his capacity as host, and the prince's brother, tried to talk sense into the inebriated challenger.

"He's not really a French Musketeer, Edward. It's a masquerade costume," Frederick explained. "Put your sword away before you do yourself an injury."

"Who is it, then? In the name of the king I demand that you remove your mashk."

Georgina, closely followed by Francis Russell, eagerly joined the spectators. When she saw it was her seductive French Musketeer who was involved in the quarrel, she was horrified.

Prince Edward could not be pacified. He reached up and snatched the mask from the Musketeer's face.

Georgina, and everyone watching, gasped when they saw the man before them was John Russell.

With jaw clenched and his hand on the hilt of his sword, Russell took his leave of the company.

The whispers began immediately. "The decadent devil. He's only just buried his wife," Lady Jersey stated.

"Good riddance, from what I've heard. Rumor has it he helped her to the grave," Lord Jersey, wearing a devil's costume, added.

"That's a damned lie," the Duke of Bedford declared coldly to Prinny's whore and her cuckold spouse. "My brother was deeply in love with his wife. John was a devoted husband. He came tonight at my insistence. His mourning has almost consumed him."

"I humbly beg your pardon, Your Grace." The devil withdrew immediately, dragging his advocate after him.

Georgina shuddered. *Is it possible he had a hand in his wife's death?* She didn't want to believe it, and yet she suspected that deep down he was a dangerous man, perhaps capable of violence.

She had heard Francis defend his brother vigorously. Her dark suspicions melted away as Bedford's words echoed in her head: *My brother was deeply in love with his wife. John was a devoted husband. His mourning has almost consumed him.*

Georgina closed her eyes. *What must it be like to be loved like that by your husband? That's the sort of marriage I want!*

The masquerade ball resumed, as did the delicious, scandalous whispers. All agreed it was the height of decadence to party when one was supposed to be in mourning. As the rumors spread, they became embellished with dissolute details about both Russell brothers. It was obvious that the Gordons had ensnared the Duke of Bedford and lured him away from making a match with the Devonshires' daughter. Secret wagers were placed on whether Lady Georgina's virginity would induce Bedford to give up his bachelorhood or whether he would steal the prize without a firm commitment to marriage.

Chapter 18

John Russell held my breast in his hand and kissed me! Did some part of me know it was he behind the mask when I willingly went to the secluded gallery with him? Georgina's heart fluttered erratically. *I behaved wantonly, going weak when he murmured French words and falling into his arms the moment he touched me.*

Her fingers brushed across her lips; then her hand moved lower and cupped the breast he had held. *We are antagonists. He provokes me to madness. Yet in spite of it, I am sexually attracted to him.* Georgina asked herself: *In spite of it, or because of it?* She shook her head. "That's absurd!"

"The whole of society is absurd." Francis took her hand and led her onto the ballroom floor. Their hostess had ordered the orchestra to play a lively tune, and she announced a mazey dance in hopes that the unfortunate episode would be forgotten.

Georgina became progressively light-headed and preoccupied with disturbing thoughts. During the dance, when Francis spoke to her, she didn't hear his words, she simply smiled.

An hour later, she found herself alone with him in one of the galleries and couldn't remember how she got there. When he drew her into his arms to kiss her, she protested. "Please, Francis, you mustn't."

"Georgina, I must. I'm afraid I've fallen in love with you."

"That's absurd!"

"Yes, I know. I've never wanted a woman as much as I want you. I can't wait any longer. You're driving me mad. Come with me."

"Come where?" she asked, as dismay rose up in her.

"To my chamber, of course." His hand caressed her bare shoulder. "You are ripe for love tonight."

She tried to organize her thoughts. "We . . . we cannot go together, Francis."

"I'm sorry. I forgot you've never done this before. I'll go first; then after a few discreet minutes, you follow. You do know where my chamber is?"

"Yes, yes, of course."

The ride back to Woburn Abbey cleared John Russell's head, though it did little to cool his temper. He was livid that drunken Prince Edward had unmasked him, and equally furious with himself for attending the masquerade.

He laughed bitterly at his own folly. "Lady Georgina Gordon doesn't even pay lip service to chastity! There was absolutely no need to worry that Francis would take advantage of her. The prey becomes the hunter . . . huntress," he amended with disgust.

John stabled his horse and sought his chamber. Knowing that sleep would not come easily, he immediately began to pack for his journey to Tavistock. *The moment my brother returns from Kimbolton, I shall leave.*

Georgina awoke with a start, and immediately looked to see if she was in bed alone. She heaved a great sigh of relief as her head cleared. "I remember now." She had watched silently until the Duke of Bedford disappeared into the shadows; then she had hurried back to the ballroom and found her sister.

"I'm afraid I've had too much to drink. I feel unwell. Will you please walk me to my room, Susan?"

Georgina felt a bit guilty. She had inferred to Francis that she would go to his room when she had had no intention whatsoever of doing so. *The Duke of Bedford will be furious. But look on the bright side—perhaps now he'll stop pursuing me.*

She avoided going down to breakfast by asking for a tray in her room. When her mother arrived, she realized she was trapped.

"What are you doing in your chamber? I've searched everywhere for you, and never in a million years did I expect to find you holed up here." The Duchess of Gordon plucked the toast from her daughter's fingers. "These three days of the Duke of Bedford's visit have been arranged for your benefit, as you are well aware, my lass. The duke has been pacing this past hour, watching the staircase for a glimpse of you." Jane paused for a breath. "It's all very well to play the elusive game to arouse his interest, but once his appetite is whetted, it is no longer a game, but a deadly serious mission."

You sound exactly like the Duchess of Drinkwater. "Yes," Georgina said earnestly, "we must strike a blow that will palsy every effort of our rivals."

"That's the spirit." Jane was deaf to the mockery. "They don't call us the 'Gey Gordons' for nothing."

"Mother, gey means overwhelming and self-important."

"Exactly—a Gordon and a Russell are a perfect match!"

"I shall dress immediately and come downstairs."

"Be sure to wear something . . ."

"Something that will give him a palsy?"

The duchess gave her daughter a level look. "If by *palsy* you mean something that will shake him to the core, that will do very nicely, Georgina."

"You look absolutely radiant." Francis kissed her hand.

God Almighty, you're not even drawling your words in that irritating, arrogant fashion. You are all earnest this morning. Georgina decided a lie was in order. She touched her brow. "I don't feel radiant. I almost passed out last night from drink. I don't remember a thing, but my sister Susan tells me she had to put me to bed."

"Pauvre petite," he commiserated.

Oh, please don't speak French. It does strange things to my innards. With a straight face, she said, *"Je ne parle pas français."*

"You are such an irresistible contradiction, Georgina." With adoring eyes he gazed down at her diaphanous morning dress that concealed so little of her youthful curves. "You have the quick mind and luscious body of a woman, while your virginity traps you in childhood."

Damnation, it's my virginity that lures you. I warrant that's quite a novelty to you, Bedford. Georgina embarked on her second lie. "Pray don't deceive yourself, Francis. I am far from pure."

She saw the bulge form in his riding breeches. *Hellfire, everything I do and say arouses you. Shall I hint that it was a footman to put you off me?* She warned herself not to be completely stupid. "I have been ardently wooed, you know, and turned down more than one proposal of marriage."

"I take it your suitors were not dukes." His drawl was back.

She gave him a coy glance. "A lady never tells."

"I believe the adage is: A *gentleman* never tells."

She laughed in his face. "From what I hear, if a gentleman makes a conquest, he believes it gives him bragging rights."

"That would prove him no gentleman. Dukes of the realm are a different breed, my dearest Georgina."

"You forget, Francis," she said dryly, "my father is a duke." Georgina glanced out the window and saw Charlotte's children playing in melted snow with Susan's offspring. "Oh, I cannot resist jumping in puddles. Would you care to join my nephews, nieces, and me for some fun and games, Your Grace?"

"The fun and games I have in mind do not include melted snow."

Her wicked juices stirred. "Are you sure? A rub-down with some ice might be rather stimulating." She opened the casement window and shouted to Mary, "I'm coming out to play." She flicked a glance at Francis and warned, "Gird your loins."

Georgina avoided the duke until dinner. Since it was to be his last night at Kimbolton, she did not have the audacity to absent herself. All the Gordon daughters and their noble spouses sat down to the late meal with the exception of Louisa. Marquis Cornwallis was in France trying to negotiate a peace treaty, so Louisa and her new husband were coming to spend Christmas with the rest of the family but were not scheduled to arrive at Kimbolton until the following day.

The conversation was lively and often downright bawdy with the duchess and her loquacious, vivacious daughters recounting the lion's share of entertaining anecdotes, while the men laughed, drank, and tolerated injuries to their pride when it was their turn to be the butt of jokes.

As Georgina watched Francis Russell, she was dismayed that he seemed to bask in the family fun as if it were a unique experience for him. He laughed at the broad jokes and totally drank in the flattery that Jane Gordon heaped upon him.

"Lady Georgina, you promised me a tour of the galleries to see all the art that this splendid castle boasts. Shall we?"

You are a shrewd sod to invent a promise I made and announce it to all. I cannot call you a liar before my mother, and I cannot refuse to accompany you without seeming churlish.

"I should be delighted." *Should be, though I am anything but.* "I'm afraid you may be disappointed, Your Grace. Kimbolton's paintings cannot compare to the art collection at Woburn Abbey."

"You must come to Woburn to view my paintings, since you are an art aficionado. Your mother has told me of your many talents."

"Not all of them, I hope," she murmured. She saw desire kindle in his eyes and dreaded what might come when they were alone. *It's my turn to gird my loins.* She picked up her paisley shawl and wrapped it about her in a way that covered her breasts.

When they arrived in the first gallery, he stopped walking. Francis drew her into his arms and kissed her. His mouth tasted of brandy, and she tried to pull away after the first kiss.

Francis sighed at her reluctance. "I know you want marriage, Georgina. You play a clever game of advancement and withdrawal, and though I hate to admit it, I am caught in your web. After much consideration, I've decided to make you the Duchess of Bedford."

You haven't even asked me. You have simply decided.

"Your Grace . . . Francis . . . I am aware of the great honor you do me, but I am afraid that I cannot marry you."

The duke, taken aback, stiffened. Then he laughed and took her hands. "I have overwhelmed you. You think yourself unworthy of such an exalted position. But I'm in love with you and want you for my duchess."

You are about to learn that you cannot have everything you want. "I'm sorry, Your Grace. I cannot accept your proposal."

"I refuse to take no for an answer, simply because I know you do not mean it."

She withdrew her hands from his. "You are delusional."

"Damn it, Georgina, are you going to make me court you like some pathetic lovesick swain?"

"Francis, that is not my intent." *You need no help from me to make you pathetic.*

"I invite you, and your family, of course, to come to Woburn for the New Year's celebration. Please don't refuse, Georgina."

You think dangling the prize of the great abbey will

make me change my mind. 'Tis plain you think me mercenary, and that is an unforgivable insult.

"I'm sorry, I should extend the invitation to the Duchess of Gordon. You totally distract me and make me forget my manners."

"You will find her in the drawing room." Georgina curtsied. "Good night, Your Grace."

"I didn't expect you tonight. I was writing you a note." John was surprised when Francis arrived home after dark. He had assumed his brother would return to Woburn the next morning, and had ordered his carriage be ready early so that he and Johnny could be on their way to Tavistock before Francis returned.

"And I didn't expect *you* at the masquerade," Francis said.

"My curiosity about Kimbolton overcame my better judgment."

"Lady Jersey called you *decadent*." He chuckled. "*You*, of all people. I was infuriated that Prinny's whore and her pathetic cuckold of a husband hinted you had a hand in Elizabeth's death. I was so affronted that they dared pass judgment on a Russell, I called him a liar in front of the whole company."

"Thanks, Francis. I can fight my own battles."

"Oh, I didn't go as far as challenging him to a duel. I simply lied through my teeth. I loudly announced that you deeply loved your wife. Told him your grief had almost consumed you. That should put a stop to the whispers."

John's jaw clenched. "Not if I know the gossipmongers." He kept a rein on his temper. "I hope the incident didn't ruin your stay with the Gordons."

"Not at all. The courtship is going swimmingly, old man."

"You are officially courting Lady Georgina? With a view to marriage?"

"Marriage? Well, I wouldn't go that far—not yet. But one thing is certain. The young vixen is madly in love with me."

Why the hell did I ask? "The boys opened their Christmas gifts from me earlier. Johnny and I will be leaving at dawn, so I shall wish you happy Christmas now. Good night, Francis."

"I know you're the Lord of Misrule, George. But who are you dressed up as?" Charlie Cornwallis asked his wife's brother.

"Good King Wenceslas, of course," Huntly replied, tipping his crown over one eye. "Here to hand out the presents."

The Gordon clan was gathered around the Christmas tree in the great hall at Kimbolton. Georgina was flanked by her sister Louisa and her favorite niece, Mary, and each lady's pile of gifts grew apace. She was curious about a present that simply said it was from *Father Christmas*. She tore off the wrapping eagerly, but was appalled when she saw the contents: a frilly white corset, lace stockings, and a pair of silver sequined garters. "Bloody hell!" she muttered.

"What did you get?" Mary's curious eyes shone with excitement.

Georgina quickly covered the box. "Just some stockings, darling. What did you get?"

"It's a hat! A grown-up hat with lovely feathers. Georgy, it must be from you!"

"Didn't you read the card?"

"I don't need to read the card. Only you know the wishes inside my heart," Mary said worshipfully.

"Rubbish. I only gave you a hat of your own so you won't ruin all mine."

When the gifts were opened, Louisa showed Georgina all the lovely things she'd received, and Georgina displayed her presents for Louisa . . . except the one from the bloody Duke of Bedford. She smiled to mask her growing anger.

"You missed the masquerade ball." Georgina gathered her gifts to take them upstairs to her chamber.

"People in masks frighten me," Louisa confided. "How did the visit with Francis Russell go?"

"It lived up to Mother's expectations, if not mine."

"What about *his* expectations?" Louisa asked anxiously.

"The duke is doomed to disappointment," Georgina said flatly.

"Good . . . he is a complete sensualist," she whispered confidentially.

Georgina glanced down at the boxes she held. "I never would have guessed."

When Georgina reached her chamber, she was seething and sat down to pen a note.

Father Christmas gave me this gift by mistake. I am returning it to you so that you may rectify the insult. This sort of present is simply not acceptable. I would suggest jewels.

"If I make it plain I am only interested in his wealth, the disgusting swine will stop pursuing me."

She rewrapped the box, addressed it to the Duke of Bedford, Woburn Abbey, and asked the Manchesters' majordomo to see that it got to its destination first thing in the morning.

As darkness began to fall the following day, a small package was delivered for Lady Georgina by a footman from Woburn Abbey. Her mother took delivery and brought it to her immediately.

"Well, aren't you going to open it? It's from the Duke of Bedford," she said breathlessly.

He's called my bluff. She tore off the paper, and lifted the lid of the small velvet box. The ring was a large oval amethyst surrounded by diamonds. Georgina's heart sank. Then she summoned her bravado, slipped it on her right hand, and said, "Very pretty."

"It's an engagement ring! It goes on your left hand, Georgy. It is the official Russell colors of purple and white."

"Mother, it is *not* an engagement ring. It's a mere trifle. It is a little joke between Francis and myself."

"A secret shared by two." Jane could not hide her excitement.

Dear God, she'll have the news spread from Land's

End to John o' Groat's, unless I can think of something to stop her. "Mother, you must not say a word, or you will ruin everything."

"I know how to keep a secret."

"I gravely doubt that. If word gets out, the Duke of Bedford will end the friendship immediately."

"My speech will be short and sweet." John Russell held up his hands for silence. "My son and I could not have spent a happier Christmas anywhere in England than right here in Tavistock."

The parish hall was crowded to the rafters with the constituents he represented in the House of Commons, from young babies in arms to elderly, weathered ancients bent over their walking sticks. Many had offered him their condolences on the death of his wife, though they had never met her. They accepted death as a natural event and did not overly dwell on it. John's people loved and revered him because each and every year he had made their lives easier with the bountiful gifts he bestowed.

"You make my work worthwhile. When I see you happy, healthy, and prospering I'm rewarded a thousand times over. It's a great honor to wish each of you a merry Christmas and a happy new year."

John had a lump in his throat as he watched his son run about in a paper hat, laughing and playing with the other children. His older sons would not have mingled well with these sweet, innocent village boys and girls, for already William and Francis had an air of sophistication bred into them at the elite Westminster School. But Johnny, hungry for laughter and companionship, was having the time of his life.

An image of a laughing Georgina Gordon came full blown into his mind. *She has a vivacity and* joi de vivre *that few noble ladies possess. 'Tis no wonder my brother is attracted to her.* His mind conjured her as he had last seen her . . . green eyes, half closed with desire glittering through the slits of her mask. He could still feel her silken breast in his palm, still taste the wild honey sweetness of her mouth. *If Francis proposes, she will become my brother's wife.* John refused to think about such an eventuality. He vowed not to conjure Georgina Gordon again.

That night when he slept, however, he had little control over his conscious will. John experienced his recurring dream again, and again his female companion's identity was no longer hidden. When he kissed Georgina, her mouth tasted of delicious laughter and sensual anticipation.

Chapter 19

"I believe you've gone queer in the head, Georgina. Why on earth would you not wish to go to Woburn for New Year's?" Jane did not give her daughter time to answer. "The Duke of Bedford made a point of asking me personally, and was generous enough to include all members of our family for the New Year's Eve celebrations tomorrow night, and to stay over for breakfast on New Year's Day."

"I don't feel well." Her excuse was feeble and she knew it.

"You were well enough to lead the children on a ghost hunt last night . . . all of you dressed in white sheets and shrieking your heads off. You were well enough to climb over all the furniture this morning, playing a game of mountaineers and yodeling at the top of your lungs."

"Perhaps that's why I don't feel well."

"Not another word. This is my chance to thoroughly acquaint myself with Woburn Abbey. Playing hard to get is becoming tiresome. You must move on to the next phase of the campaign."

I thought becoming engaged to Bedford would be a lark. But suddenly it's not so funny when he expects me to marry him. "What is the next phase of the campaign, pray tell?"

"Why, he lays siege to your castle's defenses, of course."

"Ah, this is where I pour boiling oil on him."

Her mother fixed her with agate eyes. "This is where you surrender, Mistress Impertinence."

In a pig's eye! "I will go on condition that Charlotte and Charles's brood and Susan and William's children are included, and are allowed to stay up to watch the fireworks to welcome in the New Year." *There is safety in numbers.*

"His Grace assured me that all the Gordons were invited. You'll have to ask Charlotte and Susan if their offspring have permission to stay up until midnight."

Georgina was off in a flash. *I've always been able to talk my sisters into anything, and today will be no exception.*

When they arrived at Woburn Abbey in the early evening of the next day, Georgina was delighted that they were not the only ones invited to the celebration.

"Henry, Beth, I had no idea you would be here," Georgina cried.

Lord Holland kissed her cheek. "Your radiance will outshine the fireworks." He looked at the children who spilled from three coaches. "The Gordon ladies are certainly prolific breeders."

"Isn't Charlotte due any day?" Beth asked. "The fireworks might bring on labor, and she'll give birth at Woburn Abbey."

"Not a chance! Who else is invited?" Georgina asked.

"Prinny and Lauderdale. We were making a race out of it, and when our carriage passed theirs, George shook his stick at me."

"Good God," Georgina exclaimed. "I hope he keeps his stick away from me, especially if it's the one with the big knob."

"You are so wicked," Beth said, laughing.

Mary slipped her hand into Georgina's and her aunt introduced her to Lady Holland. "This is Mary, Mary, most contrary. I'm presently giving her lessons in how to be wicked."

"You have the perfect teacher, my dear," Beth declared. "Since the weather turned so mild, we are dining al fresco tonight. The buffet tables are set out on the terrace overlooking the west lawn. It's so pretty; all the trees are lit with Chinese lanterns."

"Let's go and have a look," Mary urged.

When the pair reached the west lawn, they encountered young Francis and William Russell, who were helping Mr. Burke light the candles inside the lanterns.

Damnation, I forgot that John and his family might be here.

"I remember you," Mary said. "You are the old man's sons."

"Old man?" William puzzled.

"That's what my aunt Georgy calls your father."

"Ah, yes I remember." He looked at Georgina and laughed. "That day at the river, you shouted, '*Go to the devil, Old Man.*' "

While Georgina tried not to look embarrassed, Mary asked eagerly, "Is your brother Johnny here?"

"Not yet. He's been to Tavistock with Father, but we expect him to return tonight. It'll be a shame if he misses the fireworks."

Georgina went still. *Dear God, John will be here tonight. That's two Russells I must try to avoid.* She looked up and saw her mother approaching, holding the arm of the duke.

"Welcome to Woburn, my dear Lady Georgina. I am delighted that you accepted my invitation." He glanced down at her hands, saw that she was wearing his ring on her right hand, and took it to his lips. "I see my gift was acceptable."

"Mmm, very pretty," she said lightly. "You must excuse me, Your Grace, while I take Mary back to her mother."

"I will do that, Georgina." The duchess took a firm hold of her granddaughter's hand and led her away. Over her shoulder she said, "I shall leave you in the capable hands of your host."

Mr. Burke and John's sons had moved off to light

the rest of the lanterns, and Bedford slipped his arm around Georgina. "Happy New Year, vixen."

She touched one of the paper lanterns. "I had no idea it was Chinese New Year. What is it? The year of the *pig*?" She removed his arm. "Or perhaps they call it the year of the *boar*?"

"You are a wicked tease. Is that to pay me back for calling you vixen?"

"No, Your Grace. I haven't gotten around to that yet. But when I do, you won't be left in any doubt." She saw the Prince of Wales and Lauderdale approaching. "Here comes your fat friend," she murmured outrageously.

"Never let him hear you," Francis warned. "Even I wouldn't dare refer to his girth."

"I am relieved to know there is something you wouldn't dare."

"Your Highness, thank you for coming. The celebration wouldn't be the same without you," the duke said with deep sincerity.

By engaging Prinny and Lauderdale in amusing conversation, Georgina ensured that she and Francis were not alone for the next two hours. When the fireworks began, Georgina excused herself. "I promised to watch the display with my niece and nephew. I cannot break my word to them."

She found Mary and Charles and they sat down on the terrace steps to watch the illuminations. It wasn't long before Johnny Russell joined them.

"Lady Georgina, I'm so happy to find you at Woburn."

Her breathing became uneven. *I wonder if your father is watching us?* "Thank you, Johnny. Did you enjoy your trip to Tavistock?"

"Oh, yes. I had the best Christmas ever."

Johnny and Charles renewed their friendship and, refusing to be ignored, Mary joined in. While they were occupied, Georgina cast surreptitious glances about the crowd of guests gathered on the wide terrace. Suddenly, she drew in a swift breath. The tall, dark figure standing alone, his back leaning against the wall, was John Russell. She felt as if a skyrocket had exploded and showered her with stars.

Suddenly, she found the Duke of Bedford at her side and she stood up so he wouldn't sit down beside her. He carried a fox fur wrap and, moving behind her, draped it about her shoulders.

"My duty as host is to keep you warm," he murmured in her ear.

"You are too kind." *And much too close.* Brilliant blue, red, and green balls shot into the air, followed by a loud explosion. Georgina gasped, pretending to be startled, and stepped back onto the duke's foot with the high heel of her boot. She turned around to apologize. "Forgive me, Francis." Her spirits sank as she saw that John Russell was no longer there.

At the finale, the sky lit up with a brilliant display and everyone began to shout and cheer. Francis swept Georgina into his arms and kissed her soundly. "Happy New Year, my love!"

Suddenly, John Russell was beside her. Their eyes met for a brief moment. "Come on, Johnny. You've seen the dawn of the New Year—it's time for bed."

"Happy New Year, Father." He looked at Georgina and his uncle Francis with a frown between his eyes, and then moved toward the house with his father. "Are they going to get married?"

"I don't know," John said quietly. "I don't want to know."

Georgina's mother and sisters gathered around her, wishing everyone a happy new year, and at the same time the Prince of Wales and Lord Lauderdale clapped Francis on the back and proposed that they drink a toast to the year that had just dawned.

When everyone held a glass of champagne, Francis proposed something dear to Prinny's heart. "I declare this a good year for a Regency."

Prinny preened, and Lauderdale said, "I'll drink to that."

"You'll drink to anything," Georgina teased.

Lauderdale winked at her and, in his thickest Scots' brogue, led the guests in singing "Auld Lang Syne."

When their glasses were drained, she excused herself on the pretext of helping put her sisters' children to bed.

"They have nursemaids for that," Francis protested.

"Yes, but I want to make sure Charlotte gets to bed too."

Mary, who had been avidly listening to their conversation, said, "Mother is going to have another baby—I hope it's a girl."

Francis glanced down. "I'm sure she hopes for a son."

"You're the old man's brother—what do you know about it?"

Georgina hid her amusement. "You'll have to forgive her, Your Grace. I have been giving her wicked lessons."

He squeezed Georgina's hand. "Go and put the chit to bed, then come back and give me wicked lessons."

When Georgina returned she stayed close to either her brother, or her friends Henry and Beth. It was four in the morning before the party broke up and everyone retired.

Francis, who had impatiently bided his time, took her elbow. "As your host I claim the privilege of escorting you to your chamber." He took her the long way around, and the moment they were alone, he stopped walking and took her hands.

"So elusive, but I fully intend to have you for my duchess. Georgina, you know I'm in love with you."

"Francis, I don't want to hurt you, but my answer is still no."

"Why the devil is it *no*?" he demanded.

"Because I'm not in love with you." She pulled her hands from his, removed the ring he had given her, and gave it back to him. "Good night, Your Grace."

Breakfast was served at eleven the next morning, and afterward the Duke of Bedford asked the Duchess of Gordon if he could have a private word with her.

Jane's heart began to hammer with anticipation. "Your Grace, it would please me above all things. I have enjoyed my stay at Woburn, brief though it has been. We must do this more often."

"Lady Gordon . . . Jane . . . my feelings for your daughter run deep. I would like to recruit you as an advocate, if you are willing."

"Your Grace . . . Francis . . . you could not possibly find a greater advocate than myself. Our interests are one and the same."

"When we return to London, your daughter and I will meet at myriad social events where I will openly court her. But what I need is time, some *private* time, where I am free to woo Lady Georgina and we can get to know each other more intimately. I cannot invite her to Woburn without her family, so I ask your help in arranging a rendezvous in a romantic setting where we can find a little solitude and further our relationship without the world looking on."

"I will give it my full attention, Francis, and I shall be in touch with you when all the arrangements are in place."

"Lady Georgina is lucky indeed to have a mother who has her best interests at heart. Your daughter is rather elusive, which is an admirable quality in a maiden. I'd prefer it if you didn't mention our plans to her. I would like it to be a surprise."

"My dear Francis, you are a romantic at heart," she said coyly. "You may leave it all to me."

Jane could taste victory. She was convinced that if she arranged a private rendezvous for the couple, Francis Russell would propose marriage. There was no doubt in her mind that the duke had chosen Georgina to become the Duchess of Bedford.

The moment she returned to London, she told her closest friends, in the strictest of confidence of course, that Francis Russell had given her daughter a ring. She told them that the duke was such a private man that he wished to keep the engagement a secret until they made a formal announcement in the press.

Within hours, the Duchess of Devonshire heard the devastating news and rushed to her friend Lady Melbourne. Both women were outraged. The duchess had lost to her greatest rival the prospect of a ducal son-in-law. It was also a bitter pill for Lizzie Melbourne to swallow, that the man who had been her lover had succumbed to the charms of a young virgin who was thirty years her junior.

By the middle of January, Georgina had attended four balls where she had had no dance partners other than Francis Russell, Prince Edward, and Lord Holland. She thought that George Howard, heir to the Earldom of Carlisle, was about to ask her to dance, but he walked past her and partnered her friend Dorothy Cavendish instead. This was the umpteenth ball where she felt like a wallflower, and when she mentioned it to her friend Henry he explained it to her.

"The Duke of Bedford has made it plain to the young nobles that if they partner you, they're encroaching on his private preserve."

Georgina was furious. "His arrogance is beyond the pale! It is barefaced audacity. He has no claim on me whatsoever! How you can be a close friend to such a man is beyond my understanding."

"Well, actually, it is John who is my close friend. Francis and I are friendly acquaintances who move in the same circles. Georgy, if he hasn't asked you to marry him, I'm sure he will."

"But I don't want to marry him."

"Are you sure, my dear? There has not been a young Duchess of Bedford for three decades. You could not achieve a greater match in all of England or Scotland."

"I am aware that Bedford is England's premier duke, and Woburn Abbey is the most magnificent holding in the country, but titles and wealth do not guarantee happiness."

"Perhaps you are too young to realize it, but nothing guarantees happiness, Georgy," he said gently.

"Yes, I *am* young, and I don't see why I have to

rush into marriage in my first Season." *Your wife, Beth, did that and then she fell in love with you and ended up in a messy divorce.*

"My best advice is to trust your own instincts."

"Thank you, Henry. You are very kind to listen to me."

She agreed to take supper with Francis, then to spite him, granted Prince Edward's request to escort her. The two friends bristled and made cutting remarks to each other. *This is a cockfight, and I caused it.* She vowed not to do it again.

On the carriage ride home in the early hours of the morning, she told her mother, "I'm weary of balls. In London you meet the same people over and over until you want to scream or die of boredom. I understand why Father spends his time in Scotland."

"You need a little change. It's Susan's birthday on February 2. Why don't you visit Kimbolton Castle? There was such a crush of people there over Christmas, you never got to visit with your sister."

It would be a wonderful chance to escape from London. "Yes, Mother, I would enjoy that. We are going to have an early spring; the snowdrops and crocuses should be in bloom by then."

"I don't think I'll come. I don't find London society boring. I find it stimulating. Dear Henry Dundas has invited me to the theater on Friday. But you sound like you need a change."

Aha, that's why you want me out of the house. "Let's go shopping tomorrow. I want to get Susan something special for her birthday. You'll have to lend me some money."

"We shall have the bills for Susan's birthday presents sent to the Duke of Gordon. After all, he *is* her father."

Jane went directly to her writing desk the moment Georgina went upstairs to bed. For the second time in a week she wrote a letter to Susan, and then penned a separate letter to her son-in-law, William Montagu, Duke of Manchester.

* * *

"My compliments on your driving, Toby. You got me to Kimbolton in record time."

The young coachman grinned. "That's because the Duchess of Gordon wasn't on board, Lady Georgina. Would you like me to carry your luggage inside?"

"No, you take care of the horses. You can leave the large box in the stables, and I'll get one of the Manchester footmen to come for my luggage and the other two boxes." It was the first day of February, and she wanted to give Susan her present early. The gifts from her mother and brother could be opened tomorrow on her actual birthday.

Susan, waiting for her at the front door, embraced her warmly. "It's lovely to have you alone . . . I mean without Mother."

"I know what you mean. Though I love her dearly, I needed a breather away from her. She is constantly pushing me to make a commitment to the Duke of Bloody Bedford, and throws a fit if I as much as look at any other man."

Susan changed the subject. "You are just in time for lunch."

"Good. After I unpack, why don't we go for a ride? We could take young Jane with us. The woods must be teeming with wildflowers. I love it when spring comes early. The birds are already building their nests."

"That sounds marvelous. I'll leave howling baby George with his nursemaid. This outing will be strictly for us ladies."

After lunch the two sisters changed into their riding dresses, then made their way to the stables, with seven-year-old Jane chattering excitedly.

"Happy Birthday, Susan! I want you to open my present today."

The wooden crate held a red leather saddle decorated with silver bells. "Georgina! It's absolutely beautiful. Now I know why you wanted us to go riding."

When the stablemen had readied their mounts,

Georgina tucked her drawing materials into her saddlebags, and the two sisters, with Jane riding between them, rode toward Kimbolton's woods.

"I want some jingling bells, Mama."

"Ask your father," Georgina said, laughing. "He is Mr. Moneybags."

They came to a small glade in the woods that was carpeted with bluebells. The heady scent and brilliant color were irresistible, and the three dismounted. Jane bent to pick some, and her hands became sticky with sap from their soft stems.

"Go and wash your hands in the stream," her mother instructed.

"Jane, I'd like to sketch you sitting amid the bluebells," Georgina said. "When we get back, I'll paint in the colors."

The three spent a happy hour, talking and laughing, while Georgina did a sketch of her niece, then one of Jane and Susan together. Jane was delighted that her aunt had drawn her as a flower fairy with delicate wings, and in one corner was a baby rabbit peeping from under a burdock leaf.

The sketch of mother and daughter was more serious and showed the marked family resemblance.

That night Georgina asked to give two-year-old George his bath.

"Georgy, you will make a far more devoted mother than I will ever be," Susan said.

"I truly envy you your children, Susan."

"I just found out I'm having another," her sister confided. "I enjoy making them, but carrying them for nine months is a tedious business. William soon loses interest when I start to expand."

Georgina sighed with sympathy. "That's why I'm in no hurry for a husband. I'd rather wait until I find one who truly loves me."

"No point in waiting, Georgy. All males have roving eyes . . . and hands . . . and cocks!" she declared.

"Cynical at only twenty-six," Georgina teased.

"Twenty-seven tomorrow."

* * *

Around ten o'clock that night, Georgina decided to explore the atmospheric chambers where Katherine of Aragon had spent the last months of her life.

At the foot of the gallery staircase that led up to Queen Katherine's private chapel was a large oaken chest in which she had kept her clothes and jewels.

Georgina went down on her knees and traced her finger over the royal cipher, made up of Katherine's initials that decorated the lid. "Your unhappiness still lingers. The very air up here is melancholy," she murmured with a shiver. "You put your faith and your life in your husband's hands, and he betrayed you for another woman."

Georgina sat back on her heels and thought about Anne Boleyn. *Anne didn't love Henry. She kept him at arm's length for more than seven long years. It was her family that pressured her into giving in to him. I surely know what that feels like.* She laid her hand on the lid as if it were a Bible. "I swear I shall never give in to the Duke of Bedford," she whispered passionately.

The next day Georgina and Jane made special plans for Susan's birthday dinner. They made arrangements with the head cook for all her favorite dishes. They ordered a cake with twenty-seven candles, they gathered early spring flowers to decorate the table, and planned the special music that Kimbolton's musicians would play throughout the meal. They carried all her gifts into the formal dining room and piled them on a refectory table.

William Montagu returned from hunting and went upstairs to bathe and change. Georgina went to her chamber and put on one of her new gowns, a primrose silk embroidered with white rosebuds. One of her sister's tiring women helped her with her coiffeur and threaded loops of white satin ribbon through her dark curls. She chose pearl earrings to complement the outfit, picked up her fan, and hurried downstairs.

"At last!" William declared in his usual hearty manner.

"We have a lovely surprise for you," Susan announced.

Georgina stopped dead on the bottom stair, her happiness melting away like snow in summer. Standing between the Duke and Duchess of Manchester was the Duke of Bedford.

Chapter 20

Georgina put on a false face and assumed an air of politeness that was at odds with the way she felt inside. "This *is* a surprise. I didn't know you had invited a guest to dinner."

"Woburn and Kimbolton are so close, we are practically neighbors," William said in a bluff voice.

Francis Russell offered Georgina his arm. "Once more unto the breach . . ."

"I had no idea you were a military man." It was a stinging rejoinder. She knew damn well he had never served.

"*Militat omnis amans* . . . every lover is a soldier."

She took his arm and looked up at him. "Isn't that Ovid?"

"It is, my dear. I am surprised, yet utterly delighted, that you are familiar with his frankly sensual writing."

Francis helped her into a seat opposite Susan. Georgina stared pointedly into her sister's eyes as if to say, "What the bloody hellfire are you trying to do to me?"

Susan pretended not to notice her discomfort.

During dinner, the conversation, carried on mainly between the two dukes, ranged from hunting to rowing. William Montagu was a champion oarsman with a strong, athletic build, and Georgina couldn't help but compare their physiques. *Both men are devastatingly attractive to women—I can understand William's appeal, but I'll be damned if I know what the ladies find irresistible in Francis. Beyond his title and his immense wealth, of course.*

Georgina pointedly ignored her sister, and conversed mainly with seven-year-old Jane, who had been permitted to attend the birthday dinner only because she had helped plan it.

At last it was time for the cake to be rolled in on a cart, and Georgina stood up and lit the candles.

"You must make a wish, Mama. And if you blow out all the candles, it will come true."

Susan stood up and smiled uncertainly. "Oh, I have no idea what I should wish for."

Fidelity from your husband comes to mind! Georgina glanced at Francis. "I know what I would wish for."

"Your wish is my command, dearest lady," he said with a leer.

Then begone! She waved her fork as if it were a magic wand. Then she touched her napkin to her lips. She had almost said it out loud.

Jane wolfed down her cake. "Now it's time to open your gifts." She shot up from the table and began to carry the presents over from the refectory table and place them at her mother's feet.

The first one Susan opened was a lap robe in Black Watch tartan and all knew it was from her mother before she read the card.

Her brother, George, had sent her a pair of riding boots he'd had made especially for her by Hobey, because he knew that she rode almost every day of her life.

Jane handed her a flat package. "Oh, this is the sketch Georgy made of us in the bluebells. You've painted it for me. Thank you. I will treasure it."

When she opened her daughter's small present, it was a pair of warm slippers Jane had knitted herself. "Grandmother taught you to knit, and you do it well, my dear. Thank you so much."

"Do you really like them?" Jane asked anxiously.

"They are perfect. I shall put them on this minute."

Georgina wanted to hug her sister. *I almost forgive you for inviting Francis Russell. Almost.*

Susan opened her husband's present, and when she saw the ruby bracelet, she went still. "Whatever did I do to deserve this?"

Oh Lord, she thinks he gave it to her because his conscience is pricking him . . . and I wager she's right.

"Being a duchess has its rewards," William said gallantly.

Georgina wondered if that remark was aimed at her.

Finally, Susan opened the last present, which was from the Duke of Bedford. It was an antique silver goblet with blue lapis lazuli decorating its foot. "Oh, it's beautiful, Francis. Thank you so much. I shall christen it this moment." She signaled a footman, who filled the goblet with champagne. He filled Georgina's glass with the sparkling wine and served the gentlemen brandy. "Shall we repair to the drawing room?" Susan smiled at her daughter. "Time for bed, Jane. Thank you for helping make my birthday dinner so enjoyable."

As Georgina watched her young niece leave, she felt she was losing her only ally present tonight. She took a deep breath and allowed Francis to escort her from the dining room. The disturbing suspicion that this whole thing was a conspiracy had been growing throughout dinner. She quickened her steps and caught up with Susan. "Did Mother pressure you into inviting him?" she demanded, sotto voce.

"It was William who invited him," Susan murmured, relieving herself of all responsibility.

It was around ten o'clock, and Georgina wondered how she would get through the next two hours until midnight when she could retire to bed without giving offense. *I must make an effort to be polite. I don't want to ruin Susan's birthday by sulking.*

The men spoke of a race meet they would be attending at Newmarket at the end of the month, and that led to a discussion of the Prince of Wales. Both

William and Francis were Whigs and in favor of a Regency.

Georgina remarked, "I'm surprised you married a lady from such a staunch Tory family as ours, William. I would think a match between a Whig and a Tory would be like mixing oil and water." Of course she was alluding to the mismatch of herself and Francis.

"Susan has no interest in politics," William replied.

"Politics is one of my consuming passions," Georgina declared. "I hope Pitt regains his prime ministership soon." She threw down the gauntlet, hoping for an argument, but no one picked it up.

Next she brought up the contrasts between the English and the Scots, cataloguing their differences in a transparent attempt to distance herself from the English Duke of Bedford.

"I find that opposites have a fatal, irresistible attraction," Francis confessed.

Georgina was tempted to drop the name of one of his mistresses, but realized she was completely indifferent to his women. *I must stop this charade. Since Francis Russell becomes more insistent each time I refuse him, I will have to confront Mother and demand that she stop her matchmaking. I warrant it will mean a terrible row, but I have to make her understand I will never wed Bedford.*

Georgina yawned. "It's been a lovely evening, but I cannot keep my eyes open. I'm off to bed. Good night, all."

Susan drained her goblet "I'm off too. Good night, gentlemen."

The sisters climbed the stairs together. "I know you planned all this with Mother. It was her idea that I come to Kimbolton for your birthday," Georgina accused.

"We want only what's best for you, Georgy. It's quite evident Francis is mad about you."

"I'm mad too. Blazing mad. Don't ever do this to me again!"

"I must go and check on the children. Good night."

Georgina made her way to the guest wing, relieved that at last she had escaped and was finally alone. Her anger toward her sister abated a little. *What Susan said is true. My family does want what is best for me, but they put social position and wealth at the top of the list. They think it my duty to wed England's premier nobleman. They don't realize how unhappy I would be.*

Georgina removed her gown and hung it up in the wardrobe. She kicked off her satin shoes and sat down on the bed. Then she took off her garters and her stockings. In her shift she walked over to the washstand and poured water from the jug. She glanced in the mirror and raised her hand to remove the loops of ribbon from her hair when she heard the door open.

Thinking it was one of Susan's maids, she turned. And then she gasped. "What the devil are you doing?"

Francis Russell winked at her. "What do you think I'm doing?" He locked the door, slipped the key into his pocket, and set the bottle of champagne he was carrying on her dressing table.

"Leave my room this instant!"

"Don't pretend to be angry, puss. You knew I'd come."

"I knew no such thing." Her voice rose in alarm. "Don't come any closer! I want you to leave immediately."

He removed his coat, threw it on a chair, unfastened his neckcloth, and closed the distance between them. "This intimate liaison was arranged a week ago. I know this is all new to you, but there's no need to be afraid." He reached up, plucked the ribbon from her hair, and watched it fall about her shoulders.

Georgina pulled away until her back was against the washstand. She couldn't believe this was happening. Her heart began to hammer and her temper began to rise. "Surely you don't expect me to join the ranks of Marianna Palmer and your other mistresses!"

"Of course not—you will be my wife."

"Your Grace, if you do not leave instantly, I will scream for my brother-in-law."

"Who do you think gave me your key? Scream away, vixen. The walls of this castle are thick. None will hear you."

Georgina was stunned. "William gave you the key?" *Oh, God, William saw me at the brothel in Pall Mall where Francis Rotten Russell lured me before Christmas. He thinks we are intimate.*

Francis slipped his arms about her waist and pulled her toward him. "You need to be wooed to a giving mood, my love." He slipped her petticoat strap from her shoulder and placed his lips against the satin skin. "I think this calls for a private lesson in what's known as foreplay."

She pushed him away. Now she was not only angry, but also a little bit afraid. "Are you insane, Bedford? I have no intention of marrying you. I've told you, I don't love you. Hellfire, I don't even *like* you!"

He laughed. "You will be begging for marriage before I'm done with you, my love." He took hold of her petticoat, and when Georgina pulled away, the material ripped. He tore the remnants of the flimsy white material from her body and tossed them aside.

Georgina screamed at the top of her lungs. She wore only a small busk that concealed her breasts, and tried frantically to cover the lower part of her body that was now completely nude. She screamed again, and kicked out at him.

He lunged at her, and his arms went about her like a vice. With deft fingers he unfastened her busk and rendered her naked.

She threw back her head and screamed again as he calmly undressed.

It slowly dawned on her that no one was going to come to her rescue. This rendezvous had all been prearranged, with the full approval of her mother and the Duke of Manchester. Even her sister was complicit in the plan.

When he picked her up and carried her against his naked body to the bed in spite of her wild struggles, she realized just how strong he was. *He's going to ravish me . . . He's going to have his way with me. My denial makes him only more rampant!* Her eyes flooded with tears, and she was about to beg him to stop. But when he dropped her on the bed and hovered above her, something inside her snapped. He came down on top of her, and when his erection slid against her mons, Georgina's fear was blotted out by her raging fury. "You bastard!" She brought up her knees, and when he drew back she kicked him in the groin.

He yelped in pain and said between clenched teeth, "If you were a man, I'd kill you!"

"If you were a *half* a man, I'd be afraid!"

She was off the bed in a flash. She placed her hands on his shoulders, dug in her nails, and brought up her knee to jab him in his balls and his belly. Bedford curled over in agony; then he fell to the carpet and rolled about. "Cockteasing bitch! You've asked for it, and now you're going to get it!"

Georgina realized she was locked in with him, and he was dangerous. Like a wounded animal, he was mad with pain and rage and lust. She watched in horror as he rolled to his knees and began to get up. Her thoughts flashed about, looking for a way to escape. Her eyes caught sight of the bottle of champagne, and she made a dash toward it. She picked it up, raised it high, and hit him. She managed only a glancing blow to his temple, but the Duke of Bedford dropped like a stone.

She went down on her knees, frantically searching through his pockets until her fingers closed on the key. She got up, ran to the door, and unlocked it. A sob of relief broke from her throat. She was about to bolt from the chamber when she realized she was naked. She ran back to the bed, wrapped the eiderdown about her, slipped on her shoes, and fled.

She ran to the servants' wing and shouted, "Toby!

Toby! I need help! Where are you?" She ran to the end of the hall before a door opened and Toby came out, holding a candle.

"Whatever is the matter, my lady?"

She pushed him back in his room. "Get dressed, we're leaving."

"You want to leave now? In the middle of the night?"

"Yes . . . Now . . . This minute." None of the servants had answered her distress call, and she knew they'd been given their orders.

Toby quickly donned his clothes, fastened his boots, and put on his heavy driving coat. "Ye'll freeze out there, my lady."

She tore a blanket from his bed and thrust it into his arms. "Hurry, Toby. You're the only one I can trust to help me."

In the darkness, they made their way to the stables. A stable boy roused and lit a lantern. He gaped at the Duchess of Manchester's sister wrapped in an eiderdown. "Is there a fire?"

"Help Toby harness our carriage horses. We have to leave." She climbed into the coach, and as she leaned back against the squabs, she became aware of the soreness of her breasts and thighs and realized the brutal struggle had left her bruised.

When the horses were harnessed, Toby came to the coach door.

"Take me to Scotland."

"I daren't drive the carriage to Scotland, Lady Georgina. I'd lose my job. The duchess expects her coach and horses back tomorrow. I'd best take you home to London."

"No! I'm not going home!" *The last person on earth I want to see is Mother. We'd kill each other!* She searched her mind desperately for some place she could go.

"Take me to my sister Louisa. She lives at Brome Hall in Suffolk. You're not afraid to drive to the next county are you?"

The taunt worked. "I'll take ye to Brome Hall, my lady."

As the carriage rolled away from the castle and began to pick up speed, Georgina lifted her feet onto the seat and pulled the blanket over herself. In the darkness she relived the past hour. When she recalled how his naked body had slid against hers, her gorge rose. *The thought of him makes me want to spew!* She wiped a tear from her cheek, and her hand brushed against her ear. She realized she was still wearing earrings. *Pearls are for tears.* The words of the old adage strengthened her resolve. *I'll be damned if I'll shed one more tear over the lecherous swine.*

As dawn began to lighten the sky, Toby stopped the carriage at a crossroads, unsure of which way to drive.

Georgina opened the door and read the signpost. "Take the road that points to the village of Eye. Someone there will tell you how to get to Brome Hall. It's on the River Dove."

It was another hour before the coach pulled into the driveway of the hall. Georgina stretched and rubbed a cramp from her leg when the horses stopped. In the courtyard and stable area were several servants. Toby climbed down and opened the door.

"Explain to the grooms that these animals belong to the Duchess of Gordon. Make sure that they get fed and rubbed down."

A liveried house steward came down the steps, and when he looked inside the coach, his eyes widened at the sight of a female wrapped in an eiderdown. "Can I help you, madam?"

"Is Marquis Cornwallis still in France?"

The steward looked horrified. "I'm afraid so, madam."

"Good! Go and tell Lady Brome that her sister Georgina has arrived. You may kindly bring me one of her cloaks."

In a few minutes, Louisa came hurrying down the front steps, and the steward followed her with a velvet cloak over his arm.

"Good heavens, Georgy, was the journey so cold that you needed to wrap yourself in an eiderdown?"

"I'm naked under this, and I have no clothes to put on."

Louisa, used to Georgina's eccentricities, took the cloak from her steward and sent him back into the hall. She watched as her sister unwound the bedcover from her body. "Your breasts are bruised . . . Whatever have you done to yourself?"

Georgina wrapped herself in the cloak and stepped from the carriage. "Toby will need a place to sleep tonight. We've driven all the way from Kimbolton. The first thing I need is a bath."

"Were you set upon on the road?" Louisa asked anxiously.

"I was set upon all right. But by a bloody duke of the realm, not a highwayman."

Louisa took Georgina up to her own bedchamber, then asked the housekeeper to order a bath be made ready. While her sister went to the bathing room, Louisa opened her wardrobe and took out one of her prettiest afternoon dresses. She laid it on the bed and added undergarments, stockings, and garters.

Georgina finally finished her bath and returned. "I almost scrubbed my skin off until I realized it was a pointless endeavor." She put on the petticoat Louisa had laid out, then drew on the stockings and garters.

"Tell me what happened." Louisa's voice was hushed.

"At Mother's suggestion I went to Kimbolton to celebrate Susan's birthday. Little did I know it was a bloody conspiracy to throw me into the arms of Francis Russell!"

Louisa sat down on the bed, her eyes wide with apprehension.

"I cannot believe how naive I was. I was unpleasantly surprised when the duke showed up for Susan's birthday dinner. When I accused Susan, she blamed William. I got through the evening and retired around midnight. That's when I got the shock of my life. Bedford came into my room and locked the door with a key he said William had provided."

"The duke ravished you!" Louisa whispered.

"He assaulted me and came bloody close to ravishing me. How did you guess?"

Louisa's face went chalky white. "He . . . he . . . forced me."

"He *what*?" Georgina demanded.

"Francis Russell forced himself on me. I . . . I didn't fight him. I thought he was going to marry me."

"Why didn't you tell me?"

"I was too ashamed. I didn't want anyone to know. The swine lost interest immediately, and my reputation would have been ruined forever if I had said anything."

"Where did this happen?" Georgina was stricken.

"It happened at Susan and William's . . . not at Kimbolton . . . at their London house in Whitehall. Mother recruited Manchester in her matchmaking scheme. I don't like William Montagu." Her voice broke; she covered her face with her hands and began to sob.

Georgina went down on her knees and gathered her sister into her arms. "Louisa, darling, I'm so sorry. Cry . . . get it all out." She cradled her sister until all her sobs had subsided.

Louisa dabbed at her eyes. "How did you get away from him?"

"I hit the salacious swine with a bottle of champagne. I was amazed when it knocked him unconscious."

"Do you think you might have killed him?" Louisa whispered.

"No such bloody luck!" Georgina managed to put a weak smile on her sister's face.

"I've missed you so much, Georgy."

"Well, I'm staying for a while. Toby can take the coach back to London tomorrow. If I confronted Mother right now, my temper would explode like a volcano."

"I should have said something. If Mother had known what happened to me, she would never have pushed you into his arms."

"No guilt, Louisa. I suspect Mother would sacrifice anything to make me the Duchess of Bedford."

Georgina donned the lovely lavender silk afternoon dress Louisa had laid out for her, and the pair eventually went downstairs.

Charles Cornwallis came from the library where he had been doing his accounts. "Lady Georgina, I am delighted you have come to visit us." His cheeks flushed pink. "Louisa has missed you."

"Thank you so much, Charles. Brome Hall is very welcoming."

"By Jove, your tastes are similar. I do believe Louisa has a gown just like the one you are wearing."

Louisa rolled her eyes at her sister. "I believe you are right, Charles. How very observant you are."

Chapter 21

At Woburn, Francis Russell, his hand pressed into the side of his belly, dragged himself across the library and sank down in the leather wing chair behind his mahogany desk.

Mr. Burke, used to the duke arriving at all hours and in all states of disarray, came to the library door. "Is there anything you'd like, Your Grace?"

Francis pointed to the brandy on a side table.

Mr. Burke placed the decanter and a glass on the desk. "Anything more, Your Grace?"

The duke pointed to the door. Burke bowed and withdrew.

Francis poured himself a full glass of brandy and drank it down quickly. After a few minutes, he could no longer feel the throbbing tenderness in his groin, but the pain from the wound to his pride was still raw and unendurable. He muttered a filthy oath and lifted the decanter to his lips.

No woman had ever denied his advances before. It was beyond his comprehension that a female could resist him, especially one for whom he lusted and had singled out for special attention. His mind totally rejected the idea that Georgina Gordon did not want him. "She refused to become my mistress because she feared I would not marry her if she did," he rationalized. "She flung Marianna's name at me. The other women in my life are the real obstacles she cannot tolerate. Georgina is shrewd beyond her years, and believes I will never make her the Duchess of Bedford once she gives herself to me." The thought mollified him and assuaged his tattered pride. He took another gulp of brandy, and as the comforting warmth spread through his body, he remembered regaining consciousness in her bedchamber and finding her gone. He knew that they had had a violent struggle—he had the wounds to prove it. Rather than face accusations from the Duke of Manchester, he had left Kimbolton before dawn.

"God knows what tale she will tell her sister. I had better inform William Montagu of my intentions."

Francis took a sheet of paper embossed with his ducal crest from the desk drawer, dipped his pen in the inkwell, and wrote:

My dear William:

I thank you for your warm hospitality at Kimbolton.

It is my duty to inform you that my intentions toward your sister-in-law are completely honorable. I wish to confide that I asked Lady Georgina to become my wife. Though she vowed her love for me, she refused to accept my proposal because of my relationship with Mrs. Palmer. I fully intend to remove the obstacle that prevents Lady Georgina from agreeing to marry me, and assure you that the liaison is over.

I would like you to give her my pledge that when I return to London, I will strictly follow correct protocol. I will make a formal call upon the Duchess of Gordon and, with Georgina's permission, declare our engagement publicly.

Francis Russell, Duke of Bedford

He folded the letter, addressed the envelope, and secured it with sealing wax. After he consumed more brandy, he took a book from his desk drawer. It was a private journal where he recorded his sexual encounters in graphic detail. The combination of the prurient words and the brandy blurred his perception of reality and fantasy. As he perused the pages, it restored his manhood, and bolstered his belief in his superior virility. He dipped his pen and scrawled *Georgina* across the top of a new page. Then he embarked on a wild flight of imagination, describing how the young beauty had fallen deeply in love with him due to his unmatched seductive powers. In salacious detail he wrote of how he had aroused her passion and made her beg to be fucked.

Francis put down his pen, his pride restored. As a feeling of exaggerated omnipotence filled his brain, he laid his head down on his arms and fell asleep.

At Kimbolton, Susan left the servants' hall and ascended the stairs to apprise her husband of what she had just learned. She spied a buxom maid taking him a breakfast tray. "I'll take that," she said firmly, and noticed the look of disappointment on her face. *No doubt he's been bedding you every chance he gets.*

Montagu stretched his arms and sat up as Susan set the breakfast tray on a side table. "I heard the virginal screams last night, so I assume the relationship is well consummated."

"Bedford didn't sleep in his room, but Georgina's chamber is in shambles. When I could find no sign of either, I questioned the servants. It seems the lovers left before dawn."

"He most likely carried her off to Woburn to continue their tryst in private. Once the dirty deed was done, I warrant they couldn't keep their hands off each other. I remember how hot you were for me after the first time," he said with a leer.

"I'm still hot for you."

He heard her sultry laugh. "How hot? Come, let me feel."

Susan closed the distance between them, avid for his touch.

His hand went beneath her skirts and slid up between

her legs. "Mmm, temptingly hot, and already wet at the thought of me." He removed his fingers and licked them.

She held her breath as she watched his hands slide the bedcovers down his well-muscled body to reveal his upthrust cock.

"Too bad you're dressed," he teased.

"I can soon disrobe." She kicked off her shoes, already aching with anticipation.

His hand squeezed her buttock. "No need for that. I know you can't wait. Just hoist your skirts and bestride me."

Eagerly, Susan lifted her petticoats and straddled his hips. When he pulled her down and thrust his erection up inside her, she cried out with pleasure.

William held absolutely motionless, relishing the fever heat.

She feared he would deliberately make her wait because he enjoyed being in control, but she was so aroused, she began to move up and down, riding him.

He partially withdrew, and clamped his hands about her hips to hold her still. "What do you want? Say it, Susan."

She bit her lip, trying not to beg, but she knew his will was stronger than hers. If she didn't say the things he liked, he was quite capable of leaving her wildly aroused but unsatisfied.

"Please, I want you to make love to me," she whispered.

"I can't hear you, Susan."

"Hurry, I need you to love me, William."

"You have to say it, Susan."

"Take me, William! I love the feel of your cock inside me. Please make me come." *You cruel, faithless bastard!*

He laughed, and surged up inside her. He was a powerful man, and he rolled her beneath him, thrusting his hard erection in and out like a ramrod.

* * *

Later that day, when a letter was delivered from the Duke of Bedford, Montagu read it and went in search of Susan.

"It seems Francis didn't sweep Georgina off to Woburn after all. By the sounds of this, the shrewd little cocktease held him at bay and didn't even let him fuck her."

"How do you know?"

"Apparently, she's refused to spread her legs for him until he gets rid of his mistress Marianna Palmer. Francis is so avid to bed Georgy, he's willing to offer her marriage. By refusing to let him dip his dick, Georgina has brought him to heel."

"If she isn't at Woburn, where the devil is she?"

"Obviously, she screamed in outrage at his randy demands, issued her ultimatum, and ran home to Mother."

Susan took the letter and read the last sentence aloud: "*I will make a formal call upon the Duchess of Gordon and, with Georgina's permission, announce our engagement publicly.* Oh, Mother will be over the moon! We certainly did our part to bring about this incomparable match. I hope Georgina appreciates it."

"I take it Georgina has decided to extend her stay at Kimbolton. Thank heavens she sent you back with the carriage, Toby. I cannot abide riding around London in a hackney. It is a most unsuitable mode of transportation for a duchess. I've been on tenterhooks for news. I can't wait to read her letter."

Toby looked at her expectant face and knew his words would wipe away her smile. "I have no letter, Your Grace."

"Georgina didn't write to me? How exceedingly thoughtless! She could have at least told me how she enjoyed the birthday celebration and how long she intends to stay at Kimbolton."

"Lady Georgina isn't at Kimbolton, Your Grace. She insisted that I drive her to Brome Hall, in Suffolk, to visit her sister."

"Why the devil would she leave Kimbolton?"

Toby was not about to divulge that Georgina had fled in the middle of the night, nor inform the duchess of his suspicions. She would not take kindly to a servant knowing anything of an intimate nature regarding her daughter.

I know only too well why she left! The stubborn, thankless girl has run off to Louisa to avoid the Duke of Bedford. After all the carefully laid plans for a private rendezvous, this is how she repays me! She dismissed Toby. "Give the horses a rubdown."

Jane was furious, not only with Georgina, but with Susan and Louisa as well. *Daughters are a curse! They are vexing, thankless creatures!* For the next two hours she slammed doors and reprimanded the servants for the slightest provocation. She canceled her plans for the evening because she could not face her friends. Instead, she went to bed early, nursing a headache.

The next morning, when she received a letter bearing the ducal crest of the Duke and Duchess of Manchester, she tore it open, and her mood began to lift as she read Susan's words.

Dearest Mother:

William and I were at a loss when we discovered that Georgina had left Kimbolton in the middle of the night, without so much as a thank-you for the rendezvous we arranged for her benefit. Yesterday, however, we received a letter from Francis Russell, thanking us for our hospitality and declaring his intentions.

Georgina will be most gratified to learn that her shrewd ploy has worked miraculously. I don't know how much the devious little minx has told you, but reading between the lines, it seems that when the Duke of Bedford proposed, she refused his amorous advances, gave him an ultimatum, and left with her virtue intact.

The duke is completely enamored, and so hungry to have her that he is willing to meet all her demands, and vows to end his affair with his mistress Marianna Palmer. Francis informs us that when he returns to London, he intends to make a formal call upon you in Pall Mall and then announce their engagement publicly.

Congratulations, Mother. Yet another daughter is about to attain the rank of duchess.

Your loving daughter,
Susan, Duchess of Manchester

Jane sat down quickly, quite overcome with her achievement. Her lips curved into a satisfied smile as she reread the letter. *My clever little Georgy. Daughters are such a blessing!*

John Russell left the benches of the House of Commons in disgust. He turned when he heard Henry, Lord Holland, call his name. "Attendance today was shameful. You and I have been here every session this week, but where the hell are the other members?"

"It's mid-February and nothing has been done since we broke for Christmas. The members should have returned by now. Perhaps the early spring has enticed them to remain at their country estates."

John thought of his brother. Something was keeping him at Woburn, but John suspected it was visits to Kimbolton rather than spring that was attracting him. He expected Francis to return to London any day, announcing he'd asked Georgina Gordon to marry him. John dreaded the news. Contemplating such a match was anathema to him. He deliberately thrust the thought away and returned to his conversation with Henry.

"I believe the problem lies with Henry Addington. I warrant neither Whigs nor Tories want to serve under him."

"When Pitt was prime minister the benches were always filled."

"That's because the members of both parties respected him."

Henry sighed. "Perhaps in time they will accept Addington."

"Never! You are deluding yourself. There *is* a solution." He gave his friend a speculative look. "We could ask Addington for a private meeting, tell him bluntly how matters stand, and ask him to resign for the good of the country."

"Ask the prime minister of England to resign? That would take a great deal of courage."

John laughed. "I'll do the asking, if you will accompany me."

"I'll willingly act as your silent partner."

"Thank you, Henry. I knew I could count on you. I'll formally request a private meeting with him, and start work on a speech that will move the man to tears and persuade him to step down so that Pitt can be reinstated."

That night, when John began to make notes of what he would say to Addington, thoughts of Georgina stole to him and filled his senses. For the first time he admitted how much the vibrant young beauty attracted him. After the bleak years of his marriage, he secretly hungered for a vivacious companion who was filled with laughter and a passion for life. *The minute I was free, I should have gone to her and told her how I felt, instead of pushing her away.* He cursed himself for a fool. *Now it's too late. Francis will capture the prize!* Shame washed over him that he was jealous of his brother. He resolved to put an end to his yearning for what could never be. *Thou shalt not covet thy brother's wife.*

Francis Russell was in no hurry to leave Woburn. Because his towering pride would not allow Georgina Gordon to thwart him, he had made up his mind to have her at any cost. But the price was high. The thought of giving up Marianna Palmer filled him with frustration and made him feel impotent. Luckily, there was a cure close at hand. To restore his manhood, and prove his virility, he had turned to Molly Hill.

"Francis, you're early tonight. I haven't finished dinner."

"Stand up, Molly. I have a raging appetite that needs satisfying." His riding crop swept the dishes from the table.

She was used to servicing his sexual needs in odd places, whenever the desire came upon him. They often went for bruising gallops across his fields, where he would abruptly draw rein, pull her from the saddle, and mount her beneath a hedge on the hard ground. But lately his lust had increased alarmingly, and his demands were taking a toll on both of them. Last night's bed sport had begun well enough, but he had been unable to stay hard. For hours, she had tried to satisfy the duke's frenzied demands, using her fingers and her mouth to stimulate him, but nothing she did produced the results he desired.

Molly watched him open his breeches and saw his cock spring up, ready for action. "You are insatiable, Your Grace."

Francis bent her over the table and flung up her skirts. He thrust himself inside her and scythed in and out with a vengeance. Though he kept at it doggedly, his shaft became flaccid, and when he could not spend, he cursed savagely.

Molly had run a London brothel in her younger days. Nothing shocked her, and she knew all the tricks of the trade. "Francis, you need release. I will find a way to give it to you."

He grudgingly withdrew, and Molly rolled off the table. She went to a cabinet, measured a liberal amount of powdered dog's mercury into a glass, and filled it with brandy.

Within half an hour of consuming the potion, the duke's cock began to swell. Molly helped him disrobe and led him to her high bed. He climbed on and lay down, watching impatiently as she undressed. Her breasts were huge and bounced about like balloons. Her thighs were thick and firm with saddle muscles from her frequent riding. "Lie prone, so I can give you a rubdown."

Molly poured some scented oil on her hands, and began to massage his buttocks. Her palms moved in ever smaller, tighter circles. Then she slid a polished ivory rod into the cleft between his bum cheeks. His entire groin began to throb, and he arched his bottom off the bed. "Christ, that feels good. I'm randy as a stallion. Lie down and open your legs—I don't want to waste it."

Molly spread herself on the bed. He mounted her and began to buck and thrust like a wild bull. He achieved a hard, throbbing climax and moaned, "Christ Almighty, it was over too fast."

When he collapsed onto her, she sighed with relief. "Don't move. Just close your eyes, and you'll be asleep in no time."

In less than ten minutes his shaft turned as hard as marble, and the head of his cock began to pulse. Molly realized with dismay that she'd given him too much of the herbal stimulant. She'd known cases where the effects had lasted for days.

He mounted her again for a lengthy ride, and when she'd had enough she brought him to climax by manipulating the polished ivory rod. By midnight, Francis had never felt as potent and virile in his life. He had the sexual stamina of ten men. Eventually, he fell into a deep sleep filled with erotic dreams, and when he awoke in the small hours of the morning, he was ready to start all over again.

After he had made use of every orifice on Molly's body he began to feel sated. He hauled her up from the floor and lifted her onto the bed for one last tumble. He fell on her like a ravening beast, biting her breasts. Then he rose up and took his cock in his hand. But before he could plunge down, a scream erupted from his throat; he brought his knees up to his belly and rolled in agony on the bed.

"What is it, Francis?" Alarmed, Molly jumped off the bed.

"Christ!" He pressed both hands to his groin. "It's my bloody hernia!" He moaned, tried to rise, and fell back in terrible pain. Slowly, he lifted his hands to reveal a swollen lump protruding from his abdomen. He pressed his hands back to his belly and cried, "Go and get Mr. Burke. Hurry! I'm in agony!"

"Burke, thank Christ! Get me up to the house—I need a doctor. The pain is excruciating!" Francis groaned uncontrollably.

One glance at the naked man rolling on the bed told him that the duke was in dire straits and needed help. Burke immediately took charge. "Mrs. Hill, get a footman down here and tell the head groom to ride into town for Dr. Halifax."

Burke looked around the plush chamber and spotted a lacquered bamboo screen that would make do as a stretcher. He removed one of the panels, brought it to the bed, and lifted the tortured man onto it. He covered Francis with a blanket, and when the footman arrived, they carried their writhing, moaning burden up to the house and deposited him on his own bed.

Amid screams and curses, Mr. Burke washed Francis, dressed him in a freshly laundered nightshirt, and propped him up with pillows. Then he poured him a large brandy, hoping to ease his suffering until medical help arrived.

Within the hour, the duke's physician appeared, and Mr. Burke led him upstairs. "His Grace is in agony, Dr. Halifax. He suffered an injury while playing a strenuous game of tennis. We managed to carry him up to bed, but he has been writhing in pain since the unfortunate incident occurred."

Halifax could see for himself that Francis was in acute misery. He raised the duke's nightshirt and saw the protrusion on his abdomen. "Good God, Bedford, you've twisted your bowel!"

"For Christ's sake, help me, Halifax!"

"I'll give you something to ease your pain." He took a bottle of laudanum from his leather bag and handed it to Mr. Burke, who immediately administered a dose. The doctor waited a minute or two for the opiate to start working, then gently placed his hand on the swollen bulge.

Francis screamed.

The expression on the doctor's face turned grave. "This is an extremely serious matter, Your Grace. I'm afraid I shall have to call in a colleague who has experience in internal medicine."

"No! I can't wait. Untwist the damn thing—you cannot put me in any more agony than I am in now," Francis cried.

"It cannot be corrected from the outside. You need an operation that must be performed by a surgeon, Your Grace."

"Operation?" Bedford's eyes filled with fear.

"I have a colleague in Northampton who is a renowned surgeon. I'll summon Dr. Kerr immediately. You may put your trust in him."

"No! I'll not see the damned sawbones." He drew up his knees, trying to relieve his misery. "Nobody is going to cut me open!"

Chapter 22

John Russell fell in step with Lord Holland as they left the floor of the House. "Prime Minister Addington has given us an appointment in his private chambers for four o'clock tomorrow afternoon, after the session."

"He's in for a shock, I'm afraid."

"The situation is untenable. By now, even he must realize he doesn't have the qualities necessary to lead the government."

Henry grinned. "I warrant he'll realize it once you catalogue his shortcomings."

"Join me for dinner. I'll practice my speech on you."

When the two men arrived at Russell Square, John found a messenger from Woburn awaiting him. A feeling of dread assuaged him as his brother's servant handed him the letter.

Devil take you, Francis. I don't want to read this, if you are sending me news of your engagement to Georgina.

John opened it with reluctance, but he saw immediately that it was not from Francis. "It's from Mr. Burke."

Lord Tavistock:

I am taking it upon myself to send you this urgent message. Yesterday, your brother suffered an injury and is in acute pain. Dr. Halifax diagnosed the protrusion in his abdomen as a twisted bowel and insists a surgeon is necessary. Over the duke's objection, he has sent to Northampton for his colleague.

I fear His Grace may refuse to see the surgeon. Halifax administered a sedative, which has only partially relieved his agonizing distress. It is my opinion that your brother is in no fit state to make medical decisions. We would all benefit from your presence. We need someone with a cool head who will take charge and convince him to take the doctor's advice—someone who is not afraid to overrule the Duke of Bedford's authority.

James Burke, Steward

"I'll come at once," John told the messenger. A vision of Francis the day he had beaten him at tennis flashed into his mind, and he felt remorseful. He handed the letter to Henry.

"I'll come with you." Holland scribbled a note to his wife, and John dispatched a Russell footman to deliver it.

John drove his phaeton to Woburn at top speed, covering the forty miles from London in record time. When he arrived, he could see Mr. Burke's relief was palpable.

"Lord Tavistock, I am most grateful you have come." He glanced at Henry. "I'm sorry, Lord Holland, but His Grace refuses to see anyone."

"No, no, I'm here for John. Don't worry about me."

As Mr. Burke ascended the magnificent staircase with John, he confided, "Dr. Kerr, the surgeon, arrived from Northampton two hours ago, but His Grace adamantly refuses to see him."

"Where is he?"

"I put him in a chamber in the main wing and sent up dinner."

"I'll speak with him once I've seen Francis."

John opened his brother's door and strode to the bed.

"John, thank Christ!" Francis pulled down the bedclothes and lifted his nightshirt. "Just look at this bloody bulge."

John was shocked at the size of the protrusion, but he schooled his face to hide his alarm from his brother.

Dr. Halifax stepped forward. "My lord, I have given His Grace an opiate to lessen his pain, but that is the extent of my expertise. I have called in a surgeon, but . . ."

"They want to *operate*! I'll have none of it!"

"Doctor, I'd like a word alone with my brother." John waited until the doctor withdrew and closed the door. He knew Francis had a willful, stubborn streak, but for his own good, John knew he must persuade him to listen to reason. "Halifax is not qualified to treat this condition, Francis. The man is out of his depth. The doctor who has been called in from Northampton is familiar with this type of injury. We need his diagnosis. It only makes sense to have a second opinion."

Francis groaned with frustration and with pain. "I'll let him look, but you stay here with me. I won't be cut open."

John went to the door and asked Halifax to bring in Kerr. The surgeon introduced himself, then examined the patient. John had to steel himself. Francis writhed in agony as Dr. Kerr placed his hands on the tender bulge and felt all around it with his fingers.

"Your Grace, Dr. Halifax is correct in his diagnosis of twisted bowel. The medical term for this condition is strangulated hernia. A loop of bowel has broken through a weak area in the wall of the abdomen, and it is being pinched and squeezed to an unbearable degree. Nothing could be more painful. Unfortunately, it cannot be corrected without surgery."

"No! If they cut me open, I'll die! Help me, John."

John felt his brother's suffering, and his fear, and

wished with all his heart he could take them away. He felt extremely protective toward him. Francis had never known adversity and was ill equipped to handle it. "I'll talk with the doctors. Try not to shout, Francis. It will only worsen your pain." He led the doctors from the room so he could have a frank discussion about his brother's terrible plight.

"I must operate without delay," Dr. Kerr said emphatically. "It is the only solution."

John, though greatly alarmed, was inclined to agree with the surgeon. "Tell me what is involved, Doctor." He listened intently to everything they said. After asking some questions, he returned to his brother's side. He sat down in a chair, hoping to create a calm atmosphere while he had a quiet talk with Francis.

"The operation you need is not overly dangerous. It has been successfully performed many times. It is a simple matter of gently pushing the protruding bowel back in place and stitching up the hole. Francis, you are a man in your prime who enjoys excellent health, and you will undoubtedly heal quickly."

"I'd rather leave it alone and see if it goes back on its own," Francis gasped, stubbornly refusing to take anyone's advice.

At least he's no longer shouting no at the top of his lungs. "Delaying the procedure is far more dangerous than the operation itself," John explained quietly, still trying to convince him.

"How so?" Francis demanded, his face gray with pain.

John, loath to add to his brother's terror by describing in graphic detail how a strangulated bowel could easily burst, took a more persuasive tack. "The pain will get steadily worse. Your body will weaken. The operation is sure to relieve your agony."

"Let's wait and see. I can put up with it awhile longer."

John could see that his paralyzing fear took precedence over his suffering. *Poor Francis—a long night of agony will surely change your mind.* "I'll have the doctor give you another dose of painkiller, and I'll stay here with you tonight. Perhaps you'll be better able to make a decision in the morning."

Once the opiate took effect, Francis stopped moaning and rolling about the bed, and for a short time he dozed. John sat vigil, knowing the inevitable decision had only been postponed. The short respite merely delayed the hard choice that must be faced come morning. John silently agonized for his brother.

The effects of the drug wore off long before dawn, and John brought Francis a drink of water, helped him relieve himself in the chamber pot, and rubbed his back in an effort to ease his suffering. To distract his brother, John talked about their childhood and the dogs they'd had.

Francis begged him for brandy, and John did not demur. But the fumes took his breath away and brought on a coughing spell.

"This cannot go on, Francis. You must give the surgeon permission to perform the operation."

"Who is this Kerr? I don't even know him. I never heard of him until two days ago." The fear was back in his eyes.

"You are right, Francis. I suggest we send for the royal surgeon, Sir James Earle. He's the top man in the country. If he decides an operation is necessary, I warrant both of us will have more confidence if Sir James agrees to perform it."

"Yes. I'm entitled to the best. Send for him, John."

John joined Lord Holland in the breakfast room and explained his brother's plight. "Francis has a strangulated hernia and he needs immediate surgery to correct it and relieve the pain. He refuses to let Dr. Kerr touch him, but he has agreed to see the royal surgeon, Sir James Earle. Henry, would you be good enough to drive my phaeton back to London and fetch Sir James with all possible speed? I'll write a letter describing in detail the Duke of Bedford's dangerous condition."

"Write your letter. I'll ready the phaeton and leave

immediately. He can't put himself in better hands than the surgeon to the royal family."

John, Mr. Burke, and Dr. Halifax did all they could to help Francis endure hour after hour of pain. When Dr. Kerr finally lost all patience and insisted the operation should be performed immediately, the Duke of Bedford became furious and banished him from the chamber. His shouting brought on a coughing fit, and suddenly Francis felt something shift internally.

By morning, there was no longer a hard lump protruding from his abdomen, and his pain had lessened considerably. Much relieved, Francis closed his eyes and slept for a few hours. John kept a faithful vigil, hoping against hope that the operation his brother dreaded would not be necessary.

It was late in the day before Lord Holland and Sir James Earle arrived at Woburn. When the royal surgeon came into the duke's chamber, Francis declared, "I'm much improved, Sir James. I don't believe I need the services of a surgeon after all."

"I shall be the judge of that, Your Grace."

Sir James examined him and his expression became grave. He confirmed the diagnosis of strangulated hernia and told the Duke of Bedford an operation was absolutely imperative. When Francis began to argue with him, the surgeon took John Russell aside. "Your brother must be operated on immediately."

"The protrusion was much worse and his pain has lessened."

"That is temporary. I'm afraid his bowel has burst."

John and Sir James spent hours trying to convince Francis that he was in the utmost danger unless his perforated bowel was repaired. By morning, the duke's temperature had begun to rise and John instructed Sir James to prepare the chamber for an emergency operation.

Francis was in a full-blown fever before he relented and gave the royal doctor permission to perform the surgery.

John took a seat outside his brother's chamber, silently praying for a successful outcome to the dreaded operation. But when the doctors finally emerged hours later, he could tell by their demeanor that the news was not good. His heart plummeted, and he was filled with anguish.

"His Grace waited too long," Sir James said grimly. "The section of his intestines that ruptured has become gangrenous, which is always fatal, I'm afraid."

The blood drained from John's face. "There's no hope?"

"None whatsoever. He cannot survive more than a few hours. I'd appreciate your presence when I break the news to him."

Word of the Duke of Bedford's condition had leaked out, and many of his friends gathered at Woburn, along with his solicitors, accountants, and stewards. But Francis refused to see anyone except John in his final hours. As his life slowly ebbed away, his fevered brain was obsessed with the female who'd rejected him.

"Lady Georgina is deeply in love with me. This will break her heart. She is so young, so lovely—she will never recover from such a cruel blow. Her greatest desire was to marry me, and I was on the brink of proposing. Sadly, I never asked her. John, promise me that you will take Georgina a lock of my hair."

"I promise, Francis." The lump in his throat almost choked him.

"Carry me to the couch."

Gently, John picked him up and carried him across the room. When he looked down, he saw that his brother had died in his arms.

Stunned and grief stricken, he finally descended the stairs to break the tragic news to those gathered below.

Lord Holland gripped his friend's shoulder. "Your Grace, you did everything you possibly could for him."

John recoiled. "Don't call me that! I don't want to

be the Duke of Bedford." But it slowly dawned on him that whether he wanted it or not, he had inherited the dukedom along with all the heavy responsibilities it entailed.

The Duchess of Gordon arrived at Brome Hall distraught at the ill tidings she had to impart. "Georgy, my poor darling. Brace yourself; I have the most dreadful news."

Georgina's hand flew to her breast. "Not Father?"

"No, no, it is far more disastrous than that!" Jane's bosom heaved as she tried to catch her breath. "My poor, dear child. The Duke of Bedford is dead!"

"Dead?" Georgina's face paled, and her hand moved to her throat in a defensive gesture. *Lord God, I killed him!*

"Are you sure?" Louisa demanded. "It's not just a rumor?"

"No, no, London is agog over the tragedy. The Prince of Wales has canceled all his engagements and shut himself up at Carlton House. The funeral arrangements are being planned . . . His obituary is expected in tomorrow's *Times*."

Louisa glanced at her sister. "How did he die?"

"I was told in confidence that it was a ruptured bowel. Somehow he suffered an acute injury. The royal surgeon, Sir James Earle, operated, but could do nothing to save him."

Georgina felt sick, as guilt washed over her. She sank down into a chair and covered her face with her hands.

"It is nothing short of a calamity. All our fine plans dashed to smithereens. Instead of a wedding, we get a funeral. It is more than the heart can bear. My poor, poor darling!"

Louisa's husband hurried forward with a decanter of brandy and poured a measure for Georgina.

"Thank you, Charles. A restorative is just what I need." Jane swept the glass from his hand and drained it in one gulp.

"Please excuse me," Georgina whispered, and ran from the room.

Louisa followed her. She led her sister into the library and sat her down before the fire. "It's not your fault, Georgy."

"But it is! I kicked him and kneed him in the groin."

"That was the only way you could protect yourself from the lecherous swine. Besides, that happened a month ago and couldn't possibly have killed him." Louisa knelt and took her sister's hands. "I know you feel guilty, but you must never let anyone know what you did, not even Mother—especially not Mother. In fact, you must never say anything disparaging about Francis Russell, or utter one word of criticism. It is an unwritten rule of society that you must not speak ill of the dead."

"All the world loved him and will mourn him, with the exception of you and me, Louisa."

"But you must mourn him too, or at least put on a show of mourning him. All of London knows the Duke of Bedford was wooing you and will expect you to be devastated."

"But I *am* devastated. Though I despised the man, I am not so wicked that I wished him to die. Louisa, whatever shall I do?"

"My best advice is to look sad and keep your mouth shut."

The Duchess of Gordon swept into the library. "There you are, my poor darling. We must return to London immediately. You have an appointment with the dressmaker first thing in the morning."

"Dressmaker?" Georgina murmured, at a loss.

"You need a new wardrobe entirely in black."

Georgina was no hypocrite, and opened her mouth to protest. She saw the warning glance on Louisa's face, and the words stuck in her throat. *If I go into mourning, it will keep me off the marriage market and protect me from Mother's matchmaking.* The self-serving thought only added to Georgina's feelings of guilt.

* * *

Numb with grief, John Russell wrote his brother's obituary for the *Times* and made all the funeral arrangements. The service was held in the church at Chenies, and the duke's empty carriage followed the hearse. The streets were lined with Francis's tenants, staff, and hundreds of local people who came to pay their last respects. Friends, acquaintances, and fellow politicians, both Whigs and Tories, swelled the crowd to four thousand.

Once the funeral was over, John immersed himself in the business of running Woburn. He spent endless hours with the solicitors and accountants. Since Francis had neglected to make bequests in his will to reward his staff for their loyal service, John made sure every house servant, gardener, and stable worker received a generous amount in his brother's name.

Next, John called in the land stewards and pored over the reports they submitted. He took the time to speak with every tenant on Woburn's vast acres. He toured the home farm, personally took stock of all the animals, and then visited every farm on his land. Francis had never taken more than a cursory interest in Woburn's holdings or its hard-working people, leaving all the decisions to stewards. But John, who always shouldered his responsibilities seriously, took a personal interest in running the immense estate, checking the account books, paying the bills, and listening with respect to those who worked for him.

Last, but by no means least, was the matter of his brother's women. John was shocked and disgusted when he found a journal in the desk drawer that described in flagrant detail Francis's sexual excesses. He was stunned when he saw the last entry was a page entitled *Georgina.* Cursing his brother, he tore the page from the journal and burned it in the fire.

Since Woburn was now John's home, and where his sons would live when they were not at school, the problem of Molly Hill had to be resolved. He was surprised to learn that Francis had suffered his fatal injury in Mrs. Hill's bed, and in return for a signed statement swearing she would keep the matter private, John bought her a small house in London.

Next on the list was Marianna Palmer. John was shocked that Francis had made no provision for his illegitimate son and daughter by that lady, and immediately had his solicitor draw up generous annuities to be paid when the children came of age, along with a separate annuity for Marianna to be paid yearly.

The numbers of females who claimed to be the late Duke of Bedford's mistress and petitioned John for money were legion. Though he was skeptical in a few instances, he did not delude himself. Francis had indeed led a profligate life. He paid off the women without demur, but made it plain there would be no more money forthcoming.

Most nights John fell into bed exhausted, but work helped to assuage his grief and keep his guilt at bay. Though dog-tired, he often lay awake for hours before sleep claimed him.

I don't want to be the Duke of Bedford. The title excludes me from the House of Commons and prevents me from representing the people of Tavistock. Being an elected member of parliament was a worthy endeavor that gave me deep satisfaction. I don't want to sit in the bloody House of Lords. It is filled with do-nothing, privileged aristocrats!

Why the devil didn't I insist that Francis have the operation immediately? It suddenly dawned on him that he resented his brother for dying and making him the Duke of Bedford. The stark realization added to his feelings of guilt.

I did not genuinely grieve for my wife, so fate has punished me by taking my brother's life. John chided himself for thinking such superstitious claptrap. But he realized the dark thoughts were prompted by remorse over Elizabeth and guilt over Francis.

He thought of Georgina and the grief she must be suffering. *I resented my brother's relationship with her. I wanted her for myself and felt a raging jealousy over her affection for him.* The admission filled him with shame.

When John fell asleep, however, and he began to dream, shame played no part whatever in the passionate interlude he shared with the vivacious, emerald-eyed beauty.

Chapter 23

"Two black gowns are more than enough, Mother," Georgina insisted. "If I am in mourning, I won't be attending any social functions, and you won't be entertaining here at Pall Mall for some time."

"I've been thinking about that. As the leading Tory hostess, entertaining in my home is expected of me. Since *you* are the one who is in mourning, I think it will be more seemly if you grieve in private at one of your sisters'."

More convenient, you mean. "You should have left me in Suffolk with Louisa instead of dragging me back here to London!"

"I shan't take offense at your sharp tongue. It is a manifestation of your grief. Perhaps Kimbolton . . ."

"Absolutely and emphatically not Kimbolton. I am not even on speaking terms with my sister Susan or the bloody Duke of Manchester!"

"Then I shall send a note round to Charlotte at Fife House."

Just after lunch, Charlotte arrived in Pall Mall. The pleading look in Georgina's eyes hinted at how miserable she was. "I have a suggestion. Since Charles's parents gifted us with their lovely house at Richmond-on-Thames when I had the baby, the two of us can go there for a month. The peace and quiet will do us both good, Georgy."

"A perfect solution to our dilemma," Jane declared. "Someday, all the estates of the Duke and Duchess of Richmond will be yours, Charlotte. You have me to thank for marrying you into such a wealthy and prestigious family."

"Yes, Mother. We all owe you a debt of gratitude," Charlotte said dryly. "Go and pack your things, Georgy."

The moment her sister left the room, Charlotte thrust a printed handbill at her mother. "Have you seen this? They're being sold on every corner! Your manipulative matchmaking has made my poor sister the butt of jokes."

Jane stared at the Gillray cartoon in horror. The caption read: *Chasing the Bedford Bull.* It showed a fat and florid duchess adorned in Black Watch tartan chasing a bull. Her beautiful daughter followed, crying, "Run, Mither, Run. Oh, how I long to lead the sweet, bonny creature on a string."

"How dare they print these malicious caricatures? Such obscene lies are deliberately designed to defame and damage me in the eyes of the *ton*!"

"It is the damage to Georgina I care about. It will expose her to public contempt and ruin her reputation."

"Bedford did the chasing, and so I shall inform everyone."

"Don't add fuel to the fire, Mother. The fastest way to make it go away is to treat it with silence. Say absolutely nothing! I don't want Georgy to see that cartoon; nor do I want her exposed to all the rumors that will run rampant about her and Bedford. We must protect her from the slanderous tongues of the *ton.* That is why I am taking her out of London."

The Duchess of Gordon made it her business to inform everyone in her social circle that Francis Russell and Lady Georgina were engaged to be married when death suddenly snatched him away.

The late Duke of Bedford's closest friends denied that he was engaged. Sir Robert Adair contradicted the story, and when Lauderdale said that Jane had fabricated the whole thing, they had a vicious quarrel. Soon she was speaking only to the people who believed that Georgina and Francis had been engaged.

Jane's archrival, the Duchess of Devonshire, assured all her friends that her dearest "Loo" would never choose a Gordon to fulfill the role of Mistress of Woburn. London society became divided in its opinion. Some fervently believed the private engagement theory, while others hotly disputed it. Before the end of March, Georgina Gordon was the talk of the town.

Furious that John Russell had not come forward to confirm his brother's engagement to her daughter, the Duchess of Gordon wrote him a letter of reproach.

"When I go to London, I must hire a secretary." John Russell sat in Woburn's library, going through the post that Mr. Burke had piled on his desk. "Condolences are still pouring in." He added today's to the others stacked in boxes on the floor.

John's heart skipped a beat as he picked up an envelope embossed with the ducal crest of Gordon. *Georgina.* He tore it open and felt a stab of disappointment when he saw the signature.

Your Grace:

It is with a heavy heart that I must beg your pity and your protection for my daughter. By keeping silent about Lady Georgina's engagement to your brother, Francis, you are allowing the world to malign her. You must believe, as I do, that the Duke of Bedford's intentions toward my daughter were pure and honorable. Your silence, which is taken by society as denial, has added to the deep sadness of one already destined to suffer eternal unhappiness.

Jane, Duchess of Gordon

"Damn and blast!" John crushed the letter in his fist. *I've thought of Georgina every day since Francis died, aye and every day for months before, if I'm being truthful.* He could hardly abide the thought of her joyful laughter being silenced by sadness.

John was quite aware of the controversy raging over his brother's marital intentions, and he considered it the height of bad taste for Francis's friends and the Duchess of Gordon to be publicly arguing about the matter so soon after his death.

That isn't the only reason I've kept silent. The thought of Georgina being engaged to marry Francis is abhorrent to me. Though I loved my brother, I was not blind to his faults. He led a profligate life.

John clung doggedly to his brother's dying words about Georgina: *Sadly, I never asked her.*

John, at a loss how to answer the letter, set it aside and picked up one from his friend Henry. When he opened it, he found a handbill of the Gillray cartoon, with a short note attached.

John:

This scurrilous cartoon, which made the rounds after the Kimbolton masquerade ball, has resurfaced with a vengeance.

"Goddamn the scandalmongers!" John strode across the room to throw the offending cartoon into the fire, then thought better of it. "Mr. Burke, I shall leave for London immediately."

When John arrived at the printers with his solicitor in tow, he made no effort to hide his cold, black fury from the owner. "While my brother was alive, he was fair game for the press. But I will not allow you to deliberately exploit his death to make money by printing and selling this or any other salacious cartoon.

"You will send a runner around to all your street vendors and order them to return every last handbill you have printed. Then you will burn them. If any are still on sale by six o'clock tonight, I will not only sue you for libel, I will buy this building and put you out of business.

"If, on the other hand, you diligently comply with my demands, I will compensate you for your losses. I need your sworn oath that you will immediately cease and desist. My solicitor has prepared an affidavit for your signature."

When John returned to Russell Square, he paced about the house like a panther. Today's action had been taken to protect Georgina. He had an overwhelming desire to see her, but the thought of going to Pall Mall and speaking with her in the presence of the Duchess of Gordon was distasteful to him. *I'll send a note to Charles Lennox and ask if he'll arrange for his sister-in-law to come to Fife House, so Georgina and I can talk in private.*

"Lord, it's almost seven o'clock. He'll be here any minute, Charlotte. Do you think I can get away with this gray gown, or is black absolutely mandatory?"

"I've never seen you more indecisive, Georgy. Perhaps you should change into the black. John is in double mourning for his wife and his brother, both of whom he loved dearly." In spite of Charlotte's efforts to protect her, Georgina had seen the Gillray cartoon, and knew everyone must be whispering about her. "You mustn't say anything outrageous," her sister cautioned.

Georgina's heart hammered. *Charlotte isn't obtuse. She suspected long ago that I was hopelessly attracted to John, even before he was widowed.*

"John must be livid that his brother is the subject of so much gossip and speculation." Charlotte handed Georgina the black gown and hung the gray one in the wardrobe.

"Encouraging Francis Russell to court me was the most reckless thing I've ever done, especially when I detested the man. Now I'm the talk of London." She bit her lip to stop it from trembling.

"You mustn't let John know that you despised Francis. It would wound him to the core. Promise you won't speak ill of the dead?"

"Surely you know I would never hurt John. I assure you I won't say or do anything inappropriate or improper."

"I hear a carriage. John asked Charles to accompany him when he learned you were with me at Richmond-on-Thames. I'll go and greet them—don't wait too long before you make your appearance."

John watched Georgina descend the stairs. He was shocked at her subdued appearance. In the black dress, she was as pale as a wraith, and looked so small and vulnerable, it tore at his heart.

"I am so sorry for your loss," she murmured softly.

I am bearing the loss far better than you, little girl. He fought the urge to take her in his arms and comfort her. He glanced at Charlotte, then at Charles, and an awkward silence descended.

Georgina sensed John wanted them to speak in private. "If you would care to accompany me . . . we could walk down to the river."

"Of course." He watched Charlotte wrap a black velvet cloak about her sister, and then miraculously they were outside alone. They walked along the river as darkness descended.

Guilt lay heavily on her heart. What she had done to Francis likely contributed to his untimely death. If John ever learned of her perfidy, she knew he would recoil from her.

"I am sorry that the gossip and speculation has added to your sorrow, Lady Georgina."

If you have seen that cartoon, I will die of shame! She did not dare tell him how she really felt about Francis. She looked up at him with beseeching eyes. "Please, it is too painful for me to speak of it."

"Then we will speak of other things."

A shiver of relief went through her.

"You are cold!" He stopped walking and took her hands.

"No . . . yes. I can't seem to get warm these days.

I warrant I must feel the cold more than other people. I love Scotland with all my heart, but I cannot bear the Highland winters."

John removed his coat and wrapped it around her. It was far too long, but he was determined to keep the cold from her. "You would love Devon. It is warm all year round, and its lush vales are filled with flowers, butterflies, and songbirds."

"It sounds like paradise," she said wistfully.

He suddenly realized that was the place in his recurring dream where he and Georgy always rode through the sun-drenched meadow as a prelude to their passionate lovemaking. John was acutely aware that such thoughts were shockingly inappropriate when the lady of his dreams was in mourning for his brother.

The specter of Francis stood between them like a barrier that was insurmountable at the moment. They were the two people most affected by his brother's death, and all they could share was sorrow and bereavement. John wished with his whole heart that it was not so. "I had a letter from your mother."

Her lashes flew up, revealing how apprehensive and vulnerable she was.

How can I tell her that her mother is making matters worse by insisting she and Francis were engaged to be married? John resolved to tell the Duchess of Gordon himself.

He hastened to relieve her anxiety. "Your mother sent her condolences and expressed her deep concern about you. That's what prompted my visit. I hoped to ease your sorrow by sharing it."

"Thank you." Her voice was barely above a whisper.

"Georgina, perhaps it will comfort you to know that Francis's last thoughts were about you." He watched her beautiful eyes flood with tears, and realized it was too soon to speak of such things. Her grief touched him and, though he wished it were not so, he finally accepted that she had fallen in love with Francis.

* * *

When John returned to Russell Square, the first thing he did was write a letter to the Duchess of Gordon.

Your Grace:

I regret that my silence gives you offense, but I am sure you will understand that it is dictated by the respect I owe my brother's memory.

There can be no doubt that Francis held your daughter in the highest esteem, and I agree with you that my brother's intentions with regard to Lady Georgina were entirely pure and honorable. As proof of his tender feelings, Francis requested that a lock of his hair be given to your daughter.

I am sure that a lady with your delicate sensibilities must agree that keeping a respectful silence will quell the gossip and speculation. This will protect your daughter from suffering more pain, which I know is the thing a loving mother desires most.

He signed his name, John Russell. He still could not bring himself to use his ducal title, Duke of Bedford.

When the Duchess of Gordon read John Russell's letter, she was chagrined that he had neither confirmed nor denied the engagement, but at least he had put in writing that Francis had requested a lock of his hair be given to Georgina. To Jane this was proof positive that the Duke of Bedford had intended marriage, and she dug in her heels. This time she would take her campaign to the highest authority.

She attended Queen Charlotte's monthly Drawing Room at Saint James's Palace, and took a gift of fresh salmon for His Royal Highness, King George. She told the queen, and all the other noble ladies present, her story of the private engagement, and added intimate details of the love affair between Georgina and the duke that had been carried on in secret at Kimbolton Castle. "With his last dying breath Francis asked that a lock of his hair be taken to his beloved." She waved the letter from John Russell to verify the truth of her story.

When she returned home, the duchess wrote to Susan. She told her daughter it was imperative that she and Manchester back up her story if anyone questioned that an engagement had taken place at Kimbolton. Then she gave vent to her anger, and condemned John Russell. *The new Duke of Bedford has it within his power to confirm the engagement and put an end to the speculation. Instead, the wretched man remains stubbornly silent, which puts me in the embarrassing position of having to defend Georgina's reputation.*

The following day Jane wrote a long letter to the Prince of Wales. It was filled with heartfelt sympathy for the loss of his dearest friend the Duke of Bedford. *Only one who bore him such deep love and affection can understand the grief my daughter is suffering. Francis proposed to Georgina in private, and he wrote to the Duke of Manchester, declaring his intentions to publicly announce their engagement. Then tragedy struck.*

Jane finished the letter with a cunning mixture of sympathy and flattery, and knew that the Prince of Wales would not be able to resist sharing the story with his friends.

Unfortunately, Prinny's mistress, Lady Jersey, read the letter. She had no love for Francis Russell, since the embarrassing encounter at the masquerade ball held at Kimbolton, and she saw an opportunity to blacken his name. She told anyone who would listen that the profligate Duke of Bedford had taken Lady Georgina Gordon as his mistress before he died and had no intention of marrying the wanton beauty.

Gossip about Georgina's abortive engagement was spreading like wildfire. When Prince Edward visited Brooks's Club and, as always, had far too much to drink, he confessed to his friends that he and Francis had a thousand-pound wager to see which of them would be the first to bed Lady Georgina Gordon.

When these rumors were repeated with relish to the Duchess of Gordon, she finally realized that all the gossip was doing irreparable damage to her daughter's reputation. Scandal was the surest way to ruin Georgina's future marriage prospects. Jane, who knew she had a crisis on her hands, began to panic. It was a dilemma that she could not solve.

It was at this precise moment that fate stepped in. News swept through London that England and France were no longer at war. The *haut ton* became consumed with talk of politics, peace, and Paris. Celebration became the order of the day, and the fashionable people of London lost interest in the doleful affair of Georgina Gordon and Francis Russell.

"We are going to Paris!" Louisa's voice rang through the Pall Mall house as she tossed her cloak and hat to a footman.

With a proud smile lighting up his face, Charles Cornwallis followed his wife into Jane Gordon's sitting room. "My father signed the peace treaty at Amiens with Napoleon, ending the war with the French Republic."

"The Marquis Cornwallis—of course!" The Duchess of Gordon smiled for the first time in weeks. "It is most gratifying that my daughter is married to the son of the king's top general."

"Where is Georgy? I can't wait to tell her."

"She is in seclusion with Charlotte at Richmond-on-Thames while she mourns. It has been a difficult time for your sister, and a most trying time for me. I've done my utmost to be discreet and shield her from the dreadful gossip and speculation, but in spite of my efforts, I fear her reputation has been sullied."

"I can't bear to think of Georgy being the butt of scandalmongers. She must be devastated. Perhaps she should come to Paris with us and put the whole thing behind her."

Jane seized on the suggestion immediately. "Paris

is a marvelous idea, Louisa! You have just solved my dilemma. I will close up Pall Mall and rent a house in the French capital for the spring and summer," the duchess declared. "London will pay the price for maligning my daughter. Let's see how the powers that be manage without their leading Tory hostess."

The Gordons were not the only society ladies to descend upon Paris. It suddenly became the fashionable thing to do. The royal family sent Anne, Duchess of Cumberland and widow of the king's brother, as their representative. The Prince of Wales suggested his ally Charles James Fox take his wife, Elizabeth, to Paris, and offered to pay all their expenses in return for weekly reports.

Lady Bessborough and her daughter Caroline were among the first to arrive. Unfortunately her sister, the Duchess of Devonshire, came down with an attack of gallstones and was distraught that she had to remain in London.

Lady Georgina's sister Susan was pea green with envy that her mother and sisters had gone to Paris. Because she was expecting a child, her husband would not allow her to cross the Channel.

It's all John Russell's fault! If he'd been a gentleman and acknowledged my sister's engagement, it would not have been necessary to get Georgina out of the country to salvage her reputation. The longer she thought about it, the angrier she became. *The sheer arrogance of the man is beyond all bearing. He thinks the Russells are a breed apart, and the Gordons not good enough to be linked with their noble English name.*

"Sorry to interrupt, Your Grace. You have a visitor."

John Russell had plans to bring his sons to Woburn for the weekend and had refurbished three bedchambers with their personal belongings he'd had shipped from the Russell Square house. He wanted to make the boys feel that Woburn was their family home. He had just finished hanging a portrait of their mother above the sitting room fireplace when Mr. Burke made his announcement.

"Who is it?" John climbed down from the ladder.

"The Duchess of Manchester. I put her in the main reception room." Burke picked up John's jacket and helped him put it on.

An image of Georgina flashed into John's mind at mention of her sister. He masked the feeling of apprehension that gripped him as he strode into the reception room. "Good afternoon. May I welcome you to Woburn, Lady Susan?" He saw that she was rounded with child. She was also tapping her foot with impatience and did not return his smile. "I'm sorry if you've been kept waiting. Please have a chair."

"This isn't a social call, Bedford. I'm here on business."

She's bristling with animosity. He stood politely and waited for her to continue.

Susan pulled a letter from her reticule and thrust it at him. "Do you deny that this is your brother's handwriting?"

He took the sheet of paper embossed with the ducal crest, and immediately recognized his brother's negligent scrawl. He saw it was addressed to the Duke of Manchester and dated February 3, a month before Francis had died.

My dear William:

I thank you for your warm hospitality at Kimbolton.

It is my duty to inform you that my intentions toward your sister-in-law are completely honorable. I wish to confide that I asked Lady Georgina to become my wife. Though she vowed her love for me, she refused to accept my proposal because of my relationship with Mrs. Palmer. I fully intend to remove the obstacle that prevents Lady Georgina from agreeing to marry me, and assure you that the liaison is over.

I would like you to give her my pledge that when I return to London, I will strictly follow correct protocol. I will make a formal call upon the Duchess of Gordon and, with Georgina's permission, declare our engagement publicly.

John felt his gut knot. *You bastard, Francis! With your dying breath you swore to me you had not asked Georgina to marry you.*

He handed the letter back to Susan. "I assured your mother that Francis held Lady Georgina in the highest esteem and that his intentions were honorable." John cursed silently. "Obviously, I should have said more. When I am in London tomorrow, I will call upon the Duchess of Gordon and apologize."

"Your call will be in vain. My mother has closed the Pall Mall house and been forced to take my sister out of the country to quell the scandal that you could have so easily prevented. Georgina's reputation has been torn to shreds. Her prospects for a future marriage have been ruined. You are duty bound to restore her honor!"

John's heart sank. "Your sister has gone to Scotland?" he asked bleakly.

"Scotland, my arse! The little vixen has gone to *Paris.*"

Chapter 24

"You are welcome to stay here in Russell Square with me while your wife is in Paris," John told his friend Henry. "The place seems so empty, I'd appreciate your company."

"Thanks, John." Holland threw down his napkin and picked up his glass. "Since your chef is superior to mine, I *will* stay for a couple of days. Have you taken your seat in the Lords yet?"

"Not yet—later in the week, perhaps, when I've taken care of some business. I've decided to ask Humphrey Repton to landscape the gardens at Woburn. They are in a dreadful state of neglect." John picked up his glass. "I shall miss the Commons. Perhaps I can work behind the scenes to help get William Pitt reinstated."

"Damn good idea. Under Addington, parliament is dysfunctional."

"Well, at least one thing got done this spring—Cornwallis negotiated the Peace Treaty of Amiens with France's first consul."

"According to my wife's letters, half of London flocked to Paris, all clamoring to meet Napoleon and the Bonaparte family. They apparently hold court as if they were royalty."

"Either they don't see the irony, or don't give a damn."

"The English aristocrats or the Bonapartes?"

John laughed for the first time in weeks. "Both, I suppose."

"The nightlife is more spectacular than anything in London. Beth is invited to a ball or dinner party every night."

"No doubt her dress bills will be astronomical."

"Undoubtedly. She reports the English fashions are outdated, and though the Paris gowns are shocking, all the ladies are buying them. She is trying to persuade Lady Georgina to stop wearing her mourning weeds and go shopping with her."

At mention of Georgina, John remembered how pale and wan she had looked in the black gown. "I hope Beth succeeds. I wish Lady Georgina could regain her vivacity. Perhaps Paris will diminish her sadness." *I want Georgy to laugh again, and flirt, and say saucy, outrageous things.*

"According to Beth, Georgina has already made a conquest. Napoleon and Josephine's son, Eugene Beauharnais, is hopelessly lovesick over the young beauty, though she discourages him."

John's dark brows drew together, and he felt the familiar knot in his belly. "The Duchess of Gordon should protect her daughter from unwanted attention."

"If I know Jane Gordon, she will do everything in her power to secure Eugene as husband for Georgina."

John was stunned. "You cannot be serious?"

"I'm perfectly serious. The Duchess of Gordon is a ruthless matchmaker. She's made it her life's work to marry her daughters to men of high status. Napoleon and Josephine's son is the equivalent of a French prince. Jane won't be able to resist."

John changed the subject, and they discussed politics until it was time to retire. But once he was in bed, thoughts of Georgina flooded his imagination. *Eugene Beauharnais is her own age. By all accounts he is handsome and has proved himself on the battlefield. She is bound to find him attractive.*

The disturbing thoughts kept him awake for hours.

He wanted her to stop mourning Francis, yet perversely he did not want her to give her heart to any other man. Though he had tried to curb his longing for Georgina Gordon, he had not succeeded.

"I want her for myself." For the first time he said it aloud. The admission added to the guilt he felt at desiring the woman his brother had chosen. John thumped his pillows in frustration, and vowed to stop being obsessed with her.

Next morning at the breakfast table, John realized his obsession was stronger than ever. "Henry, at the risk of offending you, may I broach a subject that is personal?"

"I don't offend easily."

"When Beth's husband divorced her, how did the two of you survive the scandal?"

"She suffered a great deal of shame and guilt, and I was powerless to stop the gossip. But, amazingly, once we were married and she became Lady Holland, we were accepted back into society as if it had never happened. Surely you know there is nothing more hypocritical than the British aristocracy?"

"You are right, of course. When my wife died, I was completely ostracized by her sisters. But the moment I became the Duke of Bedford, both Lady Bath and Lady Bradford wrote me ingratiating letters, suddenly expressing belated concern for my motherless sons and hoping they would be welcome at Woburn." John laughed bitterly. "Not a bloody chance."

"What prompted you to ask about Beth's divorce?"

John glanced at Henry and their eyes met. "There is a lady I am interested in. She has been touched by scandal, and I am deeply concerned for her. Since I am in double mourning, I am afraid my attentions would be deemed decadent and fuel horrendous gossip—I do not wish to cause her more pain." John looked away.

Good God, you are in love with Georgina Gordon. Henry chose his words carefully. "Tongues will wag, of course. But if you make the lady Duchess of Bedford, the *ton* will fawn upon her."

John was suddenly filled with misgivings. First and foremost was the fear that she would refuse him, and on top of that, he wondered what possible excuse he could have for showing up in Paris. Yet he knew his longing was eating a hole inside of him. John cursed himself for a coward. *What the hellfire is the matter with you? If you want her, go and get her!*

"Georgina, you cannot go to the Tuileries Palace reception in that drab gray dress. You look like a dowdy old maid." The Duchess of Gordon was garbed in sapphire-blue lace with an ostrich feather fan dyed to match. "Ah, here is Louisa. Look how deliciously feminine your sister looks in her lavender tulle. Go and change at once, Georgy."

Louisa spoke up quickly. "There's no time, Mother. Marquis Cornwallis and Charles are waiting in the carriage to give you a ride. We cannot be late."

"Mother, go with Louisa. I shall stay home."

"Stay home? That is out of the question. You know Eugene Beauharnais is smitten with you. He's been dancing attendance on you for a month—we cannot let *this* one slip through our fingers."

Louisa looked from her mother to her sister. "Did I miss something while my eyes were rolling?"

"She's at it again . . . shoving me into the arms of another suitor before the last one is cold in his grave."

"Georgina, this is the chance of a lifetime. Josephine Bonaparte will give her son anything he wants, and it's perfectly obvious to everyone that he wants you. Go and change."

"There's no time. It's rude to keep the marquis waiting."

"Off you go, Louisa. You may tell Marquis Cornwallis to send the carriage back for us. Georgy and I will be fashionably late."

When they were alone, Jane rounded on her youngest daughter. "You have a rare opportunity to outdo all of your sisters in the marriage market. A connection with Napoleon Bonaparte's family will be a *dynastic* match. All London will be agog!"

"I'm already the talk of London," Georgina said with asperity. "Eugene is a boy . . . this is just an infatuation."

"A boy your own age. You should be able to wrap him around your little finger and have him panting to get you into bed. If you'd just seduce him, you could be the most envied woman in England and France. I shall wait for you while you go and change into something that will—"

"Make him pant?" Georgina asked sweetly. "In that case, Mother, you will be waiting until dawn."

"Welcome to Paris, Your Grace." Lord Charles Whitworth, the British ambassador, shook John Russell's hand warmly. "I have had a suite prepared for you here at the embassy."

"I appreciate your kind hospitality, Charles."

"I know it's short notice, but having the Duke of Bedford accompany me to Napoleon's reception at the Tuileries Palace tonight will lend me a good deal of consequence."

"I would be honored." An invitation to the Tuileries on his first night in Paris could not have fit in better with his plans.

When John and the ambassador's party arrived, they ascended the Tuileries stairs, which were guarded by double rows of French grenadiers. Then they passed through three antechambers where uniformed musicians were playing military music. In the gold salon he was presented to Josephine, who was arrayed in diamonds. John was amused that her slumberous eyes frankly assessed his tall physique, and her sensual smile told him she liked what she saw.

As they moved into the great hall where they would dine, liveried footmen lined the walls.

"This is far more ostentatious than anything at Saint James's Palace." John's polite smile hid his amusement.

"The formality of Napoleon's court *is* rather extraordinary," Whitworth conceded.

John's glance swept the mirrored chamber, searching among the guests for Georgina. He longed to see her, yet at the same time he hoped she would not be in attendance. The ambassador stopped to speak with Marquis Cornwallis and his son, Lord Brome. John's eyes were drawn to Brome's beautiful wife, and he realized it was Georgina's sister Louisa. She wore a diaphanous gown in the latest Parisian style, which exposed her breasts in a daring fashion. John's amusement deserted him.

Whitworth introduced him to Markoff, the Russian ambassador, and then a fanfare of trumpets silenced the guests as Napoleon and Josephine entered the glittering chamber. As the first consul escorted his wife to the dais and John saw that she stood head and shoulders above Bonaparte, some of his amusement returned.

Once all the guests were seated, the liveried footmen moved as one to the long tables and began to fill the glasses with French champagne. Napoleon proposed a toast to his guests, and then the servers began to bring in the first course.

The Duchess of Gordon swept into the chamber, not disconcerted in the least that she and her daughter had arrived late. She marched down to the dais, sank into a curtsy, and with great aplomb took a seat on the front row.

John's gaze was riveted on Georgina. She was wearing a gray silk gown with a demure neckline. Her eyes were downcast, and her lashes formed dark crescents on her pale cheeks. His heart went out to her as he silently cursed Jane Gordon's brazen audacity.

He was surprised to see a young man and a young lady eagerly jump up as Georgina approached. The pair guided her to a seat they had obviously been saving for her.

John immediately identified the young man as Eugene Beauharnais, and guessed that the young female was his sister, Hortense. John's heart sank. Their attentive familiarity showed that they adored Georgina.

It was easy to see that young Beauharnais was enamored of the English beauty, but John was shrewd enough to suspect that Bonaparte's insatiable thirst for power would drive him to seek a marital alliance for Eugene with a European princess. *The boy's heart may be broken, but he will obey Napoleon's orders.*

After dinner, the guests mingled in yet another sumptuous chamber of the Tuileries Palace. Whitworth introduced John to many foreign dignitaries, but after having to politely greet three French generals, he excused himself. *They were our bloody enemies only two months ago.*

Determined to see Georgina, he spotted the Duchess of Gordon and her daughter Louisa holding forth with Josephine Bonaparte. Some distance away, Georgina stood talking with Hortense and, as luck would have it, Lady Holland. John did not approach them, but stood quietly, content to simply admire her from a distance.

As if Georgina sensed his presence, she raised her lashes and gazed at him in amazement. "John." She moved toward him, mesmerized. "You came to Paris." Her eyes were filled with wonder, and a light blush tinted her pale cheeks.

Lady Holland turned and saw him. "John, darling!" she cried happily. "How lovely to see you. The change of scene will do you a world of good. Where are you staying?"

"The British ambassador was good enough to put me up at the embassy." He glanced at Georgina. "It's just a short visit."

"How marvelous. My apartment is nearby on the Champs-Élysées. Well, actually, all of us are there. It's the most beautiful avenue in the world. Number 15. Promise you'll visit me tomorrow?"

John lowered his voice. "As a good friend, may I ask a favor?"

"Why, of course."

"I'll come at four, if you promise to invite Lady Georgina."

Beth's eyes widened. "I will arrange it."

Georgina brought her young friend forward. "It gives me great pleasure to present Hortense Beauharnais. This is John Russell, the Duke of Bedford."

He greeted the girl in French and gallantly kissed her hand.

The lovely gesture took Georgina's breath away. Garbed in elegant black, wearing his own dark hair, he looked more French than English. *Is it possible he came to Paris to see me?* His nearness made her pulse race, and she shivered.

"You are cold, Lady Georgina." Eugene Beauharnais seemed to appear from nowhere, and solicitously placed a velvet wrap about her shoulders. "May I bring you wine, *mon cher ami*?"

Georgina murmured, "No, thank you," and stood by quietly while Hortense introduced her brother to the duke.

John looked at him closely. The young man had an easy smile, and he wore his dark hair clipped close in the style of a Roman statue. *When he fought the Austrians, Napoleon made him a colonel. What lady wouldn't find him irresistible?* He bowed to the company. "I believe my host is preparing to leave, so I will bid you *au revoir*, ladies." His glance met Georgina's and held for long moments. "Until we meet again."

"Good afternoon, ladies. It was most kind of you to invite me, Beth." John was relieved to see that Georgina was in Lady Holland's sitting room when he arrived. He had not been at all sure she would come.

"I trust you left my husband well?"

"Extremely well, though I know he misses you. He is happy you are enjoying yourself, and bracing himself for your dress bills."

Beth laughed. "What brings you to Paris, Your Grace?"

"Woburn is in need of refurbishing. The Paris shops are incomparable. This morning I bought some clocks."

"Shopping is one of life's pleasures. It lifts the spirits." Beth saw his attention was elsewhere. "If you'll excuse me, I shall go and see about some tea."

John took a chair close to Georgina. Her black silk dress emphasized her pallor. "Beth is right, shopping does lift the spirits. I think it's time you set aside these mourning weeds. I know wearing black is supposedly a sign of respect, but outward appearances aren't what count. It's what you feel on the inside. Georgina, you are not a widow. You are not compelled to drape yourself in black."

"You would not think ill of me?" she asked uncertainly.

"I could never think ill of you, Georgina. Both of us loved Francis, and we will always miss him. Like me, you would probably prefer to mourn him privately, in your heart. But you are far too young and lovely to grieve for the rest of your life."

You would think ill of me if you knew I detested Francis! Privately, in my heart, there is room only for you. Georgina lowered her lashes, afraid that John would read her thoughts.

"Mother is hosting a ball tomorrow night. She insists that I attend, but I told her it wouldn't be proper."

He smiled at her. "You never used to pass up an opportunity to be improper. That's the Georgina I long to see."

Her heart skipped a beat, and she looked at him from beneath her lashes. "I will attend the ball if you will come."

"I will come only if you promise to dance with me. Let's be improper together?" he invited.

She caught her breath. *John Russell, are you flirting with me?*

"Tomorrow you must go shopping with Beth and buy one of these outrageously sophisticated Parisian gowns that will make every female green with envy, and every man rabid with desire."

You are *flirting with me!* Georgina's heart began to sing.

Lady Holland returned wheeling a tea cart. John conveyed a smile of thanks for giving him time alone with Georgina. To be polite, he accepted a cup of tea and a slice of gâteau.

He set down his empty plate. "This has been delightful. We must do it again before I leave."

"When will that be, Your Grace?" Beth asked.

John glanced at Georgina. "When I have everything I came for." He stood up to leave. "May I escort you home, Lady Georgina?"

"Yes . . . thank you," she said quickly, and bade Beth good-bye.

When they were outside, she said, "Our house isn't far. It's this way, toward the Place de la Concorde."

He held out his arm, and she placed her hand on it, hoping he could not hear her heart hammering in her breast. They strolled beneath the shade trees along the Champs-Élysées as the carriages drove by and dusk began to fall. "Paris in the springtime is so lovely and romantic. I want you to enjoy every moment of it."

"Mmm, I can smell the chestnut blossoms."

"Your senses are reawakening."

His deep voice sent a delicious frisson of happiness spiraling inside her. *You came to Paris to see me . . . I know you did!*

The Duchess of Gordon's ball was well attended by the English who were visiting Paris. Even those ladies of the *ton* who gossiped about Jane behind her back were eager to rub shoulders with the new elite members of French society. Lady Bessborough's daughter Caro was making her debut tonight, attending her first grown-up affair, and the Duchess of Cumberland had persuaded Charles James Fox and his wife, Elizabeth, to accompany her.

The Duchess of Gordon preened as she introduced Madame Juliette Recamier and the Duchess of Abrantes to her English guests. At ten o'clock came the moment everyone had been waiting for. Josephine Bonaparte, along with her son and daughter, arrived and it was Jane's crowning achievement. Tonight, she had become the leading London hostess in Paris.

"John, I've been watching for you," Lady Holland chided him. "It's almost midnight—I thought you had changed your mind."

"May I partner you in the contradance, Beth?"

"That will more than make up for your tardiness, Your Grace."

"I expected reels and strathspeys would dominate the evening."

Beth laughed. "Nothing so indecorous. The Duchess of Gordon is bent on impressing the first consul's lady with her elegant grace and dignity."

"Did you persuade Lady Georgina to go shopping?"

"I did. You may not approve the results, however. Her new gown has caused quite a stir among both the ladies and the *men*."

"I don't see her." John's glance again swept the ballroom.

"Eugene Beauharnais has escorted her to the supper room." Beth watched for his reaction, but his dark eyes told her nothing. "Jane Gordon is watching us. She seemed shocked when you arrived, but now she looks quite smug."

Across the room, Lady Bessborough asked Jane, "What on earth is Bedford doing at your ball? The man is in double mourning."

Jane Gordon had asked herself that same question when he had appeared, but the obvious answer had come to her immediately. "John Russell is on a noble errand, fulfilling his brother's last request. With his dying breath, Francis asked John to deliver a lock of his hair to Georgina. This will finally put an end to any doubts that the pair was engaged to be married."

With satisfaction, Jane watched Henrietta Bessborough hurry off to speak with Lady Susannah Stafford. Her son was Granville Leveson Gower, and Jane knew Susannah's letters to London would convey every detail of what she had seen and heard tonight.

John saw Georgina return to the ballroom, accompanied by both Eugene and Hortense Beauharnais. He hung back until the next dance was announced, and then he walked a direct path to her. She was wearing a blush-pink empire-style gown that was deliciously diaphanous. Her upswept hair was styled in a profusion of tiny curls, held in place with pink rosebuds. *She looks like the icing on a cake.* He had an overwhelming desire to taste her.

She did not see him until he bowed before her. "John." When she said his name, it was half whisper and half sigh.

"May I have this dance, Lady Georgina?"

She hesitated slightly. "It is a *waltz.*" This was the latest dance sweeping Paris. It was considered extremely bold and daring because the gentleman held his partner in his arms.

"That is precisely why I have chosen this dance." He held out his hand in invitation.

Georgina placed her hand in his and felt his fingers curl about hers possessively. Then he wrapped his arm about her and swept her onto the ballroom floor. Her breasts rose and fell with the thrill of being held close in John's arms, and she was breathless from the excitement of dancing the waltz with everyone's eyes on them. "You make me feel very wicked."

"You are the most beautiful lady in the ballroom, nay, in all Paris, tonight. Your eyes are shining like stars."

Georgina had never waltzed before and had been afraid she would misstep, but John held her so securely and led her around the floor with such assurance that her fear quickly dissolved. "Thank you. You have restored my confidence."

"I have a carriage waiting outside. Do you feel wickedly confident enough to steal away from the ball and take a ride with me along the Seine?"

Georgina drew in a swift breath, and the music filled her heart as she swayed in his arms. "I do, John." *I do, I do, I do!*

He smiled down into her eyes. "I shall draw everyone's attention by dancing with Josephine Bonaparte. It will give you a chance to get a dark cloak, and slip away unnoticed."

Chapter 25

"I'm sorry to keep you waiting." Georgina was breathless. "My friend Hortense diverted Mother's attention so I could slip away without being seen."

John helped her into the carriage and sat down facing her. He knew if he took the seat beside her, he could not trust himself to keep his hands from her. "You didn't take long to make friends."

"Hortense needed a sympathetic ear to listen to her troubles. Her stepfather has chosen to marry her to his brother, Louis Bonaparte, and she has been given no choice in the matter."

"Napoleon has decided Hortense must marry for position, and I believe he will make the same decision for his stepson Eugene."

"You feel you must warn me, but you need not. I have no interest in Eugene Beauharnais, except as a friend."

"He makes no secret of his feelings for you, Georgina."

"Eugene is a boy who has mistaken infatuation for love."

"Your mother is doing her best to promote a match between the two of you. I don't want you to be hurt again."

"I am aware of my mother's matchmaking ambitions, John. I don't intend to be hurt again. I will make my own decisions about my future."

"Your future is what I would like to discuss." He warned himself to go carefully. He had visions of her bolting from the carriage. "I am a good deal older than you, Georgina," he began tentatively.

She caught her breath. He had stolen her heart long before he became widowed. Whenever they met, sparks had ignited, and there had always been an unspoken attraction between them. Was it possible his feelings had deepened into something more? "I find maturity a most attractive quality in a man."

"Flattery, begod."

She laughed softly, remembering she had once said those saucy words to him.

For God's sake, don't tell her you are in love with her. She's still in love with Francis. He leaned forward. "Georgina, I don't want to spend my life alone. I need a political hostess for Woburn, and I can think of no other lady who would fit my needs so perfectly. You enjoy politics as much as I do."

You're going to propose! Inside, she was bubbling with joy.

"My two older sons don't really need a mother, but my youngest son does. Thankfully, Johnny already loves you."

Ask me . . . Just ask me! She wanted to scream with excitement.

"I have recently lost my wife and my brother. People will whisper that I am a decadent devil, and the last thing I want is for you to be hurt by more gossip. But if you'll have me, Georgy, I promise to do my utmost to make you happy."

Her heart melted with love. She reached out and touched his face tenderly. "I'll have you, old man," she whispered.

Relief washed over him. He captured her hand and kissed it. "You had to say yes after we danced the waltz in front of everyone. I deliberately compromised you."

"You *are* a decadent devil!" *No, John, you are a*

romantic at heart, but your secret is safe with me. "Stop the carriage! Let's get out and walk."

John glanced through the carriage window, and when he saw where they were, signaled the coachman to stop. He alighted, asked the driver to follow them, and then helped Georgina from the coach. They were on the wide boulevard that ran between the Tuileries gardens and the Seine. With a protective hand at the small of her back, John led her from the deep shadows of the Linden trees toward the river.

She took a deep, appreciative breath. "It's such a beautiful night. The air is soft and warm . . . May is surely the loveliest month." *And Paris is the most romantic city in the world!*

He hated to speak of practical matters, but it must be done. "I know all brides long for a grand wedding with hundreds of guests invited to celebrate the nuptials, but that would mean waiting a year until the mourning period is over." He looked down into her eyes. "I don't want to wait that long." Georgina was such a tempting marriage prize. He feared she would be snatched away from him if he waited.

He loves me so much he cannot bear to wait. Her spirit soared with happiness. She had always vowed that she would never marry unless she loved the man with all her heart, and now her dream was about to come true. "You are right. A big wedding would cause a scandal, but if we have a private ceremony, surely we don't have to wait a year?"

John was relieved that she was amenable to a discreet exchange of vows. "All your sisters had grand weddings—are you sure you won't have regrets, Georgy?"

"Absolutely, positively sure."

John was amazed that she seemed not only willing, but also eager to fall in with his plans. *Marriage is the only way she can escape her mother. The wretched woman dominates her life.* He vowed to cherish her and give her all the freedom she craved. *That is the surest way to win her heart. I will give her lots of time to get over Francis. Then I will woo her with a vengeance.* "How about a month from today?" He pressed for a firm committment. "Will that give you enough time?"

"June is traditional for a wedding. June twenty-third will be perfect."

John took hold of her left hand and slipped a ring on her finger to seal their engagement. The large pear-shaped diamond took her breath away. He bent his head and placed a tender kiss on her forehead. "I swear you won't regret this, Georgy."

She yearned for a real kiss, but knew he held back out of respect for her feelings for his brother. It was a charade she must keep up for the present, but once they were married, she would show John that she loved him to distraction.

"I'll make a formal call on the Duchess of Gordon tomorrow."

"Oh, John, can't you wait for a few days so I can savor the secret?"

"I should return to London. There are so many pressing things I must see to before June. Apart from my Woburn obligations, I have to take my seat in the Lords, and I am obliged to get back before my sons' school year ends." He smiled down at her. "Now that I have everything I came for, there is no need to stay in Paris." A sudden thought occurred to him, and his dark brows drew together. "You're not afraid your mother will refuse me, are you?"

Refuse an offer to make her daughter the Duchess of Bedford? Not bloody likely! "It is not her decision to make, John. It is mine, and I have made it."

Little girl, I love and adore you.

"The Duke of Bedford?" Jane Gordon was pleasantly surprised that John Russell was paying a formal call. "Show him into the sitting room and ask Lady Georgina to join us." She checked her appearance in the mirror, liked what she saw, and went downstairs.

"Your Grace, I truly appreciate your thoughtfulness in coming all the way to Paris to fulfill your brother's last wish."

"My brother?" John was at a loss.

"The lock of hair you have brought for Georgina will give her so much comfort."

"Last night I asked Lady Georgina to be my wife."

The Duchess of Gordon's jaw dropped. She rapidly recovered from her astonishment. "Ah, now I understand perfectly. The lock of hair was a symbol. It was your brother's way of asking you to take care of Georgina. How very noble and selfless you are, Your Grace. I am quite overcome by such gallantry."

Her explanation for his proposal made John feel anything but gallant. He was about to enlighten her when Georgina entered the room. The sight of her made him forget about Jane Gordon.

"Good morning, John." *It really happened . . . it wasn't just a dream!* She felt her cheeks grow warm.

"Georgina, the Duke of Bedford has come to ask my permission to propose marriage."

"No, Mother. John has come to tell you that he proposed to me last night, and I accepted him. Our wedding will be June twenty-third."

"But that's less than a month away!"

"It will be a short engagement." Georgina raised her hand to display her diamond ring. "John has to return to England."

"Well . . . well . . . it seems the two of you have come to a mutual agreement. Congratulations, Your Grace. We are highly flattered at the honor you do us. May I say that nothing in the world could give me greater satisfaction." Jane held out her hand.

John bowed and kissed her fingers. "Thank you, Lady Gordon."

"I'm sure you will both excuse me," Jane said smoothly.

When they were alone, John fought the desire to sweep Georgina into his arms. "Your mother sounded pleased."

"Her words were completely sincere. We *are* highly flattered at the honor you do us," she said breathlessly.

John placed a finger against her lips. "Hush, Georgy. The honor is mine. I'm leaving tomorrow, so I won't see you again until you return to London. Let me know the moment you are home." His arms went about her to draw her close. *"Au revoir, ma petite."*

When he spoke French, her very bones melted.

"Georgina, I am speechless with admiration. After all our hopes of your becoming the Duchess of Bedford were cruelly dashed to smithereens, you have wrought a miracle! But, darling, how on earth am I to pack up everything, return to England, and plan a grand wedding in less than a month?"

"We are not having a grand wedding. We will exchange our vows in a private ceremony with just the family present."

"But you are marrying the *Duke of Bedford.* All London should be there to celebrate the nuptials."

"Mother, have you forgotten that John is in mourning? It would be in execrable taste to have a big wedding. There will be gossip enough that we are not waiting a year."

"A year? Heaven forbid! You cannot risk losing another duke."

"Has someone else died?" Johnny asked his father.

John had picked up his sons at Westminster School and brought them to Russell Square for dinner so he could tell them he was getting married. He saw the apprehension on his youngest son's face and quickly reassured him. "No, Johnny. Everything is fine. I have some news to share."

"Is it about Napoleon Bonaparte?" William asked eagerly.

John smiled. "No, it's about me. I have decided to marry."

Francis exchanged a look with William, and it told

their father that the news did not sit well with either of them. "Why do you want another wife?"

The blunt question could be taken two ways. Either they didn't want another woman taking their mother's place, or they equated females with unhappiness. John feared it was the latter.

"Is it Lady Georgina?" Johnny asked hopefully.

"Yes, it is, Johnny. You are very perceptive. The wedding will be in three weeks, on June twenty-third, so we can all spend the summer together at Woburn."

His two older sons seemed less antagonistic now that they had learned the lady's identity. "That will make Lord Lennox our uncle. I rather like him," William said.

"You'll have lots of new aunts and uncles," John added.

"That won't make up for losing Uncle Francis," his namesake declared.

"Of course it won't. No one can take Francis's place."

"Charlie Lennox will be my cousin. We had great fun together," Johnny said. "Although Lady Mary tries to rule the roost."

"That's the trouble with females. They are all bossy," William told his younger brother. "You have to put them in their place."

"Is that what they teach you at school? I hope you will act like gentlemen and treat Lady Georgina with respect."

Late that night Johnny came into his father's chamber and climbed on the bed. John lifted the covers so his son could slip in beside him. "Is something troubling you, Johnny?"

"No, Father. I want you to know how happy I am that you are going to marry Lady Georgina." Then he blurted, "I'm glad she didn't marry Uncle Francis. Is that wicked of me?"

"I'm glad too—it's not wicked at all." *Are you sure, old man?*

* * *

Two days before the wedding, John and Georgina had dinner with Charles and Charlotte at Fife House in Whitehall. The couple had accepted the Lennoxes' offer to have the wedding in their home.

"It's most generous of you to let us exchange our vows here at Fife House, Charlotte. I hope your mother isn't offended."

"Lud, Mother was the one who suggested it. She's up to her eyebrows in plans for the grand entertainment she's throwing at Pall Mall two days after the wedding."

Georgina threw John an apologetic look. "She's invited half of London. I couldn't talk her out of it, John. She sees nothing wrong with having it both ways—a discreet marriage ceremony here at Fife House, and as soon as we leave London, she'll hostess a reception at Pall Mall for the *haut ton*."

"You can't ask a leopard to change her spots," Charlotte said.

"In truth, Georgina and I are flouting convention, so your mother has my blessing. After all, she made a great sacrifice returning to London, when she found Paris so rewarding."

Huntly grimaced. "I was quite enjoying Mother being out of the country. Living here at Fife House gave me total freedom."

Georgina winked at her brother. "Make the most of tonight. It will be your last chance to indulge in depravity."

"We're going to White's, not *La Maison Rouge*," he said dryly.

Georgina blushed. Not because her brother referred to a brothel, but because she had actually been there.

After dinner, Charles and George withdrew to the entrance hall to give the betrothed couple a chance to say good night. They were taking John to White's Club, where they had arranged for Lord Holland to join them in a traditional gentleman's night out for the bridegroom's last taste of freedom, so to speak.

John took Georgina's hands. "I won't see you again

before the wedding. Do you have everything you need?"

"I will have if Father arrives tomorrow." Georgina gazed down at the powerful hands that held hers. She suddenly realized she no longer needed Alexander Gordon to make her feel secure. John Russell's love would keep her safe forever.

When they arrived at White's, Lord Holland was there before them. Henry was talking to the Prince of Wales and Lauderdale, and all three men came forward to greet John. "Congratulations, Bedford. I have only just heard your news. Lady Georgina is a favorite of ours." Obviously thinking of his friend Francis, Prinny gave a heartfelt sigh. "Life must go on."

Henry steered John away from the prince, who had a tendency to steep himself in bathos. A liveried attendant took the men's order for drinks, and they moved into one of the gaming rooms.

"Devil take it, I haven't seen so many Whigs in one room in years. I thought they preferred Devonshire House to White's."

"They do," Charles Lennox declared. "But unfortunately, the duchess is suffering from bad health and is unable to entertain."

At least a dozen members of parliament offered John their sincere congratulations, and he was glad that he had agreed to come tonight. One man who didn't come forward was George Villiers, Earl of Jersey. John hadn't seen the man since that unfortunate encounter at the masquerade ball. *Francis overheard Jersey remark that I had a hand in my wife's death and called him a liar before all the other guests. There is certainly no love lost between us.* John was secretly amused that when he and his companions sat down at the faro table, Jersey got up and left.

At first John was lucky, but gradually Georgina's brother began to win, and there was no stopping him. After two hours, John told his future brothers-in-law that he was going to try his luck in the next room at the baccarat table, and his friend Henry decided to join him.

In the corridor, John came face-to-face with Prince Edward. Though he had been a great friend of his brother's, John felt only contempt for the young royal who had said scandalous things about Georgina. He nodded coldly and was about to pass when the prince sneered, "I hear you are marrying your brother's leavings."

John was enraged. "You have maligned the lady one too many times." He fought the urge to thrash him within an inch of his life then and there.

"The *lady* bet me she would become the Duchess of Bedford. It was the title she craved, not poor old Francis. Now she is about to achieve her goal. I bow to the *Dupe of Bedford.*"

The slap was so sharp, it left finger marks on Edward's florid cheek. "I will meet you in Saint James's Park in two hours. Lord Holland will act for me. Pistols or swords—the choice is yours." John turned on his heel and strode away, his barely controlled fury smoldering.

While Lord Holland stayed behind to work out the details with Prince Edward's second, Lennox and Huntly accompanied John back to Russell Square. He dismissed the servants, led them to the library, and lit the lamps himself.

Huntly felt extremely gratified that his sister Georgina was about to marry a man who cherished her and was willing to fight for her honor.

Lennox remarked, "You are the only man I know, other than myself, who is reckless enough to challenge a royal prince."

"Well, Charles, if I acquit myself as well as you did, I will have satisfaction," John declared. "If you will excuse me, I will go up and change my clothes."

More than an hour had gone by before Henry arrived. He eyed John's white shirt and silver-gray waistcoat. "You will make a perfect target. He chose pistols."

"Too bad. I would have enjoyed slicing him open." John went to the gun cabinet and took out a leather gun case. "Who is acting as his second?"

"Lord Jersey; wouldn't you know it?" Henry replied.

"That was predictable." John opened the gun case, counted the lead balls, and handed the pair of dueling pistols to Holland. "They were cleaned before they were put away, but it's some time since they were last used."

Henry inspected them and put them back in the case. "We don't have much time left." He checked his watch. "Ready, gentlemen?" John's companions did a credible job of hiding their apprehension. They were not the least worried about Bedford's marksmanship, but they were uneasy that the duke's target was a royal prince.

They arrived in Saint James's Park with ten minutes to spare. All four men got out of the carriage and walked toward the pond. After twenty minutes had passed, John became impatient and began to pace. More than half an hour went by before they heard a vehicle approaching.

The Earl of Jersey got out of the carriage, and Lord Holland went to meet him. They spoke for a few minutes, and then Henry returned to John. "Jersey says that Prince Edward is so inebriated, he cannot even stand, let alone shoot."

"Peste!" John swore. "The drunken sot is beneath contempt. Kindly inform Jersey that I will accept a written apology." He watched Henry approach Jersey; then saw the earl return to the carriage. Finally, after a wait of ten minutes, Lord Jersey brought Lord Holland a piece of paper. Henry read it, nodded his acceptance, and brought the paper to John. It read: *I apologize for defaming a certain lady's name. The accusation was false.* The words were legible and obviously written by Jersey, but the scrawled signature after the initials H.R.H. was authentic.

John's companions returned him to Russell Square

and drank a hearty toast to the victor before they departed. All in all it was the best possible outcome to an impossible situation.

An hour later, John lay sleepless in the dark. *Could the accusation be true?* He was well aware that Georgina loved to make wagers. *Is it the title Duchess of Bedford she craves? If so she is about to achieve her goal.*

Though he'd tried to suppress it, John vividly remembered their first encounter after his wife's death. *Whatever makes you think I'd be interested in a mere lord when I can attract a duke to offer me marriage? We both know the duke I have in mind.*

He quit the bed and paced to the window. *Is it possible that both Francis and I were duped?*

Chapter 26

"This is the happiest day of my life!" Georgina stood before the mirror as her sisters fitted on her bridal veil. She looked radiant and her eyes were luminous. "Oh, Louisa, I remember you saying those exact words before your wedding."

"And do you remember laughing at me?" Louisa asked.

"Yes, I do, and I apologize profusely. I hadn't the faintest notion what love was." Both Louisa and Charlotte knew her secret, that she had detested Francis Russell and had been attracted to his brother, John, from the beginning.

"I feel positively giddy. How on earth will I act with decorum on this very solemn occasion?"

"For your groom's sake, I hope you can restrain yourself from saying or doing anything inappropriate," Charlotte cautioned.

"I shall strive to behave during the ceremony, but I make no promises after that."

"Ah, well, you'll be a duchess by then, and impropriety is mandatory, if Mother is any example. And, of course, once the deed is done, John cannot back out of it."

"Why would he want to back out of it? John is marrying me because he loves me!"

Louisa whooped with laughter. "Love has absolutely nothing to do with it. You're a Gordon—rank is the only thing that counts."

Georgina joined in her sister's laughter. "What an insufferable little cockroach I was back then!"

"What makes you think you have changed?" Charlotte asked dryly.

The Duchess of Gordon swept into the bedchamber. "It's after five, and the rector from Chenies hasn't arrived. There's no sign of Susan yet, either. It's a good thing your father brought a good supply of whiskey to fortify the men while they wait."

I'm ready to forgive Susan for what happened at Kimbolton, but forgetting is a little more difficult. "I'm sorry Madelina won't be here. We haven't seen her since Louisa's wedding."

"Madelina has no title. She is acutely aware that she cannot compete with the rest of you," Jane explained.

"It's not a competition," Georgina declared.

"Yes it is, Georgy," Charlotte contradicted, "and you won."

"You are a dreadful tease, Charlotte, but nothing in the world can spoil my happiness tonight."

The sound of a carriage caused Jane to peer through the window. "I believe the clergyman has arrived, and if I'm not mistaken the Manchesters' coach is here too. I shall allow you fifteen more minutes; then you are to present yourselves in the grand salon."

When the three sisters descended the stairs, the Duchess of Gordon awaited them. "The carriage ride brought on Susan's nausea. She begs us to carry on without her. It will give her a chance to lie down and recuperate."

The moment Georgina entered the salon, she had eyes only for John. Their glances met and held as she took her place beside him. Her heart sang with happiness and overflowed with joy. His dark, compelling looks were so irresistible, they took her breath away. *You are the most attractive man I've ever met. I am the luckiest woman in the world to be loved by you.*

* * *

"Dearly beloved . . . " Georgina heard the first two words, and then she was lost in a reverie of sheer bliss. John's tall, powerful presence at her side filled her with euphoric happiness.

"I will."

She looked up at him and realized he had just pledged to love her and forsake all others forever. His dark head was bathed in candlelight, and the solemnity of his voice touched her deeply. Then she heard the rector ask if she would obey John, serve him, and love, honor, and keep him. She looked up into John's eyes and without hesitation vowed, "I will."

Alexander, Duke of Gordon stepped forward, and placed her hand in John's, symbolically giving her to her husband. The gesture brought a flood of tenderness for a father she had always loved.

"I, John, take thee, Georgina, to my wedded wife."

Those are the loveliest words you've ever said to me. She listened closely, then plighted her troth to John softly, sweetly, and meant the words with all her heart.

John slipped the wide gold band onto her finger. "With this ring I thee wed, with my body I thee honor, and with all my worldly goods I thee endow."

The rector solemnly pronounced them man and wife.

It's done . . . We're married! She lifted her veil, and when John bent his head and brushed his lips against hers, it sent a delicious frisson along her spine.

The bride and groom were surrounded immediately. The men congratulated John, and Charlotte enfolded her young sister in her arms. "I wish you great happiness, Mrs. Russell."

"Thank you. Georgina Russell is such a lovely name!"

Louisa hugged and kissed her, and then it was her mother's turn. "I want you to know I could not be more proud that my daughter has just become the Duchess of Bedford."

Georgina saw Charlotte roll her eyes, and the two sisters dissolved in laughter.

Across the room, the Duke of Gordon was conversing with his new son-in-law. When Georgina joined them, Alexander took his daughter into his arms and embraced her in a bear hug. He admonished the bridegroom, "Look after my little girl."

Georgina and John smiled into each other's eyes. *He called me little girl the first time we met, and now uses it to tease me.*

The nannies had been given strict instructions to keep the children occupied in their own wing, well away from the evening wedding. Georgina had promised Mary she would come upstairs to show off her wedding dress before the candlelit dinner was served.

"You look beautiful, Georgy." Mary stroked the silk taffeta. "Did you marry the old man so you could be Johnny's mother?"

She was taken aback. "I suppose that was one of the reasons."

"Will you still love me?" Mary asked anxiously.

Georgina picked her up and swung her around. "Darling, of course I'll still love you. You will always hold a very special place in my heart." She pulled a delicate white rose from her bridal bouquet and gave it to the child. "I'll save you some wedding cake. Superstition says if you put it under your pillow and make a wish, it is sure to come true."

"Do wishes really come true?"

"Yes, absolutely. I made a wish, and today mine came true."

John held his bride's chair when they all sat down to the wedding supper. He hadn't slept the past two nights because of the vile accusations Prince Edward had made about Georgina. He had finally come to the conclusion that Edward was jealous. The young swine had dangled after Georgina since her coming-out ball, and John was almost certain that Edward had made a wager with Francis over which of them could seduce her. Obviously Francis had won, and the dissolute prince was infuriated.

As John took his seat beside his wife, he was ashamed of a fleeting thought that had come to him last night: *Perhaps it was Georgina who seduced Francis in order to become the Duchess of Bedford.* Now, as he listened to her witty ripostes to her brother's teasing, John realized that it didn't matter. This was the woman he wanted in his life. If he had any chance of happiness, he would find it with this vivacious beauty who had stolen his heart. *I just vowed to cherish her for the rest of my life, and I meant it.*

John listened to Alex Gordon talk about Scotland. It was obvious he loved the country life and had little use for London society. Next, he observed Jane as she dominated the conversation with ribald stories of the Parisians, and wondered how two such opposites had become attracted. *It was lust, pure and simple,* John concluded. *Flesh calling to flesh.* Georgina's enticing fragrance stole to him, and he became instantly aroused.

John glanced at Louisa and her husband, Cornwallis. *She is the dominant partner in that relationship, yet they seem happy enough.* His glance moved on to Susan, who had been unwell when she arrived. She had a petulant look of dissatisfaction on her face, and though she was carrying Manchester's child, he seemed utterly indifferent to her. *In most marriages, one loves more than the other.* He glanced down at his new bride. *In our marriage, I warrant that role will be mine, at least in the beginning. Someday, if I'm lucky, I'll win her heart.* John looked at Charlotte and Charles. Their union seemed completely comfortable and compatible, and yet he did not want that with Georgina. He wanted more, so much more.

"It's only midnight, but I believe we have monopolized the newlyweds long enough," Jane declared. "At Pall Mall we can carry on the celebration until dawn, though Susan looks ready to drop."

Georgina suddenly felt guilty. Since the night she had fled from Kimbolton, she had harbored deep resentment against Susan. But tonight her heart overflowed with happiness, and she wanted to share her joy with her sister. *I must tell Susan that I love her.*

As the wedding guests made their way to the entrance hall, Georgina beckoned her sister into the sitting room.

"It was so sweet of you to come all this way when you're not feeling well." Georgy embraced her sister. "I'm so happy, Susan."

"You have me to thank for your happiness. When you were forced to flee the country to escape scandal, I was absolutely livid. I drove straight to Woburn and confronted John Russell with his brother's letter."

"What letter?"

"The letter Francis wrote to William after your rendezvous at Kimbolton. Bedford told us that he had proposed marriage to you, and that he intended to make a formal call on Mother, then declare your engagement publicly. I made it plain to John Russell where his duty lay," Susan declared.

"Duty?" Georgina whispered. The room suddenly felt cold.

"John Russell and his friends denied there was an engagement and subjected you to public humiliation. After I showed him irrefutable proof that Francis had asked you to become the Duchess of Bedford, Russell clearly saw it was his duty to restore your reputation and honor you with the title you had been promised."

Manchester appeared at the sitting room door. "Where the devil are you, Susan? You're not going to be sick again, surely?"

"I'm coming!" She lowered her voice. "Men are so bloody impatient." Susan kissed her sister's cheek. "Don't feel guilty, Georgy. You deserve to be the Duchess of Bedford. Good night."

Georgina's knees felt so shaky, she sank down into a chair. *John asked me to marry him because he loves me.* Her luminous happiness shimmered all about her, and she clung to it desperately. Her mind flew back to that romantic night in Paris when he had proposed.

I need a political hostess for Woburn. I can think of no other lady who would fit my needs so perfectly. You enjoy politics as much as I do.

My older sons don't need a mother, but my youngest son does. The last thing I want is for you to be hurt by more gossip.

Georgina felt ice-cold fingers steal about her heart. She shivered. *John made no declaration of love. He kissed me on the forehead.* Her joy became ephemeral, like mist, and floated away from her. Her happiness shattered into a thousand shards.

"We've been looking for you." Charlotte turned up the lamp. "What on earth are you doing sitting here in the dark?"

Georgina could not answer because of the lump in her throat. She saw the anxious look on John's face as he stood at the door.

Charlotte took her hands and pulled her from the chair. "They've all gone . . . finally! Let me take you upstairs, Georgy." As they passed John, Charlotte murmured, "Bridal nerves . . . I'll take care of her."

The two sisters ascended the stairs, then turned into the guest wing where the bridal chamber had been prepared. Georgina could feel her legs trembling, and sat down on the bed.

"Is something wrong, darling?" Charlotte asked with concern.

Georgina shook her head.

A Lennox maid came in to help the young bride prepare for bed, but Charlotte dismissed her with a kind word of thanks. When they were alone, she busied herself making sure there were fresh towels and other toiletries; then she pulled the heavy drapes closed across the tall windows. She picked up the delicately embroidered nightdress from the pillow and set it down beside Georgina. "Let me help you out of your wedding gown," she said gently.

As if she were in a daze, Georgina allowed her sister to remove her dress and her undergarments and slip the white nightdress over her head. Charlotte led her to the dressing table, gently pushed her down so that she was sitting before the mirror, then began to brush her hair. "Are you afraid, Georgy?"

Their eyes met in the reflection of the mirror. "You needn't be afraid. John loves you very much."

Georgina's eyes flooded with tears, and Charlotte hurried across the bedchamber to a table that held decanters. She passed over the wine and picked up the brandy. She poured a liberal amount into a glass and brought it to her sister. "Drink up. It will banish your nuptial jitters."

Georgina took the glass and held it. She looked like she was in shock, or some sort of a trance, and Charlotte concluded she was lost in her thoughts. She remembered the night Georgy had caught her performing an intimate act on Charles, so she knew her young sister wasn't completely ignorant about sex. "Darling, you are worrying over nothing. Just drink your brandy, and John will take care of everything else. All right?"

Georgina nodded, but Charlotte could see she was still immersed in her own deep thoughts. She couldn't think of anything else to do, so she withdrew and quietly closed the bedchamber door.

At the top of the stairs, Charlotte encountered John. "I'm afraid her happy, vivacious mood has changed completely. It's just a case of nerves. I assured her there was nothing to worry about. Good night, John."

Georgina stared down into the glass of brandy. She set it untasted onto a bedside table and sat down on the bed. She felt numb, stunned like a bird flown into a stone wall. *My husband doesn't love me!* She wanted to laugh, but knew she was closer to sobbing. *I swore I would never marry without love. How foolish I must seem to everyone. It feels like a nightmare, except it's real—I'm not asleep.*

Georgina jumped as she heard the door open.

When she saw that it was John, dismay overwhelmed her. Surely there was no greater humiliation on earth than having to show gratitude to someone who felt obligated to do his duty.

John smiled at his beautiful bride when he saw her sitting on the bed in her nightgown. He removed his coat, his waistcoat, unfastened his neckcloth and removed it too, before he moved across the room toward her. As he got closer, he saw the unhappy look on her face that was close to panic. He had sensed something was wrong when he and Charlotte had found Georgina sitting in the dark. John knew the last person she had spoken with was Susan, and he suspected it was something her sister had said that had changed her happy mood.

His bride looked so impossibly young, it gave him a feeling of disquiet. He realized he must seem very old to her at this moment. "Georgy, you're not afraid, are you?"

Her eyes went wide. Her throat was so tight, she could not answer. Instead she shook her head uncertainly.

"Perhaps *afraid* is the wrong word, but you *are* feeling a little apprehensive." He gave her a reassuring smile. "Georgy, it's only natural. I imagine every bride feels this way on her wedding night." He reached out to ruffle her dark curls and tried not to feel rebuffed when she drew back from his hand. *She looks so forlorn and vulnerable, it breaks my heart.*

"Do you want to talk about it, sweetheart?" he asked kindly.

She shook her head vigorously.

He noticed the untouched brandy on the bedside table. Though he knew she would benefit from the "tiger frightener," perhaps it was too strong for her. "Would you like some wine, Georgy?"

Once again she shook her head.

"Why don't you get into bed," he suggested. When he saw her hesitation, he turned the lamp down to a faint glow. John was relieved when she slowly arose, lifted the covers, and slid into bed. She sat motionless as if she were in a trance. He removed the studs from his shirt and sat down on the bed. Propped against the huge pillows, his bride looked small and fragile.

His hands cupped her shoulders, and he drew her toward him to place a kiss on her forehead. The moment his lips touched her silken skin, he felt her stiffen. *She's thinking about Francis. I must give her time . . . I must be patient.*

John smiled down into her eyes. "You're not up to this tonight, are you, Georgy?"

Her lips trembled as she swallowed hard and whispered, "No."

"I understand—truly. Get some sleep." John tenderly tucked the covers about her. He moved away from the bed, turned out the lamp, and sank down in the overstuffed bedroom chair.

Georgina lay awake in the dark for hours before the numbness gradually seeped away. It was replaced by anger. Hatred for Francis Russell rose up inside her with a vengeance. He was the root of all her trouble. Georgina was also furious with her mother for constantly pushing her into the dissolute swine's arms.

It was doubly infuriating that her sister Susan and Manchester had aided and abetted her mother in the sordid seduction plot. Lastly, she was angry with John Russell. He had married her under false pretenses, and shattered all her lovely dreams.

The dominant devil had no trouble persuading me to do exactly as he wished. He took complete charge at a time when I was most vulnerable. My instincts should have told me that the imperious, domineering male wanted God-given dominion over me.

She lay in the dark with one unhappy thought chasing another in an unending circle. But gradually it began to dawn on her that she had no one to blame but herself. *I was the one who flirted with Francis Russell, luring him and toying with him so that he would come panting after me. I did this in spite of my brother warning me a dozen times that the duke was a womanizer.*

I should have made it plain to Mother that I detested the man and had no intention of marrying him. I could have taken Susan into my confidence and told her it was John Russell who attracted me while Francis repelled me.

Georgina pictured her new husband sleeping in the chair across the room. The thought of John marrying her out of duty, rather than love, was devastating. But there it was. It must be faced. *I am wed to a man who does not love me, in spite of vowing never to get trapped in a loveless marriage. I must stop feeling sorry for myself. My future happiness is up to me. All I have to do to make my dreams come true is make John Russell fall in love with me.* In the darkness, Georgina's mouth curved into a secret smile.

Chapter 27

Georgina opened her eyes and realized it was morning. Someone had opened the curtains, and sunlight was streaming into the chamber. In that instant everything came back to her, and her glance flew to the bedroom chair. It was empty, and her heart sank.

John has left! And no bloody wonder. Any self-respecting bridegroom who'd been made to sleep in a chair on his wedding night would be miles away by now!

The door opened, and John came in carrying a tray. "Good morning. I thought you might enjoy breakfast in bed."

She sat up against the pillows. "My behavior last night was appalling . . . I'm sorry, John."

"Nonsense." He set the tray before her and sat on the bed.

Her green eyes shone with admiration. "You are such a civil man. Civil is short for civilized, I suppose, which is something us Gordons could never claim to be."

John lifted the silver covers from three platters of food.

"Good heavens, I'll never be able to eat all that."

"I should hope not! Most of it's for me."

"Greedy devil. And here's me calling you civilized."

"I have a man's healthy appetite." His glance was

drawn to her lush breasts, enticingly visible through the filmy nightgown. *In all things, and I'm starving.* He gazed at her hungrily and couldn't quite catch his breath.

Georgina had been trained her entire life in how to attract the male of the species. It wasn't enough to be feminine and alluring. To make a man fall hard, a lady must also be provocative and elusive. Men always wanted what they could not have. They enjoyed the chase, and found a challenge irresistible. *I must not let John know I am head over heels in love with him.*

She reached for a piece of bacon with her fingers, but John got there first. "Do you like bacon, Georgy?"

"I do," she admitted, "especially if it's crispy."

He reached across the tray and held it close to her lips. She smiled into his eyes and allowed him to feed her. "I just learned a secret . . . you cannot resist temptation."

"Of course I can."

He picked up another piece and wafted it before her. Its tempting aroma was irresistible. Georgina succumbed, and allowed him to feed her all the bacon on the platter. Sharing the breakfast resulted in much laughter, and John was immensely pleased that Georgina was in a happy, playful mood.

Though he was fully aroused and longed to make love to her, he controlled his rampant desire. He was wise enough to realize he must go slowly in his courtship and win her to a giving mood. The last thing he wanted was for his beautiful wife to draw back and retreat from his advances.

"I must get dressed. I can't wait to put on my lovely traveling suit. I bought my entire trousseau in Paris." Her eyes sparkled. "I couldn't resist the temptation of French fashions."

"Our people in Bedfordshire are most discerning, and are certain to appreciate them," he teased, "but I can't guarantee that our people in Cambridge and Northampton won't simply gape at you."

"But I *love* to be gaped at. Why do you think I wear such outrageous hats?" she demanded.

"To steal every other woman's thunder and make yourself the center of attention, of course. I'm learning all your secrets."

"Ha! That will take forever."

John smiled into her eyes. "We have forever, Georgy."

You have a gift for saying exactly the right thing. It's no wonder I'm mad about you.

Two hours later, Georgina, in a spectacular primrose-yellow traveling dress and matching coat, stepped up into the Duke of Bedford's carriage and threw good-bye kisses to Charlotte and her niece Mary. The newlyweds would spend tonight at Woburn and leave on a short trip tomorrow.

"I'm sorry the time is so short, Georgina. I must visit the Russell estates in Cambridge and Northampton, and be back at Woburn when my sons finish their school year."

"You needn't apologize, John. As the Duchess of Bedford, I look forward to sharing all your responsibilities. I have an insatiable curiosity, and love visiting places I've never been before and meeting new people."

"They're new to me too. I haven't visited the Russell estates since I was a boy. I don't intend to be an absentee landlord. I need to make sure the stewards in charge of the estates are not stealing me blind, or making the lives of my tenant farmers hell on earth." He grimaced. "Such an exciting honeymoon."

"Duty before pleasure," she teased, "is a mark of maturity and a quality that is most desirable in a husband." Georgina suddenly blushed as she realized their marriage had not yet been consummated. They were husband and wife in name only. Tonight was the night when all that would change. She experienced a moment of panic, as she wondered if John would find it a duty or a pleasure. *I won't think about it now; I'll think about it later.*

When they arrived at Woburn Abbey it was late

in the afternoon, and Mr. Burke had assembled both the inside staff and the outdoor workers to greet the Duke of Bedford and his new duchess.

Georgina asked the steward to introduce each servant by name. She stopped each maid from curtsying and, instead, shook her hand. Then she offered her hand to every member of the male staff and repeated his name.

"Thank you for your warm welcome. There hasn't been a duchess at Woburn for three decades, and I warrant that most of you are apprehensive about catering to a female. I just want everyone to know that I'm apprehensive also. Being a duchess is new to me, and I ask all of you to help me fulfill my role."

Mr. Burke and the Duke of Bedford looked at Georgina with approval and admiration. Then John swept her up into his arms and carried her over the threshold. The women clapped and the men cheered. All were clearly delighted to be part of the age-old romantic custom. Before he could set her down, Georgina gave in to a sudden impulse. She wound her arms about her husband's neck and lifted her mouth to his. When he took possession of her lips, the entire staff applauded. Georgina ended the kiss first; then she smiled mischievously and whispered, "Thank you. One more kiss on the forehead would have undone me."

Helen Taylor stood in the entrance hall at the bottom of the magnificent staircase. She had arrived at Woburn a week ago, bringing all Lady Georgina's clothes, personal effects, and possessions. She helped the new mistress of Woburn from her coat. "Ye've never looked more lovely, ma lamb. I'll take yer hat and coat upstairs."

"Thank you, Helen." Georgina tucked her arm into Mr. Burke's. "I put myself in your capable hands, sir. While my husband deserts me for his office to tend to important business matters, I beg you to show me around my new home."

John hid a smile as he watched the pair disappear

from the hall. *Mr. Burke is about to succumb to Georgy's irresistible charm, and if I'm not mistaken she already has the rest of them eating out of the palm of her hand.*

Burke took Georgina into the main reception room and then led her through two smaller chambers into the sitting room.

She moved toward the fireplace and stood gazing up at the painting that hung above the mantel. "What a beautiful lady. Who is she, Mr. Burke?"

"The Duke of Bedford's first wife, Elizabeth."

"Oh." Georgina licked lips gone suddenly dry. As she stared at the portrait, all her newfound self-assurance melted away. *I had no idea John's wife was so exquisite.* She remembered Francis saying, *My brother was deeply in love with his wife. John was a devoted husband. His mourning has almost consumed him.*

Georgina could not help comparing herself to the tall, slim, fair-haired Elizabeth. *I'm too short, too dark . . . I could never take her place in his affections.* In less than a minute, all her confidence vanished and was replaced by a mass of insecurity.

Mr. Burke poured a glass of claret and pressed it into her hand. Their eyes met, and Georgina knew she had found a staunch ally. As she sipped the wine she realized that making John love her might take longer than she had first anticipated.

Upstairs, Helen opened the doors to the bedchamber that had been prepared for Georgina. Her own familiar furnishings from Pall Mall took away some of her uncertainty.

"I chose this chamber because it has a spacious dressing room for all yer lovely clothes, and also because it adjoins the duke's bedchamber," Helen explained.

"I didn't know we'd sleep in separate rooms."

"Ha! There'll be little sleepin' done. Ye'll be able to make love in one bed then move to the other."

Georgina felt forlorn. "Helen, I've just seen a portrait of John's wife. I'm afraid he's still in love with her."

"Rubbish! In any contest ye'd win hands down."

"Whatever makes you think that?"

"She's *dead*. Georgina Russell is living flesh and blood. Moreover, yer the bloody Duchess of Bedford. Never forget it. Never let *him* forget it!"

Georgy smiled tremulously. "I'm so glad you're here, Helen."

The newlyweds ate an intimate dinner for two that had been especially prepared by the chef. They lingered over the food and wine for two hours. John did not want Georgina to feel rushed, and since she was experiencing a shy reticence laced with a good deal of anxiety, she was content to let him set the pace.

When dinner was over, Georgina went to the kitchens and complimented the chef and his assistants. Pleased at her thoughtfulness, he asked what she would like for breakfast and if she would like it served upstairs.

She tried not to blush. "No, no, we will eat in the small dining room we used tonight. We are leaving for Cambridge after breakfast."

Georgina went upstairs and found Helen in the spacious dressing room, packing the things she would take on her honeymoon trip.

"Yer new Paris gowns are a wee bit scandalous, though beautiful nonetheless. I'm glad ye chose some vivid colors. This jade green is the same color as yer lovely eyes."

"I was so tired of those insipid debutante shades." *To say nothing of the drab mourning monstrosities Mother foisted on me.* "I don't want you to pack my new Paris gowns. I shall save them for when we entertain here at Woburn. But I will need some of my old clothes . . . a couple of riding skirts and jackets. I'll be meeting John's tenant farmers on the various estates and flimsy tulle empire dresses would make me a laughingstock. Don't forget walking shoes and riding boots. When you're finished packing, summon a footman. I don't want you carrying any heavy luggage, Helen."

"One thing I can say fer Woburn—there's no dearth of male servants. Some of 'em are braw, attractive buggers too."

They heard John in the adjoining bedchamber, and Helen winked. "Speaking of braw, attractive buggers . . ."

"Leave the rest of the packing, and finish in the morning."

"It's all done. Shall I help ye undress, ma lamb?"

"No, thank you, Helen. I'll look after myself."

As Georgina removed her shoes and stockings, she was gripped with apprehension. Her husband had behaved in a civilized manner last night, but she knew she dared not deny him her body tonight. Her mind flew back. The first time she'd seen him she thought him dangerously threatening. What daunted her was the deep suppressed anger in his black eyes that he kept reined in. She had thought: *If he ever unleashes his rage, it will be like opening the gates of hell.* She'd always thought John Russell had a dark, dangerous side, and suspected the dominant devil was capable of giving her a thrashing if he was pushed beyond his limits.

By the time John opened the adjoining door, Georgina had donned her nightdress, brushed her hair, and was sitting up in bed. He walked a direct path to her, drew back the covers, and lifted her into his arms. He carried her into the other room. "This is our bedchamber, Georgy. We'll both be more comfortable in here."

Her heart began to hammer so loudly she feared he might hear.

The chamber was large and luxuriously furnished in black and gold. There was a fire burning, and the huge fireplace and hearth were decorated with red Oriental tiles. Soft-cushioned chairs and a sofa sat on a thick-piled red and gold carpet. A carved, black oak games table sat in front of the fire, and a deep window seat held a chess set. The curtained bed was massive and so high, there was a stepping stool beside it.

John pulled back the covers and slipped her into the bed. He turned out the lamp, and other than a soft, flickering glow from the fire, the room was in shadow. He took off his bed robe, and saw the reflection of the flames in her eyes. "Georgy, you're staring as if you've never seen a naked man before."

"I haven't seen many," she confessed. She had caught fleeting glimpses of two of her sisters' husbands, but had averted her eyes instantly because of the intimate sexual acts involved. "And none as splendid as you."

"Flattery, begod," he teased, and she laughed nervously.

John climbed into bed beside her and drew her into his arms. If he wanted to make his young, beautiful wife fall in love with him, he knew he would have to bring her pleasure. Searing desire flared in him, but he leashed it tightly. He must not fall on her and ravage her as his hunger urged him to do; rather he must woo her with his lips, and his hands, arouse her slowly, gently, and savor her.

The heat of his body shocked her, but it also thrilled her. The male scent of his skin was tantalizing. She fought the desire to lick him and taste him. She felt his breath upon her skin and suddenly she wanted this man more than anything she had ever wanted in her life. Then his mouth took possession of hers, and her lips clung to his and opened softly under the seductive pressure of his sensual kiss.

He kissed her for an hour. Tiny, quick kisses to her temples, eyelids, and the corners of her mouth. He kissed her hair, her ear, then traced his lips along her cheekbone and down to her throat. He heard the quick intake of her breath and knew she was becoming aroused; then his mouth sought hers, and they lost themselves in the bliss of a hundred slow, melting kisses.

Georgina floated in a warm sea of pleasure; then soon her skin began to tingle, and a thousand pleasure points of fire and ice raced through her.

When he withdrew his mouth, he gently touched her lips with his finger. She suddenly lost control and took his finger into her mouth and sucked on it. This told him she was eager for more, and this time when he kissed her, he parted her lips and slid his tongue into her exciting mouth. He thrust in and out, imitating what his body wanted to do with hers.

When he drew back and released her lips, he heard a little moan of protest that told him his wooing was bringing her pleasure. He took her hand, dropped a kiss into her palm, and closed her fingers over it to keep it captive. Then his lips traced across her wrist, and he trailed kisses along the soft flesh on the inside of her arm. When she shuddered with pleasure, he cupped her breast and stroked his thumb over its tip. Through the silk of her nightdress, he felt her nipple ruche, and he could no longer control his hunger to feel her naked flesh against his body.

Starting at her ankles, he slid both hands beneath the silken garment. His palms stroked up her legs, caressed her hips, skimmed up over her rib cage; then he pulled the nightgown over her head. Though the light was dim, he gazed down at her naked body and worshipped her with his eyes. His fingers followed his glance as they caressed her lush breasts, slid across her soft belly, and toyed with the dark curls that covered her mons.

Georgina gasped as John's fingers touched the private place between her legs, but it felt so pleasurable she arched her mons into his hand as her senses whirled, and she could feel every slow beat of her heart. She cried out as he slid a long finger inside her. A protest rose to her lips and melted away in a sigh as delicious, hot strands spiraled deep inside her to her woman's core and she began to writhe.

Georgina's sheath was fever-hot and tight as it

closed upon his finger. Her shocked reaction, followed by her blissful sighs, told John that these sensations were completely new to her, and implausible as it seemed, he suspected that Georgina was innocent. The thought inflamed him. That he would be first was a precious gift he had not dreamed of. He withdrew his finger and heard her small cry of protest. Then his hands encircled her waist and he lifted her onto his hard body. He groaned as her dark, silken hair cascaded onto his chest.

When John's powerful hands lifted her onto him, she went weak at the raw brute strength he possessed. His hard, muscled legs felt like granite against her soft thighs, and his marble-hard cock lay pulsing against her hot cleft. Her breasts were cushioned on his broad chest, and his crisp chest hair teased her nipples with every breath she took. When his palms stroked down her back and his hands cupped her bum cheeks and pressed her even closer, she wanted to scream with excitement. Then his fingers dipped into the cleft between her buttocks and she cried, "John!"

"You think you are ready, little girl, but this first mating will hurt," he warned.

"I don't care!" She was panting. Her breasts rose and fell.

John took her hand. "Feel me. Gauge its size. I don't want to shock you." He slipped her hand between her legs and felt her fingers curl about his hardness. He almost came out of his skin as her fingers tightened. His whole body quivered at the exquisite sensations her touch brought him.

For a moment she was shocked at the size of his engorged phallus, but she was aroused, reeling with need, and her senses told her that this hunger could only be satisfied if John filled her and completed the mating. "Now, John, please."

Gently, he lifted her to the bed and came over her. "Open your thighs, Georgy." He slid the head of his cock inside her and held still, watching her face for any sign of pain. Then slowly, firmly, he thrust his shaft into her satin sheath until he was seated to the hilt.

She cried out once at the initial pain, but then as their bodies fused, she became aware of the fullness, and she shivered at the delicious weight of his powerful body.

"Wrap your legs around me, Georgy." He began to move, slowly at first; then he thrust faster and harder, knowing he should not draw it out endlessly this first time. Heat leaped between them, and though it was silken torment, John did not allow himself to spend until he felt her first tiny pulsations begin; then they both dissolved in liquid tremors.

He rolled to his side, enfolded her in his arms, and held her tightly. With his lips pressed against her hair, he could feel her body gradually soften. A wave of deep content washed over him. He had been without warm, loving intimacy for a decade, and he reveled in Georgina's generous response. He felt like a starving man who'd had a feast laid out before him. He was aware he had given her pain, but he knew he had also given her pleasure. His love for her had tempered his raging need, and if he could control his dark passions by cherishing her and teaching her to enjoy her own sensuality, perhaps he would be able to bind her to him forever.

In the dark, Georgina smiled her secret smile. She had not denied him. She had swallowed her fear and met his body's demands eagerly. The pleasure he had brought her was far greater than the pain, and she could tell that John was entranced with her body's response. Mating had tamed the beast within, at least for tonight. Georgina knew they had a strong physical attraction. *John is certainly in lust with me. Perhaps that's the secret key to making him fall in love.*

Chapter 28

"The dean was clearly enchanted by you. I haven't seen such bowing and scraping since Napoleon Bonaparte introduced Josephine at the Tuileries reception."

Georgina was flattered. Before they went to the Russell estate in Cambridgeshire, they had stopped at Cambridge University, where John's eldest son, Francis, would be attending in the autumn. "He hung on my every word because I am the Duchess of Bedford."

"No, it was your beauty and your charm that captivated him. There isn't a doubt in the world that he'll make room for Francis at Trinity College, even if he has to turf out another applicant."

"I controlled my inappropriate impulses to make a good impression," she confessed.

"What were you tempted to do?"

"I wanted to hike up my skirts and go wading in the River Cam."

"You're in luck. Part of the river runs through our property." John pictured her naked in the water. "Perhaps I'll join you."

"Whatever would your tenants think of us cavorting like . . ."

"Newlyweds?" He grinned. "The part I was thinking of is quite secluded, if I remember. Perfect for a moonlight swim."

* * *

The manor house on the estate was lovely. Its mellow walls reminded Georgina of the ancient university buildings. As she had done at Woburn, the new duchess charmed the staff, and they were eager to do her bidding. She selected a young maid to help her unpack, and with a few shrewd questions she learned that it was a smoothly run, happy household. The master bedchamber was not as magnificent as the one at Woburn, but it did have a fireplace and a large comfortable bed.

John went out immediately with the head steward, and didn't return until dinner. This gave Georgina plenty of time to tour the house, visit the kitchens, and then take a leisurely bath.

After dinner, the duke went directly to the desk in the library to go over the estate account books. Georgina went with him, selected a book, and made herself comfortable in a leather chair. Though she was reading, she was acutely aware of her husband's compelling presence. She noticed that his attention continually strayed from his accounts to watch her. She finally realized that John found it difficult to concentrate while she was in the room and decided to quietly withdraw so he could focus on his task and get it finished before midnight.

Upstairs, she undressed and got into bed to continue reading. Before she got to the end of the page, John arrived. Her pulse beat wildly. She hadn't expected him for hours. "Are you finished checking the accounts?"

"Nowhere near finished—I was distracted." He removed his coat.

She smiled. "I could tell. That's why I left the library."

"That only made matters worse." He unfastened his neckcloth.

"How so?"

"The thought of you in bed stole my senses, and I was consumed by fear." He took off his shirt and bent to remove his boots.

"Fear?"

"Terrified that you'd fall asleep before I had my way with you." He plucked the book from her hands and tossed it onto the table. He disrobed quickly and turned out the lamp. The room was cast in dark shadows, relieved only by the flickering firelight.

Georgina was thrilled that he could not keep away from her until a disturbing thought stole to her. *He turned the light out again so he can't see me. In the darkness does he pretend that he's making love to Elizabeth?*

As John's arms came around her, she stiffened.

His lips brushed her temple. "It shouldn't hurt as much tonight. I'll try to be gentle."

After the first kiss, her resistance melted away, and she exulted in the feel of his hard, powerful body. She couldn't bear the flimsiest barrier separating her from his hot, naked flesh, and her eager hands helped his to remove her nightgown. The rough slide of his tongue as it feathered over her breasts heightened her desire, and when he licked and tasted her nipples, she cried out at the tantalizing sensations his tongue aroused. "Your mouth is *wicked*," she whispered breathlessly.

"Do you *like* wicked, Georgy?"

"*Like* is too timid a word to describe what I feel."

John smiled into the darkness, hoping she would not resist the sensual foreplay he longed to perform. He drew down the covers and pressed kisses on her belly. With his tongue he traced a circle around her navel, and when she clutched his shoulders and drew in a shuddering breath, he knew she was becoming highly aroused. He blew on the dark tendrils that covered her mons, and when she arched with pleasure, he ran the tip of his tongue along her hot cleft. Then he plunged into her honeypot and groaned.

Georgina was shocked, but at the same time thrilled. It felt like forbidden pleasure, but if so, it shouldn't be. The hot, sliding thrusts evoked dark, erotic sensations that were more exquisite than anything she'd ever experienced. John's lips and tongue worked their magic and awoke a sensual hunger that compelled her to be splendidly uninhibited as she writhed and arched up into his possessive, demanding mouth. She felt the flames rise, and with a blissful cry she reached her peak and dissolved in long, hot shudders.

John moved up over her and kissed her deeply. She tasted herself on his lips, and the intimacy of what he'd done to her melted her very bones. She felt the rippling muscles of his chest press against her breasts and realized with wonder that she was becoming aroused again. As he slid his tongue into her mouth, and began to thrust, she opened her thighs, tempting, luring, and commanding his marble-hard cock to work its magic.

John could not believe the generous response of his young, beautiful wife. She was a voluptuous woman, and he believed that soon she would fulfill his craving for a mate whose passion matched his own. He rose and sank into her forcefully, thrusting deeply, powerfully, penetrating her over and over, withdrawing almost completely, then smoothly sinking his hard length until he was gloved in hot velvet. Buried deep inside her he could feel the throbbing of his cock and her sheath as the rhythmic penetration filled her and thrilled her until they were both reeling from the surging wave of passion that engulfed them. His promise to be gentle was long forgotten by both.

Georgina felt a scream building in her throat. She thrashed her head from side to side on the pillow; then unable to control her fervor, she sank her teeth into his flesh and bit his shoulder.

In spite of his longing to make their pleasure last forever, her passionate bite catapulted him over the edge, and he surged like a tidal wave, pouring himself into her.

Georgina's body instantly responded, and she surrendered her will to his body's commands. As her climax exploded, a thousand slivers of silver spiraled through her belly, spread up into her breasts, then pierced her heart. As she lay motionless, clasped in his arms, she felt triumphant. It didn't matter that for John it was lust, pure and simple. That was more than enough for now. But for her, it was all-encompassing love, and she reveled in it.

John knew he had lost control, and hoped Georgina would not conceive. There were several reasons why he preferred not to impregnate her so early in their marriage. Apart from the fact that he already had three sons and was in no hurry to add to his family, he considered Georgina too young to be a mother. He could not dispel the underlying fear that childbirth would affect her mentally and emotionally, as it had Elizabeth. *Georgy is so deliciously tempting. I must use more control and learn to withdraw.*

The next morning after breakfast, Georgina accompanied John and the head steward as they visited all the tenant farms on the Cambridgeshire estate. Dressed in her comfortable country clothes, she conversed with the farmers' wives and their rosy-cheeked children. She saw with her own eyes that they were thriving, and was glad that they were flourishing. Compared with the poor Highland families on the vast Gordon landholdings, John's people were prosperous.

Later, over lunch, John discussed with her his plans, to add to the livestock on the larger farms.

"It was so good to see the children laughing. Your people seem quite happy and content, John."

"They are not *my* people; they are *our* people," he insisted.

"With all my worldly goods I thee endow," she said lightly.

"I intend to fulfill my wedding vows."

She gave him a saucy glance. *Especially the part about honoring me with your body.* Georgina sighed wistfully. *How long will it take to fulfill your solemn vow to love me?*

"I ordered a couple of horses saddled. This afternoon we'll ride out over all our acres."

Side by side, they cantered past fields of ripening grain and sun-dappled hay fields ready to be scythed. They saw pastures filled with dairy cows, while others had sheep grazing on the hills. There were copses filled with beech trees and woods where rabbits and game birds flourished. They followed the river through the trees, and by the time they came to a secluded clearing, rain clouds had gathered. John looked at the sky ruefully. "I wanted to bring you here for that moonlight swim tonight, but it doesn't look like the weather will cooperate." Just then raindrops hit them. "We can outride it if we hurry."

Georgina lifted her face to the rain. "Why wait till tonight? I'm not afraid to get wet!" Laughing, she slid down from her horse and began to throw off her clothes.

John sat stunned. Was she actually going to swim nude in broad daylight? He watched her dance naked as the summer rain drenched her gleaming flesh. His heart began to fill with joy. *This is the vivacious, impulsive, laughing mate I've always longed for.* He jumped from the saddle and quickly removed his wet clothes. Then he made a dive for her.

She nimbly eluded him, and ran toward the river.

"Wait for me," he ordered.

"Go to the devil, old man!" She jumped in and swam toward the opposite riverbank. Before she got there, she felt a tug on her leg and gasped as John pulled her under. They bobbed up to the surface, laughing and splashing. Suddenly the scudding rain clouds were swept away, and the sun came out, turning the surface of the water to shimmering gold. He captured her in his arms and lifted her high against his heart. She slid her arms around his neck and wrapped her legs about his hips. John placed his hands firmly beneath her round bottom and carried her from the water.

She bit his ear and whispered, "A guinea says you're going to have your wicked way with me."

"That's one bet I'm happy to lose, Mistress Impulsive." He sank down to his knees, then rolled with her until he had her pinned beneath him in the wet grass. When he captured her soft, warm mouth, it tasted of delicious laughter and sensual anticipation, just as it had in his dreams. It was heady intoxication to know that she wanted him as much as he desired making love to her. The reaction her eagerness stirred in him was a potent spur to possess her body and soul and lure her to surrender her essence to him.

After they made love, Georgina felt exultant as they lay sprawled, slick with rain. *It's broad daylight. This time John could not possibly pretend I was Elizabeth.*

John, too, was elated. *Georgina is bubbling with happiness. Her vivacity and mischievousness have returned. Her sadness over losing Francis is far less acute—marriage has diminished her sorrow. And mine, thank God!*

When they decided to get dressed, they discovered their clothes were still wet. John laughed as she grimaced and shuddered at the feel of the soaked garments against her delicate skin. He lifted her into the saddle; then the pair of them made a mad dash back to the stables.

The moment they reached their bedchamber they began to disrobe. When Georgina reached for a towel, he plucked it from her fingers. The thought of rubbing her dry sent fire snaking through his groin. "Let me do that." He knew his need for this beautiful female was insatiable. He'd been starved so long, he could not keep his hands from her. The miracle was that Georgina welcomed him eagerly, lavishly, which in turn inflamed him as nothing else ever had.

"Playing in the afternoon has untold rewards," she teased. "I've been longing to see you naked in sunlight, so I can explore every inch of your splendid male body." She reached out and stroked a fingertip down the length of his upthrust cock, and laughed with delight when it began to buck. Suddenly, she was tempted to taste it, and since she usually followed her impulses, she slid to her knees and dropped a kiss on its impudent head.

John almost came out of his skin. He threaded his fingers into her hair and arched against her teasing lips. She grasped his shaft firmly with one hand and ran the tip of her tongue around the head of his cock, then sucked it into her mouth like a ripe plum. The hot, wet slide of her tongue aroused him to madness. With an iron will he fought the urge to push her to the floor and impale her. Instead, he swept her up in his arms and carried her to the bed. For the next hour he unleashed the fierce desire that had been riding him for months.

After dinner, John went to the library to finish the accounts. Each time his thoughts strayed to Georgina, he forced them back to the business of the estate. When he was done, and everything tallied to his satisfaction, he took the stairs two at a time. By the time he got to the bed, he had removed most of his clothes.

John looked down at Georgina and realized she was sound asleep. His mouth curved tenderly as he gazed down at his beautiful wife. He lifted a dark curl from the pillow and marveled at its silken texture. He knew he was the luckiest man alive. "I love you, little girl."

While Georgina familiarized herself with the staff at Northampton, another vast Russell estate, John went out with the head steward. The next day, she and John rode out over the acres and stopped to visit each tenant farm. While John conversed with the workers, Georgina spoke with their wives. She sensed that there was an undercurrent and encouraged a couple of the farmers' wives to voice any grievances they were harboring.

She gained their confidence, and that night at dinner she divulged everything to John. "The head steward has been coercing some of the younger wives for sex. When one of the farmers challenged him, he turned the family off the land."

Georgina had never seen John so incensed. He stood up from the table so abruptly, his chair crashed to the floor. "Christ Almighty, why didn't the workers say something to me?"

"John, you are the Duke of Bedford. On top of that, you have a dark, dangerous look about you that is rather intimidating. Because of the head steward, the men mistrust authority and the women fear it."

He stalked from the house and returned with the understewards for a meeting in the library. Then they all left, and John didn't come back until almost midnight. Georgina had already gone to bed, and when John joined her, he took her hand and apologized. "Some bloody wedding trip. I'm sorry, Georgy."

"You made me the Duchess of Bedford. The welfare of our people is a shared responsibility. Please don't think you have to shelter me from any unpleasant or sordid things that happen. My position gives me many rich rewards; it is only fair I share some of your burdens."

The next day, one of the women told her what had happened.

"His Grace of Bedford dismissed the evil swine on the spot, m'lady, but not before he thrashed him within an inch of his miserable life."

As Georgina digested the information, she realized she was not surprised. She'd always sensed that John was capable of violence if the circumstances warranted it.

The Duke and Duchess of Bedford were back at Woburn for only one day before young John started his summer holiday from school. Because Johnny was exceptionally clever, his teachers decided he need not write exams and gave him a passing grade in all subjects.

"I'll have Johnny all to myself for a week before Francis and William are finished school," Georgina said on the drive to London. "I'll need the carriage to go shopping."

John's dark brows drew together. "I hope you mean shopping for yourself. I would prefer it if you didn't spoil the boys."

"Rubbish! I fully intend to spoil them."

"You delight in flouting my authority. I know you are a saucy baggage, Georgy, but I won't allow you to ride roughshod over me," he warned.

She looked contrite. "I promise to listen carefully to all your orders and commands, Your Grace." Unable to resist a challenge, her lips curved. "Then I shall do exactly as I please!"

"Incorrigible wench," he muttered.

When they arrived at the house in Russell Square, John got out of the carriage. "I'll have a footman accompany you to carry your purchases."

She raised her chin and said pertly, "I'm not sure one footman will suffice. I have a great deal of shopping to do."

In a few minutes the footman arrived. A maid, who curtsied and said her name was Annie, accompanied him. When the pair took their place in the carriage, Georgina smiled graciously. But inside she was seething. *If he thinks I'll tolerate a chaperone, he is deluding himself. When I return, I will speak my mind!*

Georgina spent the next four hours buying books, maps, art supplies, games, and puzzles. She stopped at a confectioner's and bought boxes of marzipan in the shapes of fruits and animals. Then she went to an emporium and bought waterproof slickers and half a dozen pairs of rubber boots in various sizes.

When she returned to Russell Square, John checked his timepiece and frowned. "You're late."

"How can I possibly be late when my time is my own?" she challenged. "And while we're at it, I haven't the faintest idea why you sent Annie along, unless it was to spy on me."

"Georgina, it is customary for a lady to have a maid accompany her when she ventures onto the streets of London."

"I intend to dispense with that custom immediately.

I'm not a child; I'm a married woman. I don't need a chaperone. Surely marriage has its privileges, or what's the bloody point of my becoming your wife?" She turned on her heel to walk away.

John grabbed her by the seat of her skirt and stopped her in her tracks. "Marriage doesn't give you the privilege of being insolent to your husband. If you're not a child, stop acting like one," he admonished. "Speaking of children, it's time to pick up Johnny from Westminster. Are you coming with me?"

Georgina immediately forgot their quarrel and was overcome with uncertainty. "Oh dear, are you sure Johnny won't absolutely hate having a stepmother?"

"Are you brave enough to find out?"

She swallowed her anxiety and turned on the charm. "With you beside me, I am courageous enough for anything."

Georgina sat in the carriage and waited while John went inside Westminster school to get his son. When the pair emerged, their driver helped the duke load Johnny's trunks, and then they climbed inside. Johnny looked from one to the other. "Are you really married?"

In the fading afternoon light, Georgina saw the glint in John's eye. "For better or for worse."

Georgina took Johnny's hand. "Yes, we're *really* married."

"I'm so glad, but I don't know what I should call you."

"Lady Georgina would be best," John said.

"Best when your father's around." She squeezed Johnny's hand. "When we're alone you can call me Georgy."

John hid a smile. *She really is incorrigible.*

Back at Russell Square the three of them ate dinner together, and it was obvious that Johnny was relieved that his school term was over and excited that he would be spending the summer at his new home of Woburn.

Georgina listened raptly as he catalogued all the things he wanted to accomplish on his holidays. He was also thrilled that he would celebrate his tenth birthday in August.

"When can we go home?" he asked eagerly.

Georgina looked at John. "I vote we go tonight."

"Me too!" Johnny agreed. "May we, Father?"

John threw up his hands in mock surrender. "Since I'm outnumbered, what choice do I have?"

"Hooray! Hooray!"

Georgina gifted her husband with a radiant smile. "Thank you."

It was late when they arrived at Woburn, and Johnny was sound asleep on the seat of the carriage. John carried his son up to bed, and Georgina helped to tuck him in.

"I'm going to bed too. Tomorrow will be a busy day . . . I can't wait for the fun to start!"

John picked her up and carried her to their bedchamber. "You don't have to wait until tomorrow for the fun to start. I've never slept with a stepmother before. A guinea says it will be a rewarding experience."

"Bedford, you are becoming addicted to gambling!"

Chapter 29

"Are these really mine?" Johnny asked with disbelief, as he sat up in bed and gazed at the pile of books.

"Look inside." Georgina had smuggled in the complete works of Shakespeare before he had awakened.

He opened the cover on *King Henry the Fourth*. "It says: *To Lord John from Lady Georgina.* Who is Lord John?"

"*You* are Lord John . . . Lord John Russell. Didn't you know?"

"I never thought about it, but since Father is a duke, we get courtesy titles. I can't wait to tell Francis and William."

Georgina smiled at his innocence. "Believe me, those two young devils will have been insisting on their titles with all their friends since your father became the Duke of Bedford."

"Thank you so much for the books, Georgy. You couldn't have given me a better birthday present."

"They aren't a birthday present . . . they are one of your coming home presents. Hurry and get dressed. When you've had breakfast, we'll go and pick out a pet for you."

His eyes filled with excitement. "May I choose my own?"

"Within reason. I don't suppose your father would approve of a nanny goat running loose in the hallowed halls of Woburn, but you certainly have permission to choose any dog you fancy."

"How about a cat? I made friends with the stable tabby cat last time I was here. She's a lovely old girl."

"Excellent choice. What about a name for your feline?"

"Mmm, since Woburn used to be an abbey, and cats like to rule the roost, I think I shall call her the Abbess."

Georgina laughed with delight. "You take after your father, Johnny . . . You have a sly sense of humor!"

"During the week Johnny has been here, the two of you have become inseparable." John lifted his wife from the saddle after she and his son had spent the afternoon riding.

"Isn't it wonderful? I absolutely adore him."

"The feeling is mutual. Last night when I tucked him in, he asked me if he could call you Mother."

Aghast, Georgina's hand flew to her throat. "I'm so sorry, John. Elizabeth will always be your sons' mother and your beloved first wife. I would *never* presume to take her place."

John's face turned hard. "We won't speak of her."

Georgina hid the hurt she felt and quickly changed the subject. "Francis and William will be finished their exams tomorrow. Why don't you go to London to get them, and I'll wait here? It will give the three of you some private time together."

"Thank you . . . that's most thoughtful, Georgy."

The next day, Georgina and Johnny were enjoying lunch in a small, private chamber adjacent to the large formal dining room. All at once the door opened and closed by itself. A minute later, a door on the opposite wall opened and closed. A look of fear came into Johnny's eyes, and he dropped his soup spoon with a clatter. "I've seen doors open before . . . Woburn is *haunted*!"

Georgina wanted to dispel his fear immediately. "Yes, I believe we do have a ghost," she said matter-of-factly. "But he's quite invisible and totally harmless. When I was growing up in Scotland, we had a ghost at Gordon Castle."

"Weren't you afraid, Georgy?"

"Not after we gave him a name. It took away his power to alarm. Why don't you think of a name for our ghost?"

Johnny picked up his spoon and thought about it for a minute or two. "Oh, I know. Shakespeare has a wild exotic character ruled by magic and emotion. Let's call him Glendower!"

"That's a fabulous name, and it has a lovely Scottish ring to it. When your brothers are frightened witless, you can simply shrug and say, *Oh, that's Glendower . . . nothing to be alarmed about. He's quite harmless.*"

Johnny almost choked with laughter. "I shall enjoy having one up on Lord Francis and Lord William!"

The first few days at home, John's two elder sons held themselves aloof from Georgina, but after she encouraged them to choose pets and allowed their pair of greyhounds to chase after them through the mansion, they began to let down their barriers.

She joined her husband and his sons when they went trout fishing in the river that ran through their Woburn land and challenged them to swimming races across the lake. She encouraged them to learn how to row a boat, construct and fly kites, and she gave them lessons in drawing and painting. By making wagers with them, they all put on rubber boots and learned how to plant and grow their own separate gardens and how to tend sheep and goats.

"At our farm in Kinrara, I was always the goat girl," Georgina informed them. "You need eyes in your arse, because the playful little buggers love to come up behind and butt you."

John watched in amazement as his quiet, reserved sons turned into raucous, mischievous devils who had fun from dawn till dusk. Boisterous laughter and dog barks rang through the hallowed halls of Woburn, egged on by their precocious, young stepmother. John applauded the change in his sons. It was obvious that they were more outgoing and healthier, but most important, they were happy.

Late at night, after Georgina had fallen asleep beside him, John often gazed down at her in wonder. *Thank God I found her. How drab and gray our lives would be without her.*

"Don't rush off with the young devils, there's something I want to discuss."

Georgina sat back down at the breakfast table and fed the Abbess a morsel of kipper.

"Your birthday is July eighteenth, and I think we should celebrate the event in grand style. I believe it is high time we put our mourning for Francis aside and began entertaining at Woburn."

Georgina was at a loss for words. Though she knew John mourned his brother, she did not, and it covered her with guilt that she had perpetuated the myth that she loved Francis. She was living a lie, and it troubled her constantly, but how could she tell her husband that she hated his brother without deeply wounding him? "It's very generous of you to want to celebrate my birthday, John. Are you sure it's not too soon to start entertaining?"

"Absolutely sure. From now on we will hold Francis in our hearts, rather than mourning him publicly. Make a list of those you would like at your party, and get one of the secretaries to help you with the invitations."

"Why don't we have two parties? One in the afternoon for all the children, and one in the evening for the adults?"

John's lips curved with amusement. "And which party will you attend, little girl?"

"Both, of course!" She jumped up and kissed him.

"The dancing will last until dawn. Are you sure you're up to it, old man?"

On Georgina's birthday, the carriages began to arrive shortly after breakfast. The first guests to arrive were Susan and William from nearby Kimbolton. The Duke and Duchess of Manchester brought all their children, who were soon running wild with the Russell boys. Next to arrive was Jane, Duchess of Gordon. Georgina threw her arms about her mother. "You are up early!"

"No! I'm up late . . . I haven't been to bed yet."

"Frightened of missing something, I warrant," Georgy teased. "I shall turn you over to Mr. Burke, who has plenished a special chamber for you, overlooking the lake."

"I am delighted that you are throwing a party. I hope this is only the first of many lavish entertainments hosted by the Duke and Duchess of Bedford at your magnificent Abbey of Woburn. I brought you a case of Scotch whiskey . . . Think of it as a birthday present from your father."

"I'd rather have him, but I won't say no to the whiskey."

Charlotte and Charles arrived with young Charlie and Mary. A second carriage held their younger children and their nursemaids. "You have more guts than brains to invite my entire brood."

"The more the merrier, Charlotte. Wait until I have my own."

Mary looked aghast. "You're not having a baby, Georgy?"

"Not that I know of. But my own children won't stop me from loving you, darling," Georgina assured her favorite niece.

Charlotte rolled her eyes at her daughter. "Brace yourself, Mistress Inquisitive. A baby is inevitable."

"I fervently hope so," Georgy murmured wistfully.

In the afternoon, Dorothy and Harriet Cavendish

arrived and brought their brother Will, Lord Hartington. He was fourteen, the same age as young Francis Russell. Since both boys would be attending Cambridge in September, they had become fast friends.

"Thank you for inviting us, Georgy. I've always wanted to visit Woburn," Dorothy declared. "Caro sends her regrets."

Harriet winked at Georgina. "She came down with an acute case of duchessitis. Poor child turned quite green."

"Goose-shit green, I sincerely hope," Georgina jested.

When her brother, George, arrived, he picked her up, swung her around, and wished her happy birthday. "Marriage seems to agree with you, or is being a duchess what makes you sparkle?"

"Marriage does agree with me—I highly recommend it. The Duchess of Devonshire's daughters are here, if you are looking for a wife," she teased.

"Alas, my heart is reserved for another."

"Who is she? I promise not to breathe a word to Mother."

"Her name is Elizabeth Brodie. She is very shy."

"I never heard of the family."

"Her father isn't titled. He's an India merchant."

"You are most welcome to bring her to Woburn, George. John and I will keep your secret," she promised.

Georgina turned and found her mother at her elbow. "Is there something you would like?"

"Yes, I'm off to Kinrara in a couple of days, while it is still summer. I'd like to take Helen with me. Since you have myriad servants, I'm sure you can manage without her."

"Helen will love a trip to Scotland. I envy you both."

The afternoon party was a roaring success, with the Russell boys acting as hosts. They dined outside, with tables laden with food and desserts that would appeal to young appetites. Because Georgina knew that children loved to dress up, she provided the boys with shields and wooden swords and the girls with fairy wings and magic wands. They played musical chairs on the lawn, followed by blind man's buff and pin the fiery tail on the dragon. They had sack races and three-legged races, where Georgina tied her leg to Mary's. They fell down no less than six times, and laughed so much, they managed to come in dead last. Then Georgina's brother, George, led the older children on a treasure hunt.

"I didn't realize that having uncles and cousins could be such fun," Johnny told his father at the end of the party.

"I'm glad you enjoyed yourself. Perhaps we can do it again on your birthday next month." *It warms my heart to see Johnny so happy. He's been overly shy and quiet for too many years.*

In the early evening the musicians arrived. While they were setting up their instruments in Woburn's gilded ballroom, Georgina went upstairs to dress. She was sitting at the dressing table in her own bedchamber having her hair dressed by one of her new maids when John came in from the master bedchamber and dismissed her attendant. Their eyes met in the mirror.

John set three large velvet boxes before her on the dressing table. "Happy birthday, Georgy."

Her eyes widened as she realized he was giving her the famed Russell family jewels. As she opened the boxes, the sight of the brilliant diamonds against the black velvet took her breath away. There were necklaces, earrings, broaches, bracelets, and rings. "No one has worn these in three decades, and I warrant no one as beautiful as you in a century."

"John, they are so splendid. I thank you with all my heart." She put on a diamond necklace, and John fastened the clasp for her. "I won't wear one of my Paris gowns. They won't do my jewels justice. The white and silver gown from my debutante ball will show off my diamonds to perfection."

John bent and kissed the nape of her neck. "I heartily wish all our guests at the back of beyond at this moment. I'd like to drape you in diamonds and carry you to bed."

She laughed up at him. "And prevent me from being the belle of the ball? I think not, Bedford." She tied his neckcloth and touched her lips to his. "You'll have to wait until dawn. After the Scottish dances, I'll need you to carry me to bed."

In the ballroom, all the ladies gathered around Georgina to admire her jewels.

Lady Holland lifted Georgina's right hand to look at the exquisite solitaire ring. "The Russell diamonds are legendary. At long last there is a worthy Duchess of Bedford to wear them."

Jane Gordon whispered to her daughter behind her fan, "I once told you if you could capture Bedford, the rewards would be beyond your wildest dreams."

Her mother's words threatened to take away some of her pleasure. *You don't even remember that you were speaking of Francis.* Georgina closed her eyes. *I absolutely refuse to let the ghost of Francis Russell spoil my birthday.*

"So this is where you are all hiding!" Georgina stood with hands on hips at the library door as she surveyed the room. John, Henry Holland, William Montagu, Charles Lennox, and her brother, Huntly, were smoking and drinking brandy. A sudden suspicion crossed her mind. "You weren't talking politics, were you? Oh, damn the lot of you for excluding me!"

The men laughed good-naturedly.

"Methinks the lady has designs on becoming a political hostess," Henry declared.

"She'll get her chance sooner than she thinks." John winked.

"Tell me, you devious devil!"

"While the government is in summer recess, we're going to host a get-together for Whigs and Tories at Woburn in a fortnight."

Georgina gave her husband a radiant smile. "How exciting . . . I can't wait." Scottish music floated from the ballroom. "Come quickly. They are playing the first strathspey. At midnight I've ordered them to play the 'Gey Gordons' when I intend to partner the decadent Duke of Bedford. Politics can wait."

The men hooted. "Decadent, is he?"

Georgina rolled her eyes. "You have no idea."

Two hours before dawn everyone gathered outside to watch a spectacular fireworks display.

Georgina leaned back against her husband, enjoying the brilliant colored illuminations that burst upon the dark sky. "This is a lovely surprise."

"It was Mr. Burke's idea, but I'll gladly take credit for it. Happy birthday, Mrs. Russell."

"I'm ready for some private skyrockets," she teased. "You may carry me to bed now, Mr. Russell."

The moment all the guests departed Woburn, Georgina began making plans for the political gathering on the first day of August. She consulted John about the guest list. "Politicians always have an agenda. What is it you hope to achieve?"

"You're a shrewd little minx. Why don't you tell me?"

"I suppose your ultimate goal is to get rid of Addington and replace him with Pitt as prime minister."

"Trust you to get right to the heart of the matter. However, it won't be easy. It will take a deal of maneuvering. Henry tells me that Pitt seldom attended parliament before it recessed."

"A clever tactic." Georgina bit back *Absence makes the heart grow fonder*. She didn't want John to think of either Francis or his wife Elizabeth. "Pitt is wise enough to realize you never know the worth of water till the well goes dry."

"I wonder if Pitt will accept our invitation to Woburn."

"Why don't I write a note to Mother's dearest

friend, Henry Dundas and ask him to persuade William to come?"

"That just might be the spur he needs. Write your letter."

"Why don't you invite Pitt and Dundas to come a day early so you can discuss things in private before the others descend?"

"Your idea has merit. Holland should be here too—I will drop Henry a note."

"I'm afraid we won't be able to dine *en famille* tonight. William Pitt and Henry Dundas are coming to dinner," Georgina told her stepsons.

Francis spoke up. "William and I don't mind. Unlike Johnny, we find politics rather dull and boring. Be sure to look under the table to make sure the little pissant isn't there."

Georgina was pleased to see Johnny give Francis a good thump over disparaging his lack of height. She had been urging him to stick up for himself all summer. "Johnny doesn't need to hide under the table—he knows I'll tell him everything that's said."

"Ah, it's a conspiracy of the little people," Francis teased.

Georgina gave her oldest stepson a box on the ears.

He grinned down at her. "If I grow any taller you won't be able to reach me."

"Then I shall simply kick your arse!"

John overheard the exchange. He hid his amusement and asked sternly, "Have you been teaching my wife to use bad language?"

They hooted with laughter. Georgina had taught them to swear.

"Congratulations on your marriage, Bedford. I've known Lady Georgina since she was a child. You would have to search far and wide for a more accomplished mistress of Woburn."

"Thank you, Mr. Pitt. I realize my good fortune."

John poured him a glass of claret since he did not drink strong liquor.

"Since I had no wife to fill the role, the Duchess of Gordon generously acted as my political hostess for years. She has uncanny powers of persuasion that even the king cannot resist."

John nodded. *Georgina has all her mother's virtues, and none of her vices.* "Ah, here she comes now. My wife has the power to charm the ducks off the water."

Georgina had Henry Dundas on one arm and Lord Holland on the other. She had been showing them the landscaping that Humphrey Repton had designed. When she saw Pitt, her face lit up. "William, how lovely to see you!" She went up on tiptoe and kissed his cheek. "It is my pleasure to welcome you to Woburn."

She tucked her arm into his, led the way to the dining room, and seated the former prime minister of England on her right, between herself and the Duke of Bedford.

"I miss the House of Commons," John lamented. "The House of Lords deals with frivolous matters. Last time I was there, they were voting on a bill of divorce for one of the members." When William Pitt made no comment, John wondered how he could lead him into a discussion about the political situation.

John watched his beautiful wife work her magic. By using subtle flattery, she soon had Pitt talking about himself.

"I seldom attend parliament these days. My time is better spent at my house in Wimbledon than the House of Commons."

"You aren't the only one, Mr. Pitt," Henry declared. "The members had sparse attendance before the recess."

"When you were prime minister, William, the benches were all filled, and there was standing-room only in the gallery," Georgina said with admiration. "Your oratory skills are unmatched."

"From what Lord Holland tells me, the Tory members are reluctant to give their support to Addington," John said.

"Addington asked me to join the cabinet, but I declined," Pitt confided.

Georgina gave Pitt her undivided attention. "Why did you refuse, William?"

"If I joined the cabinet, I would be unable to express my criticism of the government."

"Is there something to criticize?" she prompted.

"Indeed there is, my dear. The government's mounting debt will soon be unmanageable. Changes are needed to the tax system, but the Whigs and Tories cannot agree, so nothing gets done."

John jumped in with a leading question. "Mr. Pitt, are you opposed to a strict partisan political system?"

"I am indeed, Your Grace. I'm referred to as a Tory, but in reality, I am an independent Whig."

The amazing admission prompted Georgina to glance up at her husband. John's eyes met hers, and she knew they were thinking the same thing. When dessert was served, she skillfully changed the subject to opera, knowing Pitt was a devotee.

After everyone had retired, Georgina sat up in bed, impatiently waiting for John. When he arrived, the subject returned to politics. "Do you think Pitt could be persuaded to join the opposition?"

"Your thoughts mirror mine exactly. If Addington loses his parliamentary support, he will have to resign."

"Will you suggest it to Pitt?"

"I'm not sure I could persuade him." John slid his arms about her and drew her close. "You did your job as hostess exceedingly well tonight. Enough politics. Concentrate on your job as wife."

She closed her eyes and offered up her mouth. Suddenly, she withdrew from the kiss. "I have it! Charles James Fox should be the one to invite Pitt to join the opposition."

"What took you so long to think of it? You *did* invite him?"

"Of course I invited Fox. Not only is he leader of the opposition, he's Henry's uncle. Charles Fox is a particular friend of the Gordons—we spent a lot of time together in Paris."

"Yet another male rendered weak by your fatal charm." His possessive mouth erased all other men from her mind.

After they made love, however, Georgina lay in the dark feeling acutely vulnerable. Not for the first time, at the climactic moment of passion, John had withdrawn. *He doesn't want me to be the mother of his children. He doesn't love me enough. That honor is reserved for his angelic Elizabeth.*

Chapter 30

"I love the smell of new-mown hay." Georgina had ridden out with John's sons so they could watch the harvesting. The men scythed the tall oats and grass, and the women followed, gathering up huge armfuls and binding them into sheaves. "Are you sure you want to stay in the fields and help?"

"It's work to the farmers, but it's a novelty for us to make haystacks," Francis assured her.

"Are you sure the attraction isn't the pretty farmers' daughters?" she teased. "I have to go and get ready. The government is about to descend on Woburn en masse." She refrained from asking the two older boys to keep an eye on Johnny. She wanted him to become independent.

When Georgina returned to the house, she went into the formal dining room to inspect the table settings. "You've outdone yourself, Mr. Burke. The flowers are particularly striking." Arrangements of spiky asters in the Bedford colors of purple and white decorated the side tables and filled the empty fireplace.

"You can put out the Scotch whiskey that Mother brought me. Politicians are particularly partial to a dram of whiskey." She switched a couple of the place cards, moving Prime Minister Addington away from William Pitt and putting him next to Lauderdale.

She went upstairs, took her bath, and went to her dressing room to choose a gown. She was glad it was a warm evening since the material of all her Paris gowns was diaphanous. She decided to wear the pale green empire dress. She pinned a single white rose into the low décolletage, and put on dangling diamond earrings.

Georgina was admiring her reflection in the mirror when John came in from the other bedchamber through the adjoining door. She turned and pirouetted prettily for him.

"You cannot wear that. Our guests are all male. It is most unsuitable, Georgy."

"What on earth do you mean?" She turned back to the mirror.

"The material is almost transparent . . . I can see the shape of your body through it." His tone was forbidding.

"But it's the very latest style from Paris," she protested.

"French women are known for their tasteless, seductive displays. English ladies are more refined, more respectable."

"Really? You are a walking authority on refined English ladies, having been married to one. What is your opinion on Scottish ladies, pray tell?"

His dark eyes narrowed. "This particular Scottish lady is a precocious minx who likes to flaunt her beauty. I know you enjoy being deliberately flamboyant, Georgy, but I would appreciate it if you would change your gown. Our guests are arriving."

She wanted to fly at him and scratch his arrogant face. Instead, she hung on to her temper and tried to see the situation through his eyes. *He made it plain he was marrying me because he needed a political hostess for Woburn.*

Georgina wanted to dig in her heels and assert herself against her husband's dominant, controlling attitude. But because she knew tonight was extremely important to him, she acquiesced to his demands gracefully. "I'll change my gown. You go and greet our guests."

Georgina changed into a rose-colored rustling taffeta and went downstairs. It was against her nature to be petulant. All her life she had been taught to use her feminine charm, and it flowed naturally from her.

John watched his beautiful young wife as she welcomed the politicians to Woburn. She moved among them with such ease, he couldn't take his eyes from her. Whether she was speaking with Lauderdale, who was rather coarse, or to Adair, who was effete, she enchanted them. When she engaged a gentleman in conversation, she concentrated her charm upon him as if he were the only man in the room, and it never failed.

The atmosphere she created at Woburn was at once elegant and comfortable. The dinner was a resounding success, and the whiskey helped the politicians of both parties to relax their guard and converse affably.

After dinner, Georgina gave John a speaking look, then proceeded to engage Prime Minister Addington. "I need your help and your advice, if you would indulge me, Mr. Prime Minister."

"It would be an honor, Your Grace."

"I have turned the stillroom into an apothecary of sorts. Since you are such a renowned medical man, could you come and look at the electuaries and herbal remedies I have concocted and tell me which are most effective in treating the minor ailments of our tenants?"

John joined his friend. "Henry, my wife has deliberately spirited away Addington so we may bring Fox and Pitt together. Let's hope the union bears fruit."

That night, in the privacy of their bedchamber, John's eyes were filled with admiration. "You were superb tonight, Georgy. I believe we made great strides toward accomplishing our mission, and you deserve a good deal of the credit."

Georgina's wicked juices were bubbling. "How gratifying. Imagine what I could have accomplished if I'd been allowed to wear the Paris creation."

"You make me sound like a controlling devil," he protested ruefully.

"You *are* a controlling devil. Irrational demands come only from irrational people. I let you get away with deciding what I could and could not wear tonight, but I warn you that's the last time, Bedford. Marriage should be a partnership, not a dictatorship."

"How about a Tory-Whig alliance?"

"Only if I'm allowed to be an *independent* Tory." When he laughingly agreed, she went into his arms and kissed him.

Georgina began a portrait of Johnny for his birthday, and he decided he wanted the Abbess to be in the painting. The cat sat beside him on the sofa, purring loudly as he stroked her back.

"Who would you like me to invite to your birthday party?"

"My cousin Charlie and Uncle Huntly."

"No, I mean your friends from school. Francis is inviting Will Cavendish and the Abercorn boy, and William wants his friends Jack Rawdon and Teddy Lister."

Loud purring filled the silence, and she stopped sketching.

Johnny finally murmured, "I don't have any school friends."

Cold fingers stole about her heart. "What about the boys in your class at Westminster?"

"I don't want to invite them. They laugh at me because I like to read and make cruel fun of me for being short."

Georgina was outraged. "The bloody louts have been bullying you! Give me their names, Johnny."

He smiled sweetly. "It doesn't matter, Georgy."

It matters a great deal. I intend to make this your happiest birthday ever. "If you had a wish, what would it be?"

"I wish . . . I wish . . . I'd like to go to the theater."

Georgina sensed that he had been about to wish for something else and was too shy to express himself. "Your wish is my command. I shall arrange for all of us to go into London and attend Drury Lane. Did you know the theater is on Bedford land?"

"Does that mean we may attend anytime we want to?"

"Indeed it does, Johnny."

Johnny's birthday, on August 18, exactly one month after Georgina's, was celebrated with gusto by all the Gordons, the Russells, and their friends. John, after much trepidation, gave in to his wife's pleading and presented his youngest son with his own horse. It was a young chestnut gelding, a far cry from the plodding Grey Lady that Johnny had ridden all summer.

"Thanks so much, Georgy. I know it was your idea. I've decided to call him Titus."

Georgina winked at him. "What'd we do without Shakespeare?"

The next day, John and Georgina took the boys to a performance of *A Trip to Scarborough* by their friend Richard Sheridan. The play pricked the pretensions of people who were above themselves, and the duke thought the comedy would teach a valuable lesson.

The following week whenever Francis did something high-handed, Johnny dubbed him Lord Foppington, to the great delight of the rest of the family.

At the end of August, John took his eldest son up to Cambridge. "I'm going to miss Lord Foppington," William declared, "but I can't wait for school to start. I've waited four years to be a senior at Westminster and enjoy all the privileges. I stand a good chance of becoming captain of the cricket team."

"Your father and I will come and watch you play, William. Better start packing your trunks. Would you like me to help you?"

William flushed. "No, thank you, Lady Georgina. Mr. Burke has taken charge of it for me."

"Then I shall help Johnny, though I doubt I'll be as efficient as Mr. Burke." Georgina noticed that Johnny had suddenly become quiet and withdrawn now that the new school term was only two days away, and her heart went out to him.

On the morning they were to leave for London, Johnny became nauseated and threw up his breakfast. Georgina put him to bed and promised to come back and sit with him until he felt better; then she went downstairs to speak with his father.

"John, why don't you take William back to Westminster and leave Johnny here for a few days? He may be coming down with something. And William is chafing at the bit to start his senior year."

"What about tomorrow night? Would you rather we postponed the dinner we planned?"

"No, of course not. Parliament opens in a couple of days, and we need to get the members together before that." The Duke and Duchess of Bedford had made plans to host another political gathering, but this time they had excluded Prime Minister Addington and his close Tory allies.

"I'm glad you're feeling better." Georgina watched Johnny eat his supper, and she helped herself to one of his quince tarts.

"I enjoyed walking the dogs. I think the greyhounds miss Francis and William. Will you watch over the Abbess for me when I go back to school, Georgy?"

"Of course I will. I'll feed her kipper every day. Now I must go and get ready. William Pitt is always punctual."

Georgina bathed and had Jenny fashion her a new coiffeur. Her silken black hair was pinned up with diamond combs, except for one long curl that fell to her shoulder. She thanked the maid and told her she wouldn't need her further. Georgina planned to wear one of her Paris gowns, and she braced herself for her husband's objections.

From her dressing room, she heard John enter her

bedchamber. "Ah, just the man I need. Would you fasten the back of my gown?" She saw his dark brows draw together as the storm clouds gathered.

"I'd rather you wore something else," he said bluntly.

"But I love this pale lavender muslin. My purple slippers and gloves contrast perfectly. I thought you came to escort me downstairs, not line me up for inspection!"

John was not amused. "You have failed the inspection. You may wear this when we dine alone, but not when we entertain a houseful of gentlemen."

She raised her chin. "Few of them, including the host, are gentlemen!"

"Guilty as charged. Change your gown, Georgina."

Her stubborn demeanor vanished, and she heaved a deep sigh, as if she would capitulate to her husband's demands.

"Good girl. I'll go down and greet our guests."

"You'd best go and say good night to Johnny first."

Georgina knew it would take a few minutes for him to go up one floor and cross to the wing where his sons' bedrooms were located. She pulled on her gloves, picked up her fan, and went downstairs.

Charles Lennox was the first to arrive and she greeted Charlotte's husband with a welcoming hug. Charles James Fox arrived with his nephew Lord Holland. "Henry, you've managed the impossible . . . you're here before Mr. Pitt. Charles, let me get you a dram of whiskey."

Fox took her hand to his lips. "You look exquisite, my dear. You are one of the few ladies I know who do justice to the Parisian fashions."

John entered the drawing room in time to see his wife bestow a radiant smile on Fox. His eyes narrowed dangerously as he surveyed Georgina's gown. He walked a direct path to her and took a firm hold of her arm. "Would you excuse us, gentlemen?" He led her from the room, then gripped her more firmly and ushered her upstairs to her chamber. "You agreed to change your gown."

She pulled away from him. "I agreed to no such thing. I don't respond well to orders, Bedford."

John made an effort to control his rising anger. "Then I shall ask you kindly. Please change your gown, Georgina."

She turned and glanced through the window. "Oh, William Pitt has just arrived. How disrespectful that we are not there to greet him. Please offer my apologies and tell him I'll be down directly, John."

When Georgina arrived in the drawing room she greeted Pitt effusively. "William, I hope you won't mind being my dinner partner again? I would rather sit next to you than any other man in England."

The muscle in John's jaw clenched like a lump of iron. He poured two glasses of claret and brought one to Pitt. He was about to hand the other to Georgina when it slipped from his fingers and the dark red wine splashed down the front of her gown.

"How clumsy of me. Forgive me, Georgy."

She smiled sweetly. "Accidents happen. Please excuse me, gentlemen."

Upstairs, she rang for Jenny. "I've had an accident. Perhaps if you soak it in some cold water, the stain won't set." Her maid helped her from the gown, and she kicked off her slippers and hurried into her dressing room. Georgina knew exactly which dress she would change into.

When the vision in the pale green empire gown with the low décolletage appeared, the men gave her a round of applause.

"Thank you, gentlemen. This dress is John's favorite." She smiled her secret smile. "I believe dinner is served."

By midnight, the last guest had departed. The dinner had accomplished its mission. William Pitt had accepted Charles James Fox's invitation to join the Whig Opposition Party. The two men made a pact to become increasingly critical of the government's policies when parliament opened two days hence.

"That was a shameless display of wanton behavior. You flaunted yourself like a bold young hussy. I forbade you to wear the first gown, so you deliberately donned the green one that revealed your body even more blatantly."

She shrugged her shoulder. "I contemplated coming down naked."

"Stop it! You love nothing better than playing the spoiled, precocious hoyden. Your family encouraged you, but I will not. I demand your obedience, Georgina."

"Obedience?" She planted her hands on her hips. "Perhaps your angelic Elizabeth obeyed your demands. Georgina Gordon will not."

"We will not discuss my first wife." His tone was dangerously forbidding.

Her fury flared. "One more word and I will take down her portrait from over the fireplace and smash it to smithereens!"

Georgina's temper was high, and it gave her satisfaction to see she had provoked his anger. She had always wondered what it would take to goad him into unleashing the controlled fury that lurked beneath his polished surface.

He saw the flash of her green eyes. "Stop behaving like a wild little hellcat."

She drew her lips back from her teeth. "Make me!"

He grabbed her by her shapely shoulders and shook her fiercely.

"Bloody brute! You've wanted to give me a thrashing since the first day we met. Is this how you kept your first wife in line?"

Her words provoked the guilt he had buried beneath the surface. John's hands dropped to his sides as he tried to leash his rage.

"I refuse to play second fiddle to any woman—dead or alive!"

She turned on her heel and ran through the adjoining door into her own bedchamber. She pulled off her diamonds and stuffed them into their black velvet boxes; then she gathered them up and returned to the master bedchamber.

Georgina dropped them onto the bed. "Keep your bloody Bedford diamonds." She slapped his arrogant face. "I'd rather have a child than all the jewels in Christendom. But I'm not good enough for your precious seed!" She stormed from the room, slammed the door, and locked it.

John stood motionless for a full minute, stunned by her tirade. Then he strode to the adjoining door and rattled the knob. "Open this door. *Now!*" The savage tone of his voice warned of violence if she dared to disobey.

Georgina chose to ignore the warning. "Go away! I cannot abide imperious, domineering men who think they have God-given dominion over their wives."

John's inner demons took control. The frame splintered as he kicked in the heavy door and left it hanging by one hinge. He stalked across the room and towered above her. "Never lock a door against me again. You may choose to sleep alone—I would never force myself on an unwilling female, but there will be no locks between us, *now or ever.*"

Georgina raised a defiant chin, but she knew she had pushed him to the limit of his control. She felt a measure of relief when he strode from the room, but her heart ached with rejection. She undressed slowly, hung up the exquisite green creation and wondered how something this lovely could cause such unhappiness. *I always knew John was a dominant, controlling devil, but I thought my love would change him.*

She climbed into bed and glanced toward the master bedchamber. The ominous silence made her shudder. *Am I willing to do battle with him every time I want my own way?* She hesitated, on the brink of tears. Then Georgina dashed away her tears, swallowed the lump in her throat, and thumped her pillow. *Yes, and yes again. I have the temperament for it!*

Chapter 31

When Georgina opened her curtains, she saw a falling leaf and knew autumn had arrived. She murmured the words of an old Celtic spell, "September blow soft, till the fruit's in the loft."

She glanced toward the master bedchamber with its adjoining door hanging in shards. She heard no movement in the other room, and knowing John was an early riser, knew he would already be downstairs working. *I'll never enter that room again until my husband apologizes to me. He may not love me, but by all that's holy, he will treat me with respect or this marriage is over.*

She went upstairs to Johnny's bedchamber. The door stood open, and she quietly watched him as he struggled to close his trunk. His shoulders slumped with hopeless resignation, and she sensed an aura of infinite sadness about him.

Her smoldering anger suddenly rekindled and blazed anew. She withdrew as silently as she could, then rushed headlong down the two flights of stairs and marched into the library, ready to do battle.

"And while we're at it, you might as well know that he isn't going back!"

John sat immobile behind his desk. Georgina spoke as if they were still in the midst of a battle royal, and most likely they were. "*Who* isn't going back *where*?"

"Johnny isn't going back to that wretched Westminster boarding school. He already knows more than those idiotic professors whose claim to fame is turning titled young men into utter snobs."

"Which school do you suggest, pray?"

"No school. I want him to remain at Woburn with me. I can't bear to see him so unhappy. You can hire tutors for him. He needs love more than he needs lessons in Latin."

"Don't we all," John said with irony.

"Like it or not, I'm going upstairs to tell him to unpack."

John didn't try to stop her. This summer he had watched Johnny come out of his shell as Georgina had lavished her love on him. He knew how lonely his youngest son was at school and had toyed with the idea of keeping him at Woburn. Now that he knew his wife was amenable to such an unconventional arrangement, John felt immense relief.

He walked down to the stables and told the coachman that the plans had changed. He would not be driving to London today. John saddled his horse, intending to ride out to make sure all the hay fields had been harvested. It would give him time to think about the accusations Georgina had thrown at him last night. He admitted that their angry row had been as much his fault as hers. *Jealousy makes me too possessive of her. I'm jealous of her love for Francis and fearful that she might find other men attractive. The thing I don't understand is why she thinks I have tender feelings toward Elizabeth. I can't bear to say the woman's name. I think the time has come for me to confess that my first marriage was a living nightmare.*

"Johnny, you are not going back to Westminster. Let me help you unpack your trunk."

He stared at her, not quite believing. "Are you sure I don't have to go back to school? What about Father?"

John may not love me, but he most certainly loves Johnny. I'm certain he will do what is in his son's best interests. "I suggested he get you tutors. He didn't refuse."

Johnny threw his arms around her. "Georgy, you're the best mother in the world!"

She glanced at his breakfast tray and saw that he hadn't eaten a thing. "Why don't we go downstairs and have something to eat? Then we'll take the dogs for a run. The leaves are starting to fall—we won't have many more glorious days like this one."

He smiled from ear to ear. "It *is* a glorious day!" He stroked his cat's ears. "Come on, old girl."

On the way to the breakfast room, they were joined by one of the greyhounds. The Abbess hissed at him, and his tail went between his legs. Georgina and Johnny laughed because she was able to hold her own against the tall hound.

After the pair had eaten, they called the dogs and set off on a long ramble across Woburn's parkland. "Maybe I will sit in with you on some of your lessons, Johnny. My spelling is atrocious."

"Perhaps we can read some books together. I think I'd like to try Jonathan Swift's *Gulliver's Travels*."

They walked for about two miles, whistled for the dogs, and started back. The greyhounds ran ahead of them all the way to Woburn. In the front garden the dogs spotted the Abbess sharpening her claws on the trunk of an ancient oak, and together they made a mad dash for her. Outnumbered, the tabby cat ran up to the top of the tree to escape.

"Damn you, dogs! We take you for a walk, and this is the thanks we get." Johnny was upset that they had chased his pet.

"I'll put the dogs in the house. You try to coax her down."

When Georgina returned, her heart went into her mouth. Johnny was halfway up the tree. "Come down! Your father would have a fit if he saw you."

"But she's afraid to climb down. She tried, but lost her nerve. She made the mistake of climbing too high."

"Please come down, Johnny. I know you're brave

enough to climb to the top, but if you get hurt, I will be blamed."

"But I can't leave her up here. It's the worst feeling in the world to be afraid."

"Yes, I know. Only those who've experienced fear know what it feels like. If you come down, I'll go up and get her."

"Do you know how to climb a tree, Georgy?"

"I climb like a monkey. Just watch me."

Reluctantly, Johnny came down. When his feet were safely on the ground, Georgina called the cat and tried to coax it down. When it refused, she hiked up her skirts and began a slow ascent. She left the main trunk and climbed out on a limb, just below where the cat sat huddled. She reached up and lifted the Abbess into her arms.

Suddenly, there was a loud crack. Terrified by the noise, the cat sprang from her arms and headed down on its own. The large branch on which Georgina was standing split from the tree, and she felt herself falling. She tried to grab another branch, but it was too brittle to hold her. She dropped like a stone. Her head hit the ground with a sickening thud, and she lay limp and unmoving.

Johnny was horrified. "Georgy! Georgy!" He fell to his knees and touched her face, but her eyes were closed. "Wake up! Please, wake up."

Johnny saw his father riding toward the stables. He got up from his knees and started to run. "Father! Father! Come quick!" Tears streamed down his face. "I think Georgy's dead!"

John vaulted from the saddle and ran toward his son. "Where is she?"

"She fell from the big oak!" He was breathless from running.

John saw her crumpled form lying on the ground, and his heart jumped into his throat. He went down on one knee and bent over her. "Georgina . . . Georgy . . . can you hear me?" She lay unresponsive and fear knotted his gut.

He lifted her shoulders, ran his palm over the back of her head, and felt a huge duck egg. He was slightly relieved that there was no blood, but worried that she had hit her head hard enough to render her unconscious.

John gently lifted his wife and carried her to the house, dimly aware that Johnny was babbling something about his cat. "Is she alive? Father, is she alive?"

"Yes, Johnny. She's breathing, but she's lost consciousness. Open the front door for me."

John carried his limp burden through the reception room to the sitting room, and laid her gently on a couch. Georgina's maid, Jenny, and an alarmed Mr. Burke followed them into the room.

"What happened?" the steward asked.

"She fell from the big oak." John began to feel her limbs for broken bones. His dark face was grim.

"It's my fault." Johnny was as white as a sheet. "She was trying to rescue my cat from the tree," he told Mr. Burke.

"I can't find any broken bones," John told Burke, "but she could have internal injuries. She fell fifteen or twenty feet." He cupped her cheek and tapped it gently. "Wake up, sweetheart."

John removed her walking boots and rubbed her feet. Her lack of response made fear spiral inside him. "We'd better have the doctor. Would you ask the head groom to fetch him, Mr. Burke?"

Johnny went on his knees beside the couch. "Please wake up, Georgy. Tell us where it hurts."

John could clearly see his son's face was stricken with guilt. "Jenny, take him to the kitchen and get him a drink. He's just underfoot here. And bring me a bowl of water and a towel, please."

When John got the warm water, he bathed Georgina's face in hope of reviving her, but she remained limp. "Jenny, go and see if Cook has any smelling salts."

The maid came back with a small bottle, which he unstoppered and held under his wife's nose. When

Georgina did not react, he found it difficult to control his alarm. Though he was calm on the outside, on the inside he was filled with panic. He slipped his arm beneath her shoulders and lifted her so he could cradle her in his arms. She felt so small and so fragile that it tore at his heart.

"My love, my little love, open your eyes," he begged softly.

Eventually, Dr. Halifax arrived. John placed a chair for him next to the sofa, told him what had happened, and waited anxiously for his diagnosis.

"How long has Her Grace been like this?"

John tried to gauge the time. "I believe it's been close to two hours by now. I don't think she has any broken bones, and she doesn't have a fever." He knew he was trying to reassure himself.

"When it first happened, did she regain consciousness at all?"

"No, Doctor."

Halifax raised her eyelids with his thumb. "There is blood in her eyes. She has a bad concussion."

John's heart lurched. "She *will* regain consciousness?"

"That is difficult to predict, Your Grace. The longer she remains in this state, the less likely it will be. If she doesn't come to within the next hour or two, I believe it is safe to say she has slipped into a coma."

John stiffened. He dreaded the word *coma.* Elizabeth had slipped into a coma and she never recovered.

"Your wife may have done irreparable damage to her brain, Your Grace. I don't want to give you false hope."

"Perhaps she would be better in bed?" John suggested.

"I wouldn't move her, if I were you."

"Is there anything you can do for her, Halifax?"

The doctor nodded. "I shall do my best, Your Grace." He opened his leather bag and took out a cup and a surgical knife. Then he took Georgina's arm and rolled up her sleeve.

"What are you doing?" John asked curtly.

"I'm going to bleed her. It might help."

"*Bleed* her? Are you serious, Halifax?"

"It might prove efficacious—one never knows."

"Efficacious, my arse! Get the hell away from her."

Halifax was highly offended. "Your brother waited too long before he allowed us to proceed. It brought on his *death.*"

"His doctors botched the job!" John shouted. "I forbid you to bleed my wife. She will need all her strength to recover."

"As you wish, Your Grace." He put his paraphernalia back in his bag and closed it with a snap. Then he turned to leave.

"How long can a coma last?" John demanded.

"Hours, months, even years. We don't know these things."

"Then what bloody good are you?" John knew he was taking out his anger and frustration on Halifax, but he couldn't help it. It helped to keep his fear at bay.

"If you wish it, I can return this evening to check on Her Grace of Bedford," Halifax said stiffly.

"Yes, thank you. I would appreciate it, Doctor."

John paced about the sitting room. His eyes were drawn to the portrait above the mantel, and he shuddered. He lifted an armchair over to the fireplace, then climbed up on it. He took down the painting of Elizabeth and set it in the next room facing the wall. *I put it there for the boys, but it must have caused Georgina a great deal of pain. How could I have been so bloody thoughtless and insensitive?*

He returned to his wife, bent down, and shook her gently. When nothing happened, he lifted her high against his heart and carried her upstairs to their bedchamber. John removed Georgina's dress and her stockings, but left her in her petticoat. He was glad she wasn't wearing a corset; she'd been mauled about enough.

He poured a glass of water, knowing she must be

thirsty. But when he put it to her lips and tipped it up, she didn't swallow. He didn't try again, fearing that she might choke.

He gazed down at her, hoping and praying that when the contusion on her head went down, she would awaken. He knew it was his only hope.

Johnny knocked and opened the door a crack. "Is she awake?"

"Not yet. Would you like to come in for a while?"

"I brought a book. If I read to her, do you think she will be able to hear me, Father?"

"That's very thoughtful." *Dear God, neither one of us could survive without her.* "She may be able to hear you, Johnny."

He sat down on the window seat and opened his book. "This is one of our favorite speeches from *Henry the Fifth:*

"Once more unto the breach, dear friends, once more,
Or close the wall up with our English dead!
In peace there's nothing so becomes a man
As modest stillness and humility:
But when the blast of war blows in our ears,
Then imitate the action of the tiger;
Stiffen the sinews, summon up the blood,
Disguise fair nature with hard-favor'd rage;
Then lend the eye a terrible aspect;
Let pry through the portage of the head
Like the brass cannon, let the brow o'erwhelm it
As fearfully as doth a galled rock
O'erhang and jutty his confounded base,
Swill'd with the wild and wasteful ocean.
Now set the teeth and stretch the nostril wide,
Hold hard the breath and bend up every spirit
To his full height. On, on, you noblest English!
Whose blood is fet from fathers of war-proof;
Fathers that, like so many Alexanders,
Have in these parts from morn till even fought,
And sheath'd their swords for lack of argument.
Dishonour not your mothers; now attest

That those whom you call'd fathers did beget you.
Be copy now to men of grosser blood,
And teach them how to war. And you, good yeomen,
Whose limbs were made in England, show us here
The mettle of your pasture; let us swear
That you are worth your breeding; which I doubt not;
For there is none of you so mean and base
That hath not noble lustre in your eyes.
I see you stand like greyhounds in the slips,
Straining upon the start. The game's afoot:
Follow your spirit, and upon this charge
Cry 'God for Harry, England, and Saint George!' "

John was stunned at the passage Johnny had chosen. It was so militant. Then he understood. "Those are very bracing words, Johnny. We need to stiffen the sinews and summon up the blood to get us through this ordeal."

"Georgy too . . . I hope she heard me. I don't want her to die like Mother and Uncle Francis." He closed the book and hung his head as if he were praying.

"I won't let her die, Johnny." *God help me, I shouldn't make promises I may have to break.*

When his son left, John thought about King Henry's speech. "I do that: *Disguise fair nature with hard-favored rage, then lend the eye a terrible aspect.* I've done that to you, Georgy." Then he marveled, "It didn't intimidate you in the least."

That evening Halifax returned and Mr. Burke took him upstairs. When he saw that the duchess had not regained consciousness, he shook his head. "Against my advice, you have moved her. You were lucky. Her Grace could have a blood clot in her brain. If it shifts, it could kill her." He felt for a pulse. "Didn't your first wife die under mysterious circumstances?"

John was incensed. "How dare you?" He took a threatening step toward Halifax. "Leave my house. Now!"

When the doctor left, John tenderly tucked the covers about his wife, then paced to the window and stared out with unseeing eyes as darkness descended. *I freely admit that I am not blameless in Elizabeth's death, but Georgina is different. I love her with all my heart and soul. I would gladly walk through fire to help her.*

Fleetingly, he wondered if he was being punished. Having Georgina fall into a coma, as Elizabeth had, was totally devastating, and a pitiless punishment if the gods wished to be spitefully cruel. He banished the ridiculous thought at once.

When Mr. Burke brought him a supper tray, John thanked him. But he knew that he would not be able to swallow one mouthful past the lump in his throat. He sat down beside the bed, and took his wife's small hand in his own. "Georgy, stay with me."

He watched her all night, never closing his eyes once. It was the longest, most agonizing night of his life. He willed her to awaken, stroking her hand, but he did not resort to shaking her.

When morning sunlight filled the room, he lifted a dark strand of hair from the pillow. It curled about his fingers, and his eyes filled with tears. *I never told her I love her.* Impatiently, he wiped away the tears, vowing not to give up hope.

Mr. Burke brought him a breakfast tray and removed the one he had left last night. John drank the tea but left the food untouched. Though he acknowledged a supreme being, John did not believe in a personal God. But he prayed now—prayed fervently that Georgina would awaken.

An urgent knock came upon the door. "What is it?"

"It's Jenny, Your Grace. Johnny is upstairs sobbing his heart out. But he has locked himself in and refuses to answer."

John opened the door. "I'll tend to him, Jenny. Will you come and sit with my wife? I don't want her to be alone."

He went upstairs and rattled the knob. "Open the door, Johnny. What happened was an accident. It was *not* your fault!" John knew how destructive feelings of guilt could be.

Georgina slowly opened her eyes. She was completely disoriented. When she tried to sit up, a blinding pain in her forehead made her feel nauseated.

"Oh, Your Grace, you're awake!" Jenny cried.

Georgina sat up slowly, holding her head. "Where am I?"

"You are at home . . . at Woburn, Your Grace."

"At Woburn?" she puzzled. "Why do you call me *Your Grace*?"

"Because you are the Duchess of Bedford, ma'am."

"No! That cannot be! I refused to marry him. I hate and detest the Duke of Bedford. I would *never* marry him."

Jenny looked distraught. "I must go and tell the duke you are awake, Your Grace."

"No! I forbid you to leave this room. Help me up. I must get away from here," she said desperately.

"Oh dear, you mustn't get out of bed, Your Grace."

"Damn you. Stop calling me that. Where are my slippers?" She sat on the edge of the bed, and Jenny bent down and put her slippers on her feet. "You cannot leave, please, ma'am."

Georgina stood up in a panic. "I must get away from here!" She rushed to the door and flung it open, then began to run.

"You cannot go out in your petticoat, Your Grace," Jenny cried. She hurried to the door, but the Duchess of Bedford had already descended the stairs. The maid was in a dilemma. She hesitated, not knowing whether to follow the duchess or run upstairs and summon the duke. Finally, her trembling hands lifted her skirts, and with her heart hammering, she hurried up the staircase.

She knocked on Johnny's door, and when the duke opened it she gasped breathlessly, "My lady is awake, Your Grace."

"Thank God!" John rushed past her and down the stairs.

Jenny hurried after him. "She isn't in her right mind, Your Grace. She doesn't know who she is. Lady Georgina said she had to get away from here. Begging your pardon, Your Grace, but she said she hated and detested you!"

Chapter 32

"Georgina!" John shouted his wife's name as he strode from room to room. Mr. Burke hurried from the kitchen when he heard John. "Did you see her, Burke? Did she leave the house?"

"I didn't see her, Your Grace, but I thank heaven she has regained consciousness."

John was out the front door like a shot. *If Georgy's leaving, she'll go for her horse.* He ran through the courtyard and headed toward the stables. He caught a glimpse of her white petticoat through the trees. "Georgina! Georgy!"

She turned and looked at the man who was running toward her. A look of pure relief transformed the fear on her face. "John!" She put her hand up to her head as he reached her. "You must help me, John. I must get away from him!"

His arms went about her. "Get away from whom, sweetheart?"

She clung to him desperately. "Francis!"

John felt his wife go limp in his arms. "Stay with me, Georgy. Don't faint." He slipped his other arm under her legs and lifted her high against his heart. With great care, he carried his wife back to the house and took her upstairs to their bedchamber.

He laid her on the bed and gently propped her up against the pillows. "You regained consciousness once, sweetheart, you can do it again. Open your eyes,

Georgy." He removed her slippers and massaged her feet. Then he took her hands and held them tightly.

As the minutes slowly ticked by, John held his breath. Finally, he saw her eyelashes flutter; then her tongue licked dry lips. She opened her eyes and blinked. "I'm so thirsty."

Almost reeling with relief, he brought a glass of water and held it while she drank.

"My head hurts." Her hand massaged her forehead. "What happened? Oh, I remember . . . I fell out of the oak tree."

Johnny came rushing into the room. "Is she awake?"

"Of course I'm awake. Are you all right, Johnny?"

"I am *now*." He caught his breath on a sob of relief.

Georgina held out her arms and Johnny rushed into them.

"Hold on!" John cautioned. "She has to be kept quiet."

"Why?" Georgina asked.

"You've been unconscious for twenty-four hours. You had a very bad fall, my love." He took her hand and placed it on the back of her head. "You had a terrible concussion and slipped into a coma. When you awoke earlier, you didn't know you were at Woburn. You were so horrified that you were the Duchess of Bedford, you tried to run away. When I found you by the stables, you implored me to get you away from Francis."

Georgina sighed heavily and lowered her lashes to her cheeks.

"I think she needs to rest quietly, Johnny. Why don't you go down and let everyone know Georgy is awake and that she's going to be just fine?"

When they were alone, John sat down and took her hand. *I won't press her about Francis. She'll tell me when she's good and ready.* "Georgy, the night before you fell from the tree, do you remember that we had a terrible row?"

"Yes, I remember. I was absolutely furious with you

for being dominant and controlling." She veiled her eyes. "And for other things."

"You accused me of being a brute and wanting to beat you. I want you to know I would never hurt you, Georgina."

"I defied you deliberately, wanting to goad you into unleashing the dark fury that sometimes lurks beneath the surface."

"You managed to come pretty damn close. Not when you flung your diamonds at me or slapped my face. It was when you locked the door on me and rejected me that my demons took over."

"When you smashed the door down, I knew I had pushed you too far," she confessed. "I'm sorry, John."

"No, I am the one who must apologize. When you lay unconscious and I feared losing you, I realized how petty my jealousy was. You are the center of my life, Georgy. If freedom makes you happy, I will never deny you again. Can you forgive me?"

"Of course I forgive you. I deliberately provoked you."

In a little while, Mr. Burke brought up some broth. "I took the liberty of lacing it with wine to give her nourishment."

"Thank you, Mr. Burke, and thank Cook for me." John took the bowl and lifted the spoon to her lips.

Georgina looked amused. "I can do it myself."

"Let me feed you, little girl," he said tenderly.

Each time John looked into her eyes, Georgina looked away. She knew she was going to have to explain herself about Francis, and she was trying to muster the courage.

John put the empty bowl down, and then he bathed and shaved and changed his clothes.

"I don't want to stay in bed," Georgina declared.

"You have to stay quiet," John explained.

"I can stay quiet sitting on the window seat." She pushed the covers aside, walked across the chamber, and sat down so that she could see outside. She gazed out at the garden for a long time, and then her eyes sought John's. "Come and sit down."

He took a chair facing her and waited.

"I've been living a lie. You thought I loved your brother, Francis, and I let you believe it. It isn't true—I hated him."

John's dark brows drew together. "Hated?"

"Oh, not at first. After my coming-out ball, when he began to pay attention to me, I was completely indifferent to him. When you and I met, sparks flew between us, and against my will I found myself irresistibly attracted to you. But you were married, and I knew it was wrong. When your wife died, I hoped there might be a chance that you would return my feelings. Then you rebuffed me, and I wanted to make you jealous. I deliberately set out to become engaged to your brother. It was wicked of me, because I had no intention of marrying Francis."

"I know he proposed to you," John said quietly.

"Many times, and though it would have pleased Mother above all things, I always said no and made it plain I didn't love him. I wanted to get away from him and from London, and went to Kimbolton for my sister Susan's birthday. Unbeknownst to me, my family had arranged a rendezvous for Francis and me."

Georgina hesitated, and John kept a wise silence, hoping she would continue.

"I tried to be civil because I didn't want to spoil Susan's birthday. I was relieved when midnight arrived, and I knew I could retire. The next thing I knew, Francis came into my bedchamber. He said Manchester had given him the key." She paused and took a deep, steadying breath. "Francis tried to ravish me. I kneed him in the groin and kicked him in the belly. He rolled to the carpet in pain. It made him furious. When he got up and came after me, I hit him with a bottle and fled naked from Kimbolton."

"The degenerate swine!" John, appalled at Francis, sat down beside her on the window seat and slipped his arm about her.

"My coachman took me to my sister Louisa, in Suffolk. A short time later, Mother arrived with the dreadful news that Francis was dead. I was covered with guilt because the injury I inflicted on him led to his death."

"The injury that led to his death happened in the bed of his whore Molly Hill," John said between clenched teeth.

"I hated him because Louisa told me Francis did the same thing to her. But I never wished him dead, John."

The depraved bastard boasted to me that he had bedded Louisa.

"When Mother insisted that I go into mourning for Francis, I kept my mouth shut and donned weeds, knowing it would keep me off the marriage market."

Georgina began to cry softly, and John enfolded her in his arms and rocked her. "Hush, darling, hush. He isn't worth your tears."

"But when we married, I knew you loved and mourned your brother, and I pretended to do the same. It was very wrong of me to deceive you like that."

John laughed softly. "I was madly jealous of your love for Francis. Though I tried to control it, I found it impossible."

"The only one I loved . . . *ever* loved . . . was you."

John's heart soared, hoping against hope that what she said was true.

"When you came to Paris and asked me to marry you, I was overjoyed. I had made a pledge to myself that I would never marry a man who didn't love me. Even when we stood before the minister and exchanged our wedding vows, I was convinced that you loved me. Then Susan dropped her bombshell, and told me you were marrying me out of duty to restore my reputation and honor me with the title I'd been promised. It shattered my dreams and crushed my happiness."

John knelt before her and took her hands. "I knew Susan had said something to you that was devastating . . . something that drained away your happiness. But,

Georgy, I swear to you that was a lie. I did not ask you to marry me out of a sense of duty. I asked you to be my wife because I loved you. I was in love with you long before I had the right."

Inside her, joy began to blossom. "Truly, John?"

"I swear it on my life. My friend Holland read me a letter he got from his wife in Paris. She said that Eugene Beauharnais was lovesick over you, and your mother was eager to make a match for you with Napoleon's stepson. It threw me into a panic. I knew I had to go to Paris and snatch the prize away from him."

Georgina's eyes flooded, and a tear ran down her cheek.

"Darling, don't cry. You've shed enough tears."

"These are tears of pure happiness, John." She slipped her arms about his neck and lifted her lips for his kiss.

He searched her eyes. "Do you feel well? Does your head hurt?"

"Not at the back, where I have the lump." She brushed her fingers across her forehead. "I have a slight headache."

"That's concussion. You must rest, but not actually sleep for a while, or you risk slipping back into a coma."

They sat together on the window seat, reveling quietly in their newfound intimacy.

In the evening, Mr. Burke brought them supper trays, and as they ate, they watched the sun set. When the orange, harvest moon rose in the dark sky, John carried his wife to bed and propped her against the pillows.

Georgina removed her petticoat and tossed it away. "I don't want anything between us tonight, or ever again."

John undressed, slid into bed, and gathered her in his arms. "Sweetheart, I've never spoken to you about my first wife because my marriage was unhappy. Elizabeth suffered from melancholia, but after Johnny was born, it became so pronounced, it affected all our lives. All she wanted to do was lie on a couch in a darkened room, and her mind was filled with such dark portents that I thought she had been touched by madness."

Can this be true? I thought she was an angel.

"When I became member of parliament for Tavistock, she refused to come to London with me. I put my two older sons in Westminster school and left her in Devon. A nursemaid brought up Johnny until he was old enough for Westminster. I should never have left him at home with her—she blamed him for her melancholy condition. When he started at Westminster, I knew he was lonely, but it was preferable to leaving him with Elizabeth and her vindictive ways."

Georgina touched John's cheek. "I had no idea. I thought you had a loving marriage and were heartbroken when she died."

"A couple of years ago, I discovered she was addicted to laudanum, which of course made her condition far worse. I forbade her the stuff, warned her maid against indulging her, but she became a secret addict. Last year, I took her to her sister Isabelle at Longleat. Elizabeth took an overdose, and when I got there she was in a coma. I revived her, but in the night she took more and killed herself."

Georgina's arms tightened about her husband. "John, I had no idea. No wonder you always looked like you were trying to control a dark, inner fury."

"I often wished she were dead, and so when it happened, I was covered with guilt and remorse."

"Guilt is a dreadful thing to live with. I felt terrible guilt over Francis."

"I think it's time we stopped feeling guilty and started to enjoy our happiness." He feathered kisses across her temple. "For years I've longed for a woman who is vivacious, who would fill my life and my sons' lives with fun and laughter and joy. When at last I found you, and was lucky enough to make you my wife, I couldn't believe my good fortune."

Georgina's heart began to sing.

"Then you fell into a coma, and I was racked with fear that I might lose you. I didn't want to contemplate life without you. Johnny was even worse than me. You are the mother he'd always longed for. You love him unconditionally, and the thought of having you snatched away was more than either of us could bear."

"It feels glorious to be loved so completely," she whispered. "Did you know that I lost my heart to you the very first time I saw you?"

"Georgy, you're fibbing. You were furious with me for ordering you to go home." He nuzzled her ear. "I remember your exact words: *Go to the devil, old man!*"

"I dreamed about you that night. I was fishing in the River Spey and almost drowned. You rushed in and saved me. When you held me safe in your arms, I had never felt that secure before in my life." She kissed the corners of his mouth. "You called me *little girl*, but it was a term of endearment. You knew very well I was a woman grown."

"Yes, I found that out when Charlotte invited me to lunch at Marylebone Manor. You were so audacious, I wanted to take you across my knee and tan your arse." He kissed her eyelids, and his hand caressed her bottom. "I couldn't stop thinking about you."

"I'm glad. Did you ever dream about me?"

"My dreams about you were so sensual and decadent, they would shame the devil."

"Tell me!" She clung to him seductively. "No, better yet, show me."

"You little wanton, you'll have to settle for cuddling tonight. You are to remain quiet. Tomorrow night is another story. The passion I will arouse in you will make you wild and wicked."

She smiled her secret smile. "I love you so much, John."

"And I love you more than life, little girl."

* * *

During the next months, the Duke and Duchess of Bedford entertained the members of the houses of parliament at Woburn on a weekly basis. With Lady Georgina as their hostess, her guests knew they could count on politics and pleasure, the two things they enjoyed most.

John allowed Georgina to wear whatever she wished, and promised her that he would make an effort to curb his need to control her.

In the House of Commons, Addington, unable to overcome the combined opposition of William Pitt and Charles James Fox, saw his majority evaporate. His previous allies joined the opposition, and when he lost his parliamentary support, Addington was forced to resign. In the spring, William Pitt was returned to power as prime minister of England, and everyone rejoiced.

Lord and Lady Holland were frequent guests at Woburn. Henry took John aside. "Prime Minister Pitt wants to see you, John, when you are next in London."

"Ah, he wants to tell me he has achieved Irish Catholic emancipation," John jested.

"That will never happen so long as King George is on the throne. I imagine he wants to thank you. It was due to your powerful influence that he is once again prime minister."

"I don't need thanks, Henry. It's sufficient to know that Georgina and I helped. Still, a request from the PM can't be ignored. I suppose I should attend a session of the Lords while I'm in London, though I will likely be bored out of my mind."

That night in bed, John and Georgina discussed all that had happened during the day, as they did every single night. It was the lovers' private, special time together, when they lay in each other's arms and whispered for hours.

"Henry said Pitt wants to see me. Will you and Johnny come with me to London?"

"The Abbess is about to have her kittens. Neither

Johnny nor I want to leave Woburn at the moment. *I mustn't tell John I threw up my breakfast this morning, or he won't go to London.* "You go, darling, if you can bear to drag yourself away from me."

"Vain little minx."

She bit his shoulder. "You wouldn't have me any other way."

"Bedford, thank you for coming. There's something important I'd like to discuss in private."

"It is my pleasure, Mr. Prime Minister. If there is anything I can do, all you need do is ask."

"Not so fast, Your Grace. I am about to propose something, but if you have any reservations I hope you won't hesitate to say no. You have always championed the Irish, and Catholic emancipation has been a cause close to your heart. Though we managed to pass the Act of Union, Dublin has no real political status. To compensate we must provide them with pomp and pageantry. Charles James Fox and his nephew, Lord Holland, have proposed that I appoint you lord lieutenant of Ireland."

"You do me great honor, Mr. Prime Minister." *Henry, you old dog, you didn't give me a hint.*

Pitt held up his hand. "The position of viceroy pays only twenty thousand pounds per annum. Unfortunately, the expenses are several times that amount, and only a wealthy and generous man could take it on." Pitt cleared his throat. "I can think of none more suitable for this appointment than the Duke and Duchess of Bedford. Lady Georgina's vivacious charm and political savvy would make her the perfect vice queen. If you will take this appointment, you have my heartfelt thanks and appreciation."

"Mr. Pitt, it is my great honor to accept."

Chapter 33

"Father's home!" From an upper window, Johnny had seen his father's carriage drive in. He rushed downstairs and ran to the stables. "My cat had two kittens, a boy and a girl. And I watched them be born."

"Witnessing the miracle of birth is an unforgettable experience." He handed Johnny a traveling bag, picked up the other, and the pair headed to the house.

Georgina had quickly donned one of her husband's favorite dresses and was eagerly awaiting him in the reception room. The moment Johnny carried the bag upstairs, Georgina threw herself into her husband's arms. "Darling, I've missed you so much!"

John kissed her soundly, set her feet back on the carpet, and they said in unison, "I have something to tell you."

John laughed. "Ladies first."

"We are going to have a baby!"

John was stunned. "Good heavens, I thought you were going to tell me the cat had kittens."

"That's when it dawned on me. I was telling Johnny the gestation period for a cat was six weeks, and we began to count. Then it hit me. I began to count the days since my last menses, and realized what was causing my morning sickness."

"That's marvelous, sweetheart. You look absolutely radiant." With their arms about each other, they entered the sitting room. "Georgy, why don't we get married again? The last time was just a private ceremony, but now I want you to have the wedding you deserve. The one you always dreamed of, where you invite half of London."

Georgina's eyes sparkled. "John, you are such a romantic at heart. That is a splendid idea. Oh, Mother will be absolutely thrilled to death. I must write and tell her the news immediately." She hurried over to her writing desk. She sat down and smiled up at him. "What was it you wanted to tell me?"

"I've been appointed lord lieutenant of Ireland."

Georgina shot out of her chair. "John! You devil! Why didn't you tell me immediately? This is the most exciting thing that's ever happened to me. Beyond marrying you and having a baby, of course."

He picked her up and swung her round. "Pitt thinks you will make the perfect vice queen. Your main duty will be hosting parties for Dublin society. As well as Dublin Castle, we will entertain at the vice-regal lodge in Phoenix Park, which has seventeen acres of parkland. The castle has sumptuous state apartments and a throne room."

"We'll be like royalty! We'll take Johnny, of course."

"Of course."

"But first, I must make plans for our wedding. It will do double duty as our going-away party. This is all so exciting!"

John Russell had no illusions about his appointment. He knew it would be extremely difficult to govern a deeply divided country. On principle, he was opposed to any system of exclusion, and believed concessions to Catholics were necessary for peace. Violence often flared in various counties, and it would be his job to restore calm and order.

He voiced his concerns to Georgina. "It won't be all beer and skittles, you know. We'll often find ourselves in delicate political situations."

"If we celebrate Saint Patrick's Day with a ball and

supper at the castle, it will greatly please the Catholics. I have decided to have all my clothes made in Ireland, and shall encourage any ladies who come to court to do the same."

"And give up your decadent Parisian fashions?" he teased.

She laughed. "In a few months they won't fit me anyway."

"We'll be apart some of the time. You'll have to hold the fort in Dublin while I tour the counties to encourage agriculture, and I'll have to sit in on magistrates' hearings and various disputes."

"I will dutifully support you in all things, John."

"Being the wife of a politician is second nature to you, Georgy. You've always been a champion for the underdog."

"I had a good teacher. Oh, and speaking of Mother, you mustn't mind when she arrives and starts organizing and planning for the wedding. We deprived her of throwing the wedding of the decade when we said our vows at a private ceremony. This time I want her to be able to indulge herself without any thought to expense."

"You are a most considerate daughter, Georgy. You have a generous heart."

"*Au contraire!* I have a generous husband."

"Here comes the bride!"

Georgina glided between the assembled guests, followed by her four sisters holding up the long train of her wedding gown. The ballroom at Woburn was festooned with roses and lilies, and their delicate scent perfumed the air.

Alexander, Duke of Gordon, resplendent in his Black Watch kilt, once more gave his daughter Georgina to John Russell, Duke of Bedford, and took his place beside his duchess, Jane. She was at the pinnacle of her matchmaking career, and preened appropriately.

When the bride and groom plighted their troths,

and the minister pronounced them man and wife, Georgina, hand in hand with John, turned to the assembled guests and announced, "I want to share a secret with you."

John held his breath. *I know she is an audacious baggage, but surely she isn't going to announce that she's with child?*

Georgina bestowed a radiant smile upon her audience and said, "I shall put an end to your speculation. I want everyone to know that this is Britain's greatest *love match*!"

John breathed with relief and grinned from ear to ear as the guests sent up a loud cheer.

Four chambers adjoining the ballroom had been turned into reception rooms where buffet tables were laden with copious amounts of beef, pork, lamb, game birds, and of course the famous Spey salmon. The desserts were spectacular, and the wedding cake was a triumphant tower of magnificence. The Sevres china, Waterford crystal, and ornate Georgian sterling silver duly impressed the two hundred guests.

Awash with champagne and whiskey punch, the *haut ton* danced the night away, as country dances gave way to Scottish reels, strathspeys, and finally the 'Gey Gordons.'

At three o'clock in the morning, the guests gathered at the foot of Woburn's magnificent staircase and cheered as the handsome groom swept his beautiful bride into his arms and carried her upstairs. Then the revelers trooped outside for a spectacular fireworks display.

"Shouldn't we join them for the fireworks?" Georgina teased.

John bit her ear playfully. "I'll give you skyrockets!"

Inside their bedchamber, she knelt on the window seat, watching the illuminations that lit up the sky.

John saw her close her eyes and knew she was making a wish. He slid his arms about her. "What are you wishing, Georgy?"

"I wish that we will always be as happy as we are tonight."

"I'll do my best to make it so, *little girl.*"

In bed, as a prelude to making love, they lay whispering.

"I love you with all my heart, Georgy."

"Why do you love me?" she demanded precociously.

"Because you are a joyous creature who loves and lives life to the full. You have a passion for nature, and children, and animals, and I never tire of hearing you laugh. Your silvery laughter is the loveliest thing I've ever heard."

He rolled with her until he had her pinned beneath him in the bed. "When I capture your soft, warm mouth it tastes of delicious laughter and sensual anticipation. It's intoxicating to know that you want me as much as I desire making love to you. Your eagerness spurs me to possess you body and soul, and lure you to surrender your essence to me."

"Mmm, tell me more."

"I love to lose myself in the tempting, honeyed depths of your body, where you allow me to indulge any wicked fantasy that I thirst and crave. You bring me blissful, almost unendurable pleasure that allows me to escape. Your lovemaking takes me to a place where only rich, dark sensation exists."

Georgina finished his litany because she had heard it before. "We indulge in a passion so powerful, it brings exquisite pleasure."

John took possession of her mouth, and they both abandoned themselves to love.

Epilogue

Dublin, Ireland

"It's so green! Now I know why they call it the Emerald Isle." Johnny stood at the ship's rail between Georgina and his father.

The king's yacht, *Dorset*, sailed into Dublin Bay, and the Russells disembarked. Though it was early in the morning, a huge throng had gathered to give the new viceroy and his family a rousing welcome.

The Duke and Duchess of Bedford were officially greeted by the lord mayor and the aldermen of Dublin. Then they climbed into an open carriage and set off for the castle with an honor guard of dragoons. The streets were packed with eager spectators, curious for a glimpse of their new lord lieutenant and his wife.

"This is the River Liffey," Georgina told Johnny.

"And this is Macartney's Bridge," John added.

The people were so enthusiastic they wanted to unharness the horses from the shafts and pull the carriage themselves, but the postillions discouraged them. John and his son waved, Georgina threw kisses to the crowd, and the carriage proceeded on to Dublin Castle through lines formed by the Irish military.

"What happens next?" Johnny asked. "I am going to write everything down so we have a record of our time in Ireland. I warrant we are making history."

"The Earl of Hardwicke, the outgoing viceroy, will

hold a breakfast reception to welcome us," his father explained.

"That's good. I'm hungry."

"Eat hearty. It will be a long day. Your father will be sworn in at three p.m., but I don't believe there will be any food until the levee at four o'clock," Georgina said.

"I read about the swearing in, Father. You will be invested with the collar of the Order of Saint Patrick, and receive the sword of state. I don't suppose I'll be allowed to keep the sword in my bedroom tonight?" Johnny asked hopefully.

"No, it will be kept in the castle's strong room, where it will be well guarded," his father explained.

Georgina winked at Johnny. "I shall make friends with the guard, and perhaps sometime he'll let us go into the strong room and rummage about among the regalia."

"Georgy." John threw her a glance that told her to behave.

After the swearing-in ceremony, the cannons in Phoenix Park gave the Russells a gun salute, which was answered by a volley of musket fire by a squadron of soldiers.

They only had time to hurry back to the state apartments to comb their windblown hair and wash their hands before the levee began where they would meet the leading people of Dublin.

"May I stay up and watch the illuminations tonight?"

"Of course you may, if you are still awake," Georgy replied.

"I'm hungry. May I go down and get something to eat?"

"Off you go before your father finds out I've given you permission to attend the levee."

Georgina picked up the list of entertainments she and the viceroy would be expected to host over the next few weeks. She raised her voice so that it would carry into John's dressing room. "We have a vice-regal box at the theater. I have to attend benefit concerts for all sorts of charities. I think I shall enjoy our sojourn in Ireland."

Georgina removed her shoulder cape to reveal her exquisite white and silver gown. She donned her magnificent diamonds and posed before the polished silver mirror.

John came out of his dressing room, took one look at her, and stopped dead in his tracks. "Georgy, the décolletage on that gown is positively indecent. And surely it's rather flamboyant to display *all* your diamonds."

Georgina threw back her head and laughed. "Accept me as I am, or go to the devil, *old man*!"

Author's Note

Georgina and John Russell were married for thirty-six years. They had ten children together—seven boys and three girls.

In their letters to each other, John often called Georgina his "darling little girl," and she called him her "dearest old man."

Georgina's youngest stepson, Johnny (Lord John Russell), became prime minister of England in 1846.

The Duke of Bedford built his duchess a palatial summer cottage at Endsleigh, Devon, with picturesque views of the River Tamar. Both Endsleigh and Woburn Abbey are now open to the public.

Acknowledgments

I am indebted to the following historical and biographical sources, which provided a wealth of information on Georgian England's society, monarchs, government, and noble families, including the Gordons and the Russells.

Mabell, Countess of Airlie: *In Whig Society*
Percy Fitzgerland: *The Good Queen Charlotte*
George Gordon: *The Last Dukes of Gordon and Their Consorts*
Elizabeth Grant: *Memoirs of a Highland Lady*
R. W. Harris: *England in the Eighteenth Century*
Lord Holland: *Memoirs of the Whig Party*
Phillip Lindsay: *Loves of Floribel*
John Pearson: *Stags and Serpents*
J. H. Plumb: *The First Four Georges*
J. H. Plumb: *Georgian Delights*
Constance Russell: *Three Generations of Fascinating Women*
Philip W. Sergeant: *George, Prince and Regent*
Charles Spencer: *The Spencers*
T. S. Surr: *A Winter in London*
Rachel Trethewey: *Mistress of the Arts*
Horace Walpole: *Memoirs and Portraits*
Spencer Walpole: *The Life of Lord John Russell*
J. Steven Watson: *The Reign of George III*

The Edinburgh City Library: *Letters and Historical Documents*
The Times of London
Britannica Online Encyclopedia
Wikipedia

Read on for an excerpt of another exciting and sensual historical romance from
Virginia Henley

NOTORIOUS

Available at penguin.com or wherever books are sold

"I cannot believe you are a woman grown, Brianna de Beauchamp. When I was last at Warwick four years ago you were a child." Roger Mortimer clasped the young girl's hands and kissed her brow, then held her away from him so he could have a good look. "I was present when you were born. I never would have believed such a scrawny little scrap would turn into a rare beauty."

Brianna raised her lashes and smiled at the darkly handsome Mortimer. He was easily the most charming male she had ever known, and her heart began to beat wildly. Her older brother, Rickard, was married to Roger's sister, Catherine, and was a captain in Mortimer's army.

"Your eyes would melt a heart of stone and render a strong man weak as water." Mortimer spoke with complete sincerity.

Brianna had the soulful, soft brown eyes of a doe, fringed by thick dark lashes tipped with gold.

"Mother doesn't think me a woman, nor does Father. They think at sixteen I am still a child."

"Nonsense! I was wed at fourteen and a father at fifteen. Your mother attended my wedding."

"You had your boy Edmund when you were fifteen?" Brianna asked in amazement.

Roger threw back his head and laughed. "He wouldn't be pleased to be called a boy. Edmund is a man of twenty-one and his brother, Wolf, is twenty. They patrol the Welsh Marches when I'm in Ireland."

Brianna's eyes lit with curiosity. "Wolf?"

"He found a motherless wolf cub a few years back and kept it. He's had the name ever since." Mortimer grinned and shook his head. "I can't believe it's been more than sixteen years since that night at Windrush. Where have the years gone?"

I was born at Windrush? Why the devil wasn't I born at Warwick Castle? Brianna wondered. Her thoughts were interrupted by her mother's arrival.

The elegant Countess of Warwick swept briskly into the hall. She encountered a servant bringing ale to their guest and lifted two tankards from his serving tray. "Well come, Roger! It's lovely to see you again." She handed him a tankard and lifted the other one to her own lips. "Is Lady Mortimer not with you?"

"Nay, she remained in Ireland. She has vast landholdings there and lives on a grand scale. I believe she prefers it to Wales."

"We've all heard of your victories in Ireland. Rickard corresponds regularly. You look every inch the conquering hero."

A year after Robert Bruce had defeated young King Edward and his English army at Bannockburn, Scotland's king had sent his brother, Edward, to Ireland to free the Irish from English rule. The King of England had chosen his fiercest Welsh border lord, Roger Mortimer, to put down the Irish insurgency. Mortimer was an outstanding military leader and within four months he had taken back Dundalk, then taken Ulster. He had remained there for the past four years as Ireland's justiciar.

Roger grinned, while his light gray eyes took in every detail of her beauty with frank male appreciation. "You have a knack for making a man feel like a conqueror, Jory." He took her fingers to his lips. "Your husband is a lucky devil."

Jory de Beauchamp rolled her eyes. "Here comes the devil now."

Warwick, now in his fifties, was still an imposing figure. The white at his temples contrasting with his black hair, and the deeper lines of his dark face, were his only signs of age.

"I've put your men in the barracks beside the armory. Your capable sons have taken charge of stabling the horses and don't need my interference. Let's sit by the fire, where we can be comfortable. There is much to discuss."

Brianna, displaying good manners, withdrew from the circle, but she had no intention of leaving the hall. She sat down in a window embrasure where she could hear everything her elders said. *I shouldn't . . . but I shall!*

Mortimer stretched his long legs toward the fire. "I was surprised to learn you had withdrawn from court."

"The Despencers are the only ones with access to the king. Father and son are determined to gain political supremacy over all the earls and barons in England." Warwick's features hardened. "Our presence there became untenable."

"It broke my heart to leave Isabelle. I have been a lady of the queen's court since she arrived from France when she was thirteen. As you well know, we became dearest friends. She adored Brianna, and they became like sisters. Then Hugh Despencer dismissed me, along with the queen's other loyal ladies."

Mortimer clenched his fists. "It is beyond belief that Edward has another degenerate favorite after what happened over Gaveston. That the queen is forced to accept him would gag a maggot."

"When we rid Edward of Gaveston, the king turned to Isabelle and fathered her children like a normal husband. At that time the elder Despencer, head of the King's Council, stood firmly with the barons. Then, last year, the avaricious swine spied his chance and made his son chamberlain of the king's household, and parliament appointed him to the council. After that it didn't take Hugh Despencer long to become the king's new favorite," Warwick said with disgust.

"Once a pederast, always a pederast!" Mortimer bit back a foul oath.

Pederast? I know not the meaning of that word, but I warrant it means something bad. Brianna decided she would ask her mother, but not in the presence of her father. *He would keep me innocent forever.*

"The avaricious Despencer is the reason I returned from Ireland. He stole two manors from young Hugh Audley by registering them in his own name, and is doing his best to appropriate certain estates that were granted to me. Hugh Despencer covets the lordship of Gower, which lies along his lands in Glamorgan. Gower belongs to John Mowbray, but Despencer claims he never got a license from the king. He's urged Edward to declare it forfeit and grant it to him." Mortimer flung out his arm in a flamboyant gesture. "Since when did a Welsh Marcher baron ever need a license from the King of England for his land? Marcher barons have had the privilege of Welsh land for centuries!"

Roger Mortimer has such a commanding, royal presence. He is exactly what a king should look and sound like, because he is a descendant of King Brutus from the Arthurian legends. She sighed.

"Obviously Despencer is trying to build a large lordship for himself in what has always been the Marcher barons' power base." Warwick made no effort to hide his contempt for the Despencers.

"Exactly!" Mortimer said grimly. "His aggrandizement is a direct threat to all the Marcher lords. Our independence and even the lands and castles we own are at stake."

"Mowbray didn't surrender his land, surely?" Warwick asked.

"He adamantly refused, so the king sent men to take it by force. I immediately went to Westminster to persuade the king from the folly of a direct attack on Marcher privileges. When he would not listen, I sought audience with the queen to ask if she would use her influence. It was then that Isabelle told me all the power is in the hands of Edward's catamite!"

"The barons hate and detest the Despencers," Warwick declared.

"They are brutal and greedy and Hugh has an insatiable desire for land and wealth," Jory added.

"The earls of Hereford, Mowbray, Audley, and d'Amory have joined with us Mortimers to form a confederacy against the Despencers. I have come to rally the barons to join us. Together we can and we *must* utterly destroy them."

Warwick nodded. "We'll go to Lancaster and enlist his support." He looked up as a tall youth fashioned in his own image entered the hall. "Here's Guy Thomas. He must have been only ten or eleven the last time you saw him. He has grown apace."

Brianna took advantage of the distraction of her brother to slip from the hall unnoticed. Her feet carried her in the direction of the stables. If a score of mounts belonging to Mortimer's men were being accommodated, she wanted to make sure that her palfrey, Venus, was kept safe from the other horses.

She got only as far as the courtyard when the sight of two snarling, growling canines who looked as if they were about to kill each other filled her with dread. "Brutus! No!" she screamed, and without hesitation threw herself between the combatants and flung her arms about her father's black wolfhound. Her eyes widened in horror as she looked at his opponent. "Hell's teeth, it isn't a dog at all, it's a wolf!"

A male descended upon her and roughly dragged her away from the two animals. "You stupid girl! Have you no common sense?"

Furious, she drew back her hand and slapped his dark, arrogant face. "How dare you bring your wild beast to Warwick?"

He grabbed her hand, forced it behind her back, and stared down at her with fierce gray eyes. "My wolf is tame, which is more than I can say for you.

They are only challenging each other to test the boundaries. Let nature take its course," he ordered.

To Brianna's amazement the two long-legged animals circled each other with their lips drawn back to show their fangs; then they stopped and stood eye to eye, growling in their throats. When both stood their ground and neither backed away, it was a standoff. She raised her eyes to stare at the intense, dark face of the male who held her in his iron grip. "Take your hands from me, Wolf Mortimer."

"You know my name." He let go of her wrist. "You have me at a disadvantage, mistress."

She raked him with a haughty glance. "And always shall." *How in the name of God could this uncivilized lout be the son of Roger Mortimer, who is the epitome of chivalry?*

"Brianna, is that you?"

She swung about to look at the tall young man who spoke her name and realized he must be Edmund Mortimer. He had been a gangling youth the last time she had seen him. "Indeed it is, Edmund. Welcome to Warwick." She gave him a dazzling smile, hoping it would affront his loutish brother. "They are serving ale in the hall. You must be parched. Come, Brutus!"

The wolfhound trotted to her side and Brianna turned and said coldly, "Keep your wild beast in the stables. He is not welcome in the castle."

"She is a bitch," Edmund corrected gently.

"She is indeed," Wolf Mortimer declared. "A bitch who needs taming." He touched his cheek where she had slapped him, then threw back his head and laughed insolently.

Brianna took Edmund's arm and walked briskly toward the castle. "Your brother is uncouth."

He looked down at her apologetically. "I'm afraid it is a Mortimer trait."

"I don't believe that. Your father is one of the most charming men I have ever met, and I'm not the only female to think so. He is renowned for his fatal attraction."

Wolf Mortimer stared after the pair until they entered the castle. The impact of the beautiful female had been like a blow to his solar plexus. The moment she slapped him, a raging lust ignited and ran through his veins like wildfire. His nature was both impulsive and decisive, and he knew instantly that he wanted her. Not only was she exquisite to look at, but she was all fire and ice. She was a spirited female who would give as good as she got, rather than being meek and submissive, and the thought excited him. *I recognize your towering pride, since I have the sinful trait myself, Brianna de Beauchamp. Your challenge is irresistible!*